I0681895

ASOKA'S ALIBI: THE COMPLETE
ADVENTURES OF BEN QUORN, VOLUME 2

BOOKS IN THE ARGOSY LIBRARY:

UP JUMPED THE DEVIL
CLEVE F. ADAMS

THE BROTHERS OF THE SNAKE: THE
COMPLETE CHINATOWN CASES OF
JIMMY WENTWORTH, VOLUME 3
SIDNEY HERSCHEL SMALL

A CLUE TO THE COPPER: THE COMPLETE
CASES OF SILVER SKULL
RICHARD HOWELLS WATKINS

KINGDOM OF THE LOST: THE ADVENTURES
OF PETER THE BRAZEN, VOLUME 8
LORING BRENT

WORTH MILLIONS
RICHARD BARRY

TIGER DICK'S DOUBLOONS
DON MCGREW

PRESIDENTS: IMAGINARY MOMENTS IN
THE LIVES OF AMERICA'S GREAT
THEODORE ROSCOE

CROSS OVER NINE
MAX BRAND

ASOKA'S ALIBI: THE COMPLETE
ADVENTURES OF BEN QUORN, VOLUME 2
TALBOT MUNDY

THE LOST PUNCH: THE COMPLETE CASES
OF GILLIAN HAZELTINE, VOLUME 4
GEORGE F. WORTS

ASOKA'S ALIBI
THE COMPLETE ADVENTURES
OF BEN QUORN, VOLUME 2

TALBOT MUNDY

ILLUSTRATED BY
JOHN R. NEILL
ROGER B. MORRISON

COVER BY
PAUL STAHR

POPULAR PUBLICATIONS · 2025

© 2025 Popular Publications, an imprint of Steeger Properties, LLC

First Edition—2025

PUBLISHING HISTORY

"Asoka's Alibi" originally appeared in the March 9–23, 1929 issues of *Argosy Allstory Weekly* magazine (Vol. 202, Nos. 1–3). Copyright © 1929 by The Frank A. Munsey Company. Copyright renewed © 1956 and assigned to Steeger Properties, LLC. All rights reserved.

"The Affair at Kaligaon" originally appeared in the May 24–June 7, 1930 issues of *Argosy* magazine (Vol. 212, Nos. 4–6). Copyright © 1930 by The Frank A. Munsey Company. Copyright renewed © 1957 and assigned to Steeger Properties, LLC. All rights reserved.

"The Elephant Sahib" originally appeared in the December 6, 1930–January 10, 1931 issues of *Argosy* magazine (Vol. 217, No. 2–Vol. 218, No. 1). Copyright © 1930 by The Frank A. Munsey Company. Copyright renewed © 1958 and assigned to Steeger Properties, LLC. All rights reserved.

ALL RIGHTS RESERVED

No part of this book may be reproduced or utilized in any form or by any means without permission in writing from the publisher.

Visit ARGOSYMAGAZINE.COM for more books like this.

TABLE OF CONTENTS

ASOKA'S ALIBI

Asoka was a mighty elephant, and none could manage him save Quorn—sometimes; nor was it carnival season, in that mad, seething India border state, the best of those times

1

THE MASTER OF ELEPHANTS

"**RECKON MAYBE I'M** nutty," said Quorn to himself. "Hell, supposing I am! So is Narada. Elephants is the only sane folk hereabouts."

To comfort himself he looked up at Asoka, the tallest elephant in captivity, whom only he could manage at the best of times. At other times Quorn had to ride him as a fury rides a typhoon.

"You, you big stiff, if it weren't for you I'd pull my freight for Philadelphia and drive a taxicab again. If I might take you along I'd join a circus. This here circus gives me the willies."

He was referring to all Narada, not merely the elephant lines. Narada is close enough to Rajputana to be soaked with a sense of worn-out history. Treaties and its mountains have kept railroads at a distance, and the news comes dim, diluted, and distressing, by mail and word of mouth, so that people are only aware that the world is changing, without knowing why, or how, or what the changes mean.

They feel backward, and resent it, but they keep up the ancient customs for lack of intelligible new ones. Accordingly, for eleven months of every year Narada is piously miserable; during the twelfth month it is impiously mad and happy—more or less—always with a feeling that happiness has to be paid for, and, though the gods are kindly, there are as many vengeful and resentful devils as there are gods.

The carnival falls at the craziest season—April, when the heat is almost intolerable and nobody has too much money, having paid the taxes and the money-lenders' interest, so there is a fine feeling of equality, with common enemies to execrate.

There is also a yearning in common to cut loose and thumb rebellious noses at authority, so the underpaid and not too numerous police receive a lesson in self-restraint; a policeman's head, struck by a long stick, cracks as easily as any one's; the police station is of wood and would make a lovely bonfire. So the police stand by, while Narada eats, drinks, dances, sees the sights, marries and gives in marriage, is irreverent, sings naughty songs, quarrels and makes it up again, wears out its finery before some of it is paid for, and does all those things that good books say should not be done—because next month it must begin all over again working for the landlord and the money-lender.

The sun beats down on that exuberant emotion and ferments it, under the eyes of Brahmin priests, who understand a little of the law of give and take. The more impertinences now, the more abject the reaction presently; the little money fines and penitential gifts will mount up to a huge sum in the aggregate. Meanwhile even the lousy sacred monkeys feel the will to be amused and steal with twice their normal impudence, acquiring wondrous and enduring bellyache from plundered sweetmeats.

Passion of all sorts blossoms, and there are more sorts of it than most men guess. Scores of species of holy mendi-

*Maraj glared at him—a monster to whom
death was life and cruelty was beauty*

cants arrive from all the ends of India; so do the astrolo-
gers, clairvoyants, ordinary fortune tellers, conjurers, snake
charmers, acrobats, sellers of love philters, preachers, teachers of how to get rich quick and gamblers to show how
swiftly to get poor again, owners of fighting quails and
fighting bantams, story tellers and proprietors of peep
shows. Each sort makes its own noise, and the din adds
madness to emotion.

Murder stalks abroad. Why shouldn't it? Life and death
are one, admits Narada. Death must have its innings. We
might even see a murder, and get excited about it, and help
to confuse the police, if we are lucky. Hot? Yes, horribly.
Dusty? Whew! We sweat, and dry dust sticks to us. But
let's go and see the sights, the free ones first.

SINCE THE LEGENDARY Gunga *sahib* reincarnated and
became Ben Quorn, and the Ranee made him superintendent of her elephants, the royal elephant lines have been
the finest circus in the world. So Quorn had thousands of

visitors all day long; and because he was homesick for the gray fogs of Philadelphia he was more than usually kindly. His strange, agate-colored eyes had frightened people in Philadelphia; but here, under a light blue turban, they suggested rebirth from the storied past, so that it was no wonder that people who believe implicitly in reincarnation should insist he was a national hero come to life again.

Was he not exactly like the image of the Gunga *sahib* on the old wall of the market place? Had he not miraculously tamed the terrible Asoka when Asoka ran mad through the city? And was Asoka not the name of the sacred elephant the Gunga *sahib* rode in the ancient legend? And wasn't it fun to know how mad the temple Brahmins were, since they had had to bow to public clamor and admit that the Gunga *sahib* truly had come to life in the body of Quorn from Philadelphia?

Some one—nobody knew who, but some one—had explained that Philadelphia means the City of Brotherly Love.

Could the Gunga *sahib* come from any better place than that?

So Quorn answered questions and wiped sweat from his face until his throat was dry and he was so weary that he had to sit down on the upturned packing case beside Asoka. There he could watch all of his four and thirty elephants, each under its own enormous tree, within a compound wall that was carved from end to end with legends of gods and men.

Since Quorn came, every one of the elephants had learned new tricks; and he was generous, he staged a fresh performance every hour or so. The Ranee was generous, too, or else Quorn had persuaded her; there was free lemonade in such amazing quantities that the mystery was where all the lemons came from; and the lemonade was pink, which was a miracle, but it made Quorn feel less homesick.

He had always loved a circus—always had loved elephants, although he never knew why and had never had dealings with them until he came to Narada as caretaker of some abandoned mission buildings. Accident, according to his view of it, or destiny, according to local conviction, had caused him to climb on Asoka's neck one day when he was idly curious.

Asoka had chosen that moment to go into one of his panics, had burst his picket-ring and had run amuck through the city. Quorn had stuck to him because there was nothing else to do; and when the elephant had stunned himself at last against a wall, it was Quorn who gave him water and a cool bath in a garden pond—Quorn who coaxed him back to sanity.

It was in response to popular clamor, and only incidentally as a political move against the temple Brahmins that Quorn had been promptly put in charge of all the elephants. Nobody expected him to make good; not even Quorn had expected it. Miracle of miracles, his love of elephants had proved to be a film that overlay his natural genius for training them.

And Quorn loved his job. But he was lonely.

There was only Bamjee with whom to be intimate—Bamjee, the ex-telegraphist *babu*, who had sat at his instrument and learned so many secrets, of so many important people, that he had finally been appointed to the lucrative post of royal purchasing agent as an inducement to hold his tongue.

The only other man to talk with now and then was Blake the British resident, a gentleman so far above Quorn's social standing that, in spite of mutual respect, anything like intimacy was out of the question. Actually, at times, Blake and Quorn were suspicious of each other.

Secretly, Blake was determined, at all costs, even at the risk of his official career, to keep the Ranee on her throne and to support her modernizing efforts. Openly, Quorn was her stanch and loyal servant, cheerfully willing to run all risks and to defy temple Brahmins or any one else in her behalf. But Blake's official position as resident agent of the British-Indian government obliged him to seem critical and sometimes even threatening, so that the two men did not always understand each other.

AS FOR THE Ranee, there was no understanding her at all. Like Alexander the Great, Cleopatra, Queen Elizabeth and Napoleon, she had blossomed at the age of nineteen and burst suddenly into full maturity of intellect and state-craft. The last of her royal race, she resembled a marvelous flower on a dying vine, whose whole strength had gone into this last effort.

Raised within the customary *purdah* that prevented contact with the outer world, she had contrived, with the aid of Bamjee, who would do anything for money, to import books and to learn three languages. She knew everything that has been printed about Napoleon, Frederick the Great, George Washington, Lincoln and Grant. She had read modern novels, and was more familiar with modern views than many people are who see newspapers every morning. And she had unbelievable courage. She had broken *purdah* and defied the temple Brahmins.

If she had been ugly it might not have mattered so much, but a beautiful young girl arouses comment, and when she rode through the streets in breeches with no women in attendance, even those who benefited by her modern views were scandalized.

She opened hospitals. She superintended sanitary improvements. She pulled down rat-infested tenements and built new houses for the poor. And—deadliest offense—she defied the Brahmins' wrath by refusing to do penance for having broken the rigid laws of caste.

In consequence, her throne was rather less secure than if it had been raised on powder barrels. The temple Brahmins were doing their utmost to produce anarchy, so that the British-Indian government would have to intervene and either reduce her to the status of a puppet queen or, possibly, depose her altogether. Everybody knew that. Quorn, in particular, knew it. That was why he staged the daily circus. They were her elephants; they should help to make her popular.

"Not that them Brahmins won't get her," he reflected. "If not one way, then another. Poison." He shuddered. He, too, had to guard against poison. "Snakes. Knives in the dark. Accident. Them Brahmins only has to drop a hint or two and some crazed ijjit sticks a knife in some one else. And if she goes, I go—same way probably."

He looked up at the elephant again. "I'd start for Philadelphia to-morrow, but for her and you, you lump! Do you know what they'd do to you if I should up and leave you? They'd order out the troops and the machine gun."

That was absolutely true. Nobody but Quorn could manage the tremendous beast. And Quorn knew that the Brahmins were trying to stir public opinion to demand the summary execution of Asoka as too dangerous to live. They hoped by that means to be rid of Quorn; he might go home to Philadelphia if his beloved elephant were dead.

Quorn's perfect understanding of that phase of the situation was another reason for his taking so much pains with the daily circus; he hoped to make Asoka as well as the Ranee more popular. But he kept constantly close to Asoka, because Bamjee had warned him that an effort might be made to poison the great elephant with something deadly inserted in a tempting piece of fruit or sugar cane.

Fortunately, Bamjee also was anathema to the temple Brahmins. As the Ranee's purchasing agent it was he who had suggested buying tons of liquid disinfectant and a spray, with which even the sacred temple precincts had been drenched for the protection of the crowds who came in carnival month.

To say that the Brahmins were annoyed with Bamjee is to understate it altogether. They were in a state of fanatical mental constipation on account of him. Nothing could restore their equanimity as long as Bamjee was alive and at liberty to pocket ten per cent commissions for inflicting what they considered outrageous sacrilege. And as long as Bamjee could pocket ten per cent commission, he would commit anything under the sun.

So it was obviously Bamjee's cue to keep Quorn posted as to developments. They quarreled very frequently about the quality and price of the corn and sugar-cane supplied

to the elephant lines, and Quorn had repeatedly earned
Bamjee's contempt by refusing to accept a percentage of
Bamjee's commission. But hardly a day passed without
Bamjee visiting the elephant compound and pausing for
a chat with Quorn. He came now. And, as usual, although
he would have hated to have to admit it, Quorn was glad
to see him.

"MARAJ IS IN town," said Bamjee.

"The hell you say! Tell the police."

Bamjee was a pleasant-looking little man, in a gray silk
suit and a turban of the same color, blinking through platinum-rimmed spectacles. But he could look as contemptuous as the devil himself. The first part of his answer was
drowned by the noise of a snake-charmer's bagpipe and
the drums of itinerant troupes of acrobats, but presently
he came closer to Asoka and sat on a box beside Quorn.

"The police would resign in a body," he said, "if they were
told to capture Maraj. Self also. Am get-rich-quick expo-
nent of materialistic fallacy of me first—fallacy because of
risks incurred in course of same. Like any other specula-
tor, might go broke. Like any other egotist, might tread on
toes of wrong rival and be disemboweled with a dagger—
funeral tomorrow afternoon, and nobody, not even you, to
pity me, because I took too many chances. But there is one
chance that I do not take. I do not monkey with Maraj."

"Hell," Quorn answered. "One mean murderer, without caste or backing—who's afraid o' that man?" He knew
better, but he wanted to draw Bamjee. "I've heard say
Maraj is one o' them Chandala people—folk that are reckoned worse than hyenas—ain't allowed in cities—lower

than sweepers—insect-eaters—bums—filthy, no account savages too skeered to look at you excep' sideways."

"They are," said Bamjee. "They are worse than that. It may be true that Maraj is one of them. But have you heard of Thuggee?"

"Thugs?" said Quorn. "Who hasn't? They were stamped out. They were the guys who used to wander about the country killing total strangers with a handkerchief—just for the love o' killing. Am I right?"

"Yes, but they were not stamped out. They invented another way of killing, that is all. Death by suicide. There is humor in that. It is better than murder. He who is murdered is not guilty of his own death, but whoever commits suicide is doomed to wander endlessly in total darkness, earth-bound on the lowest layer of the astral plane. All religions seem to be agreed on that. Even I, who have no religion, nevertheless believe it. This new form of Thuggee, there-fore, dooms its victim to almost endless misery in an astral madhouse. Maraj invented it, or so they say. His allies are the Chandala, who are allowed to rob the bodies and who cover up his tracks and run his errands. You can guess who his employers are, can't you?"

"Do you mean them temple Brahmins pay him?"

"I am not so crazy. And they are so far from being crazy that they pay for nothing. A hint—that is enough. Not even such a cunning devil as Maraj could last long unless he had protection. Nothing for nothing. How does he pay for protection? He acts on hints. He overhears two Brah-mins saying so-and-so is an undesirable. There is another suicide. Nobody guilty—nobody caught—only a whisper, and the name Maraj is more dreaded than ever."

"Do you mean he kills 'em and makes it look like suicide?"

"Not so. If he is forced to kill he makes it look like accidental death. Almost always he succeeds in making them kill themselves, and there is no possible doubt about its being suicide. All sorts of ways—clever ways. Bullets. Hanging. Poison."

"Ye-e-e-s. Maybe. But that ain't suicide if they don't know what they're doing."

"But they do know. Mr. Quorn, they do know. That is his ingenuity—his creed—his purpose—his religion. It is not enough for him to kill their bodies; he must doom their spirits also."

"That guy seems to be fixing up a lonely future for himself. Even in hell there won't be many o' his kind. Well, it's pretty near time for my act. But what's the point of all this? You aren't skeered, are you, that he'll suicide me?"

"There is no knowing," Bamjee answered. "Don't say I didn't warn you. The temple Brahmins are your enemies. Maraj is in town; and Maraj is more cunning than chemicals that make no noise but work in the dark and change something into something else."

"Mind yourself," said Quorn. "I'm going to unhitch this critter."

THE CROWD DIVIDED down the midst, making a lane along which Asoka moved with ponderous dignity until he reached the circular roped arena in the center of the compound.

Asoka's mood seemed perfect. He knew that the crowd wondered at him, and he enjoyed it. He quickened his pace as he neared the arena, as if he liked doing his tricks, and he commenced the first one before Quorn ordered it, limping around the arena on three legs.

According to Quorn, he was the only elephant in the world who could turn a somersault; he did it three times. Then he walked on his hind legs; he walked on his fore legs; he played the drum; he lay on Quorn without crushing him; he picked him up and swung him, as if his trunk were a trapeze; he sat and begged for biscuits as a dog does.

He caused roars of laughter by opening an umbrella and sauntering around the ring, holding it at the proper angle to the sun, with a two-foot dummy cigar dangling from the corner of his mouth. He was so well behaved that he ignored the oranges the children threw to him until Quorn told him he might pick them up.

And last of all—his most hair-raising trick—he pretended to get angry with Quorn and chased him until he caught him, swung him in the air as if about to hurl him to the ground, but placed him on his neck instead and started leisurely back toward his picket under the *neem-*tree.

"Not so bad, you sucker. If you make yourself all that popular," said Quorn, wiping the sweat from his face, "they're liable to forget some o' your peccadillos, such as smashing up the market place and what not else. Hey—steady now! Don't spoil it!"

But a naked fanatic whose type of holiness was dancing with a dozen snakes twined on his arms and neck had forced himself into the lane between the thronging crowd and blocked the way, giving a technically perfect exhibition of the dance of death. The crowd watched spellbound, making no room on either side of him.

Asoka began to gurgle. There is no truth in the tale that elephants fear mice, but some of them fear snakes, like a man in *delirium tremens*. Asoka hated them; they made him hysterical. Quorn shouted to the fanatic to get out of the way, but the ash-smeared, naked seeker of salvation only danced the harder, making his snakes weave themselves in writhing patterns. He even began to dance toward Asoka.

Quorn shouted to the crowd to make the fool go somewhere else, although he knew they would rate it sacrilege to interfere with any one so holy. He even yelled for Bamjee, knowing that Bamjee had no fear of sacrilege; Bamjee might have courage enough to whip the fakir off the lot. But Bamjee had vanished.

Quorn tried to turn Asoka back to the arena, but the crowd had closed in behind and on either flank; there was no room to turn quickly. And suddenly the fanatic flung his snakes straight at Asoka's face. He might better have pulled the lanyard that fires a cannon. He stood still, waiting for results, perhaps for half a second.

IT APPEARED TO Quorn—and Bamjee afterward confirmed it—that during that half second some one shouted in a strange tongue to the fanatic, who glanced, as if toward the voice, exactly at the moment when Asoka launched his charge.

Asoka may have meant to kill him, or he may have been merely hysterical and in a five-ton hurry to get home to his snakeless, comfortable picket by the *neem*-tree. It made no difference. The fanatic was in the way. He became a crimson mess that writhed as his snakes had done, crushed flat where Asoka trampled him in passing.

Quorn heard mocking laughter and knew he was meant

to hear it, since it was pitched above the din the crowd made, but he did not dare to look to right or left; he had one purpose now—to keep his elephant from trampling the crowd that was milling in mob hysteria.

There were only fifty yards to go, and he discovered that he could guide Asoka easily. The elephant responded to the least touch. He was not in one of his tantrums.

"All right," said Quorn, between his teeth, "that guy committed suicide and you, you're not guilty o' murder. But who's to prove it? They'll get the Maxim out and shoot you full o' holes, you sucker! Hell, no—home's no use to you—keep going! Keep on going! You for the tall timber!"

There is nothing on four legs faster than an elephant for half a mile. Bamjee was by the back gate; it was he who opened it. Asoka charged through like a gun going into action and Quorn heard Bamjee shout to him something about Maraj. But his ear only caught the one word, because behind him the compound was full of the din of the crowd and Asoka, too, was not moving his tonnage in silence.

Beyond, lay the open road, dusty and winding between ancient trees that were the fringe of a forest, and Asoka seemed to know he must run for his life; but to make sure Quorn emphasized the information with the goad, the iron *ankus*.

"Give her the gun now! Step on it! You great big bone-head, think up your own alibi while you run! And then tell me where to hide you! Jumping gee whiz, who can hide an elephant?"

2

INTRIGUE IN THE RANEE'S PALACE

NIGHTS ARE NOISIER than days when Narada is keeping carnival; and they are lovelier, because the colored lanterns sway amid a mystery of trees and the roofs of nearly all the ancient buildings are limned in dim fire. Shutters are closed; thieves are abroad. But doors are open; shafts of yellow light cross narrow streets; the passers-by are gaud- ily dressed humans at one moment, phantoms the next.

Friends and their families sit in the doors, adding din to the din. Men, women, children sleep in any corner they can find, or on the tiled floor of the market place, or in mid-street, reckless of the traffic; shadows are avoided for fear of treading on an unseen sleeper, or a drunken one who might have lost his feeling of inferiority and found his knife. There is even a certain amount of highway robbery; people wander in groups, and those who have no friends follow any group that has the kindness to endure them.

There was therefore something suspicious and worthy of comment in the way that Bamjee hurried through the city. He was alone, he avoided groups as much as possible and he kept in the shadows wherever he could. He knew Narada intimately, inside out, and yet he wandered like a lost man and selected streets that almost everybody knew were dangerous.

He passed by gambling houses, near which the strong-arm gentry lurked to rob the winners on their way home. Somebody snatched his watch-chain.

He was so out of breath and excited that he made the mistake of trying to elbow his way through a marriage procession. Sixteen sweating dancers paused from their contortions in the colored lantern light to hold him while their overseer beat him with a long stick; then they flung him into the crowd and the crowd bullied him, not knowing who he was, until he left his gray silk jacket in their hands and escaped down an alley, where he fell over a sleeping woman, who yelled to her husband—a lusty peasant, who gave chase, crying thieves and murder.

Bamjee had to stop and bribe the peasant to let him alone, nor was the peasant satisfied until reasonably sure that he had all the money in Bamjee's possession. If he had known Bamjee, and had not been a simple peasant, he might have suspected that Bamjee did not keep all his money in one pocket.

The strangest part was that Bamjee did not head toward his own three-story house in the bazaar, with its office on the ground floor and living quarters above, where his family were keeping supper for him. He appeared to dread pursuit and yet seemed equally afraid of running into some one who might recognize him.

When he saw a policeman he ducked down an alley as swiftly as when he saw a group of temple Brahmins and their attendants armed with staves to keep the crowd from defiling them with its touch. He avoided all the temples, yet seemed deadly curious to learn what the crowds around the temples were discussing; several times he took advantage of deep shadows to approach and listen. What he learned excited him and sent him dodging again through shadows.

It was toward the palace that he headed finally, constantly glancing over his shoulder, and now and then pausing in doorways to make sure he was not being followed. He did not go through the main gate, where the men on sentry duty knew him and the officer was so involved with Bamjee in intricate schemes for grafting off the public treasury that one might suppose he would have to be friendly. Friends may be as dangerous as enemies—especially that sort of friend.

When Bamjee passed the main gate he took advantage of a four-wheeled, tented wagon going the same way to screen himself from observation. Out of breath though he was, tired though he was, he displayed the agility of a youngster when he came to a part of the wall where stones were missing and the branches of a huge tree offered means of descent on the other side.

However, his wits were tired, too. He forgot that that tree stood in an inclosure in which a sacred white bull cultivated boredom and a loathing of all bipeds. The bull was hardly larger than a big dog, but at least as active and not at all in love with being awakened in the night.

Bamjee fell almost on top of him. There was sudden and tremendous noise. Bamjee went out over the six-foot wall of the inclosure faster than a monkey, thanking a whole pantheon of gods that he did not believe in, because his pants and not his thigh muscles had caught on the bull's horn.

One pants-leg was still intact; by holding onto the other as he ran, he could make himself believe he looked presentable. It is what we believe that matters—until there is collision with a stronger disbelief.

HE FLED LIKE a ghost through the trees in the palace garden, skirting the portico and the terraces until he reached the servants' quarters and the back door used by underlings. There was nothing normal about that; Bamjee, as official purchasing agent with a position to keep up before the world, had never felt he could afford to be admitted to the palace by any except the front door. Suspicion reared itself against him, blackmail springing from it, as naturally as Minerva from the brow of Jove.

He was greeted by a *hamal*, which is a kind of go-between servant who normally does all the butler's work, and gets and deserves all the blame for whatever goes wrong. The *hamal* refused to recognize him at first, although he did concede the advisability of standing in the dark to talk. Blackmail abhors witnesses as absolutely as nature abhors a vacuum.

"I am Bamjee!"

"By Siva's necklace, that is an easy thing to say and any one might say it in the dark. But Bamjee *sahib* has the name of being a liberal gentleman."

Bamjee had to feel under his shirt for money, and it was so dark in that corner behind the butler's pantry wall that he could not see the denomination of the bills he drew forth. He had to guess.

He guessed wrong. It was too much money for a *hamal*.

"Son of an immoral mother, hide that in your belly-band and take my message."

But the *hamal* turned toward the light. He saw a fifty-rupee note. He hid it with the swiftness of a roadside conjurer.

"But, Bamjee, *sahib,* my day's work is over. I am not even allowed to enter the kitchen again until to-morrow morning. Will to-morrow not do?"

"Do you know what *now* means? Ingrate! If the nowness of the now does not make you act swifter than dynamite I will see to it that you have no job to-morrow morning. You are out—a screech-owl screaming in a wilderness of debt with a wife on her way to another man's arms and your children following the chickens through the streets to pick up food, unless you take my message now! Now, do you understand me? Go before I beat the teeth out of your head!"

"But, *sahib*—"

"Very well. I will make a great noise and summon the butler. I will tell him you offered to sell me some of the palace silverware for one-fifth of its weight in rupees."

"*Sahib,* the butler would demand at least two hundred rupees to take such a message at this hour. Whereas I, if he should catch me before I whisper to one of the maids, could bribe him with only fifty. So give me fifty more and I will do it. Thus I shall have only forty for myself, because I must give the maid ten—at least ten."

Bamjee paid him in the dark and was so impatient and excited that he never knew that he had given the man an extra hundred by mistake. He sat down in the dark and waited—endlessly it seemed to him, while the *hamal* sent the message up in relays to the roof, each relay offering excuses and objections until the last possible cent had been squeezed from the man below and the *hamal's* hundred and fifty dwindled to a hundred.

It appeared there was a party on the roof; it was no time to interrupt a royal lady, even though she was breaking every canon of tradition by entertaining men in her palace, and of the two men one an Englishman. Even Bamjee, the contemptuous skeptic, shuddered at the idea of an Englishman drinking champagne with the Ranee on the palace roof. It made him repeat to himself the dark names certain temple priests were calling her.

THE MESSAGE REACHED its goal at last and there was no more lost time. It might be difficult to reach the Ranee from below, but when she commanded from above it was as if she pressed an electric button and things happened. Men leaped to obey.

A very important palace personage was sent to guide Bamjee up a labyrinth of stairs and passages; and because his pants were torn he was supplied with an Indian costume of crimson silk before he was ushered into the presence, amid a fairyland of colored lights, in a garden that bloomed in tiled flower beds, where baskets that seemed to have been fastened to the stars swayed gently in the night air, drenching it with the scent of musk, and a splashing fountain filled the air with music.

There was other music also; women behind a marble lattice-work were playing flutes; a man was singing the love-song of the bride of Krishna. Bamjee, stepping out of darkness with the colored lamp-light on his crimson costume looked no longer like a *babu;* he resembled an ambassador from Araby, bringing news of caravans loaded with spices and slaves and jewels.

He even forgot his nervousness to some extent, because Marmaduke Brazenose Blake was seated smoking in a lounge chair, dressed in a black dinner jacket, with his monocle fixed in his eye and an air of bachelor enjoyment like an aura all around him. It was such a scandal that Blake should be there that Bamjee grew for the moment almost superior to his surroundings—almost, but not quite.

Facing Blake sat Rana Raj Singh, prince of a line of Rajput blood so purple that its sources—so men say—are traceable to when the gods made merry on the earth with men and were a trifle more than merry with the women. Tall, black-bearded, handsome—graceful with the litheness of a swordsman who can hunt the gray boar with a sword on horseback, who has lived clean and neither drinks nor guzzles.

His presence was, if possible, the more scandalous. Blake, it might be presumed, might hardly understand the horror of the Indian aristocracy if it should learn that he was sitting *vis-à-vis* the Ranee on her sacred roof—and she unveiled. But they would know that Rana Raj Singh understood the significance, even as Bamjee did. It meant that the pillars of Indian aristocracy were falling—or else changing; and to some people change is as bad as decay. Rana Raj Singh was a cataclysm, not a scandal; compared to his presence there, Sodom and Gomorrah were a minor incident.

But the Ranee, even at nineteen, which is a revolutionary age, had not thrown all tradition to the winds. She had kept its substance, while throwing away the shell. She had ten of her ladies with her, five on either hand—surely sufficient witnesses to prove to any jury that she had not sinned as deeply as Mother Eve, who set the first unveiled example.

Nor had she forgotten strategy. Her ladies were as marvelously dressed as flowers in the early morning dew, but none of them was younger than herself and some were older; none was as good-looking. Her dress was the plainest and made in Paris by a magician who knew how youth should look beneath a hot night sky amid the smell of musk and the rustle of palm leaves.

Although Bamjee knew her well, and had seen her often, in that setting she made his sharp little eyes almost snap from his head, and took away all his remaining breath.

"What can it be, Bamjee, so important that you must intrude at this hour?" she asked pleasantly. But underneath the velvet voice there was a hint of iron. It might not fare well with Bamjee if his errand lacked justification. "Speak," she said. "The company will excuse you."

"Sister of the Starlight, this is terrible and secret news I bring," said Bamjee. "Is it wise to spread the scroll of evil before strangers' eyes?" he quoted.

"Who, then, is the stranger?" she asked him. "Speak, fool!"

"But, Daughter of the Dew, there are the servants—"

"Oh, very well." She clapped her hands until the chief attendant stood before her. "You and all the servants have my leave to go until I send for you again. See that none waits in hiding behind the flower pots—and now," she said, staring at Bamjee. "What is it?"

"THE ELEPHANT ASOKA slew a man."

"I know that. It is a great pity, even though the man who

was killed seems to have been almost as disgusting a reptile as the snakes that crawled like vermin on him. I am sorry to say that Asoka will have to be shot, unless—perhaps you have come to tell me some way out of it?"

"Playmate of the gods, they are saying that the man who was slain was Maraj! He was crushed out of recognition. Who shall say it was not he?"

"Who should want to say it was not Maraj? If such good news is true your intrusion is justified. We may forgive Asoka."

"Lioness of Heaven, it was not Maraj! Maraj himself has spread that rumor and the temple Brahmins are confirming it. Why? Why not? Whoever thinks Maraj is dead is less on guard against him. Nevertheless, although the temple Brahmins are helping to spread that rumor, to you they will make no such pretense. They will send to you to-morrow. They will say the slain man was a holy one and they will try to force you to order the troops to shoot Asoka. Why? Because that would cause Quorn to leave Narada and return to the United States, thus depriving you of your Gunga *sahib*, who has been so helpful in breaking the Brahmins' tyranny. This they will do to-morrow, nevertheless knowing that it was Maraj who slew that fakir with the snakes!"

"Maraj who slew him? What then had Asoka to do with it?"

"The man was suicided!"

"Hell's bells!" muttered Blake, and Rana Raj Singh scratched the chin beneath his beard.

"How do you know this, Bamjee?"

"Beloved by the Rishis, if I should dare to tell you—"

"If you should dare not to, Bamjee—do you wish to resign from your post as purchasing agent? Do you wish to leave Narada? Do you wish the auditor to publish the report that he has shown me privately?"

"Oh, my God!" said Bamjee. "This *babu* is on the horns of a dilemma! How do I know it was Maraj who suicided that abominably holy person? I know it as well as I know I also shall be suicided if it ever leaks out who told! That very holy person was the man whose poisonous serpents were employed to slay Ali Gul the Moslem money-lender, whom all hated. Was he slain? No. He was suicided. Why not? Had he not a mortgage on a property that the Brahmins said was their property? Was the mortgage found after his death? No. He also had a mortgage on a property of mine. Was that found? No. Were any of his papers found? No. How was he suicided? He was given his choice between taking a living cobra into his bed that night or being accidentally caused to break a vial of carbolic acid with his face. And how do I know that? His widow told me. How did she know? She was in the secret cabinet where Ali Gul used to hide witnesses to what were supposed to be secret conversations."

"This story sounds fishy to me," remarked Blake and Rana Raj Singh nodded, but his nod was neutral. He was possibly confirming his own estimate of Blake's neutrality. Blake turned to the Ranee. "Of course, your highness, as your guest I cannot take official cognizance of any of this. But may I ask to be excused from hearing more. It might be awkward."

The Ranee smiled as sweetly as if she were Machiavelli himself in woman's raiment. Blake, as the official representative of the British-Indian government, with authority to advise and keep watch and report, was no bugbear to her— not though on the strength of his reports the British-Indian government might send commissioners to rule in her name and reduce her to the status of a puppet-queen. He was a sportsman and a gentleman—insuperable handicaps in dealing with a woman who understood both qualities and had the wit to play the game according to his rules, but with her own rules added.

"I might need you," she said, gazing at him. "For the present let us call this a private conversation. Confidential—under the seal of hospitality. Then, if it gets too serious, I could consent to your breaking the seal of confidence, without having to tell you it all from the beginning."

BLAKE SHOULD HAVE taken his leave. But he loved her too well, in a fatherly, middle-aged bachelor fashion. She was too amusing to be left, and also too likely to do something recklessly behind his back that might cost him months of letter-writing to his government to explain away. He was lazy and hated writing letters. His purpose was to keep her on the throne in spite of her own recklessness, and in spite of all her enemies, if he could manage it by any gentlemanly means. He repeatedly risked his own good standing with his government to cover the strategic errors due to her inexperience.

"Highly irregular," he said, frowning. "However, I will stay if you wish."

And then came Quorn—at first a message from him, saying he was downstairs in the front hall threatening mayhem to the palace servants who kept him waiting there.

"Daughter of the Dawn, he uses strange oaths, yet he is not drunk."

Then Quorn himself, treading the heels of the servant sent to bring him—Quorn in his turban, with a ready-made blue serge jacket on over his Indian costume, and in his right hand the *ankus* of office, the iron hook with which he normally controlled Asoka's ponderous movements. Servants standing near him shuddered at it. The Ranee dismissed the servants.

"Miss," he began, then hesitated, being vague on the subject of etiquette. Besides, Blake's presence bothered him. He liked Blake, but he was too much a restraining influence on the Ranee to be suffered without some resentment. Also he knew that Blake disliked that form of address to a reigning Ranee.

The Ranee nodded. She liked Quorn to call her miss—it sounded so enormously more honest than titles such as Bamjee and her servants used. She valued Quorn more highly than a dozen Blakes, and at that without robbing Blake of credit. It is only fools and knaves who undervalue one man because they recognize the different merits of another. She was neither a fool nor more of a knave than any statesman has to be.

"Yes, Mr. Quorn?"

"You heard what Asoka done, miss? 'Tweren't his fault. He was behaving gentle as a lamb. That there holy feller went and beaned him with a raft o' snakes that would have made a temple statue throw a fit. And mind you, it was done a-purpose. Some one laughed. Maybe you don't know the kind o' laugh I mean! There's Brahmins at the bottom of it, them there temple Brahmins. I've been home to clean up, miss, and my Eurasian servant Moses had an earful for me. They've been bragging to him—told him now you'll have to order out the Maxim squad to shoot Asoka first thing to-morrow morning."

"Have you any suggestions to offer, Mr. Quorn?"

"No, miss—excepting, if you will pardon me, miss, and no insolence intended—I'd as soon they'd shoot me first. I couldn't tell you, miss, how much that critter means to me. And he weren't guilty. No, miss, he didn't even throw a tantrum. He was same as me or you if we'd had poison snakes thrown at us.

"And the devil who did it had time to get out o' the road, too. He was one o' these here fanatics. He chose that way o' dying. Miss, it wouldn't be fair to shoot Asoka—not for that."

"Where is Asoka now?" she asked him.

"Miss, I've got him hid."

Because she was young and not yet spoiled by life, the Ranee did not sigh relief, she smiled it. It was Blake who sighed. Rana Raj Singh grunted.

"I have heard of hiding needles in a haystack," said the Ranee. "Are you sure that no one knows where you have hidden him?"

"No, miss, I ain't sure of nothing. But I'm reasonably sure."

"How will you feed him? Can't they follow you when you come and go?"

"That's just exactly it, miss. I want leave of absence, please, and some money."

"My steward shall give you money. Yes, you may have leave of absence."

"There was something else, miss." Quorn glanced side-wise at Bamjee, whom he trusted at any time about half as far as he could see him.

But the Ranee had a trick of trusting untrustworthy people in the same way that some people skate on thin ice, going where others don't dare to go. It pays if you can do it; and if you can't you only drown, so it doesn't matter.

"Listen to this, Bamjee," she said. "Listen well. It would do your credit with me no harm if you should happen this once—this first time—to be loyal and secretive."

BAMJEE SMIRKED A protest of his loyalty. He bowed acknowledgment of trust. He opened his eyes and snapped his mouth shut, symbolizing secrecy. He threw a chest. Manfully he held his hands behind him. He deceived the Ranee as thoroughly as a child deceives its nurse at hide-and-seek.

"I will order the treasurer to hold up for the present all the money due you for commissions," continued the Ranee. "And now, Mr. Quorn, what is it?"

"This, miss. Them there Brahmins. I figure you're number three on the Brahmins' list. They mean to get Asoka first, me next, and then you. If they can force you to order Asoka shot, that gets rid o' me automatic. I'd go home. You could get along, o' course, without me, easy.

"But you can't afford to have them Brahmins bragging they put one over on you. So I'm here to say I'll stand by you and take all chances o' black magic, and snakes, and this here murderer Maraj, if you'll okay me."

"What do you mean—okay you?"

"War, miss! War to a finish! Back me until I get this guy Maraj and prove him on the Brahmins! Flynn ain't my

name. I'm no Pinkerton or Burns. I'm plain yours truly
with his goat got and his dander good and riz. There won't
be no widow or orphans if they get my number. I wrote
my will the other day. I named Asoka; he's to have my bit
of insurance money. If Asoka dies first, then it goes in a
lump to the feller that gets the crook who killed him. Only,
if Asoka should be executed, then the money goes where
it can do the most harm; I've named a gang of reformers
in the States who'll make more trouble for the Brahmins
with my bit o' money than Asoka himself could if he tore
loose at one o' their celebrations. So that's that, miss. Are
you in on it?"

She nodded. Blake looked nervous; he knew the danger
of what Quorn proposed.

Rana Raj Singh, thrusting his jaw forward, stroked it,
running his fingers through his beard.

"My God!" said Bamjee. "You bequeath your money to
an elephant?"

"Mr. Quorn," said the Ranee, "I appoint you my special
agent to investigate Maraj and his association with the
Brahmins. You may kill him wherever you find him. You
may give whatever orders you please. You may employ the
troops, the police, my palace servants, Bamjee—any one.
I will put that in writing and sign and seal it. If any one
refuses to obey you you may have him put in prison. If you
catch Maraj or kill him, and if you prove he was in any way
associated with the Brahmins, I will raise you to the rank of
Sirdar and I will use what influence I have with Mr. Blake
to get the British government to confirm the title. Does
that satisfy you?"

"Yes, miss."

"What else? You seem to have something else on your mind?"

Quorn looked straight at Rana Raj Singh—very straight indeed, but he could see Blake's face at the same time, and he knew better than vaguely what was going on in Blake's mind.

As an independent prince without a fortune, but with a tremendous reputation, who was modern enough to woo the Ranee in the modern way, Rana Raj Singh would be a deadly dangerous spark to plunge into the magazine of local politics. His interference might provide excuse for riots. On the other hand, he had a handful of Rajput followers, than whom there could not possibly be better and braver or more willing experts at hunting a murderer down.

Rana Raj Singh slowly rose out of his chair. He nodded at Quorn. He smiled at the Ranee, showing wonderful white teeth. He smiled at Blake. Then he nodded at Quorn again.

"You will need help," he said. "I will provide it. You may order me, too."

"Oh, my God!" said Bamjee.

That was reasonable comment. When a prince, whose pedigree is older than the proudest European king's, submits himself to the disposal of a man of an alien race, whose business is training elephants and whose pedigree dates from just before the time when births in Philadelphia were legally recorded, it is thinkable, even by Bamjee, that the two of them are first-class men.

Blake actually dropped his monocle, and had to screw it in again. The Ranee's ladies fluttered with astonishment.

The Ranee looked with wondering eyes from Quorn to Rana Raj Singh and then back again. Quorn stiffened himself, caught Rana Raj Singh's eye and answered him with four words:

"Sir to you, sir."

3

THE ART OF THUGGEE

SAY THIS FOR England: a Residency is a place where any one is safe, no matter who he is nor why he has taken refuge. Since '57, when they held the Lucknow Residency against as long odds as were ever laid against a garrison, it has become a part of India's superstition that a Residency is inviolable.

The upper classes recognize it as an embassy or legation, with all that implies; the lower classes don't reason about it, but even the criminals respect it as a sanctuary, where life at any rate is safe until the law determines otherwise. No violence in Residency grounds.

"Quorn," said Blake as they left the palace, "I'm going to take you up behind me on my horse and ride you to the Residency. I've a notion you may have been followed here, and they may be on the lookout for you. I will talk with you—unofficially—after we reach my quarters."

Blake's whaler mare behaved abominably, not being used to the weight of two men, and Quorn was no horseman. They clattered on the stones beneath the guardhouse gate; they plunged and lunged along the street outside, shying at every shadow; and they made so much noise that all Narada might have heard and seen and recognized them.

However, nothing happened, and Blake's servant, running alongside, reported that, as far as he knew, they were not being followed—until they left the zone of partially lighted streets and plunged into the pitch-dark lane between high walls that led toward the Residency compound. There the servant fell and smashed his lantern.

Blake reined in, and Quorn jumped down to help the man. He could hear him sobbing. He groped for him in total darkness, finding him—feeling him just as the sobbing ceased. He could feel two men. They were both dead.

"Got a match, sir?"

Blake passed him a box of matches. Blake's Moslem servant, Abdul, lay dead of a knife wound. He was lying prone on another man, who lay face upward and who seemed to have been dead for quite a little while before Abdul tripped and fell belly downward on the long, razor-edged knife whose hilt was in the dead man's hand.

"But there's another, smaller blade below the hilt, sir," Quorn reported, striking match after match. "It's one o' them there weapons that can be used as sword and dagger. The shorter blade is stuck into the dead guy's stomach; that's what held the knife upright.

"Yes, sir, Abdul is stone dead. The long blade passed clean through him—there's three inches of it sticking out of his back. If you should ask me, he couldn't fall that hard. I'd say not. There's something tricky about the way the lamp was smashed—as if it was knocked out of his hand on purpose. Would you care to look, sir, if I hold the horse? It looks to me as if some one jumped on Abdul's back and forced him down on the knife."

"Are you positive he's dead?" asked Blake.

"As dead as mutton."

"Well, the thing to do is to get his body to the Residency. Which shall it be? Will you run on and bring back any of my servants you can find? Or will you wait here while I gallop and get them?"

"Go ahead, sir. That's the quickest. Do you pack a gat, sir?"

"Do I do what?"

"Carry an automatic?"

"No, confound it. Here, are you sure both men are dead? Get up behind me then and we'll both go. That's safer."

"No, sir, I'll be all right. I'll stay here. You hurry."

It was Blake's off night. No human being ever lived who did not make a murderous mistake at one time or another. Blake rammed in his spurs and thundered down the dark lane like a whole troop of cavalry. He made enough noise to drown the shouts of ten men, and his own shouts, to his servants, as he neared the Residency, were enough to deafen them to any noises Quorn made—not that Quorn made any.

HE HARDLY KNEW what struck him. He felt a stinging blow from behind and smelled the musty stench of a burlap gag that was thrust into his mouth and wrapped around his head.

He struck out blindly with his fists, but hardly felt his wrists seized and pinioned, hardly felt his ankles being tied before he became unconscious from the blow—or perhaps from some drug with which the gag was soaked; it tasted beastly. He had seen nobody; he had heard no sound; he could not even swear that a cry had escaped his own lips.

He recovered consciousness within a dark room and lay listening to voices that, for a long time, seemed to be inside his own head. It seemed to him he was home in Philadelphia. His taxicab had been in some sort of smash-up—his first. He felt ashamed, and afraid for his license. After awhile he shook off that feeling, but the voices seemed to come from another world—inhuman, without emotion, hollow.

At last, though, he was able to recognize a few words in the local native tongue, but it was a long time before he could make any sense of what was being said. There was an argument—hot on one side, ice cold on the other. One man was urging action, to which the other appeared insolently indifferent.

"If you don't kill him now—"

"I know my business."

"He is probably listening!"

"Let him."

"Can't you understand that the Englishman, Blake, will raise such a hue and cry that—"

"I have understanding. I am not in need of advice from you."

"By Jinendra's nose, I am not giving you advice! I order you!"

"Order somebody who will obey you—some priest, for instance. I am no temple rat."

"Too much success has made you insolent."

"No. I was always insolent."

"Suppose we should turn against you?"

"That is not hard to imagine. You are sure to do it sooner

or later. I am not afraid of you. You know why. Cease talking. You annoy me. It is not safe to annoy me."

Some one took a cover off a lamp. The light hurt Quorn's eyes; he shut them for a moment. When he opened them again a man was squatting beside him, gazing at him. He was a man with a big head, crowned with a shock of shaggy hair that seemed to have been bleached to the color of new manila rope.

He had dark eyebrows and a shaggy, dark beard and mustache that half hid and yet exaggerated the coarseness of a big mouth, around whose corners a sort of humor lurked. His nose was coarse and honeycombed with pock-marks. His big, full, deep-set eyes had humor of a sort too, but it was cruel humor; they would have been splendid eyes if they had had more color, but they were so light—gray, blue, green perhaps—as to look hardly human.

"Why do you not go to the United States?"

It was the bored voice that had pleaded insolence. Quorn lay still, trying whether he could move his wrists and ankles, wondering whether he could break the man's neck if he had his arms free. He felt an impulse to kill.

Quorn was a man who had almost never raised his hand in violence; certainly he had never contemplated doing murder; he would have been willing to bet all his money, at any time, that he never would commit murder, and would never wish to do it. Yet he felt now he would almost rather kill that man who gazed at him than go on living. There was nothing to argue about, he just wanted to kill him.

"Do you wish ever to see the United States again?" the man asked him, in the same cold, incurious voice.

Quorn did not trust himself even to try to speak. He

was working hard to regain possession of his senses, which recognized, in the man who was talking to him, something vaguely suggestive of his own peculiar influence over animals.

Nevertheless, he had never pretended to understand that influence; and this man's was not quite the same, it seemed reversed, although to save his life Quorn could not have explained the difference. Black magic was the thought that came into his mind. His head felt woozy, and he knew that was only partly due to the blow, only partly due to the drug he still tasted; there was still something else that he felt he could fight and overcome.

"Understand me," said the man, and he spoke English with only a trace of accent, "you are physically at my mercy—absolutely. I can kill you slowly or quickly, however I please, in my own time, in my own way, for my own pleasure. Sit up. I will show you something else."

HE SEIZED QUORN'S shoulders and raised him until he sat with his back propped in the corner of a wall. His strength appeared to be prodigious; it produced in its victim a sense of helplessness that had nothing to do with the cords around wrists and ankles. It was like the strength of machinery.

"There is a fool here," he said, "who has wearied me."

Quorn discovered it was painful to turn his head; however, he managed it, and decided he had not been badly hurt. He was in a small square room with whitewashed walls. The only furniture was heaps of gunnysacks, that looked rat eaten, and a small glass lamp on an upturned packing case. Another man sat on a heap of sacks, whom Quorn recognized at the first glance as the individual used by the temple Brahmins as go-between, whenever they had business with persons with whom their caste forbade them to associate—a man in a long yellow robe with a variation from the Brahmin caste mark on his forehead—a sort of bastard Brahmin, a metaphysical eunuch, authorized to touch defilement in the name of holiness without infecting his masters.

"You shall watch him die."

As if he had been shot out of a catapult the other man made headlong for the door. But the door was locked.

"You would escape from Maraj? In what way are you more clever than all those others? Come here."

His panic-stricken effort having failed, the man seemed paralyzed by fear. He turned ashen gray, trembled, unable to speak. The man who had called himself Maraj reached out with his right hand, seized him by the ankle, twisted it, drew him forward, changed his hold to the shoulder and hurled him back on the heap of sacking—all with one hand and without much noticeable effort.

"I will not kill him. He shall kill himself."

At those words the man found speech at last. He jabbered, stuttered, threatened, pleaded—until his voice died to a meaningless mumble and his jaw fell.

Then Quorn spoke for the first time:

"Out with the light, you idiot!"

The advice came too late. The Brahmin did make a move toward the lamp, but the other man seized his ankle and twisted it again until he screamed and struggled like a landed fish. Maraj then put the lamp up on a beam; he had to stand on the box to do it.

"It is time to die now," said Maraj. "Which way do you

prefer? Painless, of course. They all seek painless ways, as if that made any difference! Die! Do you hear me? Kill yourself!"

He turned to Quorn: "The poor fool threatened me. He had the impudence to order me. He said he would betray me unless I slew you out of hand. He could do it, too; he could have betrayed me easily if I had let him. But he hasn't much intelligence. Let us see which way he chooses."

He sat down close to Quorn and waited, watching his victim, who seemed several times as if going to speak—and as if then the uselessness of speech occurred to him. He even seemed to try to summon dignity, but found none.

"What will you do?" Maraj asked. "You have no knife— no rope. How will you kill yourself?"

Quorn spoke again, surprised by the impersonal aloofness of his own voice, that sounded as if it belonged to some one else.

"Why not have a crack at killing *him,* you idiot!" he heard himself say to the terrified prisoner. "I'll help you if you'll loose me some way."

Maraj chuckled. "Why not?" he suggested. "Would that not be suicide? Try killing me!"

The man found speech again. Quorn's voice seemed to have stirred lees of manhood in him. He spoke in the native tongue cold-calmly, every word a concentrated curse.

"You offspring of all the dogs that ever lay in filth! You soul of stinks! You carcass of—"

HE RUSHED HIM suddenly—and died that instant. He who had called himself Maraj stepped sidewise with the skill of a toreador in the arena. No eye could have followed the speed of the silken handkerchief that licked across the

*Craftily Bamjee wrote his name in pencil
on the toe of Siva's image*

man's neck and killed him infinitely more neatly than a
hangman's rope.

It left no mark on him. It severed him from life, and was
out of sight again before the knees could yield under his
weight and let him begin falling to the floor; and yet he
fell as if there never had been life in him nor any bones to
keep him straight.

"That is the art of Thuggee, so-called," said Maraj. "Isn't
it brilliant? In a world where so many forms of death are
messy, what do you candidly think of a so-called government that tries to stamp out and abolish such a mystery
as that? Mind you, it is a mystery. It is more than an art.

"You couldn't learn it—not in fifty years—not even
though I should be fool enough to try to teach you."

He rolled the body over with his foot, then sat by Quorn
again. For a moment or two he paused as if turning over
matters of importance in his mind. Then:

"Don't you think they ought to make me public executioner? It would make me so happy. It would save them so much trouble. Often I make a victim really kill himself, but that fool's fear was of the sort that is not easy to control. He was not sentimental. You are. Where have you hidden your elephant?"

"He ain't mine," Quorn answered.

"Liar—or else imbecile! You have no bill of sale for him; therefore he is not yours, eh? Show me a bill of sale then for the death you will presently die! Will it not be your death? Ownership! Where is the elephant?"

"He belongs to the Ranee. Ask her."

"You mistake me, I think, for a worse fool than she is. Your Ranee's hours are numbered. I said hours, I should almost have said minutes. These pretty ones—young ones—they taste sweeter on the teeth of death than carrion like that thing." He kicked at the corpse on the floor. "Does she love life? Will she cling to it? Ah, then what a sacrifice to death! Mn-n-n—what an offering! You love her, don't you? And that elephant loves you? Ah! You shall kill her. Then you shall see me kill the elephant. Then I will kill you. Perfect! Look at me."

He peered into Quorn's eyes, leaning over him. If he was human he hardly seemed so. Mania, as if it were a monstrous spirit from another plane of consciousness, had entire possession of him—a monster to whom death was life and cruelty was beauty.

Not for nothing had Quorn handled elephants in all their moods; he recognized the likeness of the thing that seized Asoka now and then. Only this was more developed—had more intelligence. He had thought of it, when Asoka threw his tantrums, as the spirit of one of nature's cataclysms, weary of blind energy and seeking a sensual outlet. But this man seemed to have the spirit of all evil in him.

"Death is a devourer—hungry. One must feed death daily, if he wants to live. Keep death fed full—and live forever! Hah! Feed life—and die forever! But you are too silly to understand that. I understand it, that is the point. You shall obey me!"

QUORN LAY STILL. He was thinking elephant. How did he manage Asoka when the fits of frenzy seized him? Let him run—offer him no opposition—hang on and wait and pretend to be one with him, seeking the same goal with the same wrath. Pretend to encourage him. Get him to use his strength against some obstacle that did not matter. Get him to exhaust himself, and at the first chance get him to believe he had done all his havoc by request. It had worked all right; the tantrums were fewer nowadays. Something of the same sort might work now—maybe—a bare chance— worth trying.

"Hell!" said Quorn. "What's all the yawp about? Do you kid yourself you're tough because you kill a few poor suckers? Yah! You don't know what tough is! You should see 'em where I come from."

"You mistake me," said Maraj. "I have been where you come from. Toughness has nothing to do with it. The tough ones die the easiest. They love life and they dread death, though they think they don't. They dread passion; there-fore they are its slaves. I love passion; therefore it is my slave, even as a woman who is properly loved is the slave of a man."

"Aw, hell! That's talk. I've heard 'em on a soapbox hand-ing out a better line o' yawp than that—bolshevists and such like. Show me. Talk don't mean nothing. I can't teach a guy to drive an automobile by singing songs to him. I got to show him. Show me. I won't believe a word of it until you show me."

All the East asserts that there is no such thing as luck, yet Quorn had stumbled on something that the men of science labored for a century to find—and doubted then. To save his soul he could not have analyzed it or have put it into plain words. What he knew, by the change in the maniac's eyes, was that he had touched off something that might presently give him the upper hand. He had gained time. He had flattered cunning. Cunning proposed to magnify itself before it had its climax.

"Why not show you? Knowledge increases suffering. Suffering is cruel. Cruelty is the delicious essence of all nature. It is essence that I seek. I find it daily. Do you understand me? Essence."

"Hell," Quorn answered, "any fool could understand that, Essence? Huh!"

"You are ignorant, but I will teach you. Ignorant men don't suffer much, not even in this world, under torture—although I know tortures that are exquisite, and I will show you several. Suffering increases as the square of knowledge. Do you know what that means? The suffering of this world is as nothing to the infinite agony provided in the next. Those who suffer genuinely here take with them an increased ability to stiffer. They add to the hell— to the hell—to the hell! Do you understand me? Spiritual, mental, infinite, eternal hell! Ah-h-h! So I shall show you. I will teach you. You shall not go forth in ignorance.

You shall be a delicious morsel for the spiritual fiends of torment. What does this life matter when you have eternity in which to revel in the blistering, nervous dissonance of death?"

"It don't matter a damn—not a damn," Quorn answered. "That's an easy one."

"Where is your elephant?"

"I can find him for you any time. Say, all you've said is talk so far—lower grade stuff. You've got me interested, but you haven't proved a thing. I saw you kill that sucker, but, hell—that weren't much; I could have killed him myself with half a brick. You show me something A-1—genuine magic. I'll name the stunt—you do it. If you win, I join your gang. How'd that be?"

"You will be my disciple? You will yield your soul to me? You will try to learn what I shall teach? Hee-ee! That would be amusing. You will go mad, but never mind. What do you wish me to do?"

"I'll set you an easy test. Put one over on them temple Brahmins. Put it over on 'em good, mind. Trick 'em—trap 'em—show 'em up—bring shame on 'em—reduce 'em to a common joke. Then set yourself in place of 'em—me under you. I'm game if you are. The folks say I'm Gunga *sahib* come to life; that ought to make it easy if you have imagination. Maybe you haven't—you haven't showed me any yet. How about it?"

THERE WAS A long pause. Maniac imagination thrilled itself with ecstasies of vision—Brahminism going the way of all things mortal, only in an agony more awful than any sane man could invent. Watching the maniac eyes, Quorn played his trump:

" 'Fore I'd reckon you worth learning from, I'd have to see you out from under them temple Brahmins' influence. Hell, they've been giving you orders. They've been claiming they protect you. Yah! I'm not the thousandth o' what you are, yet I wouldn't let that gang claim they was protecting me. I'd show 'em different. You show 'em where they get off, and I'll join you, elephant and all."

Maraj looked keenly at him. Quorn's face was as innocent as any actor's. The blind spot that is in the brain of every maniac, however supernormal his intelligence may be, permitted vanity to smother cunning.

"You'd better let me go and get my elephant," said Quorn. "Come with me if you like," he added, noticing a sudden constriction of the irises of the madman's eyes. "Then you make all the plans, remember. This ain't my problem, it's yours. I'm yours if you work it out right. Anything you say, I'll do, barring that I don't have to kill nobody until the temple Brahmins quit, and fire a lee gun, and haul their flag down. Get me? After that I'll kill as many as you say."

"Tell me," Maraj leaned over him again. "Do your wrists hurt? Does the cord cut your ankles?"

If the East is right and there is no such thing as luck, perhaps luck is a form of genius. Again Quorn stumbled on the key to freedom, though he paid a high price.

"Yeah, it hurts fine. I like it," he answered.

"Hee-ee! You do? You like it? Try this. Is it exquisite now?"

He knew where to touch the nerves that carry torture to the brain. Quorn writhed, but the lamp threw shadow on him. Maraj had rolled him over on his face. Quorn's quivering and grunting might be masochistic ecstasy.

"You will do, you will do for a pupil," said Maraj. He cut the cords; Quorn almost sobbed with the relief. "That is not a bad beginning. I can teach you. You shall learn that pain is the only pleasure. Go now. Go and find your elephant."

"Are you coming with me?" Quorn asked.

Sudden fury seized the maniac. "You witless idiot!" he shouted. "Who are you to dare to question me, your master? Do you think I need to watch a fool like you? Can you escape me? Try it! Go before I—"

He made a gesture as if to produce the handkerchief with which he could kill with such consummate art. Quorn staggered to the door, in torture from his rope-raw ankles. It was locked. His wit deserted him; he could not imagine what to do. He glanced at the glass lamp on the beam. With his ankles in that shape could he jump up from the box and smash the lamp, and take a chance in darkness? He decided he would try.

He had gathered his strength for the spring when he heard voices. Something on the outside struck the door. He heard the hinges give. He saw Maraj spring, swinging for a moment like a monkey on the beam—spring like a monkey again and break an opening, feet first, through the thatched roof. Blake burst in then—Blake and half a dozen servants. It was like a dream.

"Here you are, eh? Hurt much? Had a hard time finding you. Hello—who's dead? Well, I'll be damned—another murder, eh? Oh, look out there—catch Quorn, or he'll tumble. Lay him on that sacking."

4

THE BABU AND THE BRAHMIN

RATS ARE CREDITED with instinct that enables them to leave a ship some time before it sinks. Bamjee had perhaps evolved beyond that animal characteristic without losing the desire to practice it. He was as fearful and as fearless as a rat—as full of cunning and as energetic—as suspicious and as keen on testing information for himself. What he lacked in actual intuition was compensated by peculiar alertness.

He was not at all afraid of venturing so near to a trap, or even into one, that a sneeze or a sigh would have snapped the spring. But he was difficult to catch. And being an incredulous, irreverent, observant rat he understood the ways of temple Brahmins—which is more than quite a number of the Brahmins do, since, like the rest of us, they are, generally speaking, lazy and accept as truth much untruth as their seniors believe it wise to tell them.

"My God!" said Bamjee to himself, when he had shed the palace finery and once more held his silken pants leg as he flitted through the palace shrubbery in quest of secret foothold on the palace wall. "My God! If she should order that cursed auditor to tell the truth about me—Krishna! Women in authority are worse than men. They are more cunning. They are willing to let themselves be cheated, so as to have you by the short hair. And they hang on—dammit! Dammit! Dammit! On the other hand, should she lose her throne, this *babu's* job is gone. The auditor would see to that; I should have paid that scoundrel a better percentage—maybe—maybe—but beggars on horseback ride you down. To hell with them. And if she wins this battle with the Brahmins she will probably dismiss me anyhow and try to find an honest man for my job. There aren't any. She will ruin herself learning that the honest men are too big fools to be trusted. But that won't help poor Bamjee. This *babu* must climb on fence, part hair in middle for balancing purposes and be ready to jump kerplunk into the arms of either side with nuisance value well established."

For a beginning he climbed the palace wall in total darkness, leaving his pants inside the palace grounds. He did not propose to go home yet, partly from fear that his movements might be traced. It might not matter if they were traced, but—

"If I should choose to qualify the truth a little, it might be awkward if some liar knew where I actually went. I can do my own lying, thank you. And it costs less."

So he found a small storekeeper who owed him money and who felt flattered by being aroused from bed by such an important personage. To him he told a long yarn about having been stripped by thieves—

"And if it were known that such bad thieves lurk in your neighborhood, where there is only your shop and a few stables, you might find yourself in bad with the police, who would come and search you—and you know what that means! So you had better say nothing about it."

He bought several yards of cotton cloth and dressed himself native style. He also bought a cotton turban, wrapping the silk one carefully around his body underneath his shirt, and into that he tucked his remaining money.

"Now perhaps I can venture homeward without being robbed," he remarked to the storekeeper; and having started homeward because he was sure the storekeeper would watch him out of sight, he made a circuit and went hurrying in the opposite direction.

His goal now was the Pul-ke-Nichi—the long, narrow thoroughfare on the far side of the city, that dipped down between two mounds, on which the temples of Siva and Kali stood, connected by an ancient bridge. He had no fear of not finding Brahmins awake.

"Two things would wake them anyhow," he told himself, "the chink of money; and the least little whisper of smelly, secret news—they love it."

HE WAS TIRED to the bone, but he solved that problem. To the pious horror of the temple Brahmins the Ranee had recently installed a modern hospital in that part of town in charge of a young Sikh doctor, who was nothing if not keen on getting cases. There was a motor cycle ambulance, and a night bell.

Bamjee rang the bell, gave a false name and told circumstantial details of an accident. He offered to show the way to where the victim was, and the doctor decided to drive the ambulance himself; his presence on the scene, instead of the ignorant ambulance man, might save the victim's life.

So Bamjee lay in comfort in the ambulance while the doctor drove at full tilt through the city, missing the legs of sleeping men by inches, clearing the way with his horn and breaking all the rules of even reckless driving with a confidence in destiny and disregard for risk that would never occur to any one except a Sikh intent on winning laurels for himself.

And in the dark trough of the Pul-ke-Nichi, where the bridge cast pitch-black shadows and there were too many sleeping nondescripts for even a Sikh to take that chance of killing some one, Bamjee stepped out of the ambulance to find the supposititious victim—

"Compound fracture of both thigh bones, doctor, and the ribs of both sides—one arm broken also, and perhaps internal injury—a very interesting case."

That was the last the doctor saw of him. He slid into a shadow and followed it beside the ponderous wall of Siva's temple.

There he was challenged. Two men in yellow robes ran out and blocked his way. They scurrilously mocked his glib confession of sinfulness and a desire to meditate on the omnipresence of death in life and life in death. They called him a casteless miscreant, who might go and mock his lady mother on a dung hill. So Bamjee was obliged to change his method.

"Business," he whispered, "with the high priest! You are undoubtedly 'twice born,' both of you, to make you twice as stupid as you look, but you had better tell the high priest Bamjee is here. Yes, Bamjee! Yes, Bamjee—the man who caused your temple to be defiled with Johnson's Jubilee Germ Exterminator! Bamjee with a message for the high priest—sounds important, doesn't it?"

There was whispered consultation. One man took the message and the other stayed. There followed prickly silence for a space of fifteen minutes, broken into irregular intervals by the impatient honking of the Sikh doctor's horn, until the messenger returned.

Bamjee was to be admitted—not into the temple, but into the cell across the courtyard in which virtually unclean visitors were sometimes as an act of mercy blessed through a hole in a wall of the temple basement. So he was soused with water that had been treated by incantation, hustled across the courtyard along a row of flagstones that were also immunized against the tread of ritually unclean feet, and thrust into a bare stone chamber. Bamjee shuddered as the door slammed shut behind him and he heard the bolt slide home.

"Oh, my God!" he said. "What a man won't risk to save his neck!"

On three or four walls little lamps were burning, leaving the door in shadow. In the wall that faced the door there was a round hole, showing that the masonry was ten feet thick; the hole was trumpet-shaped, its small end inward; Bamjee did not dare to examine that very closely until he had blown out two of the three lamps and adjusted the wick of the third.

"But they will hardly dare to kill me," he reflected. "Nobody knows I was not seen to enter here. Phuh—death is an unpleasant topic—let me think of something else."

HE EXAMINED THE stone chamber. There was no window. He could hear nothing except his own blood surging in his veins. He crept close to the wall and peered very cautiously into the trumpet-shaped hole, but could see nothing; it appeared to be closed at the far end. However, presently he heard a shutter slide in iron grooves at the end of the hole in the wall. A voice spoke angrily, complaining that the lamps were not properly lit in the chamber. Another voice offered to send an attendant to light them.

"No, but discover whose fault it is. Impose a heavy penance. Go now. Close the door."

"Is that the most holy and reverend twice-born confidant of gods and treasurer of wisdom who presides over all the Brahmins of this temple to be an example to men and a blessing to the world?" asked Bamjee. "Humbly then I kiss feet. Humbly I ask blessing."

Through the hole came the mumbled perfunctory formula. Then:

"Who are you and what do you want?"

"All-wise, I am Bamjee bearing bad news."

"Because, for the sake of your pocket, you defiled this temple, you are doomed for a thousand lives to be a blind worm in the belly of a dog!"

"I know it! I know it! I sinned and the sin is on my head. *(Dog of a Brahmin! Humble am I? You shall pay for it!)* But may I not commence to purge my sin? *(Purge your own, you old tyrant!)* This *babu* has had sudden change of heart. Some god has probably observed what wrong this *babu* did *(You old devil, I'd like to drown you in a tub of sewage!)* and stirred an impulse to do better and to make amends. Oh, Most Wise—*Muddle-head*—if this *babu* has wrought evil, you yourself will do worse evil unless you give him opportunity to make compensation for his ill deeds! Am contrite! Am able to do valuable service. Am, above all, ab-so-lutely bent on telling truth and nothing but truth. Pity me and listen!"

"You shall be heard."

The shutter squealed back into place along its iron grooves and there was silence again so almost absolute that Bamjee knew he would go mad if it should last long. He could hear the noises in his head that are so quiet and so intimate that we are unconscious of them until real silence stimulates hearing and imagination invents mysterious reasons for them. Silence is no sedative. It arouses self-analysis. But in Bamjee it also aroused a saving sense of humor.

"Yes, am rogue undoubtedly. Am that sort of person. But it takes *all* sorts of persons to make a universe, and I did not create myself—unfortunately. Had I done so this poor *babu* would be billionaire—most estimable personage, with lickspittles by the dozen to say to him, 'Yes, *sahib*' and 'marvellous' and 'such high-mindedness'! Instead of which, even these rascally Brahmins dare to call me a low-minded nasty crook! No, this *babu* did not build the universe. Not guilty! And by Krishna, who is a legend, and by Ingersoll and Bradlaugh, who lifted themselves by the seat of the pants in order to prove there are no such things as miracles, these noises in my head will give me religion unless I watch out! Ah!"

Somebody was coming. The door bolt rattled. Bamjee was himself again, and by the time the door opened he looked like an idol made of hardened india-rubber, squatting with his back against the wall.

"Such hospitality! Such courtesy!" he exclaimed. "You have a mat for yourself, I see. Bring two mats. This stone floor is not salubrious to sit on."

The partly opened door slammed shut again.

"High priest is one thing," Bamjee remarked to himself.

"High priest's deputy assistant walking alibi is camel of a different smell. Noose that would neatly fit neck of high priest would not make finger-ring for expert alibi. Must use ax—verbally that is—plus irritant. An irritant deputy assistant alibi is good—as ginger under horse's tail—will kick his master into difficulties. Now then—"

THE BOLT RATTLED again. A temple servant entered, threw a mat on the floor and walked out. Bamjee spread the mat and sat on it, resuming his look of molded impassivity.

A Brahmin entered, well fed, rather athletic-looking, haughty, with the self-esteem derived from a monopoly of wisdom, carrying his sacred mat under his arm. He spread the mat as far away from Bamjee as he could and sat down, muttering incantations calculated to preserve him from contamination.

"I kiss feet," Bamjee murmured with almost as much perfunctory insolence as the Brahmin conveyed with his answering, equally formal, blessing.

"You are a spy," said the Brahmin.

"I am," said Bamjee. That admission rather took the Brahmin's breath away. He blinked perceptibly. There was a long pause. Presently: "You have the impudence to try to spy on us?"

"Have No. Had? Yes. No further need. Have found out what is necessary. Business of bargain now."

"Miscreant! Who would bargain with you?"

"Any sort of half-wise, sanctimonious sweeper of crumbs of sanctity who did not want to pass up any wise bets."

"Do you know what happens to fools who are disrespectful to the Brahmins?"

"I know what happens to Brahmins who shut their

eyes to opportunity. They are just like other people—only more so. Esteeming themselves higher they fall harder and it hurts worse. This *babu* is versed in several theologies, including atheism and relativity—perfectly familiar with theory that all is illusion and nothing provable. Am possibly a hypothetical assemblage of imaginary atoms, saying nothing to nobody in a vacuum abhorred by nonexistent nature. Nevertheless, you kid yourself you are somebody very important. Self, am pragmatist with positivistic tendencies that tell me your fall from your high place would hurt your imaginary feelings more than my fall from my low place could hurt mine. So you had better get down off that high place. It is much more comfortable down here."

The Brahmin scowled. Special sanctity can endure all inflictions except ridicule.

"Concerning what do you wish to drive a bargain?"

And now Bamjee showed genius. He knew he had pitted himself against a system—a morass of metaphysical influence that could swamp any individual as surely as stone age swamps yielded and smothered the mastodons' strength. He who would prance upon swamps requires agility and wit. Metaphysics must be met with metaphysics; bludgeons are no use whatever.

"Lost in mazes of speculative philosophy, this *babu* seeks something to which to cling—something that somebody else thinks is solid, even if it isn't. If we are all kidding ourselves, why not do it in easiest possible way. You may be right. Your teachings may be right. If they are wrong, it doesn't matter, and if they are right then the sooner this *babu* accepts them the better, not only for me but for you also. If it is true that you have power to bless and curse,

I buy blessing! With money? No. Money is imaginary and evasive symbol of gross materialism—much too difficult to get—and of no importance to one of your sanctity. This *babus* services, however, are for sale, also without money payment. In other words, with swap. My definite and dangerous deeds in this world, against your hypothetical assistance in the next!

"Am, like English Prime Minister Balfour, an honest doubter, doubting own agnosticism and afraid of consequences—if any. Shamelessly, therefore, will sell to you, in this world, now, if there is such a thing as now, all secrets of Her Highness, the Ranee, insofar as they are known to this *babu*, together with this *babu's* allegiance—in exchange for forgiveness of past offenses and recognition as eligible candidate for perferment in after life, if, as, and when. Something for nothing—maybe. But your nothing may be something after all. If so, I want it."

"You speak like a man possessed by devils."

"Many devils. Mad ones. Some so devilish that if you refuse to accept my repentance and to put me on favored waiting list of applicants for spiritual bliss, I will certainly be much more devilish and instead of working against the Ranee, I will work against you. Instead of telling you what I know about her, I will tell her what I know about you. In other words, if I can save my soul, I will; but if I am to be damned, there shall be no more damnable enemy of sanctity, living or dead, than myself. So now you know. Forgive me, bless me and use my services—or look out!"

"Blessedness can make no bargains."

"**TOO BAD. BLESSEDNESS** will wish it were cussedness before I have finished, in that case. I am not afraid of you in this world. It is the next I am thinking about. You can, of course, detain me if you wish, and I know there are dark dungeons somewhere, into which inconvenient enemies of Brahmins vanish. Oh, yes, indeed. I even know where those dungeons are. And I know the names of individuals who have vanished into them. But I did not come here alone, and if I fail to reappear within a certain time there will be reprisals."

"Liar! You came in an ambulance. You gave a false name to the doctor who brought you. You are a servant of the Ranee and an accomplice of that impostor Quorn, who calls himself the Gunga *sahib*. Quorn—even at this minute—is meeting the fate he deserves. You? For you, what evil destiny is bad enough?"

"Oh, well, no use talking to you. Let me go," said Bamjee, covering his agony of fear under a very well-acted cloak of indifference. Cold sweat was bursting out of every pore in his body and he felt sick at the stomach, but he looked belligerently insolent.

The Brahmin rose, rolled up his mat and made a signal on the teak door, rapping with his heavy finger-ring. The door opened and the Brahmin stood back to let Bamjee precede him.

"To your doom!" he remarked in a strange, startling voice. "Never enter this temple again!"

"Sanctity first!" said Bamjee with a mocking bow of abject reverence. He waited. The Brahmin waited. At last the Brahmin shrugged his shoulders, began murmuring a *mantram* nasally, like an angry swarm of hornets, and led the way out.

His signal, it appeared, was misinterpreted. A long stick,

swung with strong hands by a man who hid beside the wall on tiptoe, came down like a pole-ax on his shaved crown. It broke the stick. It cracked his skull. A second stick, from the opposite side of the door, descended on him before the blood had time to burst through the broken skin or his knees had time to give beneath him. Then he fell like a steer and his blood went pouring on the paving-stones.

The apparition—the white, whirling specter that seized half the broken stick, leaped over the body and dived into the darkest courtyard shadow—was Bamjee. One of the men beside the door gave chase—until a shadow leaped to life and the point of Bamjee's broken stick so nearly disemboweled him that he rolled in silent agony, his knees on his chest. Somebody shouted to the men on guard to close the outer gate. There was a clash of chains, the hinges squealed and the gate shut with a clang in Bamjee's face. But it was pitch-dark by the gate. None saw him.

"Seize him!" a voice shouted.

"Too late—too late!" came the answer. "He escaped us."

5

LIKE A THIEF IN THE NIGHT

ONE REASON WHY Brazenose Blake had been picked for
the post of British Resident in Narada was his genius for
official inertia and strictly unofficial action. He could be
incredibly indiscreet and get away with it.

A more meticulous observer of precedent and the
proprieties would have sent for the police. Blake searched
the dead Brahmin's clothing, asked Quorn all the questions
he could think of, left the Brahmin's body lying in the hut
and took Quorn to the Residency, where, the moment he
arrived, he sent a galloper in search of Rana Raj Singh.
Then he gave Quorn a carefully measured dose of whisky,
personally rendered first aid to the tortured wrists and
ankles, bit the end from an expensive cigar, sat down and
waited, with his feet on the veranda rail.

"No use getting excited," he said. "You've twenty minutes,
Quorn, to lie still and remember all that happened. When
Rana Raj Singh comes, you can tell the whole story to both
of us at the same time. Save breath and exertion."

So Quorn fell asleep, which was exactly what Blake
intended, and when Rana Raj Singh came thundering
down the lane at last—only a sound in the night—black
suit, black boots, black beard, on a black horse—and drew

rein like a landslide at the front door, Quorn had recovered to a point where he could tell his story almost as it happened. But his account of Maraj was understated: he was afraid that if he told the whole truth, and described the maniac whose picture had been burned into his brain, neither Blake nor Rana Raj Singh would believe a word of it.

"That's all," he said at last. "The next best thing is for me to get back to Asoka before he busts loose and comes looking for me. He's liable to look good. He knows he's only got to shove down a wall to see what's t'other side."

But Blake had not finished yet. "I found this," he said, "on the dead man's body." He unfolded a slip of yellowish paper and passed it to Rana Raj Singh. "Will you read it to us? Do you mind translating it?"

Rana Raj Singh carried the writing to the lantern that hung from a hook on the porch and studied it, stroking his beard, looking almost like a disembodied phantom because the unusual black suit that he had put on shaded imperceptibly into the darkness, offering almost no outline. Then he strode back.

"Temple jargon," he remarked. "A sort of slang in shorthand that the Brahmins use for confidential communications. It appears to me to mean: 'M'—that may stand for Maraj—'bungled elephant affair. Faquir killed uselessly, since no rioting occurred and Quorn escaped on elephant. Find M and tell him he must finish Q'—that is Quorn, I suppose—'or coöperation must cease.' I suppose it means they intend to denounce him unless he kills Quorn. It might mean that. I can't think of anything else it could mean."

"Cinch," sdid Quorn abruptly. "You keep that, sir, and let's pretend I have it. Them Brahmins 'll try all the harder to get me, and we'll trap 'em that much easier."

He watched Blake fold the piece of paper in his wallet. Then he turned to Rana Raj Singh: "Maraj ain't far off. He's as mad as Nebuchadnezzar the king was in them Bible times. But maybe they didn't teach you about Nebuchadnezzar, sir. Anyhow, he's mad, and he's got it all set in his mind to make a devil out o' me. So if you watch me you'll get him easy. But that won't get them Brahmins all compromised up with him the way we want. My thought is, sir, that madmen maybe are like any other kind o' mad critter—one idee at a time but covered awful cunning, so it maybe looks like just plain random cussedness, whereas it isn't. Get me?

"This guy's got it in his head to prove himself superior to Brahmins on all points. He's all set to take a fall out o' that gang that run Siva's temple. They've used him for a heap o' dirty work and me, I heard that dead guy threaten him. They mean to double cross him whenever it suits 'em, and Maraj, he knows it. What's more, he figures two can play that game. So the Brahmins have it in for him and me; he has it in for me and the Brahmins. The Brahmins want to get me first and then him. He wants to get the Brahmins first and then have a good time turning me so crazy that even Satan 'u'd feel jealous. 'Tain't worse than a crossword puzzle. We ought to be able to work it out."

"The thing to do," said Rana Raj Singh, "is to follow you and kill him the first moment he shows himself."

"You'll pardon me, sir, if I talk back?"

Rana Raj Singh nodded. Blake bit another cigar, scowling. All three listened for a moment to a noise outside; it was difficult to guess where it came from, but it might have been close to the compound wall, a hundred yards away.

"IF THAT IS Maraj," said Rana Raj Singh, "I expect we have him. Ten of my men followed me. They are rather good at approaching a place silently."

" 'Twould be a sin to kill that sucker and let them temple Brahmins get off free," said Quorn. "I'm mean about 'em. Maybe it ain't good manners, sir, to mention your young lady, but she's my employer. I think such a hell of a lot of her I'd take a long chance for her sake and I've no sort o' use for swine that 'u'd try to make her kill a decent elephant. I'd go the limit—and there ain't no limit—just to down her enemies and leave her sitting pretty. I know her as good as anybody does. She'd say, 'Take all chances, Mr. Quorn, and let's win this! Don't let's have another drawn game?' That's what she'd say. Can't I get you, sir, to see it that way?"

Rana Raj Singh's white teeth showed in a slowly widening smile.

"I am afraid you have my promise, Mr. Quorn. You may command me. I obey!"

Before Quorn could think of an answer to that a peculiar whistle—high C, B, C sharp—thrilled out of the darkness not far off. Then a horse tripped on a stone and stumbled. Rana Raj Singh answered the whistle, vaulted the veranda rail, leaped on to his black horse and was gone like a galloping ghost.

Suddenly: "What's that, sir?" Quorn asked in a low voice.

"What?" demanded Blake. "What d'ye mean? Where?"

Any man's hair would have stood on end, and his blood run cold. The end of the veranda was some fifteen feet away, screened by woven wire and hung with creepers. Lamp-light, streaming past the edge of a carelessly drawn blind, made a fan-shaped, milky opalescence in which a tangle of wire and creepers were clearly visible.

Something as irresistible as destiny was tearing that tangle apart—opening it, as curtains are opened down the center. There was hardly any noise. Then, in the midst of the opening, full in the lamp-light, grinned a face—a human face, inhuman as a nightmare.

"God!" cried Blake. "Who is it?" He mastered himself. He had no weapon. He forced himself up from his chair, and the face vanished. Blake strode toward where it had been, and stood there staring at the broken strands of wire and of creeper that would have been difficult to cut through even with an ax.

Quorn watched him—until a hand came through the veranda railing and seized Quorn's leg in a grip that checked the flow of blood. It checked speech, paralyzing like the cold-iron grip of nameless fear.

Then the face of Maraj came up out of the dark—and the lips of Maraj smiled upward—and the eyes of him gleamed at Quorn. They were like an animal's and Quorn knew they were watching Blake alertly even though they stared so straight into his own eyes. Then the lips moved and a voice that was hardly a voice at all, and yet that carried as distinctly as sounds carry in dreams, said:

"Get your elephant and meet me—"

There was no time for him to finish. Blake was turning, starting back toward his chair. Horses were coming—clattering, cantering, scattering stones, making as much noise as Rajputs always do when they are done with ghostly silence. Quorn felt the blood flow again as the grip ceased from his leg.

"Thought we had him," said Rana Raj Singh, vaulting from the saddle and throwing his reins to a man who galloped up from behind him. "One of my men saw him, another heard him, but he gave us all the slip."

"He was here not a minute ago—there—at the end of the veranda," Blake said. "I distinctly saw him."

"Hell, I felt him!" said Quorn. "Look at this." He held his leg toward the light and drew his trousers up to show the marks where the maniac's hand had gripped. "He ain't far off."

Rana Raj Singh whistled all his men and there began a hunt amid the shrubbery that bad fair to lay Blake's garden waste. Blake ran to the other end of the veranda and slammed a window shut, then ran into the house and locked it on the inside. As he came out he slammed the door and turned the key.

"Fine howdy-do if she should bolt into the house?" he remarked. "Why haven't I a dog? Goldarn it! Never again will I live without a decent dog. Why, even a terrier would—"

HE VAULTED THE veranda rail and vanished into the darkness to help Rana Raj Singh and his companions search the shrubbery. Quorn heard the click of the Colt revolver that Blake had brought with him out of the house.

"Too bad if they get him yet," he muttered. "We've a first rate chance, if we use it right, to teach them Brahmins a lesson they won't forget—not in *her* time."

He sat considering the Ranee and his duty to her, wondering whether it was possible, in these democratic days, to be the benevolently autocratic ruler that she aspired to be. He knew there are more than a hundred different kinds of government in India, ranging from a theocratic despotism to the fringes of fascism and social-istic experiment.

"Tyrannies, all of 'em," he muttered. "Maybe she can do it." He spoke louder than he realized—and suddenly he almost leaped out of his chair.

"Of course I can!" a voice said quietly behind him.

It was the Ranee herself, in riding breeches. He jumped to his feet, but it hurt his ankles, so he leaned against the railing.

"No, you are not dreaming, Mr. Quorn. You talk aloud so often to your elephant that you think aloud when you are alone. It is dangerous. And those others all talk at the top of their voices, which is foolish; but people are ruled by being foolish, not by any wisdom in their rulers. Have you heard of Haroun-al-Raschid—and Peter the Great—and Amir Abdurrahman? Each of them was his own secret service. I follow in their footsteps, in some respects.

"Do please be seated, Mr. Quorn. I came when I learned that Rana Raj Singh had been sent for, and I have been listening. Maraj was within three feet of me—he even touched me without knowing it. Mr. Blake looked straight at me through the hole that Maraj made in the trellis. How blind men are unless they know what they are looking for! I heard what you said. Have you anything to tell me that you haven't told those others?"

"Yes, miss! You go home! This ain't no place or time o' night for pretty ladies with a throne to lose! Who came with you?"

"Nobody."

"No guards nor nothing? I'll be sugared! The President o' the United States can't move around without he's watched, and he's supposed to live in a safe country. Prince Rana Raj Singh—what will he say?"

"We will soon know," she answered. "I hear him coming."

Blake came up the steps to the veranda. Rana Raj Singh caught sight of the Ranee in the lamplight and vaulted out of the saddle over the veranda rail. His gesture as he stood before her was inimitable, blended of an Old World courtesy, a lover's privilege, anger, self-control, a sense of outraged dignity, and hopelessness of ever teaching her the elements of common sense. But he was too steeped in dignity to reproach her in Quorn's presence.

Blake had less compunction. "You?" he said. "At this hour? Have you come to claim protection? No? What do you suppose my government will think of a queen of your age who runs such personal risks in darkness? Don't you realize your enemies will represent—"

Her musical answering laugh disarmed him. "I came for sport!" she said. "Politicians are fogeys, but is there any need to lecture Mr. Blake on sportsmanship? Rana Raj Singh is another story. Listen!" She laid her right hand on the Rajput's. He seized it and the slumbering fire in his dark eyes leaped into passion, but he subdued that.

"When your ancestors in Rajasthan went forth to war," she said, "who held the castle? Women! When your ancestors were slain in battle and the enemy laid siege, who defended the castle? Wives and sweethearts! If a woman had not held your castle against the Mahratta hordes, she ever in the front rank of the fighting, until her son was born

and the Mahratta army gave up the siege in weariness—
would you be alive to frown at me to-day? You talk to me,
and rightly and proudly you talk to me, of the ancient deeds
of Rajput men and women. Would you have me something
less than they were? This little war we wage against the
Brahmins of Narada—is it something that should make a
coward of me? You—on whom I count to help me make
my throne a power and my people free!"

He bowed dramatically, with a hint of half-grudging
good humor. Not yet officially recognized as even her
future consort, he was hardly in any position to restrain
her. Besides, her logic was not answerable. Logic is exasperating stuff, which women never use unless they wish to
defend their illogical intuition. Rana Raj Singh stiffened
himself, a grim determination to stand by and face whatever consequences she might bring down on himself and
herself simply bristling from him.

"Danger and death are nothing. It is how we die and
how we meet danger that counts," he remarked.

"This is neutral territory. Let us talk things over amicably
and make a good plan," said the Ranee.

"Neutral be damned!" Blake muttered. He had his eye
on a shadowy perpendicular pen-stroke in the darkness—
nothing more important than the pole on which, by day,
the British flag was raised. He wondered how many treaties
and laws were being broken, using his neutral veranda for
a jumping-off place in a raid on Brahmins.

"AFTER ALL," SAID the Ranee, "it is me they are after.
Quorn and Asoka are pawns they think they have to take
before they catch the queen. I wish I knew where Bamjee
is. I might send Bamjee to the temple with misinforma-

tion that should cause those Brahmins to trap themselves. Bamjee is crooked and unreliable, but I can depend on him to do the wrong thing at the right minute. If you know what somebody will do, then you know yourself what to do. But where is Bamjee? No, he didn't go home. I often have Bamjee watched; it pays. But he didn't go out through the palace gate, so the watcher hunted for him and found his trousers lying near a place where an active man could climb the wall. Bamjee is up to mischief."

"So is Asoka, miss, I'll bet you!" Quorn retorted. "I hid him good, but he won't stay hid long. He has hay enough, but he'll miss me and he'll miss his warm cakes. Folks with long noses like his have a way o' getting so darned inquisitive that rope won't hold 'em. And the rope weren't none too up-to-date. Rats had et some of it. How will I get to him? I can't walk."

"Do you think Maraj would follow if you should go on horseback?" the Ranee asked. "I heard him order you to get your elephant and meet him. Did he tell you where to meet him?"

"No, miss, he was interrupted."

"He is very likely listening to us now," said Blake, leaning out over the veranda rail to peer into the night.

"No," said Rana Raj Singh. "We have searched every bush and shadow. He escaped, but my men are watching. Not a rat could get past them. He may be lurking outside their circle, but he is not inside it."

"Very well then. Somebody give Mr. Quorn a horse," the Ranee ordered. "Let it be a tame horse, one that he can sit on even if he can't ride. And let somebody give him a big white turban and voluminous white clothing, so as to make him unrecognizable. Be sure you shorten his stirrup leathers—otherwise a child would see through the disguise. Let Mr. Quorn go to his elephant and two or three men follow him on horseback at a distance, taking care not to appear to follow him. If they are half wide-awake, they may capture Maraj. If the Brahmins are watching Quorn, some Brahmins might be caught, too. If we had the luck to catch Maraj alive, and two or three Brahmins as well, and lock them into one room—and listen—"

"Don't trust luck. Luck is always with your enemy," said Blake. "Two or three men—could they take that many prisoners? It might take more than three of them to hold Maraj, even supposing they could catch him and tie him."

"I will follow Quorn," said Rana Raj Singh, "and I will take eight men. Let the others be your escort to the palace. It is no man's business to ask me whither I ride at any hour, day or night, so if any one asks—"

"Take all your men," the Ranee interrupted. She looked appraisingly at Blake. "Would Mr. Blake mind riding with me to the palace?"

"Honored. Shall we go now?" Blake answered promptly. He wanted her out of the residency before some spy should recognize her and send secret reports to the Central Government that might keep him writing explanations for a twelve-month.

AND IF THIS plan fails us?" asked the Ranee.

"Which it will," Blake interrupted. "But it's a good plan, because it sends you back to the palace out of danger."

"If it fails us, there is this: the Brahmins are sure to send a deputation to me in the morning to demand the execution of Asoka and probably, too, the dismissal of Mr. Quorn. I shall refuse, of course, and that will make them far more irritated than they are already. I will publicly arrange to send Asoka to the old hermitage beyond the river. That will be a challenge to them; they claim the hermitage as theirs, whereas it isn't. I will ride Asoka to the hermitage, and I will ride rashly without my soldiers. That should tempt the Brahmins to occupy the hermitage and to attack me on the way, or to cause others to attack me, as is more likely. Rana Raj Singh will provide them the answer to that!"

Suddenly she turned to Rana Raj Singh—touched his hand again. "You and I have quarreled, because I rode from my palace at night, unattended, to the residence of Mr. Blake, who is a bachelor! You are leaving me—riding away in disgust with all your men! I will spread that story. All Narada shall have heard it by to-morrow noon. So you shall be a surprise to the Brahmins. Watch Quorn—keep yourself and your men under cover—let Mr. Blake know where you are, so that he can find you or get a message to you without any one suspecting you are in secret touch with me." She smiled at Blake. "Everybody knows that Mr. Blake would never stoop to interference in local intrigue, so no one will suspect him—not even his government."

Blake winced. Smoking in a powder magazine is a sane, safe and comfortable form of self-preservation in comparison to overstepping the bounds of diplomatic privilege in India. However, he who coined the motto "safety first" forgot that safety is the enemy of all adventure and of all things new, as well as of the ancient virtues such as chivalry.

"Oh, damn!" said Blake. "Well, go on. What next? I'm in for it."

"Each to his task," said the Ranee. "I go home. If any

of you happens to see Bamjee, don't be too rough with him, but send him to me at the palace. Good night, Mr. Quorn. I hope your ankles and wrists will soon get well again." Suddenly she remembered she had made Quorn her special agent with full authority. "Is the plan all right? Is it a good one?"

"Yes, miss. Good as any other, I guess."

"Very well then, it stands. Mr. Blake, shall we let them ride away before you take me to the palace?"

Ten minutes later she bowed to convention enough to let Blake hold her stirrup while she swung into the saddle.

Less than thirty seconds after their backs were turned—almost before the lamp-light ceased to gleam on their horses' quarters—Blake's office window was gently raised and a man stepped out on the veranda. One of Blake's servants saw him, started after him.

The man waited and the servant rushed him. The man stepped aside. A silken handkerchief flickered almost too fast for human eyes to follow and the servant fell face forward, separated from his life as if electric energy had drawn his very nerves into itself. He did not move. He made no sound except the thump of falling. For a second the owner of the handkerchief stood on the rail of the veranda, holding to an upright, listening. Then he leaped into a shadow and was gone.

6

AT THE FEET OF SIVA

SIVA'S TEMPLE STANDS on Siva's breast, which is a hill. Kali is the dreadful bride of Siva. Kali's temple stands on Kali's breast, which is another hill.

An ancient bridge unites the two, and underneath the bridge the Pul-ke-Nichi runs—a narrow street between the hills, a few feet higher than the level of the temple basements, which were excavated century by century until the hills are like honeycombs and no man—except certain Brahmins—knows the secret of the interlacing tunnels or how deep the dungeons lie in the foundations below the basement and the courtyard level.

Nobody knows what happens in the dungeons, or has happened in them. Certainly Bamjee did not know, although he had boasted to the contrary. He only knew that the courtyard where he stood was almost at street level, but between him and the street was a teak door, possibly a foot thick, that exactly fitted a ponderous arch and frame of cyclopean masonry. There was no escape by that route.

Crouching like a rat in the shadow he listened. He heard the gatemen say he had escaped. He heard them reprimanded, heard the order given to keep the gate locked until morning—worshipers were to be told to enter the temple

by the small door on the far side of the hill. Bamjee's problem was to get into the temple, in which there was never
an hour of day or night that did not see somebody, and
normally a number of people, meditating or clicking rosa-
ries and chanting *mantrams*. From the temple he could
walk out through the small door unobserved.

There were two chief difficulties, of which the more
immediate was the danger of crossing the courtyard. There
was no guessing how many temple attendants lurked in
the pitch-dark shadows; it was a hot night and every one
off-duty probably had spread his mattress under the stars.

"And such dogs sleep with one eye open," Bamjee
muttered.

However, it had to be risked. Another difficulty was
that he had dressed as a low-caste nondescript who had no
business within those sacred walls. A caste-mark did not
matter; that would be invisible at night, but the huge white
turban and the flowing cotton garments were a problem.
He had to solve that first.

He remembered the silken turban he had coiled around
his waist, and the thought of that reminded him that he
still had money tucked away.

"Could buy a high priest if I had enough," he muttered.
"How much have I? It feels like five hundred rupees. I
remember the time when that much would have bought
me five times over. I was always better than two Brahmins.
That is therefore ten times too much for a Brahmin's honor.
He must therefore throw in something. Courage, Bamjee-
bhai! If you can escape from this place there is no reason
why something besides dirt should not stick to you. I think
those gatemen have gone to sleep."

He could hear one of them snoring; of the other he was not so certain. However, he contrived to strip himself stark naked without making any noticeable sound. Then he bound the silken turban on his head and, timing the sound to the snores of the sleeper, he tore the cotton sheeting until he had enough to make one simple loin-cloth, which he wrapped around his waist. He could now pass for a Chattrya, who had a right to worship, but no right whatever except in a certain section of the temple set apart for non-Brahmin suppliants for Siva's notice.

So far, so good. But to reach the tunnel leading to the winding stairway, hewn out of the rock, that led upward to the temple floor appeared impossible. He could dimly see shadowy forms of men sitting in groups in the courtyard. He could hear the murmur and drone of their conversation. It would be impossible to get by them unnoticed, nor did he dare to risk losing himself in any of the other passages and tunnels whose dark openings loomed like inkblots in the night.

HE CREPT TOWARD the courtyard until, on his right, he could see the flight of steps leading to a parapet from which, he knew, the bridge stretched over the street toward Kali's temple. Kali's temple would be worse than Siva's, as far as concerned getting out of it; its priests were not on speaking terms with Siva's priests, whom they regarded as loafers lacking discipline and zeal.

But Bamjee knew that the parapet, and the bridge beyond it, as far as the midway barrier erected and protected by the rival priests of Kali, was a zone where idlers often broke the temple rules unknown to their superiors.

It is not alone in Christian churches that the devil incites the sanctified to shoot craps in a vestry now and then; the critics of Christianity have problems also. Bamjee, seeing that the moonlight streamed down one side of the steps and left the other half in darkness, tiptoed silently along the shadow by the wall and climbed in search of sinners *in delictu.*

"Luck," said Bamjee to himself, "is a hole in the roller of God that otherwise crushes us. I have found one or two in my day. Maybe I find another now."

He did. There were no card parties, such as he hoped for; no surreptitious singing of immodest songs; no drinking—nothing of any blackmail value, until he peered around an image of the temple god, on whose impassive shoulders scores of pigeons slept, and saw a woman, who shrunk herself into a niche in the masonry, weeping. Never a man met misery with greater pleasure.

"Woman," remarked Bamjee, "I disagree with you. It may be you are all he said you are, and worse, but you are not the most desperate person. I am he. I, too, am made incredulous of the divine because I rashly trusted a disciple of divinity. What shall you do? I don't know—until you tell me what the matter is. First you shall tell me your sad tale, then I will tell mine. Thus we may help each other."

She was a pretty, soft-willed little woman of the sort that any rascal can seduce with words that ooze romance, and she had given all she had to somebody, no doubt of it.

But like many another little fool, she had seemed so foolish that her sanctified betrayer had dared to warm his vanity at the flame of her admiration by revealing secrets to her that he thought were safe in her simple mind, and now she only asked for sympathy to make her bubble them all forth, the last first, in the order in which they crowded memory.

She had not depth enough of grief to be ashamed; she was only sorry for herself. First come, first served; if she had known that Bamjee was an expert at uncorking secrets, she would have told hers nevertheless. She simply had to talk.

"A little cash," said Bamjee to himself, "applied at the proper moment, in the right way, heals all the smarts of ignorance. It is only knowledge that is incurable." So he applied the cash.

He pointed out to her how money pays for care at the Ranee's hospital; and he told her of the Ranee's school of industry where women became self-supporting and were protected from rapacious relatives, so that even lawful husbands could not claim them and collect their earnings. Such talk was like a fairy tale, but the hundred rupees that she clenched in her hand were true enough. So she told the truth, too—first the name of her seducer, then his temple rank, and then, to match those wonder tales of Bamjee's, one by one his secrets.

"And he will come for you? He will come for you here?" asked Bamjee.

"Oh, he must. He will come to get rid of me when he comes off duty. I can't get out of the temple without his help."

SO BAMJEE WAITED, getting her to tell the tale again until she grew suspicious and, having told it all twice over, suddenly decided to be secretive. Bamjee knew exactly what to do with that mood.

"If you say one word more I will ask the Ranee not to admit you to her hospital and to her school after your baby is born. From now on, silence! If you speak when the priest comes, I will tell him what you have told me."

It was late—hardly an hour before sunrise, when the culprit came: a shaven, well-fed, healthy Brahmin, with a long nose and a mouth less cruel than irresponsible. He did not see Bamjee, who had perched himself up on the arm of Siva's statue, disturbing numbers of pigeons that came back and slept on his shoulders. The Brahmin began upbraiding the woman, resuming a conversation where it had been interrupted when he went on duty in the temple:

"How should I know that the child is mine? And if it were, what of it? Do you know how great an honor is intimacy with one of my caste? Do you know the penalty for bringing a Brahmin into disrepute? Do you know the law against adultery? Do you know what your husband can do to you if he suspects that child is not his own? And do you know the penalty for trespassing within this temple? Do you know the sin of ingratitude? Do you know—"

"Do you know who I am?" Bamjee asked him. When he moved he disturbed the pigeons, so that up there on Siva's arm he must have looked amazing at the first glimpse; the Brahmin's imagination may have clothed him in other-world emblems of association with the gods. The Brahmin put the palms of his hands together and touched his forehead. Then he knelt with bowed head.

Bamjee stepped on to his head. He rapped his forehead smartly against the stone work. Then he squatted, and when the Brahmin looked up it was at Bamjee's platinum-rimmed spectacles.

"Who are you?" he demanded then, angrily, aware that

he had made a fool of himself. Perhaps he suspected that Bamjee was the woman's husband.

"Point is, I know who you are," Bamjee answered. "I know what you have been doing and I know what you are going to do."

Recognizing Bamjee as any rate not of Brahmin caste, the Brahmin resorted to the insolence that is the essence of the pretensions of his breed. "Dogs now and then bark at their betters, but—"

"But the betters avoid being bitten sometimes," Bamjee answered. "One thing you will do, when I am ready, is to guide me and this woman from the temple."

"Oh, is she your woman?"

"The whole temple shall know she is yours, at the top of my lungs," said Bamjee, "her lungs also, probably—unless you swallow your impertinence and listen. You will do exactly what I tell you. Otherwise you shall be known as a Brahmin who has defiled himself—and much more also. The Ranee shall learn all about your plans. Oh, yes, I know all about them. No, no, you cannot immure me in a dungeon—not for many minutes. It is known where I am. I am not at all afraid of being caught in here. I am a spy! Yes, certainly, a very good one. And I don't mind telling you who pays me: a committee of the merchants of Narada! What for? They are weary of the Ranee. They desire to know whether or not you Brahmins are concerting action against her. If so, they will be very generous to the temple treasury, but if not—"

"If not, what then?" the Brahmin demanded.

"Never mind. I know your plans now. They are good ones."

The Brahmin sneered. "You have learned them from that fool?" He glared at the shrinking woman as if eyes could burn her up. Not even the dark shadow of the overhanging statue prevented the woman from seeing and feeling his wrath. In another moment she would have denied having told anything, but Bamjee forestalled her.

"I have said I am a good spy, oh, person of small intelligence!" Bamjee was itching to get away, but he betrayed no trace of it, he appeared willing to talk until after daylight.

"Would a good spy listen to a woman? To a woman with a grievance? I have been all night listening to the twice-born groups of holy chatterers who sweat below there in the courtyard. As for the woman, I only use her as a stick to beat you with, to make you guide me out of the temple. In return I will see you well rid of the woman. I will attend to the woman. You need not give another thought to her. Give her your blessing—and perhaps a little money—"

Bamjee knew perfectly well that no temple Brahmin would give up money to a woman. Thoroughly he understood the money hunger of the men who were supposed to get along without it.

"MONEY? I HAVE none," said the Brahmin.

"Never mind. If she agrees to be silent, perhaps I myself will give her some," said Bamjee. "I have plenty. The merchants of Narada pay me handsomely, in return for the risks I undertake. How many men are there who would dare to spy into this temple? Daring and intelligence such as mine command a market price. I could even spare you some—perhaps—if you should need it."

"To the giver the reward," the Brahmin answered. "There is virtue in giving."

"Yes, undoubtedly. But"—Bamjee blinked behind his spectacles. He was taking a long shot at a venture, betting on his own imagination and the inspiration of the moment—"who is to guarantee that Maraj will perform his part of the bargain? Maraj bungled that elephant business. It is true he induced a fakir to frighten the elephant, and the fakir was silenced by instant death, but who else suffered?"

The Brahmin's breath was almost taken by the question. Leaning, almost touching faces, Bamjee thought he noticed signs of that snail-like withdrawal into a mental shell that all the East knows how to practice and that is so difficult to probe. So he went on talking, telling what he really had learned from the woman, not what he guessed:

"It is a good plan to demand that the elephant be slain and that Quorn be dismissed from her service. She will refuse both demands, undoubtedly. The next move after that is equally well considered, since she is proud and obstinate and fearless. Let the deputation say to her: 'If true that this monster is fit to live, and that Quorn can manage him, prove that to us. Ride him yourself. Order Quorn to put the howdah on him, and do you ride in the howdah.' That is excellent, and she will do it, because she is young and foolish and excitable. But who is to guarantee that Maraj will make the elephant unmanageable? Who? Who guarantees that? I have a sum of money for that man, if I can find him. Some now, more afterward. Who is he?"

The Brahmin tapped his own chest. Bamjee nodded, but produced no money yet. He knew those Brahmins.

"How will you go about it? How will you manage a maniac?" Bamjee asked.

"Easily. We would withdraw our protection—he would not last one day if he should fail us. Besides, the old hermitage has been his hiding place so long that he feels like a ghost that haunts it. Maniacs have iron minds. They yield up no obsessions. Rather than be driven from the hermitage Maraj would—anything. There is nothing he would not do rather than yield that hiding place. Part of the plan is to speak to the Ranee craftily about the hermitage, inducing her to claim she owns it. We defy her. She goes for a ride on the elephant. Somebody subtly suggests to her to ride toward the hermitage and take possession. Then I notify Maraj that she is coming to cast him forth. And there will be enough of us near the hermitage to be witnesses that she was on her way to seize temple property. Thus all Narada will know afterward that her death was a just penalty inflicted on her by the gods."

"ARE YOU SURE you can find Maraj?"

"Oh, yes, I can always find him. I have only to make a certain signal. Then I meet him at a certain place. Two of us know that signal. One of us is with Maraj to-night. He was to try to persuade Maraj to kill Quorn, but the plan appeared to me ridiculous—too risky—too many chances for Quorn to escape. I am sure he will be back soon saying that the plan failed. I hope it does fait. To-morrow's plan is better because she and Quorn will both die at the same time—Maraj also, perhaps."

"Much better," said Bamjee. "Here are three hundred rupees for you. There will be three thousand more if the plan succeeds. Will you be at the hermitage?"

"Yes. Please bring the money to the hermitage. And now

you had better go if I am to guide you and this woman without your being seen."

"Come, woman! Come!" commanded Bamjee. But before he went he wrote his name in pencil on the toe of Siva's image.

"Proof," he muttered, "proof that I have been here might help, if the Brahmins—yes, it might help either way the cat jumps."

Through a maze of passages, in darkness, up and down enormous stairs between enormous walls, they reached a narrow door at last that opened on an alley.

When the door was shut behind them Bamjee sat down on the step. He had his pencil, but no paper, so he tore a corner off his cotton loincloth, and on that he wrote a short note to his wife. He gave it to the woman.

"Take it to her," he commanded, "and say nothing until you see me. You will receive food and a bed to sleep in. But before you go to sleep, remember and remember and remember every word you heard that Brahmin say to me. Now run!"

The woman ran. Bamjee sat still on the step, his head between his hands. He was tired to the verge of hysteria.

"What next? What now? Are there any gods? I doubt it. If there were they would admire—they would inspire me! To the palace? Tell her? Certainly not; she would get the credit and Bamjee would be left out in the cold as usual. Then what? Never mind the danger—danger is the spice of profit. Who—where—what is the key to the riddle now? Quorn is!

"Can I find him? Where did he hide that elephant? Puzzle: find an elephant. Only all outdoors in which to look. And at that he may be indoors. Nevertheless if I find the elephant I find Quorn. Not there? Only have to wait, perhaps sleep—Quorn will arrive presently. If I can find him, tell him, make him understand, perhaps—oh, damn perhaps! I am a genius—I can be what that idiot Blake calls a god in a box—no, god out of a box. Critical moment, pull plug—save everybody—here—credit—thank you, Bamjee—profitable—very. Where could Quorn have hidden that abominable pachydermatous atrocity? Oh—all that distance?—walk—well—"

Bamjee walked until he found a pony that had stood all night hitched to a shop door. It had a bridle, but no saddle.

"Flagrant breach of regulation number so-and-so—duty of any citizen aware of same to take steps—pony, do you know where the city pound is? Neither do I. Let us look for it. Canter, you hairy curse, or somebody may catch us!"

7

ASOKA IN HIDING

THE OUTCAST'S LOT is not a happy one, but there are compensations. The Chandala are regarded as so untouchable that even sweepers will have nothing to do with them. They are not allowed in cities. Such villages as they have are in the jungle, where they are neither taxed nor troubled by the census taker. If they die, they die; and if they rot, they rot; it is nobody's business.

So they are as free as any sort of human being can be, and the proof that they are actually human is that they crave what they have not got—servitude.

They ignorantly ache for a red-hot religion and rules and a boss to deprive them of liberty—a fact which had made it very easy for Maraj to pose among them as a being from another world.

Quorn had merely taken pity on them and employed them to cut grass for his elephants. He had made a number of journeys into the jungle to show them what kind of grass he wanted, and on one of these expeditions he had found a ruined building, roofless but otherwise serviceable. It had been full of trash and brambles when he first discovered it, but he had made use of the elephants to clean it out, and he was using it now as a place in which to hide Asoka from the machinations of the Brahmins.

He could with fair confidence count on the Chandala not to give away the hiding place because of their ingrained, justified and lively mistrust of any one asking questions or even trespassing into their part of the jungle. It was not very far from Narada—at any rate, not more than twenty miles—and he reached it on Blake's skewbald errand pony not long after daybreak. He was rather surprised that there were no Chandala, lean and dirty-looking, perching on the walls like vultures to stare at Asoka.

He turned the pony into a roofless room beside a heap of hay and limped into Asoka's chamber, where a glance told him that nothing whatever was wrong. Asoka greeted him, gathered him up in his trunk, hoisted him up on his head, and the two went down to the creek for the morning drink and a mud bath.

That took time, because the mud had to be washed off afterward, which meant a long swim and a lot of fooling, so the sun was well up over the trees when Quorn rode back along the jungle glade and reëntered the ruin. He could see, at a bend in the glade, the broken branches that Rana Raj Singh had thrown down to mark and at the same time to conceal the trail down which he and his men had ridden to hide in the *nullah* not far away. It was probable that one man, or perhaps two, were in the trees on the alert, but it would need second-sight to discover a Rajput scout, even if you knew exactly where to look.

Quorn proposed to himself to get some sleep, although it was a poor place for it because the flies were awful. However, he gathered green leaves with which to cover himself, shook the hay to make sure there were no snakes in it, and lay down, near enough to Asoka to be awakened if the monster should grow restless.

He was watching, through a chink between the leaves, the great body swaying to the rhythm of the spheres, or whatever it is that elephants are conscious of, when Bamjee came cantering down the glade and, after turning his pony into the same inclosure with Quorn's, broke in on Quorn's peace.

"OH!" SAID BAMJEE. "I am glad to see you!"

"Can't return the compliment," said Quorn, sitting up and brushing hay out of his hair. "You're a buzzard of ill-omen. Any time you show up there's grief around the corner. What's eating you? You didn't run me down for nothing?"

"Nothing? What is nothing? If everything is nothing, as the Yogis say, then nothing is everything. Everything is enough. I have every reason. Shall I name one?"

Quorn sighed and filled his pipe. "You look like the wreck o' the Hesperus. Indecent, you, a father of a family, sporting around in a turban and cotton gee-string. I'm ashamed of the elephant seeing you."

"Nevertheless," said Bamjee, "I am the person who will cause you to become a Sirdar. Sirdar Benjamin Quorn: how will that look on the envelope? I know now what the Brahmins intend to do. You shall defeat them with my help. You shall have all the credit, but you must promise to pay me half of the big bonus that the Ranee will undoubtedly give you."

"Nix," Quorn answered. "Getting's keepings. Play your

*Then came the shudder and shock as Asoka struck
the wall with his enormous forehead*

own hand. You wouldn't offer to deal me in unless you
wanted me so damn bad you're fair busting. So shoot."

"Well, I could easily go to the Ranee with my story."

"You can soap yourself and slide to hell with it. I ain't
particular."

"If I should tell you what I have ascertained, will you
promise to recommend me also for a bonus?"

"No. You make enough off the gum you lick off postage
stamps to pay my salary twice over. When I make promises, I know why. And when I don't make 'em I know why.
You're why. Get me?"

"Well, if I should take you into my confidence—"

"You mean get me to trust you? Can't be done."

"If I should tell you what I know, and you should use
that information, and by using it should not only save the
Ranee's life, but also catch the Brahmins in their own trap,
would you see that I get credit for it?"

"Mebbe."

"Is that your best bid? Listen, Mr. Quorn. The Ranee appointed you her agent to hunt down Maraj and to connect him with the Brahmins. You may order everybody—troops, police, palace servants, Prince Rana Raj Singh, even myself. I have information, and I am willing to tell you how to solve the riddle—how to give the necessary orders and so snatch fame and reward in the very face of destiny. What will you do for me?"

"You mean if you ain't lying? If you really have that information? I'll hold you underneath that elephant while he does a Charleston on your belly—unless you tell me dam-quick every word you know. Sit down there. Spill it. Satan's high hat! You, as naked as a nigger, coming here to try and *sell* me something that might save *her* life? Act your age, Bamjee. Say all you know, and say it quick."

Even his enemies, of whom he has several, say this of Bamjee: that he knows when to capitulate, and that he does it with a good grace. He ignored Quorn's rudeness, threw all stipulation to the winds, and plunged into his story, relating in minute detail what had happened in the Brahmin temple.

"And I tell you, Mr. Quorn, that they are tired of Maraj, even though they do not say so in plain words. They are afraid of him. They are almost as anxious to see the end of him as of you and the Ranee. I think it likely they will snap him in the same trap in which they hope to catch you. All you need to do is ride into the trap and have Prince Rana Raj Singh lie in ambush; each of his men will have a Brahmin on his lance before the day is over.

"But if you tell the Ranee beforehand she will give

neither you nor me the credit. And if you tell Prince Rana Raj Singh, it will be the same story—"

A shadow fell between them. Then a hollow voice:

"And if you tell Maraj? What if you should tell Maraj?"

BAMJEE ALMOST FAINTED. Maraj had climbed over the wall and approached from behind them. His maniac eyes looked burned by lack of sleep, and his movement was almost simian, but an intelligence, mocking and masterful, glowed beneath the surface. However dry his eyes might seem, they looked indomitable. He lifted Bamjee by the neck with one hand and dumped him beside Quorn.

Then he sat and faced them both. Quorn noticed that Asoka was beginning to grow nervous.

"Snap Maraj in a trap! That is funny!"

"Hell!" said Quorn. "Of course they couldn't catch you in a trap."

"But I will catch them!"

"Sure you will. O' course you will. That's a part o' the bargain you made with me."

Genius has nothing whatever to do with education. It is a gift for recognizing the essence of things and what to do about it. Quorn knew nothing about maniacs, just as he had known nothing about elephants until he came to Narada. He could not have explained his method; it would certainly not have occurred to him to say there was something simple about a man whose manhood had been lost in a maze of egotism and murderous cunning.

He did not think about it. He acted, simply.

"Would you break our bargain?"

But Maraj was suspicious. "There is new horse-dung on the track. Whose horses?"

"Mine. Bamjee's."

"Many horses. Whose?"

"Rana Raj Singh and his men. Rana Raj Singh quarreled with the Ranee—pulled his freight. Off in a huff. Nobody knows where he's going, and nobody cares."

Something in the maniac's eyes altered. Cunning beneath cunning readjusted purpose beneath purpose. Quorn noticed a sudden blaze of anger that was instantly suppressed and hidden, under too much suavity; but he had no means of knowing that Maraj had listened through Blake's window to the whole of the Ranee's conversation.

"He is after Maraj," said the maniac.

He was being so subtle now that subtlety oozed from his lips in a conceited smile, defeating its own end. Simultaneously Quorn and Bamjee recognized that his conceit could be his own undoing.

"What do you care?" Quorn asked. "Ain't you a match for him?"

"Yes, and for the Brahmins also." He fixed his eyes on Bamjee's. "You did not know, did you, that I was listening behind the wall? I heard you say the Brahmins mean to snap me in the same trap with the Ranee. So they shall. I will be the bait. I will draw the Brahmins, too, into their own trap. Rana Raj Singh shall find them in it, and destroy them. But, first, they shall destroy the Ranee, so that he shall have the impulse to destroy them. Ho, but we will feed death! And though they close me in a trap without an outlet, can they keep me in it?"

He grinned, glaring again into Quorn's eyes. "Afterward, you and I will keep that tryst—when you have no elephant to think about—nothing to think about except me, your master."

MARAJ GOT UP and stared at Asoka, having glanced first at the ropes that held the monster's hind feet. He was well out of reach of his trunk. He said nothing—did nothing— only stared. But the elephant, already nervous, suddenly grew panic-stricken, screamed, tried to reach him and kill him. He did his best to burst the heel ropes.

Quorn's fingers were on a piece of broken masonry; the intention to crush the maniac's skull with it burned in his brain and his veins, but the stone was too heavy to lift. Maraj turned to him and grinned:

"Soon—soon now you shall learn what it means to be all-passionate, and at the same time helpless. That is agony—exquisite, exquisite agony; dew on the flowers of death. So fragrant! So delicious! Wait and see."

He sprang to the wall in three strides then, vaulted it, and vanished. Quorn went to Asoka and spent a whole hour coaxing him back to calmness.

"Did a bogy scare him? Daddy's big boy! Never mind, we'll show 'em. Nex' time, maybe, we won't have no heel ropes on—and then what?"

Suddenly Quorn turned on Bamjee: "Get a move on, you. Time enough to take it easy when you're dead. Go find the Ranee and tell her every word of what's took place. Don't you leave one word out. And if them Brahmins have already been to her with their demands, you tell her from me to give out that she'll ride Asoka to that there hermit-age to-morrow morning. I'll have him saddled and ready and at the palace door.

"She'd better order about half the troops to march

behind her, but remember: them guys aren't dependable against the Brahmins, so they'd better start late and come along slow; they're jes' for appearances. I'll see the Prince. And say, see Mr. Blake. Tell him if he wants to see sport and maybe be a bit useful, he'd better ride Asoka with the Ranee. That's all. Get your pony and get out o' here."

When Bamjee had departed, Quorn took Asoka for another mud bath and a swim.

"Lord," he muttered as he rode out of the ruined building, "do you suppose that maniac heard what I jus' said to Bamjee? Well—who cares? I'm betting on the Prince and twenty Rajputs. There'll be a picnic." Then he went on talking to Asoka: "Trouble you make, don't you? Never mind, though, you ain't guilty this time. Use your big bean, or they'll execute you day after to-morrow at sunrise.

"What you're needing is a first-class working alibi, and durn me if I know one. You killed a guy. You've got to offset that somehow. Maybe alibi's the wrong word—I ain't no lawyer. Anyhow you use your bean, you sucker, and I'll use mine, and we'll get you a verdict o' not guilty some-how—somehow. Self-defense? Extreme provocation? No evidence? Hell—none o' them won't do. We got to get an alibi or bust!"

8

A TRAP FOR ASOKA

NARADA KNEW THAT there were tantrums in the wind. It was the time of year when corn-fed elephants go *musth* and men are inflamed by all the tom-tom of the marriage drums until imagination, like a strange gas, maddens the whole mob.

It was normal in the month of carnival for slumbering resentment of a thousand years of wrongs to blaze into sudden flame and make a smoke-black ruin, of—perhaps a street of money-lenders' houses, or a mean mosque, raised by poor Mahommedans whose chaste and inexpensive minaret had too long pointed to a scorching sky.

No agitator needed to harangue hot crowds and tongue-lash lethargy into a spate of violence. It only needed murmurs—of the right sort, from the right source. And it is a strange fact that the more men mock the methods, and the servants, and the outer symbols of religion, that much easier it is for whisperers to stir them to the state where they will stab each other.

Nowhere more than in Narada are the Brahmins hated. Nowhere is it easier for Brahmins of a certain sort to stir with almost noiseless tongue the terrible volcano that resides in ignorant minds.

And so it happened that the Ranee's troops could not march on the day when Quorn brought back Asoka to the city, polished him until he shone, harnessed him with the lightest hunting *howdah*, and rode him, stately as a page of legend, through the crowded streets toward the palace. The troops were needed to the last man—fifty of them— to parade with gleaming bayonets and make rioting look like too risky a gamble.

There were two tales circulating. One was that the Ranee had defied the Brahmins, which nobody minded much, although they shuddered at the sacrilege while they secretly and even openly enjoyed the scandal.

It was the other tale that made men glower when they heard it. It was not enough that the Ranee kept and protected and used an elephant that had slain a very holy fakir. She had employed Maraj to cause the elephant to do it. The Brahmins said so.

And to show how fair and strictly truthful the Brahmins could be on occasion, had the Brahmins not admitted publicly, and now privately, that Quorn truly was the reincarnated Gunga *sahib?* The Brahmins had explained it perfectly: it was just another case of ingratitude to the gods who had provided the Ranee with agents for the accomplishment of holy purposes, in the form of Quorn and his elephant; agents which she had promptly used for unholy purposes.

There could only be one possible end to it. Quorn, of course, would have to suffer for letting himself be so misused. The elephant—the Ranee—well, whoever should kill all three of them might have to be a martyr for it, but inevitably he would turn out to be the agent of the angry gods who would mete out due reward in the hereafter.

As for Maraj, it was obvious now how he had escaped capture and punishment for all those horrible murders. Anybody could understand it now, since the Brahmins had told the truth about it. The Ranee had been protecting him all along. Her offer of a heavy reward for his capture had been nothing but a blind to deceive people. She had been making use of Maraj to get rid of her enemies.

True, many of the people murdered by Maraj had seemed unimportant and not dangerous. It was equally true that some of them had been notorious enemies of the Brahmins.

But there were plain answers to both those questions. In the first place, tyrants grow afraid of shadows, and kill imagined enemies without rime or reason, that being one of the aspects of tyranny. In the second place, people who oppose themselves to religious authority must not blame the authorities if the gods take steps to destroy such opposition.

Nobody should blame the Brahmins for the gods' annoyance. One did not have to like the Brahmins personally, or even collectively, nor need one approve of all their arrogance, in order to see the unfairness of blaming them for what the gods might do. One did not have to hate the Ranee or to call her beauty ugliness and her generosity meanness, in order to see what a fool she had made of herself, and what a wicked woman she had been to employ and subsidize Maraj.

BESIDES, THE RANEE had discarded *purdah* and neglected many of the ancient customs. She had repeatedly defied the Brahmins who are, after all, the fountain-head of wisdom. She had opened hospitals, where people died at the hands of heretical doctors in spite of all the genuine remedies that were smuggled to their bedside.

She had opened a school for women, where women were actually taught, in so many words, that they had rights as well as obligations. She had closed the brothels, which, as everybody knew, were a social safety-valve. And she was proposing to marry a man of her own choosing.

The gods don't tolerate such infidelity for long; when they are weary of it, they act suddenly and swiftly.

So the city was in an expectant, ugly mood, and there were ugly rumors, borne on the wings of nobody knew what. Everybody knew that something terrible was going to happen. Those who owned property were afraid, and those who owned none, or owed money, were belligerently watchful.

The only thing that prevented rioting from breaking out in a sort of spontaneous combustion was the gleam on the bayonets of the Ranee's infantry and the beautifully polished brass of their machine gun, strategically stationed where they could do the greatest amount of damage in the shortest possible time.

The sun beat down on all that mixed emotion like a million discordant cymbals of yellow brass, heat and noise being only different vibrations of the selfsame violence.

So as Quorn rode Asoka through the streets he did not receive his usual ovation. Children were not lifted up to look at him. No women threw him little bunches of waxy flowers. And the story of Asoka's slaying of the holy fakir had been so spread and so exaggerated that the throngs in the narrow streets melted away ahead of him; whereas it had always been Asoka's reputation that, though his temper was terrific, he was dignified and patient toward a crowd, particularly if the crowd was noisy in its admiration.

Asoka sensed the change of public sentiment almost, if not quite as readily as Quorn perceived it, and by the time he reached the palace he was already showing symptoms of uncertain temper. Quorn's voice kept him in control and he behaved beautifully under the palace portico while they set the ladder against him and the Ranee climbed into the *howdah;* but as he started off he was rumbling in a way that called for several smart raps with the *ankus* to remind him he was not his own master.

Blake was on horseback and had brought four mounted servants with him. They were a sort of superior *sais,* quite undependable except as grooms, and unarmed, but Blake's own automatic reposed in a holster underneath his shirt; he appeared ill-tempered, in a mood to use that pistol, in spite of his diplomatic status.

Blake was the type of man who, when he does get involved in indiscretion—as every diplomat worth trusting, and every diplomat who ever accomplished anything, must do at times—never retreated but, by even greater indiscretion, usually saved the day. The only thoroughly discreet men are the dead ones, and the ill-served governments are those whose agents never make mistakes because they don't dare. Blake and his servants formed the rear guard, Blake being of the reasonable opinion that his own presence, as a sort of unofficial escort, and official witness, ought to make the Ranee safer than her own troops would have done.

The advance guard was a party of the sons of the nobility, courtiers all, eight in number, beautifully horsed and splendid in their colored turbans, but unarmed because they were not Rajputs and because, by treaty, the Ranee's troops were limited to fifty men. No non-military individuals in India, except the Rajputs, are allowed to carry even their native weapons, so there was neither sword nor lance in all that party. But by the same law they had the right to suppose they would not be met with weapons.

As they swayed toward the open country the Ranee lay chin-on-elbows in the *howdah*, merely sitting up at intervals to let any one who cared to know it see that she was trusting herself on Asoka's back.

She was in riding-breeches and a turban made of cloth of green and gold. Her white silk shirt was fastened at the throat with an emerald worth her ransom, but except for the diamonds aigrette in her turban she wore no other jewelry: she was out to do things and defeat her enemies, not to adorn Narada. And as usual she talked with Quorn as if he were a minister of state who knew all her personal secrets.

"MISS," HE SAID over his shoulder, "I seen the prince, and him and me understood each other. He has all his twenty Rajputs with him. Half have lances and the other half have sabers. And if you want my guess, there's bootleg automatics under cover, but I know the law and I ain't seen nothing. The prince told me he knows a *nullah* near the hermitage where he can hide his men perfect; there's high reeds and a swamp, with the river back o' that, so you can only come at the hiding place by one track. He took along food for men and horses and he aimed to get in there last night, or early before daylight. And he says there's a kind of island in the *nullah,* quite high, with a clump o' tall trees on it, so he can watch the hermitage and know what's going on."

"Let us hope," she remarked.

"Hope, miss? You can bet your boots he's on the job!"

"I hope," she said, "there will be a job for him to do. It is not so simple in these days for a prince to prove his mettle. Do you know, Mr. Quorn, if it weren't for that—that Rana Raj Singh needs an opportunity to prove to himself that he is fit to be my consort—to himself, you understand?—I would have sought some other way of solving this problem."

"Miss, there ain't no other way. You've got to soak it to them Brahmins good. You can't argue with 'em. They've got laws and rules and spiritual reggilations every way you turn and all amounting to the same thing: Brahmins is right and everybody else is wrong, plus damn-bad, ornery and wicked. Did Bamjee tell you all he knows?"

"Bamjee never tells all he knows, but he told enough. Poor Bamjee! I have sent him to the hermitage."

"Good God, miss! What for?"

"Simply to make trouble on general principles. Since we are to have trouble anyhow, let us hive lots of it. Bamjee told me that the Brahmins have sent about a dozen of their number to the hermitage with orders not to move out of it. Rana Raj Singh shall drive them out. When the highest spiritual authorities turn crooked they always ally themselves with the lowest elements, so I don't doubt we shall have the Chandala to deal with. Maraj has probably stirred the Chandala against me. Bamjee says the Brahmins are growing afraid of Maraj and intend to betray him—"

"And Maraj, miss, he means to betray the Brahmins—"

"And the Brahmins, I happen to know through reliable spies, have taken a number of ruffians with them to the hermitage."

"There'll be hell to pay, miss—and no soldiers!"

"Yes, this looks like real opportunity for Rana Raj Singh!"

"And Asoka, miss? You ain't going to have him executed, nohow, are you? Not whatever the outcome?"

"This is his chance, too, I think," she answered.

Quorn thumped Asoka with the *ankus*. "Do you hear that, you big bum? Strut your stuff and think up your own alibi!"

The hell that was to pay began when they had just crossed the wide lower ford of Narada River. The advance-guard, laughing and chatting, drew abreast of a swamp where the reeds were ten feet higher than a man's head. The road they were to follow led around that swamp and then eastward along the river bank. On the right was a porphyry cliff with enormous bowlders at its foot, and ahead was the road to the railway station, two days' march away.

ASOKA WAS THE first to fore-sense trouble; he curled up his precious trunk out of harm's way and began shaking his ears. Quorn hardly had time to get a firm grip with his knees when one of the escort threw up his hand and shouted.

With no other warning at all, from two directions—from the bowlders and the reeds—at least a hundred water-buf-falo came charging down on them in one of those blind, irresistible rushes in which one mind, one terror governs a whole herd and whelms whatever stands in front of it.

The horsemen scattered and Asoka plunged into

the reeds, the Ranee laughing gayly as she clung to the *howdah*—until she saw a naked man on a sort of raft open the reeds with his hands, leap carefully from clump to clump of roots and jab at the elephant's rump with a spear.

Asoka screamed with anger. Three more naked spearmen tried to work their way toward him, but he plunged again out of the swamp at almost the place where he had entered and proceeded to remove himself from that scene at a speed that would have made a horse a Derby winner.

"Hang on, miss!" Quorn cried.

Fear takes hold of elephants as suddenly as typhoons smite the sea. Frenzy as well as fear took hold of Asoka, arousing his whole strength, his entire speed, blinding him, deafening him to Quorn's voice, making him almost as unconscious as a landslide or a monster in a dream.

He crashed into the jungle, smashed the *howdah* roof against a branch, thundered through undergrowth, slid down *nullahs* like an avalanche with earth-banks breaking under him, charged through clinging clumps of thorn-brush, floundered into a wallow where the buffalo had lain, came out of it smothered with mud and butted, squealing like a bucking pony, against a tree that blocked his path. The tree cracked, splintered and fell.

Then, glimpsing through his bloodshot eyes a glade beyond a bamboo thicket, he crashed through the thicket and began to lay the long leagues underfoot.

An elephant driven by terror can run for a day without stopping. Quorn was satisfied to hold on for the present. He was pleased that he had not dropped the iron *ankus*. Branches had whipped his forehead; with his free hand he wiped the blood that had streamed in his eyes; it was the blood that prevented him from seeing what was happening along the glade. The Ranee, clinging to the low brass rail in front of the *howdah* and with her feet jammed under the side-rails, leaned out and touched Quorn between the shoulders.

"Do you see?" she shouted. "Fires!"

He heard the word and used his sleeve to wipe his eyes. Men—Chandala, he could see them now, lean, rusty-skinned, filthy—had set heaped thorn-wood fires along the glade. They blazed and crackled suddenly as Asoka drew near. They were all on one side of the glade—to the right.

Asoka swerved away from them, until he left that glade where his path was blocked by a wall of sputtering flame, and tore along a left-hand opening between the trees in the direction of the river. The Ranee touched Quorn's back again.

"Can you turn him?"

"No, miss."

"I feel sure we are being driven into a trap!"

Quorn began using every faculty he had. He had been half-stunned by the whipping branches, but he threw off that sensation—or lack of it—as a fighter in the ring does in the minute's interval between rounds.

"Got to think—got to think like hell!" he muttered. "This big bum ain't thinking."

He began to encourage Asoka to run, instead of merely sitting still and letting him. Pitching his voice to the familiar note of command he urged him forward—faster!—faster!—until a shadowy, comforting sense of obedience began to invade Asoka's consciousness.

It seemed to the elephant now that he had obeyed

Quorn in the beginning; obeying him, he had outdis-
tanced horror; he was ready to obey again—presently—
presently—maybe—when he should feel quite sure.

THERE WERE FIRES again now, and more of them, at
closer intervals; and through a gap in the trees, ahead.
Quorn saw the river gleaming like burnished metal in the
morning sun. He saw where the path they were following forked; both branches led toward the river, but the
left-hand path was blocked by an inferno of crashing
thorn-bush. Certainly the trap was somewhere down the
right-hand fork. Men leaped out of the undergrowth with
burning fire-brands, taking all risks, setting the grass alight
to drive Asoka down the right-hand fairway.

And then Bamjee dropped out of a tree. It was like a
dream. He was torn, disheveled, he had lost his turban. He
stood in the midst of the righthand path and waved his
arms. He shouted. Then he fled into the jungle with two
of the Chandala following, hard on his heels.

Quorn used the *ankus* then. He used it cruelly. Voice,
knees, *ankus,* all together urged the elephant to turn left.
Once again Asoka curled his trunk. He did not hesitate.
He caught a glimpse of the river between the trees, swung
left between two blazing fires that almost singed his flanks
and scooted for the friendly water where he knew no fire
could follow.

Quorn had forgotten the waterfall. There was a fifty-
foot drop, heavy water plunging onto crags, and he could
hear the roar of it as the river bank broke beneath Asoka's
weight and the monster plunged in head-first, turning
almost a somersault, displacing tons of water.

How Quorn hung on he never knew. He was half-drowned. For awhile he was conscious of nothing except the need to cling with heels and hands and knees, and to keep Asoka, if he could, from being swept down-river and on to the crags below the fall. That thought obsessed him.

Almost the first clear glimpse he had was of the river bank a hundred yards away, and of the roaring falls not fifty feet beyond him on his left hand. He could see the pale-green film of the crest of the plunging water. In the same moment he knew that the Ranee was no longer in the *howdah*.

For a moment—just one moment—he ceased to care then whether he went over the falls or not. The universe went blank. He had not known how much he loved the Ranee. Then, as suddenly, a rage took hold of him. He beat Asoka with his fists.

"You big bum! Turn and find her!"

But Asoka was cooling his hot flanks, comfortable, careless—as indifferent to the world he had left behind as he was to waterfalls. He had fled from terror.

He had found peace, that included Quorn with no *ankus* in his hand. Quorn's fists were funny.

He submerged himself, breathing through his trunk that stuck a foot above the water, giving Quorn a bath, too. Possibly he thought his friend Quorn would enjoy that. Then, because the water, and the sense of safety, and the physical reaction made him happy, he amused himself and drove Quorn nearly frantic by pretending that the current was drawing him over the waterfall.

He let himself drift until the water thundered in Quorn's ears and the glassy curve of the descending wave was almost within hand-reach; then he slowly swam upstream—only to repeat the performance again, and again, and again. At last, when he was nice and cool and the thought of grass seemed good to him, he permitted himself to recognize that he was being ordered out on dry land.

Dry land be it, then. But not the bank where horror had pursued him. Whenever Quorn tried to turn him toward the south bank, he submerged himself, pretending he supposed Quorn wanted that; and it was on the north bank that he emerged at last, ten feet above the waterfall, as pleasant-tempered as he had been frantic half an hour ago.

Narada River is deep at that point, banked up by the dyke that forms the waterfall; below the fall it shallows to a ford a quarter of a mile wide. Far across the river Quorn could see a stream of crimson topped with billowing smoke where the thorn fires had caught the jungle undergrowth. There were no men in sight. Doubtless they had fled from the spreading flame. There was no wind just then; the fire was eating its way outward in a circle.

"Maybe I can get this fool across the ford," Quorn muttered.

9

THE LOST RANEE

THERE WAS A well-defined track down the rocks to the foot of the fail, and below that there was a footpath all along the river to the ford. Quorn rode along that, watching the troubled water, half-expecting to see the Ranee's body, mangled by the crags, floating in mid-stream or stranded. But he knew there were alligators, slimy, greedy devils; floating bodies had a slim chance; even the fords were sometimes dangerous for passengers on foot.

All that way along the river bank Quorn was sick at heart and careless even of Asoka's comfort or his destiny; however, he began to be puzzled before long by symptoms that he noticed, and he was more than ever puzzled by Asoka's willingness to cross the river when they reached the ford.

"What's eating you? What's making you forget?" he wondered.

All the way across the ford he indulged in sentimental guesswork as to whether the Ranee's death had not humiliated and broken Asoka's spirit. Nearly every one is capable at times of that sort of imagination.

However, on the far bank he got down to search for what the matter might be, and soon discovered the spear-wound in Asoka's rump. It was nothing serious, although it might be painful, and he understood then that Asoka had been merely asking for attention.

He made Asoka kneel and, having no remedies handy, made a fly-brush of grass at the end of a string that would sway with the elephant's movement and prevent the stinging flies from laying eggs in the open cut.

It was while he was tying the string to the *howdah* rail that Bamjee came. By this time the *babu* had lost his spectacles. There was hardly a shred of untorn clothing on his body and almost every inch of him was bleeding from the thorns. He was breathless and he fell at Quorn's feet. For a minute or two he lay and vomited. Then suddenly his will power triumphed and he knelt—sputtered—exploded:

"Damn! Loafer! Bloody fool! You wait here? Oh, my God! I saw you on the far bank—didn't you see my signal?"

"Looking for the Ranee," Quorn answered. Then he lowered his voice. "She's drownded."

"Liar!"

"She is. She's drownded."

"Liar, I tell you! I saw her swim—she was washed out of the *howdah* close inshore—caught the grass in her hands and climbed out—scrambled up the bank. He seized her—"

"For the love o' God, who did?"

"Maraj! Pounced on her like a hawk on a bird. He had a trap set. I warned you, and you avoided it. I had to run, and they thought they killed me, but I came back. When Maraj saw you plunge into the river he ran to the place. And when he saw the Ranee in the water he hid himself.

I tried to yell to her, but I had no voice. I couldn't whisper! And so she climbed out, and Maraj pounced on her.

"I saw him pick her up—she was kicking—he carried her—he ran—and I ran—he choked her until she left off kicking—then I saw him take her to the hermitage, which is full of Brahmins and cutthroats—and I don't know where the Prince is—and we can't get to the hermitage now—*because the whole damn jungle is on fire! Oh, my God!*"

He lay and beat the hard earth with his flat palms. He beat his forehead on the ground. Quorn lifted him, took him by shoulders and heel and hoisted him into the *howdah*. Then he climbed up to his own place on Asoka's neck, after he had broken off a short stick for administrative purposes.

"Come on now, and no bunk!"

QUORN WAS NOT even quite sure where the hermitage lay, and it was no use asking Bamjee, who was moaning and out of his senses, rolling from side to side of the *howdah*. But Bamjee had told the truth about the jungle fire; the hot-weather wind was rising and the roar and heat and smell of it were coming closer every second.

There were birds and animals in full flight—scores of them—even a leopard that passed within six feet and did not pause to look at a man on an elephant. Asoka, too, was getting difficult to manage.

So Quorn turned down-wind, but headed southward as much as possible, in order to make a circuit of the fire; but he had to make a very wide circuit indeed because of Asoka's nervousness. However, Asoka was willing, and put his best foot forward; they covered five or six miles faster than a horse could have done it, which brought them out of the zone of rolling smoke.

And when they were out of the haze of the smoke Quorn presently saw Blake on horseback on a knoll, gazing under his hand in every direction. He clapped his spurs in and came galloping the moment he caught sight of Asoka.

"For God's sake, where is the Ranee?" he demanded. "What has happened?"

Quorn was laconic. Bamjee stuck his head over the *howdah* rail and repeated Quorn's words after him—adding to them.

"Go to her—for God's sake, go to her!" he almost screamed, and then collapsed.

But in another moment he was on his knees again, and it was Bamjee who first caught sight of Rana Raj Singh and ten of his men moving westward in an extended line with the long slow-swinging canter that saves horses' strength against emergency.

"Bloody dam-fool! Go back!" Bamjee yelled. But Rana Raj Singh came on at a gallop, drew rein in a dust-cloud and sat silent, waiting for Blake to speak first.

Blake told him all that he and Quorn knew.

There was no pause between Blake's last words and Rana Raj Singh's order to his men. They wheeled and, like eleven arrows launched out of eleven bows, they sped back along the course by which they had come, Blake after them, swallowing dust, and Asoka bringing up the rear in no great hurry, since the horses' utmost limit of speed was easily within his scope.

They rode as a blast of wind goes ripping through the scrub. Jungle, *nullahs*, crags and trees went past them like a motion picture, and the horses were blowing heavily when Rana Raj Singh halted at last in full view of a building half a mile away.

It was a domed structure surrounded by a mud-and-stone wall, with plenty of space between building and wall and some trees in the inclosure. Considerably less than half a mile beyond it was another group of trees. Rana Raj Singh pointed to them:

"Ten of my men are in hiding near those trees. One man is up in a tree. They have seen us." He waved his right arm. Blake's keen eyes were not keen enough to read the answering signal from the tree-top, but Rana Raj Singh seemed satisfied; he turned to Blake again.

"I waited," he said, "and grew weary of waiting. I did not understand what was happening in that hermitage, or why the Ranee did not come. A number of Brahmins came. I was astonished; they had their high priest with them—an unheard-of thing. They also brought a lot of ruffians with *lathis [Long sticks.].* Then I saw the jungle on fire, and no Ranee. So I left ten men in hiding and rode to see what might have happened. Ah! My men come."

TEN MEN ARMED with lances rode into view from a depression near the trees. They formed into a line with wide-spaced intervals and halted, watching for a signal. Quorn drew as near to Rana Raj Singh as the nervous horse would let him.

"Did I hear you say, sir, that the high priest o' them Brahmins is in that building?"

Rana Raj Singh nodded. Quorn slowly moved Asoka forward until he was in front of all the horses.

"Me and you won't miss this, soldier! Durn your old

hide, but you was born lucky. A *habeas corpus* beats an alibi. You *habeas* the *corpus* o' that high priest and a legislature couldn't hang you!"

Rana Raj Singh signalled. The men opposite approached, extending their line as Rana Raj Singh maneuvered his ten to meet them, until they formed a wide arc of a circle with Asoka in the midst. Blake was at Asoka's left, Rana Raj Singh to right of him, and for a moment or two they halted in that position while men's heads stared at them from over the hermitage wall.

There was evidently some confusion in the hermitage. Two men who appeared not to be Brahmins let themselves down from the wall and took to their heels toward the *nullah* where the Rajputs had been hidden.

"Catch them alive," commanded Rana Raj Singh. Two of his men gave chase.

Then a gate of the hermitage opened and three Brahmins approached, waving a white cloth. Rana Raj Singh rode to meet them, Blake almost abreast of him and Quorn on Asoka keeping well within earshot.

"Halt!" commanded Rana Raj Singh. "Where is the Ranee?"

Bamjee came to life and knelt up in the *howdah*, clearing his throat to shout something, but Quorn cursed him into silence.

"She is with us in the hermitage," the Brahmin answered insolently. "She bids you go home."

Bamjee exploded, Quorn or no Quorn. "Liar!" he shouted. "Your highness, that man is the go-between who tells Maraj what to do. I know him!"

The Brahmin promptly played his trump card. "Her

Highness the Ranee has apologized to the high priest and has received his blessing. You are to take that elephant away and shoot him. The person known as Maraj has been imprisoned in the hermitage and will be taken to Narada to be tried and executed.

"We ourselves will be the Ranee's escort to Narada."

Rana Raj Singh's men came dragging prisoners. They threw them to the ground and held them there at the lance-point.

"Prince, they say the Ranee is locked into a cell. There are forty more of this sort in there, prepared to defend the place. Maraj is a prisoner, but the Brahmins have offered him freedom if we attack and he helps the defense."

They tied the prisoners back to back by necks, hands and feet. There began to be a great commotion in the hermitage—an uproar—and another Brahmin came running, but not through the gate; he climbed the wall, jumped, fell, hurt himself and limped, hurrying as best he could. He stammered; it was hard to understand him. Quorn, who could see the roof of the building letter than the rest could, understood first.

"Hell's bells!" he exclaimed. "Maraj is loose. He's on the roof. He has turned those other guys against the Brahmins! This guy wants us to go help the high priest! Can you beat that?"

"Can you break that wall?" asked Rana Raj Singh.

ALWAYS THE EASIEST thing in the world was to start Asoka smashing things. Quorn's only immediate worry was the risk of damage to Asoka's head, so he chose the mud-and-stone wall rather than the teak gate and sent Asoka charging at it like a five-ton battering-ram.

He heard Bamjee crying, "Oh, my God!" behind him—heard the thunder of the Rajput horsemen closing in behind him, two by two, to burst through the gap he should make, saw—through the edge of his eyes—Blake and Rana Raj Singh slightly to his rear, one on either flank, distinctly heard and felt the *ping* of several bullets, thought he heard Blake answer them, and was dimly aware that a man on the roof was shooting at him, but kept on missing.

Then came the shudder and shock as Asoka struck the wall with his enormous forehead—strained his weight against it—grunted—and a section of the wall fell inward in a cloud of dust.

Asoka staggered through the gap. Behind him the horsemen streamed through, wheeling right and left. And then confusion, in which Bamjee scrambled to the ground by clinging to Asoka's tail and vanished into the building.

Asoka swung a limp trunk, swaying with his eyes shut, more than half-stunned by the impact. Quorn slipped to the ground.

"Lean against that wall, you sucker. Keep your feet. No lying down or you'll kid yourself you're all in."

For a moment or two he watched the elephant, since that was his first charge. He decided Asoka would stand there—at the worst he would hardly stray far—at the utmost worst he might stagger off home to the elephant lines in Narada; but he was likeliest to stand.

He left him. There was fighting going on in every direction—horsemen charging; Brahmins and their own hired ruffians at throat-grips, some of them rolling on the ground together; other ruffians trying to climb the wall and being skewered by the Rajput lances; two men in the gap to guard

that, sabering whoever tried to slip through; and a maniac—a leaping maniac—a prancing, yelling maniac who
jabbered in an unknown tongue as he raced around the
parapet of the rambling building, brandishing an empty
Colt revolver.

"Maraj!" Quorn muttered to himself. "I guess you're my
meat!"

But he had no weapon, nor any notion how he was going
to kill the maniac. He ran all along the building looking
for an entrance. There were dozens of doors, all leading
into cells, but he came on a passage at last that led between
two cells into a dark hall under a dome, with columns to
support the dome.

He saw the Ranee leaning on Rana Raj Singh's arm.
The prince's saber was all bloody and there were several
dead men lying around the door of the cell from which the
Ranee had been rescued. The door had not been opened, it
was smashed in, but Quorn had not time to be curious how
that had happened—he saw a stairway leading to the roof.

It was narrow. Near its summit stood the high priest,
taking refuge there for fear his sacred person might be
defiled by the touch of common mortals—much more
afraid of that than of being killed or injured. In fact, he
did not appear afraid.

Quorn charged up the steps. The high priest retreated
in front of him, dreading that Quorn might bump against
him. Three steps backward, and he bumped into the door
that opened on the roof—it yielded, and there he was out
on the roof with Quorn staring at him, until Maraj came
prancing along the parapet.

The high priest looked afraid then, as Maraj paused,

grinning at him—grinning at Quorn, too; and Quorn cursed himself for a bigger idiot than any one, because he had no weapon. Maraj twisted the Colt revolver in his hands, broke it as if his hands were a gorilla's, dropped it as if he had never been conscious of it. And then human speech returned to him.

"The oh, so holy—twice born—high priest—who commanded Maraj to be tied and—handed over—in Narada—to the judge—and the executioner!"

MARAJ GLANCED DOWN from the parapet. Asoka stood beneath him, midway between wall and building, shaking his head, but with his eyes open now. Suddenly Maraj came leaping at the high priest, seized him, crushed him in a light arm that was like a vise. He caught Quorn with the other hand and nearly crushed his ribs.

"You shall come and learn what Maraj knows!"

Quorn's right hand was free; he rained blows on the maniac's face, but their only effect was to make him tighten the terrific grip. The high priest groaned with the agony of in-bent ribs. Maraj hove both of them off their feet and rushed toward the parapet, mounted it, paused there. He laughed so loud that even the fighting Rajputs looked up. Shouting something, in an unknown tongue again, and hugging his captives, he leaped, feet first for Asoka's back.

Asoka moved away from under them—by instinct perhaps, intuition, whatever it is that forewarns animals. Quorn's feet struck Asoka's forehead, which set all three men turning in the air. Maraj struggled, clinging to Quorn and the high priest, trying to turn them under him and break his own fall, but the reverse of that happened; his back struck the earth. Quorn and the high priest fell on top of him, the high priest with a broken shoulder and Quorn shaken up but not hurt otherwise.

He rolled clear. Then he dragged the high priest free, and swung him roughly out of reach of Asoka's trunk and forefoot that were dangerously close.

Maraj seemed dead—but suddenly he sat up, staring at Asoka. He seemed to remember something about that elephant.

Asoka, too, seemed to remember; he rumbled. Then Maraj saw Quorn, and then the high priest. Suddenly he tried to stand up, but his legs refused to function, so he rolled—he tried to seize the high priest by the leg. Quorn spoke quite quietly:

"There's your alibi, Asoka—soak him!"

It was only two steps forward—one foot on the belly of the maniac, the other on his head. Quorn took Asoka by the trunk and turned him around, led him to where he had left him near the gap in the wall.

"You win," he said, "you great big lucky stiff! I think you done it in a dream. I don't believe you know which end of you is your head. I hope your skull ain't split—you hit that wall a hummer."

Then the Ranee and the prince, and many Brahmins clustering around the high priest, some of them bruised and bloody, and every one of them as nervous as a wet hen because they had been defiled by the touch of low-caste ruffians.

The Ranee's voice—a stern note that Quorn had never heard before—the high priest answering, and all the Brahmins echoing him in chorus—promises, Quorn supposed—agreements, to be broken when the time came.

Pity she couldn't hang 'em all. He sat down, more stunned than he had realized he was, his head so swimming that it was several seconds before he recognized Bamjee with a big ax in his hand.

"We win, I think," said Bamjee, "both of us! I chopped the door down while the prince was slaying dragons—six men at least! Oh, my God! I chopped with all that going on behind me—think of it! But it was I who released her from the cell—can she forget that?"

Then the Ranee's voice, the Ranee's sweet young face amid a sea of others that persisted in whirling ground in a circle. Somewhere in the whirl Blake's monocle and a glimpse of Blake cleaning an automatic with his handkerchief.

"I thank you, Sirdar Benjamin Quorn. Do you think you could make Asoka understand how much I thank him?"

And then Blake's voice: "Gad! I don't know, Quorn—I might—you never know—I might be able to persuade our government to recognize that title. Do my best, old fellow—do my best for you at any time!"

THE AFFAIR AT KALIGAON

Intrigue is subtle and murderous on India's borders—and Ben Quorn, keeper of the Ranee's elephants, needs all his wits in the deadly devious games being played there

1

"THE DEVIL'S NAME IS SIVA"

THE MILES OF the Indian border state of Narada are mostly vertical, so its inhabitants have several sorts of climate—which accounts perhaps for some part of their versatility that ranges all the way from scorpion alertness to a gentle, uncritical lethargy.

Narada boasts mountain peaks covered with snow during two-thirds of the year, and steaming jungles in which wild begonias and orchids flourish in midwinter. Midway of these altitudes are square leagues of comparatively level land, tolerably cool in winter, but abominably hot in summer.

In the middle of one such level stretch, the city of Narada stands very nearly as it has stood for a thousand years. The plumbing is the same and so are many of the temples. Descendants of the same families migrate to the same summer residences in the mountains, in the same type of two-wheeled carts.

For about three-quarters of a century the same complaint has been uplifted to the whitewashed sail-cloth ceiling of the Residency office whenever a lonely and bored representative of the British-Indian Central Government has had to postpone his annual sojourn in the hills.

"Hell holds no discomfort like the plains in May," remarked Brazenose Blake. "Whisky tastes like tepid camomile tea and a good cigar like straw out of a packing case. You can't whistle because your lips are cracked. You can't sing because your throat is like a lime-kiln. The piano is out of tune and the Victrola records have all warped. You can't read because the sweat runs in your eyes; and if you sit under the *punkali* the wind blows the leaves of your book, so that you never can tell which page you're at and the stuff doesn't make sense. How do you endure it, Quorn? What do you think about?"

"I'm thinking, sir, I don't believe that part about the whisky and cigars."

"Help yourself. Don't blame me if they taste worse than I told you."

OFFICIALLY THEY TWO were as the poles asunder. So they were by birth, education, upbringing, employment, habit, and probable destiny. India has more than a hundred different kinds of governments, hundreds of religions and castes, scores of languages; and not one of them provides that the cousin of an English earl, commissioned as the representative of Viceroy and Council at the court of a reigning Ranee, shall be intimately friendly with an unlettered man from Philadelphia, whose former vocation was driving a taxicab, and who has now become the superintendent of the Ranee's elephants.

Nevertheless, they were friends—undoubtedly in part because in all Narada there was no one else of their race with whom to talk, but also because they liked each other's company.

Brazenose Blake was a sportsman of the old school, who

"Woman! You are obsessed by devils!" snarled the High Priest

could box, fence, shoot, and ride to pig as ably as any living man of his years. He knew at least nine languages, had served with fair distinction in several wars and in even a greater number of awkward political side-shows in which a moment's indiscretion or a moment's lack of it would have caused disastrously expensive trouble.

He was probably the handsomest and most wooed bachelor in India, although he had no money, and the secret of his exile in Narada was twofold—two-faced, as almost every secret is: he had offended the wives of certain very important personages by refusing to be drawn into their matrimonial or non-matrimonial schemes; and the Indian Government had felt called upon to select for the Narada Residency a man of more than usual skill in handling unusual situations.

Quorn's idea of good sport was a crap game. He could read a newspaper, write a reasonably well-spelled letter and do small sums in arithmetic; but he was not sure whether Shakespeare was a poet or a soldier, and he mistrusted

anything whatever that had to do with any kind of government, owing to certain differences of opinion that he had
had with traffic cops and courts of what is known as justice.

He wondered why he liked Blake, probably as much as
Blake wondered why he liked Quorn. However, they got
along together famously and there was almost never a day
when Blake did not visit the elephant lines or Quorn did
not look in at the Residency for a drink and some conversation.

"You haven't told me yet what you think about in this
damned hot weather," Blake insisted.

"Elephants," said Quorn. "Next after them, the mahouts.
Them heathen 'u'd swap elephants' corn and sugar-cane for
rot-gut arrack if I didn't watch 'em closer than a school-
marm watches kids. Any time left when I'm through with
that mess I use up thinking of the Ranee. Mostly I lie
awake nights thinking of her.

"She's a headful, you'll admit that, sir. Nineteen years
old come Tuesday o' next week. You know, sir, after you've
done warning her where she gets off, she's made it a kind
o' rule to send for me and ask me how to put one over on
you. That's why I lie awake nights so much. You aren't such
an easy guy to put one over on."

"WAS IT YOU," demanded Blake, "who put the notion in
her head of sending for Miss Blackstone?"

"Me, sir? What would I know about a society leddy like
her?"

"You didn't know about elephants until you came to
this country," Blake retorted. "Seems to me that when the
Narada natives looked at those extraordinary eyes of yours
and said you were a reincarnation of the Gunga *sahib* who

was killed a thousand years ago, you began to develop some kind of a sixth sense—a damned uncanny way of saying and doing the wrong thing in the wrong place at the right time and not only upsetting me and everybody else, by gad, but being right, confound you! I wish I knew how you do it. I admit I first mentioned Miss Blackstone. Was it you who suggested to the Ranee she should send for her?"

"No, sir. That was the Ranee's idee. If I remember right, I told her not to."

"Yes," said Blake, "you've brains enough to tell her not to do what you intend she shall. How did you come to talk about Miss Blackstone? You couldn't have picked a worse bet, considering the problems of this weird country."

"Well, sir, the Ranee was crabbing about how difficult it is for a queen on an ancient throne to be modern. She was saying how even the women are sore at her for going unveiled in public, and for opening hospitals and schools and what not else. And she asked me how the women in the United States behave. Well—should I have stuck strictly to what I know and told her how some of 'em behaved in taxicabs I've driven?

"You'd told me about Miss Blackstone, how she lost her money when her father died after being all that rich.

"Anyhow, me and her concocts a letter to Miss Blackstone, care of the President, Washington, D.C., please forward. Our young Ranee tells Miss Blackstone to name her own figure. All she's asked to do is to come and live here for a while and be nice and friendly.

"I've been told she answered by cablegram, and her demands were so durned reasonable that the Ranee thought maybe there's something wrong with her. However, she's a good little gambler, our young Ranee is, sir. So she puts up her money and bets—on her judgment of your judgment. Me, I haven't had a thing to do with it."

BLAKE SET HIS heels on the desk. "And in consequence," he remarked, "I have to postpone my visit to the hills until Miss Blackstone comes. How is she going to make the two-day journey from the railway station?"

"Elephants! The Ranee tells me, 'Go and meet her, Mr. Quorn, and bring her from the station with at least ten elephants.' I tried to talk her out o' it, but I can't say no when she gives me downright orders."

"No," Blake answered, "I suppose you can't. But—would you care to do me a favor?"

"Anything, sir, so long as it ain't supposed to be a secret from the Ranee. Me and her, we understand each other middling good. More than once she's bet her throne on it that I don't tell her any lies, and you'll notice, sir, she hasn't lost her throne—not yet."

"You are quite right, Quorn. No, this needn't be a secret from the Ranee. All I ask is, that on the way from the station you won't say a word about me to Miss Blackstone. I have reasons."

"What if she should ask questions, sir?"

"Be evasive."

"Very good, sir. I never yet met the woman that couldn't read her own meaning into any answer to any question, but I'll do my best… I'm going for her on Asoka; he's a beast with what you might call personality. If she should start to do some back-seat driving—well, sir, I haven't ever known him to buck, actually, but he has a motion or two that can beat that to a frazzle. She'll be too tired holding on, and too stiff at the end o' the first day's march, to ask anything but 'where's the liniment?' And the second day is usually wusser than the first, on account o' the first day's soreness."

Blake lay back in his long-armed chair and stared at the ceiling cloth, wondering how far to trust Quorn with secrets, personal and semi-official. But his next remark drew proof that Quorn knew at least a portion of one of the problems that worried him.

"Just now I'd rather see the devil here than Miss Blackstone!" he exploded.

"Sir, the devil ain't no stranger in these parts."

"You are quite right, Quorn."

"THE DEVIL'S NAME," said Quorn, "is Siva, and his hellions are them Brahmin priests o' Siva's temple. They're ag'in' the Ranee. They're ag'in' you. They're ag'in' me. And they're hell's bells and halleluja plumb dead doggone obstinate set ag'in' havin' a nice young lady here from foreign parts."

"I know it, Quorn. I know it."

"And I wouldn't put it past them Brahmins, sir, to make use o' politicians, fanatics, snakes, thugs, holy men or any other vermin. They're all scared stiff of any changes. Would it occur to you, sir, that the Ranee herself is in danger?"

"Yes, Quorn. That is why I won't move to the hills until the Ranee does. These temple Brahmins hate her. They would stop at nothing. They would like to produce anarchy, so that the British Government would have to interfere and possibly even dethrone the Ranee. They suspect Miss Blackstone will teach the Ranee any number of modern notions. But they can't prevent Miss Blackstone's coming any more than I can. The law forbids the invasion of Narada by aliens, but it permits the Ranee to invite her own guests and to employ any one she pleases, so there's nothing I can do about it."

"No, sir. Has it occurred to you, sir, they might try to get Miss Blackstone on the way here? Me—I'd better stay awake on that trip."

"Right, Quorn. Quite right. Keep both eyes lifting, but the less you say the better. Above all, don't talk about me."

2

"I'M AFRAID THAT'S HIM, MISS"

THE TRAIN CAME clanking around the curve and bumped itself to a standstill—a mixed train of miscellaneous freight and many third-class passengers whose varicolored turbans made the heat seem hotter.

From under the iron station roof peddlers of water, fruit, and sweetmeats, and scores of men, women and children who had been waiting since daybreak and now feared they might miss the train, surged forward, sweating, yelling, trying to force themselves into compartments already over-flowing.

Into that swarm, out of the only first-class compartment, at the rear of the train, stepped Virginia Blackstone.

She was one of those young women who can look cool when they are not, and she had not made the mistake of wearing white. Her frock was of cool green, as was her broad-brimmed hat. Her short reddish-golden hair was crisp and curly, her eyes mischievously curious, and her skin, of which plenty was visible, was sunburned to a deeper golden tan than most blondes can achieve. She looked as if she might have earned it by tennis, swimming, golf— perhaps even polo. She was more than passably good-looking; Quorn thought her far better-looking than any printed pictures he had seen of her, and he guessed her at less than twenty-five years old; wherein his judgment was at fault, for she was twenty-seven.

Quorn liked several things about her, and not least of them her luggage. Everything about her was practical; her heaviest boxes could have gone on horseback. There was no lost look about her, and she was not excited or nervous. Nor was she contemptuous. She appeared unhurried and not concerned as to how she should reach Narada.

Quorn had purposely left his elephants where the station building would hide them. His own dramatic instinct, that had so much free rein nowadays, had suggested the advantage of surprise to impress Miss Blackstone with the ancient strangeness of Narada.

He proposed to himself to lead her around the corner of the ugly corrugated iron station building and let her see the ten elephants suddenly, all splendid with crimson tassels and their semi-state, brass-decorated *howdahs*.

He approached her with the same peculiar mixture of respect and independence with which he normally addressed the Ranee. He was wearing the cloth-of-gold turban and official uniform. His agate-colored eyes were like no white man's she had ever seen, and it would have been strange if she had not mistaken him for a native of the country.

His bearing and the jeweled *ankus,* the elephant goad that he carried in his right hand, gave him an air of authority, however. She spoke first,

"Do you know any English? How does one reach the palace of the Ranee of Narada?"

"This way, please." He made a lordly gesture with the

ankus and a dozen men ran for the trunks. Quorn beckoned the station master, who let the train wait until he counted the luggage and released it to the porters.

QUORN, MASTER OF ceremonies, led on, and it needed no subtlety on Virginia Blackstone's part to realize that she was expected to be impressed; however, she found the part not difficult to act.

Asoka, at the first view, would have astonished any one, he being the tallest elephant in captivity as well as the most dignified when that mood was on him. He stood at the head of nine more elephants, all splendid in their trappings, looming on a glittering white road against a background of forest in which monkeys crashed through the upper branches. He was a breath-taking spectacle. Nevertheless, the effect was different from that intended. Virginia Blackstone laughed with sheer delight and beckoned sweetmeat sellers and fruit boys, bought all their wares and proceeded to win the hearts of all those elephants, Asoka's first.

She fed Asoka at least a pound of sticky sweets and a dozen oranges. The monster's first and enduring impression of her was of a girl in cool green who stepped out of shadow into the blazing light and, making obviously agreeable remarks in a strange tongue, fed him scandalous quantities of things that, next after strong liquor, he loved best.

At last Asoka gathered her up in his trunk and raised her to the seat of honor on his head.

"That's my place. Better climb back into the *howdah*, miss," said Quorn.

He was jealous. That was the first time he had ever known Asoka to do that to a stranger, of his own free will. As they started homeward, he was obsessed by a feeling of vague uneasiness, as if his thoughtfully staged surprise had failed. He hoped that Miss Blackstone still mistook him for a native of the country; there was room for a surprise there—one that perhaps might take her down a peg or two.

"Why ten elephants?" she asked him presently.

"Oh, the Ranee has lots of 'em, and didn't know how many trunks you'd bring."

Too late he realized that he was not talking like a native—not even like a native who knew English uncommonly well. So even that satisfaction had vanished.

However, Virginia Blackstone presently wearied of watching the landscape swaying past, and the line of elephants behind her. The pace was slow for one of her motor-educated race, and curiosity was working on imagination.

"What is your name?" she asked him; and he told her promptly, but sulkily.

"How many miles to Narada?"

"Dunno," said Quorn. "I never counted 'em." Then he suddenly felt ashamed, remembering that at first glance he had liked her. He also remembered his own loneliness when he had first come to Narada. So his voice changed as he added: "Folks don't measure miles or time in these parts, miss. Everything goes by habit, except the Ranee, and she reckons time by the number o' new ideas she's fooled with since breakfast."

THE DAM WAS down between them. Quorn deftly avoided the subject of Blake, however, until they topped the last rise and came within sight of the *dak* bungalow erected as a midway halting place. Then at last:

"Some one at a station down the line told me the British Resident's name is Blake. What is his first name?"

"Him and me don't call each other by our first names," Quorn answered.

"Is it Brazenose?"

"I dunno, miss." Quorn hated to lie, but he felt he had to.

"Is he a rather tall, athletic man with a prominent nose, who can box and fence and ride and talk a lot of languages? Is there a little piece missing from the lobe of his left ear that was nicked out by a bullet? Does he say 'Damme' and 'God bless my soul' and 'hell's bells' like a person in a play? Does he shoot particularly straight and seem to be particularly even-tempered when anybody else would be frightfully angry? Does he wear a gold snake-ring with ruby eyes on the little finger of his left hand? Is he—"

"I'm afraid that's him, miss."

"Oh!… Why afraid?"

"I'd sooner not say."

There was silence between them for a time; then:

"Mr. Quorn."

"Yes, miss?"

"I have never run away in all my life. I refuse to, now. But if I had known in time that Mr. Brazenose Blake is the Resident here, I would never have accepted the Ranee's invitation—no matter how badly I needed the money."

"No, miss? Well, that's too bad. But you'll find Mr. Blake's a gentleman."

"Thank you, I'm quite well aware of that. But I have excellent reasons for not wishing to meet Mr. Blake. Please tell me if he knows that I'm coming."

"Mebbe. How can he help knowing? Him that's attached

to the Ranee's court for no other purpose than to let the British know what's going on! Yes, miss, it's a safe bet he knows you're coming."

"Mr. Quorn—do you think you could do me a favor? I have no right to ask, of course, but—"

"Yes, miss—anything I can do."

"Will you kindly not discuss me in any way with Mr. Blake, if you should meet him?"

"Yes, miss. What if he asks questions?"

"If Mr. Blake asks questions, please tell him I said I would rather not meet him."

"Very well, miss."

"Thank you very much, Mr. Quorn."

Asoka knelt before the bungalow, and Virginia Blackstone vaulted out of the *howdah* before any one could bring a ladder.

3

"YOU ARE OBSESSED BY DEVILS!"

RATS ARE NO good whatever, say some of the naturalists. They, however, overlook the truth that rats are part of the destructive force of nature, without which nothing would be scrapped and there would be nothing new. Some day scientists will harness rats, as they already have harnessed microbes. There are rats on every layer of existence, and their usefulness on certain layers has already been discovered—though not by scientists.

Bamjee was a rat. He was a prosperous, sleek, well fed rat, who wore a silk suit and a platinum watch chain. Left to his own devices Bamjee would have gnawed away the very props of the throne of Narada. As purchasing agent for the Ranee he was so anxious to make commissions and to be on the winning side of every political plot and counter-plot that he would have brought himself and all his friends to ruin in six or seven ways before there was time for a plot to mature. But he was fortunate in having an employer who understood his value and how to manage him.

So Bamjee, in his best silk suit, sat sweating in a stifling closet with a dim dark lantern on the desk in front of him adding seriously to the heat, but making his stenographic notebook visible.

Beside his right ear was a slot that looked, on the other side, like an innocent grin on the face of a god who smiled from, the wall of the room in which the Ranee sat and interviewed the High Priest of Siva's temple. Being an ex-government clerk and telegraphist, Bamjee was a very swift and accurate stenographer.

The Ranee was fighting for life, liberty, happiness and the whole future of Narada; but the fight was beneath the surface, just as Bamjee was behind the wall. This was a strictly unofficial meeting with the High Priest, held after dark for the sake of secrecy, so she was not seated on the royal throne but on a chair beneath a gilded canopy that resembled a throne so closely as to keep the High Priest constantly reminded of the deference due to her.

Of course he showed no deference, but she scored her point because he had to concentrate part of his mind—say five per cent of it—on being insolent, whereas with one hundred per cent of her own efficiency engaged she was less likely to make mistakes. At the same time she had wit enough to wear a Paris frock that suggested Eastern tradition disappearing in the light of modern Western energy—one of those inspired French rhapsodies in rose and green and gold.

Siva's High Priest was an elderly gentleman sworn to chastity, so there was nothing improper about the interview except the temper in which he had approached it and his actually unchaste reputation. With his shaven skull and lean, ascetic-looking face, his splendid robes and his air of lofty insolence he seemed exactly what he stood for— conservatism grafted onto utter selfishness.

"IT HAS BEEN against tradition for a thousand years,"

said the High Priest, "that he who holds my sacred office should visit the occupant of the throne of Narada. The throne should visit the mouthpiece of the gods, with due humility. It is because you are young and inexperienced that I have consented to this exception to a rule based on the experience of ages."

"Time works wonders, doesn't it?" the Ranee answered. "I appreciate your courtesy in coming, but it was you who demanded the interview. What is it you want to talk about?"

"Woman!" The High Priest almost roared at her. He clutched the chair-arms, scratching at them with his long nails. His great, dark, angry eyes flashed malevolently. He was terrible. But she behaved as if she was not conscious of it.

"Woman! You are obsessed by devils! You are no longer clean! You are untouchable! You have disobeyed the ancient laws. You have suffered yourself to be defiled. You are incurring evil *karma* that it will take icons—hundreds of thousands of earth lives to outlive. I myself, who come to you in duty's name, incur for doing so a *karma* that I shudder to contemplate." *[The law of cause and effect which, according to the Hindu teaching, are inseparable—so that each individual eventually pays in full for his own thoughts and deeds.]*

"Your *karma* is your own," she answered. "You are not polite. And you are not telling the truth. There is *karma* for such conduct also. It was you," she continued, "who publicly released me from the law that hitherto has kept us Hindu women in seclusion, in the *purdah*. Which then is holy and true? Your law? Or your release from it? Or are law and release from it equally lies? I ask with due humility for information."

"I will inform you." The High Priest bridled his indignation, paused, and looked around him to make sure there were no witnesses. "It was to help your father who was nothing if not observant of the sacred law that I released you from *purdah*. That was done for political reasons and because by accident you appeared to fulfill an ancient religious prophecy. It was expedient that ignorant people should not be deprived of the evidences of their faith, and so I winked at trickery—your trickery—not foreseeing what advantage you would take of it. Now you associate with such untouchables as the alien who superintends your elephants!"

"Ben Quorn, you mean? But you yourself have publicly named him a reincarnation of the Gunga *sahib,* reborn after a thousand years in fulfillment of the prophecy. Deeply reverencing your wisdom, I accepted Quorn as the reborn Gunga *sahib.* And so did all Narada. Do you wish me to turn around now and declare in public that you lied?"

"YOU ARE A woman," the High Priest snarled at her. "No woman can declare judgment or hear counsel without perverting it." But he was stung. He retreated and shifted his line of attack. "Have you not sent for another *feringhee,* another foreigner, a woman this time, victim and agent in one of the devils of darkness that seek to make a desert of the land of Hind by destroying tradition and making a mockery of the ancient teachings?"

"No," the Ranee answered. "I have invited Virginia Blackstone to come and visit me. Do you wish to know why?"

"I know why. Well I know why! It is because, like any other woman, you crave excitement and novelty. Curiosity impels you. Fool that you are! Ignorant moth at the flame of materiality! Deluded dreamer on the highway to annihilation!"

"No," she said. "Nothing of the kind. I kept a copy of what I wrote to Virginia Blackstone. I wrote to her, among other things, that the priests of my country are Brahmins who claim a monopoly of wisdom; and that if their claim is true, then they are wrongfully withholding from us much that we ought to know."

"You dared to write that? You confess that you dared to write that to a casteless female of an alien race, who—?" The High Priest paused for lack of breath, he was so scandalized.

"Indeed I wrote it. I wrote also, that if my companion and inner counselor should be an American, then it would not be nearly so easy for the priests to control or corrupt or frighten her; and that the priests might not dare to use or to advocate violence toward her, because of the danger to themselves on account of her being an alien whose government would demand investigation."

Siva's High Priest rose out of his chair, a tyrant stirred to the lees of his inner being, a fanatic to whom all earth and its affairs were nothing except in reference to his dignity and beliefs.

Physical violence was no part of his own method, though he trembled visibly with the anger that raged in his veins; he understood too well the trick of stirring other men's emotion so that they would run all risks and bear all blame for what they did; himself he was a man of peace.

But there are forms of violence other than physical. There is a mental means of bludgeoning and numbing human wit until the victim cowers like a beaten dog and lives thereafter haunted by nameless dread. Some call it hypnotism; others, wondering what ails them, call it nothing, telling less than truth.

"If I should curse you in your own house—" he began. But the Ranee interrupted:

"It is true that you have no love for me, nor I any for the cruel tyranny that you represent. If you should curse me I would find sure means of turning back your curse on you and all yours! I am no such fool as not to know how surely you could cause me to die by inches so that none could prove any crime against you. Well I know it. It is because I know it that I have laid my plans so carefully."

"*Your* plans!" said the High Priest, sneering again, that being the simplest, oldest trick for causing others to betray their secrets. He was watching her with his burning eyes.

But the Ranee understood that system.

"NO, NOT MY plans," she retorted, "Mine is part of the eternal plan. If there should be black magic worked on me to make me lose my mind and my throne; or if death or sickness should befall me or Ben Quorn or Virginia Blackstone—no matter what the doctors may say is the cause—then look to yourself! Look to your temples! Look to your whole tribe of shaven priests! For you will fall in that same hour. And if you doubt that, try me! Curse me this minute—and see!"

The High Priest stared. Never before had he been met with his own venom. He did not quite dare to disbelieve her; she had already defeated him badly, more than once. She might be lying, but he did not dare to assume that.

He knew the strength and honesty of the friendship that Blake, the British Resident, felt for her. It might be that she had found some means of breaking ancient treaties and permitting hordes of alien reformers to descend on the country—preachers—teachers—investigators—scientists—all sorts of tamperers. There was no knowing what she had done. She might have thought of something he had never dreamed of.

"Why should I curse, who came to bless?" he answered, craftily assuming magnanimity.

But she was not to be put off guard so easily. "I have decided I am willing to be cursed," she assured him. "That may be the best thing for Narada and for all my people, because it would be the end of you also and of all that you Brahmins impose. So you may curse me. I am ready."

"I refuse to curse you," he retorted. "Evil though you have spoken—evil though your heart is, I will bless you. Hour by hour a hundred Brahmins shall bless you day and night, until you have a change of heart."

"I kiss feet," she assured him pertly, that being the proper formula when speaking to a personage of his twice-born sanctity: "But see to it that your Brahmins make no mistakes. For only so long as my health and my friends' health is good and my throne is secure shall they wallow in those material rewards against whose corrupting influence they warn us others."

The High Priest's blessing, as restrained and formal as a law clerk's mumbling of the oath, emerged through grimly angry lips to sweeten the world's sorrow. Then he turned his back, because that was the insolent way to leave the room and he was the High Priest, if not a gentleman.

It was not until the creaking of the wheels of the High Priest's bullock-drawn carriage had departed down the drive that the Ranee pressed a god's nose, opening a panel in the wall, through which stepped Bamjee, dripping with perspiration and more frightened than ever a four-legged rat was.

"Daughter of the Moon," he stammered, "you have challenged the anger of all the Brahmins! They will—" He finished it with a more or less dramatic gesture to suggest annihilation.

"Did you write it all down?"

"Heaven-born, it burns the paper!"

4

"IT IS BEST FOR YOU TO TURN BACK"

VIRGINIA BLACKSTONE TRIED to sleep, but the trees stood close to the rear of the *dak* bungalow and there were sounds in an Indian jungle that inoculate imagination with the virus of dread until the time comes when, after months of it, familiarity breeds contempt and careless-ness brings disaster. The new arrival on the Indian scene is much too nervous, as a rule, to be caught sleeping when the stealthy danger creeps and closes in. She tried to sleep, but lay awake and stared at moonlight making patterns on the bedroom wall. She had an automatic underneath the pillow and knew how to use it, so she was not actually afraid. Her nerves refused to be stilled; and her pyjamas irritated her, because the night was hot and the *punkah,* swinging about two feet above her nose, was inefficient.

After a while the *punkah* cord began to squeak where it passed through a hole in the wall. There is no more maddening sound than that. For a while she endured it—then pulled on her slippers and sat on a cane-seated chair by the table, smoking innumerable cigarettes.

The moonlight cast her shadow on the white wall, and the moving *punkah* shadow looked exactly like the wide blade of a big black knife that swung toward her throat, paused there for a fraction of a second without quite touching, swung back, paused and then was aimed at her again. She turned her back toward it.

That brought her facing the window, where every now and then a bat would cling to the copper screen. Like most women, she detested bats. There was a constant stream of them flitting like black darts past the window.

One of them managed to enter the room. She wondered how—wondered whether there was a hole she had not noticed in one of the window screens. For twenty minutes she tried to kill it with a tennis racket that she unpacked from a roll of blankets. But the bat flew high, and when she stood on a chair it refused to fly near enough.

Then a monkey in the near-by jungle screamed. It was a hair-raising, horrible scream. Either a panther or a python had come on the monkey while it slept.

Then an elephant made a strange noise and she heard somebody cry out *"Bagh!"* which she knew meant "Tiger!" All the other elephants grew restless; she could hear them tugging at their picket-rings, and the mahouts woke up to use what sounded like blasphemous language to them. But those sounds were almost comforting because they meant that there were humans awake and within reach. She thought she could hear Quorn's voice.

However, all grew still again and the ensuing silence was more dreadful than the monkey's scream. It was a silence made of stealthy sounds inseparable from each other.

There began to be a smell that she hardly noticed at first and that grew stronger as the minutes passed. It was a clammy, dank, unpleasant smell, quite new in her experience and unexplainably alarming, not in the least like the smell of gas or slow fire, but at least as suggestive of danger.

She could still hear the bat flit to and fro, and made three or four hopeless swipes with the tennis racket. Then she laid down the racket to strike a match, because she could not endure the darkness any longer.

THE MATCH BURNED her fingers. She forgot it in the horror of what its light revealed. She supposed there must be rats in the room, though she had never imagined rats' eyes swaying so like a pendulum and she wondered why they made so little noise.

She suddenly moved her chair, expecting to hear the rats scamper away, but there was no sound, so she struck another match. The two score pairs of eyes had not moved. They swayed a little—tiny, gleaming dots reflecting match-light. And before the flame of the second match quite reached her finger-tips, she understood.

Snakes! Snakes of all sorts and sizes. The room seemed full of them. She was surrounded. Before the match-light died she had seen one shadowy shape go writhing along the skirting board, and another had vanished into darkness underneath the bed.

She had had one glimpse of an enormous reptile—probably a python, but the others all looked like small snakes, perhaps four or five feet long, some smaller. And she had heard—she forgot who told her—that the smaller snakes are the deadliest. She drew her feet up on the chair, too terrified to shudder, thinking of the automatic underneath her pillow that she did not dare to cross the floor to get.

And what use would the automatic be? Supposing that

in the dark, and with her hand trembling, she should kill six snakes with it. There would be fifty more to deal with.

No, the tennis racket would be a lot better. She reached for it—and drew her hand back with a scream that she swallowed and stifled, wondering why she did not dare to scream. She had touched something. It was alive. It had moved. Her finger tingled with the horror of it.

Should she shout for Quorn? She knew she did not dare, although she did not know why. Something—probably her own fear—was imposing silence on her. She had forgotten the bat by that time, but the darkness seemed to be alive with crawling things that crept toward her, weaving themselves around table-legs and bed-legs—chair-legs. It seemed as if the legs of the chair she sat on were standing upright in a maze of snakes.

Then suddenly a chair moved, exactly as if a heavy snake had pushed it aside as he wove his way toward her. So the python was coming! She could even hear the monster's movement. Two or three other snakes made a sound like hissing, as if the bigger one had scared them as he crossed their path.

Then a man spoke and she was so startled that she let the match-box fall to the floor.

"Memsahib."

It was a passionless, colorless voice—like a voice from the grave, and she could not tell which corner of the room it came from. She had sense enough not to try to answer. Wit works swiftly in a crisis, if it works at all. As long as she kept silent and did not move, whoever was in the room could not know whether or not she had her pistol.

"Memsahib, why do you come to Narada?"

IT WAS A moment or two before she realized the words were English. But it was an alien accent. She began to feel more in command of herself as soon as she had noticed that.

"*Memsahib*, it is best for you to turn back."

She imagined a tall, lean man with burning eyes and snake-like arms, but she could not see even a hint of him where his voice had seemed to come from. Only she was almost sure now that his voice came from a height not much, if anything above the level of the seat of her chair, as if he might be squatting on the floor. And if he knew about the snakes—how could he help knowing?—and was not afraid of them, they might be harmless.

She began to feel better. Obstinacy, that is sometimes kin to courage, and arouses courage, stiffened her a little. She began to feel indignant and to wonder whether this was any of the Ranee's doing. She had heard stories of how swiftly Orientals can change their minds and to what expedients they resort in order to escape from a bargain.

"*Memsahib*, evil awaits you in Narada. You will not reach the palace alive. Turn back. Enemies lie in wait for you. And there are not only snakes. There are tigers—panthers— there is poison."

He was doing something. She could hear a stealthy movement on the floor. He was possibly creeping toward her.

"Stop!" she commanded, rather surprised by the calmness of her own voice. "If you come any nearer I will shoot."

"*Memsahib*, you will not shoot, because I have the pistol. Listen." Something—perhaps a pistol butt—struck the floor three times. That sound was followed by the click of mechanism; she could hear him remove the clip that held the cartridges. "There. Now it is harmless. You may have it." She heard it tossed on the bed. *"Memsahib,* no harm shall come to you if only you will turn back. But if you go forward, death awaits you—death in many forms. Turn back."

"Who are you?" she demanded.

"Memsahib, I am your friend."

"The hell you are!" remarked another voice, followed instantly by a thump and a grunt. There was a scuffle and wood thudded against wood, as if a trapdoor had been closed. Then an electric torch flashed on and she could see Quorn standing where the voice had been. His torchlight as he turned it about the room revealed a glimpse of three or four snakes vanishing under the skirting board, which had been raised about three inches.

"Too bad I didn't kick that louse harder—if you'll pardon my bad language, miss. I almost missed him when he ducked down through the trap. No, no use chasing him; there's prob'ly tunnels under there; them heathen don't take many chances; they make sure o' their get-away first, 'fore they start anything. See—here's the trap—two short boards hinging on a pivot—locked from underneath… Huh! See that? See that skirting board drop back in place? He probably had the nerve to stay and count his snakes afore he shut that. Follow him? And get myself knifed in the liver! Are you badly scared, miss? Shall I bring you a shot o' something? I've some brandy in the *howdah.*"

"WHAT DOES IT mean, Mr. Quorn?"

"I'll tell you." He lit the lamp, adjusted the wick thoughtfully, and then sat down across the room from her. "This is

India's coral strand, what hymn-books tell of. Many's the nickel I sent to India when I was young. But I ain't financing no more sermons to these heathen. Not but what I haven't friends here. And the Ranee—who employs me—she's the hornet's nosegay. Nothing whatever the matter with her."

"But what does this mean?"

"I'll tell you, miss. Don't hurry me. The Ranee, she has enemies. She's back against the wall."

"She told me in her letter that the Brahmins—"

"Sure, miss. Brahmins. And if you should ever see a straight-eight, four-shift-forward, full-floating-axle alibi with four-wheel brakes and body by Fisher, that belongs to the Brahmins. Them boys naturally aim to scare you off the lot, seeing that's less risky than to kill you when you get there. Did they scare you much, miss?"

"Yes. But I'm none the worse for it. What brought you?"

"No more than a hunch, miss. There was two tigers out there in the jungle, acting stupid, as if they was half-drugged and being driven. Maybe you heard my elephants raise hell about it. After I'd made the elephants see sense—and that ain't any picnic, but it's easier than managing mahouts—I got to thinking. I figured tigers all doped up with laudanum was kindergarten stuff they'd hardly waste on me. I wondered wasn't they maybe out to get your goat.

"So I did some pussyfooting. And I found the back door open. I'd a notion to take my shoes off, but I'm glad I didn't. As it was I caught that sucker in the mouth or in the eye—I don't know which—the mouth, I guess—I didn't hear him say much. He might have bitten off my toe if I'd been barefoot." And Quorn grinned.

"But the snakes? Do you suppose they were poisonous?"

"Su-u-u-ure. Snakes don't bother them folk—not the folk, I mean, who make that a business. You'll see stories in the home papers about how they pull the fangs out, but that's the bunk. The trick's much simpler. The guy they call a charmer keeps his coat in the bag with the snakes. They sleep in it. It stinks o' snake. By and by he wears it and the snakes won't harm him because he smells even worse than what they do. Each o' them smells of only one snake. He smells of a hundred. He's the ace o' snakes and he can train 'em easy. But it takes a heathen to go to all that trouble."

"I can't say I enjoyed this," said Virginia Blackstone, "and I don't think I can sleep. But now that the scare is over I'm beginning to enjoy the prospect. I can imagine there will be fun and lots of danger. Next time I won't be so frightened."

"Next time, they'll soak it to you harder, miss. Hell don't hold such devils. If they mean to scare you off the lot they'll act ingenious."

5

"DID I TELL YOU TO STEAL BLAKE SAHIB'S LETTER?"

"IT IS NO use your talking to me about loyalty, respectability and good faith, Mr. Bamjee. I regard you as a rat," said Blake.

"*Sahib,* that is just exactly what her highness said. Quorn also said it. So many people have said it that I sometimes wonder if it isn't true. Nevertheless, rats have their uses. I am only an ignorant *babu*—B.A. of Calcutta University; risen through sheer incompetence, of course, to purchasing agent of the royal reigning Ranee of Narada… Sense of loyalty is relative. I have a tale to tell."

"Go on then. Tell it."

"But I have already told it. There is no more."

"I don't believe you," said Blake. "Either your tale is a lie, or you are lying now. There must be more to it, or there would be no object in your telling it to me."

Brazenose Blake sat bolt upright at his desk under the office *punkah.* He scowled. He was doing two of the things that he most detested. He hated to sit in his office after dinner in the evening; and he loathed anything whatever that carried a taint of spywork.

Nevertheless he was there in Narada to keep the Central

Indian Government informed; and as a matter of nasty, naked fact it was impossible for him to do that without listening to backstairs gossip and to treasonable folk like Bamjee. Consequently he had been at pains to establish the reputation of being a perfectly safe man to whom to talk in confidence.

"But, sir," said Bamjee, "is my motive not as clear to you as that it is a hot night? If the Ranee should lose her throne, then this *babu* would lose his job—his profitable job. She is endangering her throne. I have repeated to you word for word the conversation she had with the High Priest of Siva. She has defied and challenged the Brahmins. And you, sir, do you not know what devils those Brahmins are?"

Blake scowled again. He knew those Brahmins only too well.

Bamjee went on. "Sir, they think in terms of centuries. But they do not neglect the passing moment. If they could make such trouble for Miss Blackstone—even cause her to be killed, so that the Indian government would interfere… I beg you, send that woman back across the ocean."

"I can't," said Blake. "If she were English, possibly it might be done. But she happens to be an American with extremely good credentials."

THEN BLAKE DID what he hated even more than listening to spies. He set to work to use one.

"Bamjee."

"*Sahib?*"

"What would happen if her highness knew that you came straight to me with this story of her secret interview with Siva's High Priest?"

"Oh, *sahib!* I should be a lost *babu* without a business!"

"It is the fate of nearly all spies, Mr. Bamjee, that sooner or later they become so involved in intrigue, that the only way is to go in deeper. You have reached that stage already. You must spy on the Brahmins now, and keep me informed."

"Sir, I am incompetent."

"It would be the only way to keep my confidence, and—er—your post with the Ranee."

Bamjee wilted—on the surface; but his bright eyes blinked behind his spectacles in token that he loved intrigue as drunkards love their drink. He was excited—half-flattered. He craved to be wholly flattered. He enjoyed, with a sort of masochistic glee, the sense of being threatened.

"*Sahib,* I ask no reward other than your recognition of me as a man who can be trusted."

Blake's face was half in shadow and the swinging *punkah* made the shadow leap and change each moment, so if his expression altered not even Bamjee noticed it.

"You had better be trustworthy, Mr. Bamjee! What I expect of you is that you make contact with the Brahmins without loss of time, worm yourself by some means into their secret counsels, and inform me. I shall reward you according to the results."

To any other spy than Bamjee that was almost an impossible assignment. Centuries have brought no revelation of the Brahmins' secrets. Something is sometimes learned by inference, and something by deduction, but the secrets on the whole are marvelously kept.

Bamjee left Blake's office smothering his feeling of importance under an air of benignant harmlessness, pausing in the door to bow with his hand behind him—lest Blake should see the letter he had stolen on general principles. It was a letter that Blake had written to his mother in England.

BAMJEE STEAMED THE envelope and read the letter beside a candle in his private office at the upper, more respectable and honest end of the Bazaar. There was a part in it that made his eyes blink snappily behind the gold-rimmed spectacles. It ran:

> Do you remember Miss Blackstone? The American girl whose father was disgustingly rich, but a remarkably good sort? Well, the girl is coming to Narada. Can you beat that?
>
> You seemed to like her rather well. I know I did. But, of course, I had no money and the thing was impossible.
>
> She claimed a modern woman's privilege and proposed that we get married—explained that she understood my diffidence and said the money didn't matter. To be perfectly frank, if I wasn't actually in love with her before, I certainly was then.
>
> But beggars have to be choosers, so I drew my horns in. It wasn't easy. If my diplomatic standing rested on my finesse in rejecting a sweet and honorable lady's offer to marry me, I should be out of a job and starving. Serve me right, too. Some blundering words of mine offended her. She was high-spirited and let me have it back with chilled steel shot. I took my coup de grace, of course, without a murmur and I haven't seen her or heard from her from that day to this. However, I heard that her father had lost his money and I learned from several sources how splendidly she behaved about it.
>
> Now she is coming to Narada on the Ranee's invitation! She probably doesn't even know I'm here. It will be a horri-

ble situation. She'll imagine—why not?—that I think she
came here either to annoy me or else to resume negotiations.

"Um-m!" remarked Bamjee to himself. He returned
the letter to its envelope and resealed it carefully, examining it thoroughly with a magnifying glass to make sure
there were no telltale fingermarks. Then he summoned
his servant.

"Lazy loafer without shame!" he exploded, using the
local dialect. "Blind idiot! What do I find among my
papers? Look! Blake *sahib's* letter! Imbecile! Yes, I know
there were papers of mine on Mr. Blake's desk. I know I
sent you for them—yes, I know that. But did I tell you to
steal Blake *sahib's* letter? Thou *be-shirm!* You must have
picked it up by accident along with my papers, must you?
Liar! You did it to get me into trouble! Return it to Blake
sahib's desk. Don't let anybody catch you doing it, if you
value your skin!"

But the servant did not wait to hear more. He took the
envelope and ran—inventing on his way a story to tell
the *hamal*—manservant—at the Residency about having
dropped on the floor, or perhaps into Blake's wastebasket,
an amulet for curing heaves in Bamjee's horse.

He had the amulet concealed under his cotton shirt in
the hope of curing his own warts before the horse's turn
came, so he had no doubt of finding it if the *hamal* would
only let him look.

He could spare a two-anna piece for the *hamal,* if he
must, but he hoped, if he gossiped enough, to save that
money. Hope springs eternal.

6

"HANG ON IF YOU LOVE LIFE!"

QUORN AND VIRGINIA Blackstone were firm friends by the time they were ready for the second day's journey. She watched Asoka eat his morning meal of big flat cakes with a chaser of hay. Without jealousy Quorn let her lead the monster to the brook for his morning drink. The elephant's muddy, wet trunk made a mess of her linen frock, but that was a small price for her to pay for making two firm friends.

She was too excited to eat much breakfast, so they got away to an early start in the delicious hushed calm of an Indian morning before the brazen sun had burned the color from the landscape.

And now they saw the Ranee coming to meet them! Not a soft exotic doll in old-rose silk as Virginia Blackstone's fancy had imagined her, but a lovely, lithe, athletic-looking girl in modern riding breeches and a white shirt, on a plunging Arab stallion, escorted by a dozen officers in uniform, who were hard put to it to keep pace. No formal, regal greeting, but a hand-wave and musical laughter—not a taint of shyness—nothing whatever to spoil the instant recognition by two women of each other's eagerness to make friends.

Quorn made Asoka kneel. The Ranee tossed her reins to the nearest officer and climbed into the *howdah*.

"Oh, but I'm glad you have come!" she exploded, laughing because she was out of breath in her excitement. "I couldn't wait in Narada, and I'm glad I didn't. I do like you. And your frock is muddy—oh, it's perfect! Tell me, did they make you comfortable last night?"

Perfect English—hardly any accent—not a trace of the sort of self-consciousness that snobs feel and genuine folks resent. No condescension. None of the inbred, hook-nosed *purdah*-look and sly eyes that suggest the gulf between the East and West. The Ranee might have passed for a Carolinian co-ed, with possibly a trace of Spanish in her ancestry.

"YOU LOOK HUMAN to me," said Virginia Blackstone. "No, I didn't sleep much; but I'll tell you about that later."

"I suppose you've heard often enough that nonsense about a throne being only a bore," said the Ranee. "It isn't. It's the best fun possible. Only one does simply starve for a friend who can be told everything, and trusted, and who will enjoy it with you. Will you stay with me a long time—a really long time? Quorn was homesick after the first few weeks, but now he declares he will stay forever."

They chatted and laughed, both lying full length in the *howdah* because now the sun was up and the sides of the *howdah* provided shade. Virginia Blackstone had the least to say. She dreaded lest some chance remark might bring Blake's name into the conversation. But presently the Ranee wiped that problem off the slate.

"Don't be deceived by my modern ways. They're mostly out of magazines and novels. I have a motion picture

"Hang on if you love life!" cried the Ranee

camera, too, and I've studied gesture, and walking, and
how to look as if life doesn't hold any problems that a kiss
can't solve. But I'm an Oriental, so remember I am jealous!
I shall want you all to myself. I don't mean that I won't trust
you not to tell secrets. But I know that I couldn't endure
to share you with man or woman—not for a while, at any
rate."

"It happens that I would rather not meet other people,"
said Virginia.

"Are you in love?" the Ranee asked, suspicious on the
instant.

"No. Are you?" asked Virginia.

"Yes."

Followed silence, only broken by the padding of the
feet of elephants and by the snorting and prancing of the
Ranee's Arab stallion, who objected to being led.

The officers who formed the Ranee's escort had arranged
themselves in single file on either hand; they appeared to

make rather a point of not being military men, although they wore a sort of uniform with turbans all of the same color; they were gentlemen of high breeding who helped to evade the treaty limiting Narada's army to fifty men, including officers, by constituting themselves a bodyguard of volunteers. Being Rajputs, they were entitled to carry weapons, and a saber clattered from each saddle.

Virginia Blackstone noticed that the Ranee's eyes repeatedly lingered on the man who seemed to lead the escort. Almost every time that she paused between two sentences she looked at him.

He led the right-hand file—a very splendid person, at least six feet tall, black-bearded; and he rode his big bay Kathiawari mare as if his mount and he were one graceful and extremely potent entity. He had that rare gift of appearing quiet and yet capable of instant brain-directed violence. He seemed aware of everything and master of himself and every other thing in sight, but not at all concerned about asserting his dominance.

"That is he," said the Ranee after a long pause, nodding. "That is Prince Rana Raj Singh. He owns a castle in Rajputana, and he is a proud man, even for a Rajput. He and I love each other. But he doesn't like the thought of being merely a reigning Ranee's consort. Neither do I like it. If we could share the throne together—equally—but the English won't allow that, and the Brahmins are bitter against it."

SILENCE AGAIN. A coppersmith bird in a tree near by kept up an irritating *bong-bong-bong* that refused to fit in with the sway and squeak of the *howdah* or with the footfalls. The Ranee's led stallion neighed, and Rana Raj Singh rather deliberately raised his bridle-hand, his eyes examining the dusty trail ahead. There began to be a feeling of insecurity, as of impending, unseen trouble; but the Ranee, if she felt it, took no notice.

Except for those top-boots and modern riding breeches, she might have been Titania discussing who should rule in fairyland. They passed for miles along a trail where orchids and wild begonias grew in squanderous profusion. Azure sky, flaked with swan's-down clouds, was framed in snow-clad mountain peaks clearly limned in the morning sunlight.

The song of birds, the footfall of the animals, even their own voices were now and then drowned in the rioting tumult of the almost countless waterfalls that had to be crossed by bridges flung like spider-web from lip to lip of echoing ravines. The narrow track, glittering white with mica, zig-zagged like a flash of lightning between earth and sky.

"This little land of mine," said the Ranee, "is the last place left in the world where people and things are almost as they were a thousand years ago. We are almost inaccessible. We are almost free from outside influences. We have the telegraph, but it wouldn't pay to bring in the railway. We almost never see even an airplane, because the peaks make flying difficult; and the radio is almost useless because of static. So we are left very much to ourselves, and I am hoping to introduce just enough modern innovations to make life richer without robbing us of ancient goodness."

"Don't your people all live in a dream?" Virginia Blackstone asked.

"Sometimes it's a nightmare," said the Ranee. "They are

like the weather; nobody knows what is likely to happen to-day or to-morrow. They submit with a smile to some of the changes I have brought about; other apparently unimportant innovations have made them bitterly rebellious. It's exciting. But it's dangerous, too."

THE WEATHER—THE IMPIOUS, numberless, nameless godlets that are said to govern the Narada weather may have heard that speech. A peal of thunder seemed to split the very mountains with its din in confirmation of the Ranee's words. Hurrying, black and howling, from beyond the nearest ridge, spitting forked lightning and darkening the day as if the sun were in eclipse, a hailstorm smote the smiling valley. Now the waterfalls were noiseless, there was nothing to be heard but thunder and the seething, smashed-glass shattering of tons of hail that stripped the trees of foliage and slew such luckless birds as had not been able to find shelter in the clefts of rocks.

Above the *howdah* on Asoka's back there was a canopy of light material that could have shed rain and was proof against the sun. The hail destroyed it in a second. Asoka felt the icy volleys on his rump, and wasted no time wondering what to do about it. Not his to oppose the elements; he fled before them.

Graceless, gray, enormous in the dim gray murk, Asoka borrowed wings of fear. Five tons of him, he fled like fifty feathers in a blown gray bag, while Quorn bent low along his head in torture from the hail, and the ice-filled *howdah* swayed like a small boat in a surging sea. One sound reached Virginia's ears through the din of the hail and thunder:

"Hang on! Hang on if you love life!" cried the Ranee.

7

"THE GODS REWARD THEIR AGENTS"

NOT ONLY PEOPLE such as Bamjee are rats, and not all rats are wholly harmful. There were Mazarin and Frederick the Great, both of whom left their mark on the world without the aid of covenants too openly arrived at. Bamjee went to work to prove that a rat can be a statesman.

He was possessed by one all-encompassing instinct—that of self-preservation; and he had one incorruptible loyalty—to Bamjee. Within those limits he could live and let live on a suitable sliding scale blackmail basis, ethically graded.

"Too bad," Bamjee muttered. "I am no heroic personage. I would not look well on horseback at the head of armies. People would never look up to me if I were a prime minister. But as a rat—he said I am a rat. He insulted me; nevertheless—"

It was nearly midnight, but he knew both the value of the darkness, and the habits of the priests of Siva's temple. He also knew their prejudices, so he changed into Indian garments instead of the nice silk suit of European cut. He put on sandals. He examined himself in the glass until he was satisfied with his facial expression, which could be made at a moment's notice to reflect a vast variety of moods, all simulated.

"You rogue!" he remarked. "Almost I myself would believe you if you told me two times two are five!"

He slipped quietly out of the house and walked down the middle of winding streets for about two miles toward Siva's temple. He knew that nobody would recognize him by moonlight in that costume, and the shadows, where the homeless sleep, are dangerous.

The great gate of Siva's temple opens on the street—a shadowy gap in a ponderous wall from which the graven faces of a thousand nakedly immodest godlets leer at the passer-by. The great teak door almost always stands open, but there is never a minute by day or night when watchers are not there, it being one of human nature's least encouraging peculiarities that the reputedly pious are more suspicious than confessedly impious people are.

TWO MEN IN yellow garments challenged Bamjee, and they mocked his ingenuous statement that he wished to meditate within the temple on death in life. They called him a casteless miscreant, which was untrue; he belonged to a sub-caste of a fraternity of miscreants. And they assured him he would learn all he needed to know about death's unpleasantness in due course, which was one of those simply prophetic statements that have given priests in all climes and ages a reputation for infallibility.

"Why anticipate?" they asked him. "Siva, who created you along with evil smells and similar things, will slay you when the time comes."

"I have business with the High Priest," said Bamjee at last. "If you don't believe it, one of you run in and tell him

I was behind the panel in the palace when he—when he blessed the Ranee privately."

"Your name?"

"Never mind. Go in and tell him." One man carried the message. The other watched Bamjee, and there was prickly silence for fifteen minutes, until the messenger returned with orders to admit Bamjee into the cell where unclean visitors were sometimes, as an act of mercy, blessed through a hole in the wall.

The sanctity of Brahmins was too precious, and too costly to reestablish after contact with rank outsiders such as Bamjee, to permit his being brought into the inner temple. Even as it was, the two gate guardians soused him with water that had been properly treated with incantations, before they led him across the gloomy courtyard, admitted him into a bare stone chamber and shut the door behind him. Bamjee shuddered as he heard the bolt slide home.

There was a lamp on each of three walls, leaving the door in shadow. In the wall that faced the door there was a round hole, showing that the masonry was six feet thick. The hole was trumpet-shaped, with the small end inward, so that any one looking through it from the far side of the wall could see most of the room; but at present the far end of the hole was closed with what looked like an iron shutter.

Bamjee did not dare to examine that very closely, but he blew out two of the lamps and adjusted the wick of the third, so that the cell grew very nearly dark and whoever should look through the hole in the wall would hardly recognize him.

"Nobody knows," he reflected, "that I was not followed

to this place and seen to enter here. So they will probably not dare to kill me. *Phuk*—death is an unpleasant subject. Let me think of something else."

He stood up close to the wall, where he would be invisible if any one looked through the hole. He listened for a long time, but could hear nothing, except his own blood humming past his eardrums. It was the silence of the tomb. There was no window. The wooden door was something like a foot thick; not a sound could penetrate.

The silence began to get on Bamjee's nerves.

"I must get such an office as this," he remarked to himself. "If a salesman should sit in it, say, for an hour before I interviewed him, I could learn his inmost thoughts. I could get good terms from him, I think. They know something, these Brahmins. But they don't know me—not yet."

THEN HE HEARD the iron shutter slide in rather squeaky grooves, and he heard a voice he recognized, grumbling to some one else because the lights were not lit properly. The other voice offered to send somebody to light them.

"No," came the answer, "I can manage. But impose a penance on him whose fault it is. You may go now."

And so Bamjee knew he was alone with the High Priest, although there was six feet of solid masonry between them. He crept close to the hole and peered in; there was utter darkness at the far end, so he stooped below the level of the hole, crossed the floor, blew the other lamp out, and returned.

"I kiss feet," he remarked then, just as piously as if he were a penitent in quest of guidance on the Inner Way. There was no answer. For a moment he feared he had overdone caution and that the High Priest had gone away; but he was sure that the shutter had not been slid back into place.

"I am afraid of the dark!" he complained. "I kiss feet. But why is there no light in here? Are they afraid to burn a little oil? I am too terrified to give my message."

"Speak. Who are you?" said the voice at the end of the hole.

"O All-wise! O Father of Wisdom! O Heaven-born! Truly, if my name is not as easily discernible to you as are all the inscrutable meanings of the sacred books, then indeed I might as well have no name whatever. But I have a message."

"Speak."

"Patient one! In fear, because I knew the dreadful nature of my sin, I obeyed an order—and I hid behind a panel— and I heard—I wrote down—all that was said when your sacredness went to the Ranee to reprove her for the error of her ways. I wrote all, and she has the writing. She has hidden it where none except herself can find it. I have sought for it, hoping to bring it to you, O Fount of Blessings."

"Because of this sin, for a thousand lives—"

"No, no—no cursing! Not yet! It is not too late to undo what is done. Out of your wisdom give me a command, O Heaven-born. I obeyed an order. If I sinned—and I did sin—she who gave the order is thrice guilty. Let me be an agent in her punishment? If she is to be destroyed, let my hand do it!"

"What is your name?" was the answer—an ultimatum.

Bamjee owned up, reflecting that the Brahmins would

not take long to discover his name if they decided it was worth the trouble.

"I am Bamjee, purchasing agent."

"Wait."

The iron shutter squealed along its grooves and Bamjee was left alone in such abysmal darkness that at last he struck a match to keep from losing his self-control. When the match went out he struck another, but by the time that one had burned he was feeling better.

"That," he remarked to himself, "is the last I shall hear from the High Priest. If he decides to try to use me, he will send an underling to make the compact between virtue and necessity—some one who can be repudiated along with his bargain, and can eat blame if anything goes wrong."

HE WAS RIGHT. The iron shutter did not move again, but the door opened after a while and a man came in who might have been a priest and might not. He carried a lamp with him and a rolled mat under his arm. He made sure that the door was locked, then very deliberately unrolled the mat along the floor, set the lamp beside it, and sat down cross-legged.

His skull was shaven, but he wore no caste mark on his forehead. He looked almost like a lawyer with his high-beaked nose and one ear farther than the other from his head, as if he usually stuck his pen there.

"Do you know what silence means?" he demanded, after he had stared at Bamjee for at least two minutes. "Do you know that the entrails of a dog were men once, who broke an oath of silence laid on them by Brahmins?"

"I did not know it was as bad as that," said Bamjee, pretending to tremble.

He was in his element at last. Face to face, he felt himself more than the equal of any one at this game. Let Brahmins make up all the tales they liked about the next life; Bamjee was busy with this one—busy and as blinkingly alert as any mongoose.

"I kiss feet," murmured Bamjee. "I am silent."

"Listen. Not only are you an out-caste, you are irreligious, and you have helped that woman, who calls herself the Ranee, to degrade her throne. Your share of that, and its *karma,* is on your head. Life after life you will pay for it."

"Pity me! What shall I do?" moaned Bamjee.

"Make good *karma,* imbecile! For every ill deed do a good one, thus providing blessings for the lives to come, that shall offset evil *karma* and make life somehow tolerable."

"Tell me what to do," said Bamjee.

"I will not tell you what to do. But I will tell you this for your information and your judgment, so that you may offset certain of your sins if you have wit enough to do it. She who calls herself the Ranee will cross the river at daybreak, or soon thereafter, on her way to meet a woman she has invited to come and help her throw Narada into worse confusion than already is. There will be an accident; it may be on the homeward journey. He who has cast the horoscope declares there will certainly be an accident."

"I understand you. It has been foreordained," said Bamjee.

"By the gods."

"And their agents, doubtless."

"The gods use human agency. And they reward their agents."

"Oh, affluence!" said Bamjee.

"But they punish those who try to interfere."

"Unwise, immodest fools!" said Bamjee.

"They who keep the fools from interfering, and thus leave judgment to the gods alone, incur good *karma* for their pains."

"Virtue bears its own reward, and there is no escape from justice," murmured Bamjee.

"She who is known as the Ranee has arranged that one half of her army of fifty miscreants shall march along the road toward her summer palace in the hills, to await her in the hills after making repairs to the road. The other half are to march to meet her on her way back with this foreign woman. They are lazy. They are not likely to march far. But if they should chance to be near the river when the accident takes place—"

"There might be disappointment?" Bamjee suggested.

"The gods might not be pleased. Unnecessary evil might befall those five-and-twenty infantry. Whoever should prevent that—"

"By delaying them—"

"Undoubtedly would earn reward."

"As purchasing agent I have no authority," said Bamjee. "But as creditor, to whom their officer owes more than he can pay in three years, and whose unpaid notes I hold, I think it may be I have influence."

"But are your wits about you? Go then. There is not much time. The gods take no delight in idleness."

"I kiss feet. Oh, I kiss feet. Bless me. Open the door and let me run!" said Bamjee; and he fled into the night.

TWO HOURS LATER Brazenose Blake was awakened

from bed where he lay naked under a *punkah,* tossing and swearing. He was pleased at having his misery interrupted, though he did not choose to admit it, so he scowled as he pulled on his pyjamas.

But when he entered the office and recognized Bamjee he forgot what he had meant to say. The *hamal* had lighted the lamp on the desk and Bamjee's face looked tortured with excitement.

However, there was no use in making the man more excited.

"Hello," he exclaimed, "how did that letter get there?" The letter he had written to his mother lay face upward on the blotter.

"I don't know," said Bamjee. "By Krishna! *Sahib,* what should I know about letters when I come this minute from out-Brahmining all the Brahmins under Brahma's heaven!"

BLAKE WAITED, KNOWING it was no use to try to hurry him. He put in the time making sure there were no scorpions under the rug, because he had not pulled on his slippers.

"*Sahib,*" said Bamjee at last, "it is half past three A.M; and the Ranee left fifteen minutes ago on horseback with only one attendant to meet that American lady. There is an ambush set for them on the way home—Quorn, too. I am committee of one expressly bribed with promises of Kingdom Come, also diabolically threatened with alternative incarnations into a dog's belly. My commission is to make sure that the soldiers don't march. Hurry, *sahib!* Make sure that they do march!"

"I have no authority," said Blake. "I can't interfere with the Ranee's soldiers."

He was almost sure that Bamjee was inventing a trick to get him involved politically in some way that would force his resignation. Bamjee, he knew, was perfectly capable of trying that, for reasons so obscure, perhaps, that even Bamjee would hardly know them. Incredulity was Blake's best weapon, even though he seldom used it.

"Oh my God, *sahib!* What shall I say to you! Listen! I have no proof—not a scrap of proof—no proof of any kind. But if I am lying to you, may my tongue be torn out of my head and may my wife and children die of cholera! May I eat shame all my days, if I am lying! And—may I—may I lose all my money!"

At that last, Blake began to believe him. Very coolly he struck the bell beside him on the desk.

"*Hamal,*" he said, "wake Abdullah. Tell him I want my boots and breeches. He's to look sharp. Then wake the *sais* and tell him to saddle the Waler mare. Get a move on... Now," he said, turning again to Bamjee, "where is Prince Rana Raj Singh staying? I'll go to him and send him with as many horsemen as he can gather to overtake the Ranee and protect her."

"*Sahib,* Prince Rana Raj Singh has already gone, with all his gentlemen. They are the Ranee's escort. They are probably to die, too. Do the Brahmins not hate Rana Raj Singh?"

Blake frowned. The one thing in the world that he did not want to do was to inflict himself on Virginia Blackstone. Next after that, he was anxious not to go off half-cocked and be caught interfering m local affairs without valid reason.

"Quorn is a good man," he muttered. "Quorn isn't easily

trapped." But he remembered that Quorn was only one, against a host of enemies.

"Dammit!" he exploded. "There is no law against my taking an early morning ride. Have you a horse? No? I know your house. I will come with a pony for you after I have talked with the commander of the Ranee's troops."

8

"A SORT OF DEVILS' PARADISE"

QUORN LAY FLAT along Asoka's head. He did not dare to try to look back; that would have meant exposing his face to the blinding force of the storm. The hail, hurricane-driven, came from behind in screaming blasts so nearly horizontal that the worst of its violence passed over him; but even so he felt as if his back was being numbed and then stripped of flesh.

He could look downward, but he could no longer see the track, such drifts of steaming ice were volleying before the wind. Asoka appeared to be running knee-deep in a raging river, whose every drop was separately frozen.

It was as dark as if the sun were in eclipse; but there was enough diffused, dim light to indicate rocks on the left, around which the hail surged like a raging tide-race, deafening and dreadful. On the right there was nothing visible, not even an outline of the edge of the ravine, into which trees and rocks went crashing phantom-fashion, their noise utterly swallowed by wind and hail.

So Quorn did his best to make Asoka hug the left-hand side, knowing that even an elephant's prodigious senses must be deadened and his natural surefootedness lost in that titanic uproar. Quorn preferred to crash into a cliff rather than be hurled a thousand feet on to rocks in the valley below.

So with his elbow up to shield his eyes, and with the *ankus* in his right hand tapping, tapping at Asoka's cheek to edge him leftward, he watched for the looming bowlders. Otherwise he never could have seen the skin-clad jungle pariah who dodged out from behind an almost unseen rock and, using both hands, jabbed with a long lance at Asoka as he sped by. The wetted shaft probably slipped in the man's grip, since the sharp blade hardly slit the elephant's thick skin and Asoka, already mad with terror, did not even notice it.

They raced before the wind until the hail ceased as suddenly as it had commenced and the sun shone through a rift amid the clouds onto a dazzling track that seemed spread with diamonds, inches deep.

A hundred yards ahead, where the cliff on the left hand overleaned, there was a ledge—a sort of shelf on which eagles nested; on it was perched an enormous bowlder, held in place where it had fallen centuries ago two hundred feet above the track, by debris crushed into a solid mass and cinctured by the gnarled root of a thorn-tree.

Somebody had sawed the root through. Somebody was up behind the bowlder with an iron crowbar. Somebody had calculated to a nicety, but had reckoned without the storm; and hail had undercut the debris and—a minute too soon—loosed a hundred tons of granite. The huge mass toppled, fell on the track, smashed it and took a thousand tons of track and cliffside with it, avalanching to the rocks a thousand feet below.

"And that's wi' them Brahmins' compliments, damn 'em!"

Quorn muttered; but the wind blew the words from his lips and new excitement drove the thought out of his mind. **NOW CLOSE IN** front of him a gap yawned, slippery and broken at the edges. To its left, along the cliff base, there were less than three feet of the track remaining, under-mined and possibly as fragile as an egg-shell. But there was no chance of stopping Asoka, no hope of turning him, and no room in which to turn him.

There was no hope of making him see that narrow, zigzag strip of footing, he was blind with terror—nor was there any certainty that there were no further bowlders to come thundering down. Another hail-cloud swept between earth and sun. Darkness shut down again as suddenly as if unseen hands had drawn the blinds. Bitter, screaming volleys of driving hail descended and were split apart with lightning. The valley was filled with thunder that made thought unthinkable.

"I ain't me! No, I ain't! I ain't me!" Quorn muttered to himself. He did not know he said it nor could he hear his own words, although he remembered them afterward. "Ever see an elephant with wings afore? I reckon—"

No man knows what happens to him when his brain lets go and leaves his body to the mercy of whatever unseen powers there be; but there have been men, and Quorn was one of them, who had strange experiences not explainable by any scientific code or rule of thumb.

Quorn felt an unseen presence seated on Asoka's neck behind him—felt that presence lean and touch the *ankus* in his right hand. His goad tapped Asoka's head and the elephant obeyed. Fear vanished. Almost swifter than the hail Asoka charged along that blind track, skidding the side of the *howdah* along the cliffwall, twisting like a polo pony at the zigzag turns—and as fast as he moved the track went down behind him, leaving empty nothing in his wake.

They reached the far side and the hail ceased. So real had that unseen presence felt that Quorn turned, half-believing that the Ranee might have climbed out from the *howdah* to Asoka's neck to do the guiding. He believed her almost capable of that; she was plucky enough. The incredible thing was that she could have sat there and endured the onslaught of the hail against her back.

However, one glance told him that it had not been the Ranee; she and Virginia Blackstone lay beneath the heavy *howdah* blankets with their heads protected by the thick felt cushions.

" 'Tweren't me anyhow," Quorn muttered. Then he shouted: "Hey, miss! Are you all right?"

The wind snatched her answer away; he heard only her voice, not the words, and he had no time to turn again and listen, since Asoka was still running and the trade was slippery with melting hail. But the strange thing was that Asoka appeared to have forgotten all about his panic. Normally, when frightened, the enormous beast would run until some obstacle or else sheer exhaustion stopped him; but now he was merely moving as if asked to show his top speed. There were no sudden spurts and snorts that indicated terror.

"You big bum, I believe you've gone and got religion!"

QUORN FELT ALMOST jealous. It annoyed him to believe that any other power than his own could control that huge four-footed friend of his, whom no man ever had been able to manage until Quorn came and discovered by sheer accident that he could do it.

Not that he understood the secret of his own success; Asoka's moods, though now and then predictable, were more a mystery than ever; but Quorn liked to consider himself the priest, as it were, or at least the one tolerated student of those mysteries. He proceeded to assert authority:

"Ahsti! Go slow!"

Asoka obeyed. Quorn ordered him to halt. He was obeyed again. Asoka even gathered up and chewed a tender tree-branch that had blown from probably a mile away. He had forgotten terror. If his rump was numb from having suffered the assaults of driving hail he gave no sign of it. He knelt at the word of command. Quorn even dared to get down from his neck and look for injuries to the elephant's hide and the *howdah* buckles.

He discovered that the *howdah* had been stripped and splintered by being nibbed against the cliff, and he found the long cut where a lance had slit Asoka's skin; but there was nothing to worry about—nothing that a carpenter and varnish, stitches and some iodine could not put right again.

"You managed him perfectly. You are a magician," said the Ranee.

"Yes, miss." Quorn was no man to reject a compliment, deserved or otherwise, when offered by that young woman. It was only compliments from idiots and strangers that annoyed him. Besides, he knew from intimate experience, that she would make him pay for it in full, if indirectly; he had learned that the praise of kings and queens who know their business is payment in advance for services that will

be ruthlessly exacted. Nevertheless, the praise was pleas-
ing. And he did like breaking dire news—as who doesn't?

"Miss—them temple Brahmins are on the job again.
'Twas them that tried to drop that rock on us. It was the
hail that beat 'em to it. They'd set a gang to drop that rock
on us. And in case I should see 'em and turn back in the
nick o' time they'd set a sucker with a long lance to jab
Asoka's belly and make him disobey me. 'Twas the hail
that made that sucker's hands slip; and it loosed that rock
too soon."

Virginia Blackstone's head and shoulders peered from
under a blanket, shaking loose a quantity of melting hail
that fell like squandered diamonds down Asoka's dark-
gray flank.

"DID YOU HEAR what he said?" the Ranee asked her. "You
have come into a land of enemies worse than snakes. And
there is no road back to the station now."

"It may turn out to be amusing while it lasts," Virginia
answered. "What next?"

"Nothing to do but keep on going," said the Ranee.
"My prince Rana Raj Singh probably will find some way
around, although it may take him days to do it. We are
quite likely to be killed between here and Narada unless
some of my lazy soldiers come in time. They will know that
the faster they come to meet me the farther they will have
to march home again; and our enemies understand that,
too; so the next ten miles are likely to be exciting."

By the time the Ranee ordered him to go on homeward,
Quorn had thought of no alternative. He knew the road
ahead as intimately as he knew the contents of his pockets.
He could think of no place where it would be safe to dally

until help came; and he could think of a hundred places where the Brahmins or their superstitious dupes could set an ambush or prepare another calculated accident.

In his own way Quorn was quite as difficult to deal with as his elephant. Only the Ranee knew how to manage him, and only she when she devoted to it all the skill and common sense at her command.

Left to his own devices he was likelier than not to make some arbitrary blunder, calculated in his own quixotic mind to save the day for some one else, but actually making twice the trouble he intended to prevent.

His brain worked in amazing ways. He began to think of Blake and Virginia Blackstone. Now that she was his friend as well as Blake, there was nothing he would not do for either, and if he could serve them both with one unselfish gesture he could think of nothing that could please him better, unless to serve the Ranee at the same time.

"Blake," he reflected, "doesn't want to meet her. She don't want to meet Blake. Too bad, since they're god 'uns, but it can't be helped. It's a cinch they'll meet; and they'll quarrel. That's human nature. And it's a cinch they'll get the Ranee into trouble, 'cause she's sure to try to patch things up, and that 'll give them lousy temple Brahmins all the opportunity they want. They'll oar in and sink the ship o' state. I know 'em.

"Shucks! I'd be a sucker if I took Miss Blackstone to Narada. Wisht I knew the way to Kaligaon; there's a road from Kaligaon leads to the border, where Miss Blackstone might get transportation to the railway. She's a nice young leddy, but she don't belong here. Back she goes to where she came from or my name isn't Ben Quorn."

KALIGAON WAS A sacred city more than twenty miles away—a place of pilgrimage where even pilgrims were unwelcome except during two months of every third year. At all other times the place was supposed to be so sacred that not even the Ranee herself could go there without an escort strong enough to overawe the sullenly proud priestly inhabitants.

Only a few of them actually took part in Kaligaon's temple mysteries, and none of them was of the twice-born Brahmin caste, but they gave themselves even greater airs than Brahmins.

Kaligaon was a place where servants and even merchants had to live outside the city in unsanitary shacks for which they paid ferocious rent and taxes levied in the name of voluntary contributions; yet, so solemnly ridiculous are certain elements of human nature that even those robbed and insulted merchants bore the extortion and indignities with pride and thought it a more than royal privilege to be allowed to trade within the city between dawn and sunset.

It was the sort of place that made Quorn sick to think about; however, intriguers can't be choosers.

"Mebbe, if I show her that place, she'll be fed up. Mebbe she'll believe Narada is the same sort of devils' paradise. Mebbe she'll beg for a stroke o' lightning to ride home on, so's to get gone quicker. Try it, anyway. It's mebbe dangerous. It ain't no dangerouser than the road to Narada would be with all them blasted temple Brahmins cooking tanglefoot to catch us. Hell's bells—here goes!"

9

"BAMJEE, IF I THOUGHT YOU READ MY LETTERS—"

A HERO, PROBABLY, is one who fits into the scheme of things and fills the immediate needs of destiny, which rewards him for not resisting what had to happen. So it was with Brazenose Blake and Bamjee. Neither of them ate any breakfast whatever that morning. Unfed, Bamjee was a restless rat, incompetent to think of anything but danger and how to get past it to the corn-bins of physical comfort. He was also an extremely inefficient horseman; and like all Blake's horses, this was a spirited animal.

Brazenose Blake without his breakfast was a gentleman of somewhat gloomy disposition, over-prone to ponder disagreeable tasks that he had shelved until necessity should force him to tackle them. Conscience had a way of worrying him until tea and boiled eggs should restore him to his normally genial frame of mind.

He was also a man of dignity, who was in love with Virginia Blackstone and knew that he never would love any other woman enough to link his life with hers. But he felt that he owed it to himself and to his social standing to avoid indignity whenever possible. In other words, he

would be damned rather than ask forgiveness at the risk
of being snubbed.

He was so disgusted by the danger of appearing to try to
inflict himself on Virginia Blackstone, or of appearing to
be nervous in her presence, that he dreaded meeting her.
Nevertheless, it appeared he would have to meet her unless
he should learn in the course of his ride that the Ranee's
safety was an assured fact.

Consequently, he was peculiarly open to assurance.

His before-breakfast conscience, stirred by circumstances, was busily reminding him of orders long since
received from his superiors in Delhi to investigate the
Kaligaon scandal and report as to possible ways and means
of cleaning up the place.

The motion of the good horse under him provided
impulse to his natural anger at the thought of such foul
immoralities as were the essence of the Kaligaon creed; and
the thought of the utter helplessness of the gayly determined young Ranee in her efforts to remedy conditions
spurred rising indignation. Indignation made him spur
his horse.

The harder he rode, the harder Bamjee had to ride to
keep up with him—Bamjee and an English saddle—
Bamjee and a hard-mouthed horse on a rather narrow
trail beside a yawning precipice, with hail clouds in the
offing and a cold wind blowing in his teeth—Bamjee who
had profitable business of his own in Kaligaon—in many
places.

Bamjee knew, as he knew many things, that Blake had
orders to investigate the place; and he was a *babu* full of

devious and apt excuses for doing almost anything except gallop at that breakneck speed.

THE HAILSTORM WAS his natural ally. The horses, of course, refused to face it. It was more than even human fortitude could endure to ride forward into that blizzard of sharp-edged ice that beat an eagle down and slew it within ten paces of their horses' feet, ice that stripped a tortured tree of bark as deftly as if with machine gun bullets. The horses turned their rumps toward it and fled. There was nothing to be done but turn under the lee of the first rock that offered shelter, back along the trail about three hundred yards away.

It was good shelter, hollowed almost into a cavern, dry and black with the fires of merchants who had used it for a bivouac on their way to and fro between Narada and the railway, and of pilgrims *en route* to Kaligaon; for it was at the corner of the trail that leads up stream-beds and along the shoulders of enormous cliffs to Kaligaon.

An officer of the Ranee's army, mounted to save his dignity and the important soles of his distinguished feet, had galloped ahead of his company of plodding infantry, in part to spy on Blake, whom he detested, and in part for the purpose of giving his fat horse exercise. Now he, too, turned into the throat of the road to Kaligaon and availed himself of Blake's and Bamjee's shelter.

Since he hated Blake, he tried to hide the fact beneath a smear of almost exquisite politeness about as thin as butter on a charity-school orphan's breakfast bread. Blake did his best to get rid of him by dint of flattering him shrewdly; and when the hail finally let up, the officer followed Blake's suggestion to mount the heights and look for some sign of the Ranee.

IN LESS THAN twenty minutes he was back again, reporting that he had seen the Ranee and her guest approaching on the back of Asoka, who was apparently unharmed and well under Quorn's control, although there seemed to have been an accident because the road was down behind them and he could see no sign of Rana Raj Singh and the Rajput escort.

"How far behind are your men?" Blake asked him.

"God knows. They will have taken shelter from the hail."

"But they'll march now the hail is over?"

"Certainly."

"Then I think I won't wait. My presence here might be misinterpreted. I might deprive you of the credit of having come to the Ranee's assistance. I will leave you to enjoy her gratitude."

Blake was about to ride away. The Ranee's officer, with a smirk on his face intended to suggest appreciation of Blake's courtesy, but actually signifying his contempt for Blake's ignorance of how to employ opportunity to curry favor, spurred his tired horse and was gone, full gallop, to meet the royal party and receive the Ranee's recognition of his zeal.

"She may even give him a tin medal," Blake remarked. "Well, let's be off home to breakfast."

But Bamjee was the last man in the world to waste a morning and all that physical discomfort on an empty, errand. Sore from the saddle and chilled to the bone by the hail, he proposed to himself to have the worth of all that agony.

"This road, *sahib*, leads to Kaligaon."

"What if it does?"

"No matter. But I thought your honor might like to see the place. Besides—I have business there—and—"

"And what? Say it, man, why don't you?"

"I can guide your honor. Also your honor's diplomatically sacred presence will protect me. Though they may not like your visit, the inhabitants will not dare to interfere. Also it would be a sort of surprise visit. The politicians would have no time to cover up what they may wish you not to see. And—"

"Well? What? What's at the back of your mind?"

"Kaligaon is a very interesting place. No one of your race has ever seen it, *sahib*."

"That wasn't what you intended to say. You've another thought. What is it?"

"I thought that in Narada, *sahib,* should you go there now, it might be diplomatically unwise not to call at the palace to inquire as to the Ranee's safe return. I am an ignorant *babu,* knowing nothing of such matters, but I have heard it said that etiquette compels a visit in such circumstances."

"Well, what of it?"

"It is customary, also—is it not?—to leave a card at such times for any distinguished visitor who may have temporary lodging in the palace."

CAUGHT OFF HIS guard, Blake let slip an irritated half-confession.

"Dammit, yes, I know that, naturally. But what's to be gained by postponing it?"

"*Sahib,* should the Ranee go to-morrow to her palace

in the mountains; that would be more than a short post-ponement. The inquiry could be made by letter. It might be possible to avoid a personal meeting all summer long."

"Why, dammit, Bamjee, you're a genius. Yes, that's a bright idea. We'll go to Kaligaon. We'll pretend that's what I started out to do this morning. Any chance of food at Kaligaon?"

"*Sahib*, I have a cousin who conducts a store in Kaligaon. He lives outside the gates, and will be honored to enter-tain you."

Not unwillingly Blake turned along the narrow track toward Kaligaon, spurring his horse up the cataract bed that resembled a stairway now that the season's rains were over and the regular streams took care of all the water from the snow-clad hills.

For fifteen struggling minutes the difficult trail gave him all he needed to employ mind and muscle. But at the top of the long rise he halted to breathe the horses and let his eyes survey the splendid panorama. Then it suddenly occurred to him to wonder how it was that Bamjee knew he did not wish to meet Virginia Blackstone.

"Do you read my letters?" he demanded. "Do you keep spies at the Residency?"

"*Sahib!*"

Bamjee's virtue had received a shock, no doubt of it. His ivory complexion did not lend itself to blushes, but there are other ways of suggesting violated modesty and scan-dalized indignation melting into dumb but magnanimous pity for an ignorant accuser. Bamjee used them all. He invented new ways, pantomiming rare emotions graded, like the Oriental scale of music, into half and quarter tones too subtle for the Occidental senses to perceive—or so the Oriental thinks.

But the reason why the Oriental is in bondage to an alien government is because he thinks that nobody is half so subtle as himself. Blake's subtlety was Anglo-Saxon, which is to say it was not paraded on the surface; it was heavily disguised beneath a mask of apparently humorless brusqueness.

"Bamjee, if I thought you read my letters—"

"*Sahib,* how could any one imagine such a thing?"

"No more, I dare say, than you can imagine what I'd do to you if I even half-suspected you of reading 'em. How did you know that I didn't wish to see Miss Blackstone?"

"I deduced it—from the fact that your honor did not ride ahead to meet the Ranee."

"Damn' quick answer. Clever. Like an uppercut, eh, Bamjee? Well, we'll see—suppose you ride ahead and show the way to Kaligaon."

10

"WITS IS BETTER WEAPONS THAN A BOW AND ARROW"

"IT AIN'T A fat excuse I'm looking for," Quorn muttered to himself. "One o' these here thin ones that 'ud slip through a keyhole 'ud suit me. I've a hunch to go to Kaligaon. Hunches don't need no attorneys. Arguments are a symptom that you're wrong, that's what arguments are. All I need is an ounce of excuse."

He perceived about a hundred and fifty pounds of it almost before the muttered words had crossed his lips. There was a sharp turn where the track, not more than six feet wide, was cut like a notch chafed by a rope into the wedge-shaped corner of a mountain.

Asoka turned elephant style, hugging the wall and feeling around the corner with his trunk before trusting his weight on ground that he could not see or risking a collision. He reported trouble, using the simplest signal-code; he backed away.

But it was merely some sort of trouble, not actual danger, because he went ahead again without much urging, flicking himself trunk first, head—neck—shoulders—section by section around the turn, doing the already damaged *howdah* no good as he hugged the wall.

Across the narrow track, not twenty yards beyond the turn, lay one of the Ranee's officers, shot through the back by an arrow that had penetrated lungs and heart. His horse was gone.

Three rocks lay along the track, together with tons of loose dirt and fragments that had fallen with them when some one levered them loose.

"Miss," said Quorn, facing toward the *howdah*, "that officer of yours was prob'ly on his way to warn you of traps on the road ahead. Them Brahmins are plumb determined to bump you off. I'm jes' as equal plumb determined to make suckers of 'em."

"See if he's dead," she commanded. She was used to Quorn's vocabulary and the phrases he used when excited. Hers was the royal gift of seeming to grow less excited when other folks' nerves were on edge. "If he isn't dead we will take him with us."

"Miss, he's deader than Julius Cæsar. See—the swine weren't satisfied to plug him with an arrow. They dropped rock on him afterwards."

"Where is his horse?"

Quorn tried to peer over the cliff—then saw the marks made by the horse's hoofs turning to gallop homeward. She saw them too—interpreted as swiftly.

"My troops are coming. They will hurry when they see that riderless horse. Make haste to meet them," she commanded.

"No, miss." It was the first time since he became her superintendent of elephants that Quorn had refused to obey an order. It excited him. "They can drop rocks on the soldiers jes' as easy as on us. You two leddies are in my charge. I'm answerable. I ain't going to ride you into no traps—not if I lose my job for using sense."

"Go home, I order you."

"No, miss."

GINGERLY ASOKA, ANSWERING the pressure of his knees, picked his way past the dead man and between the fallen rocks, then set his best foot forward, so that the Ranee supposed Quorn's upset nerves had caused him to answer no when he had meant yes. So she sat back in the *howdah* and began to talk to Virginia Blackstone.

Suddenly the Ranee was up on her knees. "Where are you going, Ben Quorn? Stop, I tell you!"

"No, miss."

Quorn had turned up the track to Kaligaon, and his back, as he urged Asoka up the difficult ascent, was stiff and sturdy with rebellion. The thrill of disobedience obeying inner intuition passed along his nerves to influence Asoka.

Asoka perceived there was excellent if unknown cause for putting forth his full strength and all his agility. The *howdah* became more restless than a small boat on a rough sea with the wind across the tide. The Ranee and Virginia Blackstone had to shut their teeth and cling or else be pitched out. They lay prone on their stomachs, facing backward, their feet tucked under the front rail and clinging to the rear rail with their hands.

Thus it was that they saw the disappointed group of almost naked nondescripts armed with bows and arrows who jumped from a ledge behind a rock and ran to the throat of the track, apparently in hope of loosing a flight of arrows before the range became too great. But an elephant's speed up a mountainside is one of those incredible phenomena that upset calculations; only a lone arrow winged in futile protest at Asoka's rump and fell so far behind that it was almost funny.

"Ben Quorn, you were quite right," said the Ranee when Asoka paused at last on level rock-bed at the summit to recover breath and work his big lungs like a bellows.

"Miss, I know I am."

"Where do you propose to take us?"

"To Kaligaon."

"But we ought to try to warn my infantry. They may march straight into a trap. Rocks may be dropped on them."

"Miss, if them there infantry is so blind they can't see a ambush ahead, after a riderless horse has hit 'em head-on, it's a pity they weren't bumped off sooner. Let 'em walk into a trap—then get yourself a new bunch. Let me pick the nex' lot. I'll choose you a set o' scorpions who'll sting them Brahmins proper."

"But it may be worse at Kaligaon. Even my father never dared to go there without an escort."

"Mebbe. But the Brahmins are ambushin' us between here and Narada; they know all about our goings and our comings. Kaligaon don't know. We'll surprise 'em. We're a walkin' ambush on our own hook."

"And no weapons!"

"Don't need no weapons! Weapons never was no use to a minority. You've got to use your wits, same as me and you have always had to use 'em in a tight place. Wits is better weapons than a bow and arrow."

"You are quite right, Mr. Quorn."

The Ranee sat back. There was a look in her eye that intimated resolute determination not to let one act of disobedience become a precedent, but she was a wise young woman, much too sensible to entertain a merely personal grudge against a man whose loyalty was priceless.

QUORN STARED AT Virginia Blackstone, obviously pondering her character, intuitively fathoming her state of mind. It was several seconds before he found words:

"Can you live without your luggage, miss? If I should find a way of getting you back to the railway, it might take three days. Can you rough it that much?"

"I can rough it as well as any one. But why the railroad?"

"Best skidoodle out o' here. Narada's too hot—dangerous—you'd better beat it for somewhere else."

Virginia met the Ranee's eyes. "That's where you're wrong," she answered. "I wouldn't dream of quitting. If the Ranee wants me—"

The Ranee nodded. So did Quorn, and said:

"I might ha' guessed it…. Hell's bells—what's the sense o' quittin' anyhow? He who fights and runs away is a sucker, whatever the tex'books say. Always smarter to attack. There's four of us. Asoka is the best man of the lot. Get a move on, Behemoth, we'll try our luck in Kaligaon."

11

"LOOK AT THAT TEMPLE WALL!"

KALIGAON STINKS, NOT only to the nose but metaphysically, too. It is a cesspool of superstitions that were rated rotten in the days when *suttee,* the immolation of widows, was considered civilized. The Biblical abominations of Astarte were no worse than Kaligaon's of to-day, since nothing worse can be imagined by the human mind.

Kaligaon has no glamour; it is merely vile, and knells the death of every decent thought—the doom of aspiration—the decline and fall of man from spiritual curiosity to brutish self-abasement in a dull, unlovely tyranny of sexual desire enthroned as the disgusting god of nature.

It is a place that could not possibly exist to-day except in India, and not in India unless the vested interests of jealous castes were so intrenched in the mind of priestly privilege that even a modern government must shrink from the task of digging out the roots.

It is a place whose fame among the ignorant has drawn to it by the hundred thousand, once in every three years during unnumbered centuries, pilgrims from the ends of India, for the most part tramping all the dusty miles on foot, in abject poverty, denying themselves even enough food in order to have money to give to the priests. There is

His kick sent that obscene Brahmin into
a rather graceful somersault

hardly a mile but has its scores of little heaps of stones to
mark where some one had died and reckoned life a failure
because he could not reach the shrine at Kaligaon, where
obscene symbols stand in lamp-lit gloom within a golden
crypt.

It was the last place in the world for a man like Brazenose
Blake to view with indifference. He loathed it. He was
neither Puritan nor rake, neither prig nor hedonist, but
a practical-minded sportsman perfectly aware that one
man's meat may be another's poison, and that moral codes
are geographical without an absolute relation to vice and
virtue.

He could see the virtue in the pilgrims' longing to reach
Kaligaon, since they had been told it was a place of sacred
mysteries; but, like any other man of decent mind, he could

see nothing but bottomless vice in the place itself and in the men who made their living by parading vice as virtue.

As he approached the gate of Kaligaon he began to feel nauseated because the smell was something that even an Indian official's nostrils, long used to Gargantuan stinks, could only endure by exercise of sheer will. Even Bamjee showed qualms, and Bamjee was no specialist in civic niceties; true, he had helped to clean Narada City, but that was because the Ranee ordered it, and Bamjee made a handsome profit purchasing supplies.

Even the horses snorted at the filth and at the burning *ghat,* between road and river, where the dying lay beside the dead to await their turn while mangy vultures watched them from the trees with gorged indifference.

There was a soul-chilling gray gloom in the atmosphere; perhaps it was dust, and if so the dust was dirty and impenetrable even by the Indian sun, whose magic could only change it into a misty hopelessness, through which the lepers and the cancerous sacred cattle groped like demons in a madman's dream.

IT IS AGAINST the law of Kaligaon to destroy life, but there is no obligation, expressed or implied, to preserve it; so sick beasts are left to starve along with human lepers in the streets, the animals having a shade the best of it because the humans are expelled from the city at sundown.

The beasts may stay within the gates—the grim, disgusting gates of Kaligaon, whereon all imaginable vice is carved in life-size illustration, rich in detail, and above whose triple arches stand the statues of the Kaligaon trinity, necklaced with human skulls and crimsoned with the paint that nowadays the priests must use in place of the actual blood that the paint represents.

The city walls are very high and ancient; time has undone most of the indecency that once was pictured on them, though there are piecemeal carvings left by carelessness of the fanatical Moslem conquerors with scimitar and chisel who defaced them and slit the throats of the scornful hierarchs who view such standards of obscenity with pride.

Around the walls outside the city lies an unmapped maze of dwellings, *go-downs*, brothels, workshops, stables, refuse heaps—all of which drain into the river, whence the drinking water comes and where the dying lave their feet until the cholera, or what else, kills them, and their half-burned ashes are spread on the sacred stream to be raced for by vultures and sacred fish. There was a dam below Kaligaon, which made a festering pool of the river, and though it is beautiful by moonlight the light of day reveals it as a sewer.

These sights Blake saw with his handkerchief held to his nose as he approached and rode through Kaligaon Gate, aware that he was being scowled at even by the leprous beggars who swarmed toward him, risking his horse's heels as they tore off rags to show their deformities.

An unimaginative, rather simple man in his well-bred way, Blake was stirred to a sort of prophetic anger.

"Bamjee," he said, for Bamjee rode knee to knee beside him, too afraid to adopt the single file that courtesy demanded. "I believe I understand why massacres so often followed conquest. If I should lead a victorious army into this place, I believe I would emulate Genghis Khan and would order my men to wipe it off the earth."

"*Sahib,* this is unwise—very. Am respectfully obedient *babu,* but—"

"But what?"

"Also am experienced in certain matters—as for instance, how many beans make five, if you will pardon me. Can sit serenely, *sahib,* when cinema bad-men shoot directly from the screen toward the audience. But this—"

"Nonsense. Who would dare to shoot us?"

"Let me see," said Bamjee. "There was Charley First. He was a king, I think—decapitated. There were Lincoln, Garfield, and McKinley—Presidents—important, very. And, unless the world was dreaming, there was Sarajevo and an Austrian archduke. Somebody always dares to pull the trigger, *sahib.* Nobody ever counts the consequences."

"WHAT DO YOU suggest?"

"That we turn back and visit my cousin outside the city. That we engage his services as diplomatic mediator, so to speak. That we should send him to the ecclesiastical panjandrum, with your honor's compliments and even a little present along with them. A check is negotiable, even in Kaligaon. Money talks all languages; it justifies one's dealings with the devil—or with the English, which the priests say is the same thing. I suggest that we should black-mail, browbeat and persuade my cousin—all three courses may be necessary to intrigue for the priestly permission for us to inspect the city and whichever temple they believe is least likely to drive us crazy."

"Their permission be damned. Turn around, if you're afraid, and go and find your cousin. I'm going ahead. I will bribe nobody."

"There is a difference, *sahib*, between bribing and paying blackmail. It is the latter course that I recommend."

"I never paid a shilling's worth of blackmail in my life. I never will."

"Let us pray God to pity the proud!" said Bamjee. "Meekness may cost money; nevertheless, it is not a bad investment now and then."

Bamjee was afraid to turn back. He was also afraid to lose Blake's good will by deserting him. And to his credit, he was afraid to let Blake ride alone. Bamjee did not flatter himself that he was any paragon of valor or much of a lance to lean on, but he knew that two heads and two horses are no worse than one when a riot begins. So he edged a bit closer to Blake and kept pace with him, trying to look bold and unconcerned.

"Dammit, Bamjee, I have seen some copies of the secret books and most of the worst sights of India, but nothing to compare with this. I didn't think it possible. Look at that temple wall! Colored, too—all newly painted—they can't blame that on the ancients; it looks as if it was painted yesterday."

"*Sahib*, it is painted once a month. There is a fund, contributed by pilgrims, for the purpose."

"Good Lord—do you see the vultures tearing at that bull before it's dead?"

"*Sahib*, nobody may interfere because it is wrong to take life, and to protect the dying bull it would be necessary to injure and perhaps kill the living vultures."

"What is the danger to us, then? If they mayn't kill, what makes you afraid?"

"*Sahib*, logic warns me that they are going to try to kill

us, just as lack of logic will suggest to them that we, being outside the pale of their religion, are less than animals. We are dead already; thus we may be slain without sin. Besides, they might encourage us to die without exactly, 'bump- ing us off,' as Mr. Quorn would call it. They can put us in a dungeon, can't they? They are not obliged to feed us or even to give us water. There are several ways of making life a little difficult to live. Have you a weapon, *sahib?*"

"No, I never carry weapons…. Who are those women?"

"WIDOWS, *SAHIB. SUTTEE* having been abolished and being too risky to be practised except in secret, the priests have invented the plan of marrying the widows to an image in one of the temples. They explain that the widows are legally dead, because their husbands died, and if it were not for the lawless interference of the British Government the widows would have to immolate themselves on the funeral pyres. Therefore, being dead, they are the property of beings in the next world, who are of a sort of universal nature. Consequently, the widows are to be regarded as universal property. And when they die they are so doubly dead that the priests say they cease to exist. Can anybody prove the contrary?"

"Does the Ranee of Narada know about it?"

"What can she do? Narada City was never as bad as this place, but it has taken all her courage, as your honor knows, to improve conditions in Narada; and even now the priests defy her. So how can she attempt to tackle Kaligaon? It is—"

"It's an Augean stable," said Blake.

"Was there ever a female Hercules?" asked Bamjee.

"Not that I know of. What's that building with the

wooden sides and big stone columns at the corners—that big building, at the end of this street?"

"That is the holy of holies, *sahib*. That is the sacred place so many pilgrims die before they reach. There—"

But something interrupted him, he never knew what. It was something hard that some one threw. It hit Bamjee on the head behind the right ear, so that he fell to the left across Blake's horse's shoulders and Blake caught him by the waist. Bamjee's horse bolted. Blake, with Bamjee hanging like a sack across his knees, rode full pelt in pursuit.

He cornered the runaway horse between a crowd of city ruffians and a baked clay shrine that was so obscene that he laughed in rejoicing when the horse crashed into it and knocked it over.

Now it is dangerous to laugh in Kaligaon. To be an unblessed, unenlightened foreigner is bad enough; but to be that and to laugh about it is to stir the very lees of Kaligaon's anger. Hampered by having to manage two horses and hold Bamjee, Blake was instantly surrounded by a yelling mob, which armed itself with prehistoric weapons—primitive, but ten times more efficient than revolvers in the hands of men who can't shoot. It began to rain stones. The air rattled with sticks.

Blake's trade was diplomacy. He was an old school diplomat, who believed in offering the other cheek before he smote his adversary—not that that made any difference. It seems to be the oldest rule of all that diplomats lose their heads more thoroughly than any one whenever the absurd rules of their game are upset by simple directness.

He proceeded to address the mob, in its own language, much too accurately as to grammar and pronounced with the aristocratic English accent that in the ears of annoyed opponents is like a spark to gasoline. Quite a number of acute if unimportant wars have had their origin in that accent, which is meant to be so mollifying but exasperates worse than a fist on die nose.

"Now be advised by me and don't make asses of your-selves. You won't gain anything by using force. You'll only bring down unpleasant consequences on yourselves."

TOO TRUE. TRUTH, however, is as irritating as a flick of the whip to people who have been fed so long on lies that lies are palatable. Blake was caused to cease from speaking by a dead dog thrown straight at his mouth. Whereat, like any other diplomat, old or new school, he completely lost his diplomatic standing and became a human being, governed by human motives. So the dog wrought better service dead than living, Blake being no mean strategist and no man's fool when he had done with what the governments call conciliation.

He rammed in his spurs and rode like a polo player racing for a goal ten seconds before the call of time. He scattered the mob to right and left. Aware that instinct would warn them to block his retreat, he charged straight forward.

Knowing that the heart of things is where solutions lie, and that a dagger in the heart can kill not only men but causes; seeing a new mob come surging hundreds strong up by-streets to attack him, and aware that tactics twice repeated lose the virtue of surprise, he swerved and sprang the ace of all surprises on them. He rode full pelt up the steps of the temple that Bamjee had assured him was the holy of all Kali-gaon holies. At the top of the steps, amid a maze of carved indecencies, the heavy wooden doors stood open. In he rode, into incense-heavy gloom, where guttering *ghee*-fed lanterns made a thousand pricks of yellow light.

There was a stone floor, ringing hollow as the horses skidded to the rein. There were niches, sensed rather than seen, in which the jewelled eyes of lewd gods and unchaste goddesses leered on obscenity done in the name of Kali and Siva Priests and worshippers, like rats caught stealing, scurried into darkness, swallowed by shadows that stank.

A gong rang. A man with a long beard, lean and naked, opened a brass door that glittered with light from the chamber behind him. For a moment he stood staring, one hand on the door, the other on the door post, a patina of sweat and ashes on his skin, so that he looked like a Pompeian satyr done in bronze. A woman as naked as the man stood on tiptoe to peer over his shoulder. Irritated, he elbowed her in the stomach. She cursed him. He turned to strike her—and the next he knew, two horses crashed into the door, which opened inward.

Blake let go the reins and vaulted from the saddle, lifting Bamjee to the ground. Then he kicked the High Priest— he was no less—and the High Priest did a rather graceful somersault that landed him flat on his back on the floor in the outer darkness. The woman followed unassisted; Blake slammed the door shut, bolted it, and turned to examine Bamjee, who was only stunned, not badly hurt.

There was an altar, or something like it, in the midst. Around it was a trough containing water that had proba- bly been blessed with all sorts of mysterious ritual. Blake blessed it anew; it was just what he wanted. He took from the altar a golden bowl inset with jewels and embossed with an orgy of gods and humans, dipped up water with it, and soused it onto Bamjee's face until the *babu,* spluttering, recovered consciousness and sat up.

"Oh my God!" said Bamjee.

"Pick a better god than this one," Blake advised him. He tied the horses to an indecent symbol that projected from the wall—there was no other kind—and grimly began to study his surroundings. The famous "golden" walls of this inmost shrine of Kaligaon's mysteries were actually brass, and indifferent brass at that, but they shone like gold because there were dozens of lamps, hung high and backed by mirrors of many facets that projected the light through varicolored glass.

But the account Blake had heard of the figures embossed on the walls in half-relief was not exaggerated; no man could exaggerate it; no man could invent anything viler.

BAMJEE WAS TITTERING with enjoyment of Blake's scandalized modesty.

"After all, these things are sacred. That is the important point," said he. "By being here we are committing sacrilege."

"Don't be a damned fool."

"*Sahib,* the foolishness was in riding into this place. Oh, well—even torture must come to an end, although they will make it last as long as possible. But better, I suppose, to die distinguished than like a pair of doubting Hamlets. We are the first outsiders ever to enter this place. That is one world's record—pity it won't be published. Do you realize that nearly all of Kaligaon must be in conference to decide what to do? We may live for a day and a night if

they torture us skillfully. I would give all of it for a chance
to listen to that conference. It must be funny. *Sahib,* why
am I afraid, and you not? Why are you solemn, and I not?"

"Solemn? I'll burn this temple down before I'll let them
torture us," said Blake. He pulled an automatic lighter from
his pocket, tested it, extinguished it and looked around for
inflammable tinder, but there was none; the brass walls and
the stone floor hardly lent themselves to arson.

"Dammit, Bamjee," he said suddenly, "I'm afraid I'll
have to beg your pardon. It's my fault that we're in this
mess. Maybe I can get you out of it. I'll try to bargain with
them. I will undertake to stay here pending investigation,
provided they will let you go. I will threaten to break this
holy of holies of theirs into unrecognizable pieces if they
don't agree."

"*Sahib,* they will not agree. Why should they? And
besides—"

"Well? What?" Blake asked him gruffly.

"It is the first time, *sahib,* that a gentleman of your race
ever offered to stay and die, in order that this *babu* might
go and live."

"Come, now, don't get sentimental, Bamjee."

"Dammit!" Bamjee rose to the occasion. He could not
stand yet, but he could throw his head back and square his
shoulders. "I am no more sentimental than you are, you
damned Englishman! I can die as cockily as you, damn
your eyes! You are a brave man—and you propose to treat
me like a timid woman. You are a sentimental gentleman,
and you propose to treat me like a cad who has no feelings.
You propose to rob me of the privilege of staying with you
in appreciation of—"

Bamjee's voice broke.

"Shut up. Shake hands. No offense meant. Sorry."

"I apologize," said Bamjee.

"Not at all." Horror of sentimental conversation between man and man, which is a British failing, forced Blake, who was a sentimentalist if nothing else, to tell his inmost thoughts to Bamjee. It was the simplest, the only direct means of avoiding any further blather about mutual regard; and it would serve the little man as proof that he was now accepted as a man who understood what cricket means.

"Dammit, Bamjee, a worse mess isn't possible."

"We will find a way out of it, *sahib*. God is good to men like me who have no compunctions but also not much malice. I am lucky. I will share my luck with you."

"Good of you. But the worst of it is that if we do get out of here there'll be a hell of a scandal just when I would rather eat my hat than have one."

"Pardon me, but how English!" Bamjee remarked. "*Sahib*, I have never known an Occidental who could tell the whole truth in a crisis of life and death. You are all what Shakespeare called you—actors, all of you. And you can only play one part, which is that of self-deception. I know we shall both be taken prisoners and put to torture within ten or fifteen minutes, so I don't deceive myself or you. On the other hand, you don't even mention what worries you."

BLAKE WALKED OVER to where the horses stood champing their bits. Because there was nothing else that he could think of to do at the moment, he lifted their feet to examine the shoes, speculating as to whether they could gallop on the smooth stone temple floor.

"What do you imagine it is that worries me?" he demanded.

"Miss Blackstone."

"Whatever hit you just now must have injured your brain," said Blake.

"Perhaps, *sahib*. But I think you would rather die than let Miss Blackstone find you scandalously caught investigating this abominable place. You think she will believe your secret character entices you to study such things. You feel like a man in tennis flannels who has stepped into a sewer. You would rather she should see you coming out of church or some such place."

"Dammit, what makes you suppose Miss Blackstone means anything to me?" Suddenly he remembered the letter home that he had found at midnight on his desk. "Have you been reading any of my correspondence?" he demanded. "A letter to my mother?"

"Yes, I did."

"Then all I can say is, damn your impudence."

"I bow. If my head did not ache so badly I would bow more humbly. Nevertheless—"

"What?"

"Had I not read the letter I should have been ignorant, and that would have prevented me from offering to be of service in the matter."

"How so?"

"They will presently torture us, so it might be well to make our testaments and hide them where they may be found by the investigators who will come to inflict penalties and hush up matters after we are dead. I can write in my testament that you came here to rescue me. Thus Miss

Blackstone will think kindly of you; and though I don't believe it makes the slightest difference what people think of us when we are dead, it might make dying easier."

"Don't be an idiot. Oh—I see—stupid of me—what you want is my forgiveness for reading my correspondence? All right, I forgive you."

"Dammit! I refuse to be forgiven!" Bamjee swayed to his feet unsteadily, blinked a few times and began to feel stronger. "I insist it was a damned ungentlemanly thing to do—beneath my dignity!"

Blake studied him, at a loss to see the point. Dignity and Bamjee hardly were associated in his mind. Bamjee enlightened him:

"Never mind how I have lived, you have shaken hands with me. I mean to die a gentleman, with all the responsibilities. I acted like a cad when I read your letter. What do you propose to do about it?"

"Oh—ah—why, yes, certainly, a damn' dishonorable trick. If your head weren't hurt I'd punch it."

"I would punch back."

"However, since your head is rather badly hurt, let's consider we've had the fight, shake hands and call it a closed incident"

"I confess myself defeated in fair combat. Your fists are far stronger than mine, and you can kick much harder than I can," said Bamjee. "Therefore I apologize, as one man to another."

"I accept the apology. Shake hands again. There, not another word about it. Head better? Think you can ride now? Good, I'll help you up and we'll see if we can't escape from here."

12

"IT NEEDS A HERCULES"

THERE WAS AN excellent reason why Blake and Bamjee were left so long in undisturbed possession of the inner shrine of the temple of Kaligaon, like a pair of healthy insects in the heart of a rotten fruit.

Asoka had just arrived at Kaligaon Gate, not only with the Ranee of Narada in the *howdah* on his high back, but with a cursed Western woman, too; and on his neck was Ben Quorn—a tobacco-chewing, casteless alien, reputed by fools and fanatics to be a rebirth of the legendary Gunga *sahib*. Kaligaon hated him—hated his name, his looks, his soul and his very shadow. Had not the Gunga *sahib*, at least a thousand years ago, denounced the Kaligaon creed and prophesied that in the gods' good time he would return to destroy the place along with all its human parasites?

Quorn was doubly detestable. If he truly were the Gunga *sahib* reborn, as his extraordinary eyes and his whole appearance indicated, then he was the enemy of grace and should be banished again to the infernal regions whence he came at far too frequent intervals. He should be so emphatically banished, with such torture and degradation that he would stay dead this time twice or three times as long.

If he were not the veritable Gunga *sahib*, then he was

the foulest sort of an impostor, for whom no mistreatment could be bad enough. The fact that Quorn had never claimed to be the Gunga *sahib* made no difference whatever. The fact that he had frequently denied it made no difference. Upward of a million people said he was the Gunga *sahib;* that was the important point. And here he was at Kaligaon.

Quorn did not even know that he was known by sight or name in Kaligaon. He was curious to see the place, and since Virginia Blackstone had refused to leave the Ranee, he was bent on finding a messenger to notify the Ranee's soldiers where she was.

He hoped to find a second messenger to send to Rana Raj Singh, in the hope that the prince might somehow find his way over the trackless hills; he rated Rana Raj Singh and his penniless Rajput noblemen a lot more highly than he did the Ranee's troops. And meanwhile he proposed to find the makings of a decent meal and a place where two travel-weary women might rest themselves and enjoy some privacy.

However, the abominable carvings on the gate upset Quorn's notions of propriety. It would have shocked him to be present when the Ranee saw them, although he understood that her eastern heritage had familiarized her, almost from birth, with matters that even the loosest cities of the western world keep out of sight. He knew she was a royal rebel against these degrading superstitions, and it scandalized him to have to confront her with such evidence of the hopelessness of the war she waged.

All that was bad enough. But to bring Virginia Blackstone face to face with such revolting indecency was a much greater shock to Ben Quorn than it was to her. For she was sane; she could afford to laugh at it. To her the stinks were hugely more distressing and she rode with her handkerchief over her mouth, which gave Quorn the impression that she was blushing.

The gate had been shut and bolted the moment Asoka hove in sight. Quorn shouted, and while he waited for some one to come and open it he turned to say his piece to Virginia Blackstone. He could not have been prevented had the Ranee ordered silence—not if the obscene divinities themselves had come to life and, pausing from their lewd amusements, had forbidden him to speak.

"Miss, don't you look at it. If I'd ha' knowed it was as bad as this I'd sooner ha' chanced the dangers along the high road. I'd turn back now if it weren't that we'd be benighted. There's things here as 'ud make an elephant feel shame-faced. Hide your head under the blankets, miss."

Then loyalty surged to the front. "And don't get to thinking, miss, that this is any o' your friend the Ranee's doing. Her highness is dead set ag'in' it. She's the fireman's nozzle when it comes to cleaning up—she hasn't got around to this yet, that's all."

"Needs some cleaning," said Virginia from behind her handkerchief. Then, unconsciously using the words that Blake had used less than an hour before, " 'It needs a Hercules.' It smells and looks like an Augean stable."

"Hercules?" Quorn asked her. "Wasn't he the guy who invented blasting powder?"

"No. He was the man who turned a river into a particularly filthy stable—on a bet."

"I'll bet with him that he'd lose his stake in this place.

Watch out, ladies—somebody's coming to open the gate. Duck under the blankets—please, miss—please, your highness—keep out o' sight until I get a word with 'em. A set o' guys who'd keep them carvings on a gate 'ud do most anything, so hide yourselves and hang on tight in case I turn sudden and scoot for safety."

KALIGAON'S PRIESTS, HOWEVER, did not propose to lose so easily as that such an easy prey as Quorn or such a valuable hostage as the Ranee. They had seen her from the roofs, and they knew that she had no escort. Since the gods had led her thus into their hands they proposed to make the most of opportunity, and richly she should pay for Blake's and Bamjee's sacrilege before they let her go again.

Since she had had the impudence to flaunt Ben Quorn beneath their noses and to bring with her a Western female, she should be made to witness their subjection to the same treatment about to be accorded to Blake and Bamjee. Furthermore, she should submit to the extreme humiliation of indorsing it and taking all the blame in the likely event that the British would make a fuss about it afterward. But first, she must be trapped; they did not want to kill her on the run, they wanted her alive and at their mercy.

So they double-baited their trap. Suspecting that the elephant was hungry they had heaped about a hundred-weight of good grain on some shutters pulled down from a window belonging to a holy man who had the concession for selling uncooked food to pilgrims and others within the city. And a little higher up the filthy street they had gathered a band of musicians with enough banners and temple servitors to indicate that the Ranee was welcome and was to be accorded a procession through the city.

It was a quick job, rather ably managed, and there was no sign of a mob or of ambush or of intended violence of any kind; a group of priests in full regalia stood just within the gate on either side and a priest who was plainly a man in authority gestured an invitation to come straight on in. He used exactly the correct blend of pride and politeness, and at the same moment some one threw some hot cakes on the shutters beside the heap of grain.

They were entirely right about Asoka, who was used to being fed, as a public spectacle, in every town he visited. He was hungry and hot cakes were his passion. He accepted the invitation without waiting for orders from Quorn; and the moment Asoka's tail was inside the gate it was closed behind him, although there was still no show of force or of anything whatever that should rightly arouse suspicion.

The musicians struck up an appalling tune with cymbals, drums and brass wind-instruments and Asoka approached the banquet spread for him.

But the dealer in grain had been overlooked, or at any rate not consulted. Probably embittered by the extortion of temple treasurers, who taxed his cent per cent profits down to a mere pittance, he strode down-street and saw his good grain spread on the shutters stolen from his own front windows and about to be devoured by an elephant whose owners certainly had paid no money in advance. He ran. He pulled his slipper off. He smote Asoka on the snoot.

And by coincidence, at exactly that moment, thirty or forty men emerged from buildings near the gate with obvious intent to form up behind the priests. If they had been unarmed that might have been nothing to worry about, but they all had swords and shields; so Quorn, who was as nervously alert to danger as a mongoose, struck Asoka with the *ankus* pretty smartly to bring him to attention.

Nobody could blame Asoka for supposing that was meant to arouse his anger against the fool who struck him with a slipper heel on the tip of his sensitive trunk; and besides, of all the easy ways of starting trouble, possibly the easiest in the world was to come between Asoka and his dinner.

Having registered his protest, the dealer in corn had stepped back; so, to reach him Asoka set a forefoot on the shutter. That tipped a corner of the shutter down into a mudhole in the filthy street, which spilled the corn and cakes and caused the shutter to rise and smite Asoka's legs. *Ankus* notwithstanding, instantly Asoka caught the offending culprit by the waist and hurled him through his open window, where he lay yelling.

Asoka was red-eyed now. He had forgotten dinner. He was out for bloody vengeance, further maddened by the men with swords and shields who shouted and ran to prevent him from smashing the side of the house in his effort to follow his victim and finish the job. A sudden rush from behind him, accompanied by shouting, is the one sure way of making an elephant bolt.

"HANG ON, LEDDIES!"

Quorn knew better than to make things worse by using the *ankus* now. His job was to sit tight and watch for a chance to get control again when the first burst of Asoka's fury should have spent itself. Asoka went scream-ing up-street like a five-ton cannon ball, so neatly through the midst of the musicians that they separated as a puddle splashes, half to either hand, when a big wheel crashes through it.

Up the street was a crowd that fled and left a booth unguarded—a blue and vermilion booth that sheltered the scandalous effigies of a god and goddess, whose nuptials were celebrated once a year on that exact spot because, so legend had it, it was there that they first taught the human race the impropriety of being chaste.

The sacred bulls, alarmed out of their melancholy by Asoka's onrush, fled before him straight into the open door of the booth, where they jammed between the heavy poles that formed the door-frame.

"Hang on, leddies! Duck!"

Asoka followed the bulls, but swerved to avoid collision. His forehead crashed into the latticed framework on which the painted cloth covering of the booth was hung. He went through it as if it had not been there. Quorn was caught by the top of the framework and clung to it, but the top of the *howdah* struck him from behind, the frame broke, and he scrambled back into his place behind Asoka's ears, a bit bruised but too scared and excited to know it.

By that time the sacred bulls had struggled through the opening and were milling around inside the booth with their tails in the air, upsetting scores of godlets that had been set on a shelf on three sides of the tent. After galloping two or three times around the booth they escaped through the door, but they had made their contribution to the chaos. Asoka stepped on a gilded godlet. Being made of bronze, it rolled away beneath his foot, thus causing him to bump his shoulder hard against the platform in the midst of which the god and goddess were enshrined beneath a canopy.

So he smashed the god and goddess. They were made of

clay and ivory and brass and many other substances, and they wore enough fake jewelry to have graced a wax work show. The beauty of them was that every piece would come apart when suitably attacked. Asoka shook them, pricked his trunk on something sharp, raised one and used it as a battering-ram to break the other, smashing both of them to smithereens.

After that the booth went down; he never could be satisfied to do a half job of destruction. As he pulled the framework down and trampled it he hurled the little godlets right and left into the mud of the street and against the walls of near-by houses, almost in the way that a digging terrier throws dirt around.

By that time Kaligaon's priesthood had gathered its scattered wits enough to arouse the populace and set them on to the attack like hornets; only, unlike hornets, they were rather hampered by the religious admonition not to take life. They might, and they did, make a demonstration with swords and spears. They did rain rocks and broken tiles from the roofs of houses. But, no matter what the priests said now, nor how noisily the arch-high-priest himself, with gong and ritual of curses, removed the ban on killing, superstition had sunk too deep to be repudiated.

Almost undirected, that excited and indignant mob, as it were by instinct, worked like one organized gang in an attempt to drive Asoka toward the quarry at the rear of the town, two hundred feet deep, where the sweepers dumped the rubbish from a platform that might yield beneath the elephant's enormous weight. If he and his passengers should die by that means, there would be no death guilt on the residents of Kaligaon.

They might have done it, had not Quorn been in his place on Asoka's neck. He could not stop the furious animal, but he could guide him to some extent. He caught sight of the quarry at the end of a long, filthy lane.

"So that's the little game, eh? Hell's bells! End for end, you big bum—sit tight, leddies!"

A swarm of excited laymen under the direction of a dozen priests were barricading a side street to prevent Asoka from heading in the wrong direction. As he turned he caught sight of the jumble of poles and furniture, doors, shutters, carts and what not else. He charged it instantly— went through it like a landslide—left it shattered in his wake, and swung around two corners until he brought up face to face with the wooden temple that was Kaligaon's pride.

There was a crowd on the steps, and they fled at sight of him. He paused and seemed to ponder for a moment, then mounted the steps and strode into the temple, smashing the top of the *howdah* against the heavy door-beam. And now Quorn grew genuinely worried.

"Miss," he said hurriedly, over his shoulder, to the Ranee, "look out—he's turning ugly! When he heads for the dark it means he wants to sulk. When he sulks, he's murderous. You and the other leddy climb down by his tail if you can manage. Slip in through the first door you can find. This ain't going to be no picnic."

VRGINIA WAS THE first to jump for it; she caught a lamp that hung by heavy brass chains from a beam and hung there until the Ranee climbed down India-fashion by Asoka's tail and dragged up a four-wheeled gilded box in which temple godlets were paraded through the streets.

From the lamp to the box and then from the box to the floor was an easy business, but Virginia only managed it in the nick of time. Asoka turned and smashed the box to smithereens. The women fled. They hammered on a door, but it did not yield.

"This way," said the Ranee, breathless, leading along the wall in gloom fortunately too deep to let them see the nature of the carvings into which they bumped as they felt their way along. "This way—hurry!"

They found another door. They entered and bolted the door behind them.

The slamming door startled Asoka, but as he turned to investigate the source of the noise he saw about a hundred priests and laymen running up the temple steps, so he charged them instead. They were armed with sticks and knives, but no man waited to discover what stick or knife could do against that elephant.

They fled like smoke, he after them, and one man—fatter than the rest and clothed in bright red—scooted to the right, alone, toward the river that gurgled and sang over rapids at the place where its course had been turned to make two streams, of which one became the almost stagnant pool beside the burning *ghat*. The other was a riotous, rock-staked torrent that circled around the city and became a tributary of Narada River after it had plunged down half a dozen falls.

The man in red ran like a fat, demented ghost. His speed seemed superhuman. Fear so frenzied him that his fat feet hardly touched the earth, and though he ran into the wind it seemed as if the wind was blowing him.

Asoka gave chase up a long street, gaining spurt by spurt,

and all but caught him, but the fat man saved himself by inches, diving underneath the props of the wooden wall of the embankment of the river. The props formed a sort of tunnel, being set so close together that there was hardly room to put fingers between them. They were an afterthought—a mere haphazard reenforcement of the wooden wall which supported a levee-like embankment of earth and stones, some five feet thick.

Asoka tried to follow down the tunnel, but he could not even wedge his head into the opening. He hurried to the other end to meet the fat man coming out, but the fat man remained where he was, so Asoka paraded the line to and fro, examining each prop to find a place where he could thrust in his trunk or his tusk and break an opening through which to reach his prey—Quorn talking to him all the time:

"Now, buddy, come and cool off. Come and get into the river. You don't want that fat guy. Come on, d'ye hear me?"

He whacked him with the *ankus,* using it fiercely, but Asoka was determined to reach the fat man and to drag him forth and trample him into crimson mud. He found two props that had an inch of space between them, drove his tusk in and worked like a giant beaver.

Quorn stuck to his place. There was nothing else whatever for Quorn to do, except to shout to the man behind the woodwork that shielded Kaligaon from the river:

"Get out o' there, you, and run for it—afore he breaks the whole damn' shootin'-match? You fat fool, he'll drown the city! Where's your patriotism? Come on out and run for it."

13

THE AUGEAN STABLE

IT WAS PITCH-DARK, but both women had lighters. They found themselves in a passage at the head of stairs descending to a smelly underworld. The wooden walls were painted with life-size obscenities. At the head of the stairs was a statue worse than any they had seen yet; there were three lamps in front of it, fed with rancid *ghee;* the Ranee lighted one.

"I would prefer the darkness," she said, "but it can't be helped. At any rate, now you know the worst about us. This is the element of India that I will slay, or it shall slay me. Let us look downstairs. We may find a way to escape."

Shielding the *ghee* lamp carefully with one hand, she led the way, her face like Chinese porcelain in the reflected light and her eyes gleaming with courage. There was one turn, then another short flight. At the foot she paused, holding up a hand too late to turn Virginia back. They stood together, staring, silent. Neither had ever imagined, or thought it possible to imagine, anything to equal the filth of that crypt, which was the home—the heart—the place of celebration of the Kaligaon mystery.

The floor was unguessably deep in refuse of countless generations, but that was the least offensive part of it. There were nameless horrors. Leering through the leaping shadows, groups of statuary represented vice and torture in every conceivable form.

"Turn back!" said the Ranee, clutching Virginia's arm. They climbed the stairs, their nostrils choking with the smell, their senses reeling.

"They grinned!" gasped Virginia, leaning against the wall. "I swear they did."

"No, it was the movement of the shadow."

"What shall we do? We must get out of here."

"I think we have two chances," said the Ranee. "Rana Raj Singh may perhaps have found a way across the hills. If so, he would have to come by Kaligaon to reach Narada."

"Too thin," said Virginia. "Can't you think of a better solution than that?"

"There is nobody more splendidly resourceful than my prince," the Ranee answered proudly.

"What is the other chance?"

"Brazenose Blake. He is a strange man. I have known him to do all sorts of unexpected things. Sometimes he annoys me to the point of exasperation by treating me as if I were his daughter. He might—I don't know why I think so, but he might have ridden out to meet us. He would certainly have come to meet us if he thought there were any danger brewing. If he did he will have seen the broken road. He will have seen Asoka's footprints. He may have followed and brought my soldiers with him."

"Oh, oh, I hope not!"

"Why?"

"My dear, I'm not conventional. I'm not a prude. But I

would rather die than be found by him in this place. Don't you understand?"

The Ranee nodded. She understood in part at any rate. For about two minutes she was silent, holding the lamp, staring straight at Virginia's eyes but seeming to see far beyond them.

"This place is built o' wood," she said at last.

"What of it?"

"I am going to burn it. Then, if they kill us, I shall at least have done the best I could."

"There may be people somewhere in the building."

"I don't care. Open that door—not wide—just enough so that we can escape in a hurry. It may burn faster than we think."

VIRGINIA DREW THE bolt and moved the door outward an inch or two. Suddenly she closed it—shot the bolt again.

"The whole place is full of people!"

"They will go when it burns," said the Ranee. "Draw the bolt again. You wait here, it won't take me a minute."

She carried all three lamps downstairs into the crypt, for the sake of the *ghee* that would help to start the woodwork burning, but it took her longer that she expected. Listening at the door, opening it again a fraction of an inch, Virginia heard scores of naked feet go shuffling across the temple floor toward the entrance. There was an alarm of some sort; they were in a hurry; in a moment the temple was empty again.

She opened the door wider, keeping her fingers on the bolt in case she should have to shut it suddenly. She thrust her head through, then her shoulders, peering into the gloom, a bit confused by the strong light shining through the temple entrance. Suddenly she heard the brass door on her right hand open—heard, too, what sounded like horses' footsteps. She shut the door tight and shot the bolt.

Apparently no sound could penetrate that door. She drew the bolt and opened it again, a fraction of an inch—then wider. Some one seized the door in both hands, wrenching it out of her grasp.

"Miss!" said a startled *babu,* blinking at her through platinum rimmed spectacles, "who are you!"

"My name is Blackstone."

"You! Are you alone? Where, then, is her highness?"

"Who are you?" Virginia asked him.

Bamjee came inside and closed the door, leaving only a crack that let a stream of dim light fall on Virginia's face.

"I am Bamjee—B.A.—*babu*—personal friend of—" Then he hesitated. "Where is her highness? Oh, my God, where is her highness?"

"She is downstairs."

"Doing what, for the love of Krishna?"

"Burning the place, I believe."

"And you stand there calmly? Gods, but you have nerve—and she has genius! That was exactly what I had intended to do! I was on my way to do it."

"Why? Who are you?"

"I am intimate personal friend of—of a certain gentleman. Miss—can you keep a secret?"

"Why?"

"Because—this friend of mine has confided in me—he is deeply in love—he dreads to be found in this place—by the lady whom he loves."

"But why tell me about it—and why now? Hadn't you better go and help the Ranee set the place on fire?"

"Miss, he loves you!"

"Me? What on earth do you mean? Who is he?"

"Brazenose Blake, Esquire, C.B., C.S.I., *et cetera!* But if you tell him that I told you he will kick me all the way to Bombay. How did you and her highness get here, for the love of—no matter, she'll tell me herself."

He went groping down the dark stairs, calling: "Your highness—your highness—here I am, your highness—this is Bamjee!"

The door opened. Virginia Blackstone stepped into the shadow. A voice that she instantly recognized shouted: "Bamjee? Where in the devil are you? Look sharp, like a good chap. Do you want help?"

Bamjee's voice came upstairs with the words all mixed up by the echoes. Blake took a stride toward the stairhead—stopped—stared.

"Virgie?" he gasped.

"Bray!"

"For the love of God, how did you get here?"

"The same to you! The point is, can we get out?"

"Where is the Ranee?"

"Downstairs, trying to set the place on fire. A *babu* who calls you his intimate friend has gone to help her."

Blake laughed, a trifle awkwardly. "I'd better go, too. I have horses for you and the Ranee. If the place burns, perhaps we can all escape in the confusion. We'll try at any rate. It's our one chance."

HE STRODE TOWARD the stairs, but crimson light came

forth to meet him. Framed in the glow came the Ranee, Bamjee following.

"Trust you!" she laughed. "Have you seen Quorn?"

"No, but I've horses for you. This way."

He led in a hurry, brought both horses through the brass door, tossed the reins to Bamjee and turned to help the women mount. But the Ranee vaulted to the saddle, so he held a stirrup for Virginia.

"Do you think I would go and leave you here?" she asked him. "What do you take me for?"

"You must. Oh, dammit, mount! Don't argue. The whole place will be a furnace in about a minute."

She mounted because she knew he would have lifted her unless she did. The door burst open from imprisoned gas, belching a cloud of crimsoned smoke into the temple. The horses plunged and staggered on the slippery stone floor. Blake seized the reins and led them, Bamjee clinging gamely to the Ranee's off rein.

"*Sahib!*" cried Bamjee. "What—"

Where the street had been, a torrent surged around the temple steps. It plunged down side streets. It was undermining houses. Men on roofs were watching building after building sway, heave, stagger and go crashing into its neighbor until Kaligaon seemed to fall like a pack of cards. The head of the temple steps was ten feet higher than the street, but the whole interior was now a roaring mass of flame and the heat was unendurable. A flame licked through the open door and caught the dry carved timbers.

"Ride, your highness! Plunge in!" Blake commanded. "Follow her!" he ordered, turning to Virginia. He slapped both horses on the rump. They plunged into the raging stream, shoulder deep—swam with it, feeling for bottom and leaping, dodging debris and obstructions—and were out of sight in less than half a minute.

"Come on, Bamjee, we're next. Can you swim? Lie on your back if you can't and I'll try to tow you."

"Wait, *sahib*—wait! Is that Asoka?"

There was no mistaking Quorn or his enormous elephant, heading downstream toward them.

"Crazy, mad, bewildering country—a god pops out of a box whichever way you turn," said Blake. "He has seen us, too. He's coming."

But the heat behind was unendurable. They had to wade into the water knee-deep. Then they had to duck to keep their skin from blistering. An upper floor came crashing down and burst the paving of the floor below. Flames spurted through every crack and cranny, curling upward, caught in the rising wind and blown to white heat. It was doubtful, too, whether Asoka could breast the flood and come to a standstill near the steps.

"Come on, Bamjee—better try our luck!"

Blake jumped in, seizing Bamjee by the collar, dragging him in backward.

Asoka, cooled by the water and pleased with himself for having done some truly elephantine damage, now obeyed Quorn's orders, ducking like a submarine in dread of the thunderous flames but following Blake and Bamjee—gaining on them—overtaking them where debris choked the street and made a boiling cataract. Quorn reached for Blake's hand, passed him astern toward the *howdah*, holding the half-drowned Bamjee until Blake had scrambled in, then helped Blake haul Bamjee high and dry.

"Now *juldee! Juldee!* Hurry, you big sucker!"

Asoka climbed the débris, plunging on the far side.

"They're down-street somewhere."

"Sir, I seen 'em."

There were places where the water raged so deep that Asoka could bury himself beneath it without touching bottom. But the gate of the city was built on slightly rising ground that split the stream in two, destroying buildings to right and left, but leaving a long island in the midst. The Ranee and Virginia stood there, struggling to loose their horses' water-tightened girths. They were safe for the moment.

But the city gate was closed; and on the roofs of near-by buildings an increasing swarm of Kaligaon's enraged citizens was gathering, bent on vengeance in the face of disaster. Tiles came hurtling through the air to an accompaniment of yells and curses. As Asoka set his forefeet on the firm road and came up dripping another group of men came running two by two along the city wall. Blake scrambled to the ground to loosen the girths.

"Mount!" he commanded. "Hurry! Can Asoka break that gate, Quorn?"

"No, sir."

"Turn to the left then. Look for a gap in the wall. The water must have burst through somewhere."

But the narrow street was choked with floating débris, so that even Asoka had to struggle to get by, and the only chance the horses had was to follow him and leap into the gaps he made. Pursuit began, howling and venomous, men swarming along the wall and over roofs to attack from four sides. Quorn saw a place where the wall was broken, but the gap was choked with débris, jammed tight; not even Asoka could have tackled it.

"**BETTER TURN AND** try some other way, sir."

"Keep on going!" Blake commanded. "There'll be another gap somewhere."

Suddenly a fifty yard long section of the wall tottered and fell, undermined by the flood. Asoka charged the gap, the horses following.

The men on the wall descended on the far side, meaning to attack on firm ground as the fugitives reached the open, knowing they would have to turn again to reach the high road and avoid the deep ravine that followed the line of the wall a hundred yards away. The men on the housetops followed them, hurrying like monkeys. There were two or three hundred men to deal with, armed with sticks and knives—religion down-wind—bent on murder.

As Asoka scrambled through the gap, the horses following, Blake leaned forward from the *howdah*.

"Ride straight at 'em, Quorn. Make a gap in their ranks. Then turn and keep on charging. Keep it open. Give the women a chance to break through."

"Sir to you, sir. But no need. Them's the Rajputs coming— Rana Raj Singh—jes' see that sucker ride! Sixteen—eighteen—twenty—four-and-twenty men behind him. We're all right I guess they saw that temple burning and came to get a look-see. Maybe they ain't welcome, eh? And maybe them varmints don't know what a Rajput's sabre means— look at 'em? Did you ever see men run that fast?"

It was a rather breathless meeting, Rana Raj Singh curtly answering the Ranee's questions as to how he found a road to Kaligaon.

"Was it you who burned that temple?" he demanded, smiling as she nodded. "Then make the most of it. Go home and let Narada know you did it. It will be a lesson to the Brahmins. They will yield to you for fear you may burn their own hives. Rajputs!—threes right—march—canter!"

On the way home Quorn accepted a cigar from Blake and grew communicative.

"Nice young leddy, sir."

"You mean Miss Blackstone?"

"Right. Too bad, she's sweet on some one."

"How so?"

"Her and me had quite a confab at the halfway bungalow. There was a mess o' snakes there—sort o' frightened her. I made a pot o' coffee. She and I got kind o' chummy. Lord, but old Asoka's tired—this'll serve him for a week's excitement. Wished you'd seen him go a-rolling when he pulled the props loose and the river broke through. Mighty nearly drowned him—me too."

There was a long silence, Blake crowding down his curiosity. At last he said, too casually:

"Of course. I forgot for the moment that you and she are both Americans. I suppose you found a lot to talk about."

"One thing mainly, sir. A leddy that's in love but don't want nobody to know it talks o' nothing else. That's human natur'. That young leddy talked around you north, south, east an' west, not mentioning your name no more than half a hundred times. It's too bad. She thinks you'll think she came on purpose for to back you in a corner."

"Oh, no, she could never think that."

"And she thinks, sir, that you'll hate her for it."

"No," put in Bamjee, sprawling in his corner of the

howdah, limp yet from his ducking, "she can never think that. I have told her, *sahib,* I enjoy your inmost confidence. I told her—"

"Oh, damn!" burst out Blake—then shouted: "Rana Raj Singh! Do you think one of your fellows would mind riding in the *howdah* and lending me his horse? I'm afraid of a chill in these wet clothes unless I can keep moving."

The exchange was made in sixty seconds. All the way home Brazenose Blake and Virginia Blackstone ambled side by side, until the Ranee left her prince's side at last and overtook them.

"You two!" she exclaimed. "You two! Why is it I can't find any one but Quorn to come and live in Narada and help me rule the place? I suppose you'll marry now and both of you will go away forever. Damn! Well, I'll meet you again in the next life. I'll probably know better by then. I will keep you quarreling instead for years and years. But what a lot a Ranee has to learn—and what a time it takes to learn it all!"

THE ELEPHANT SAHIB

*The natives of a turbulent mountain
State on India's border called Ben Quorn
a god; but the American-born master of
elephants was not mighty enough to control
the five-ton avalanche Asoka if that
whimsical giant started on a rampage*

1

"MAYBE GOD COULD TELL WHY ELEPHANTS HAS DISPOSITIONS"

THE RANEE OF Narada sent for Ben Quorn. She had a perfect right to do it. There were hundreds of people in that independent little State on India's border who would have been delighted to get wet and muddy in the last terrific downpour of the biggest monsoon of a century—delighted to ruin their best clothes, catch colds in the head and be treated snootily by palace underlings, for the sake of an interview with their young ruler. She never summoned people for nothing; always something satisfying came of it. Even her enemies liked to talk to her.

But Ben Quorn knocked the ashes from his pipe, carefully folded a month-old copy of the Philadelphia *Ledger,* stowed it in the hole in the brick wall where he kept his tobacco and matches, and swore.

He folded up the canvas deck-chair, leaned it carefully against the wall of the empty elephant stall that he used as smoking-room and office, hitched his turban straight, found his umbrella, and went into the biggest stall of all, at the end of the line, dodging the water that splashed from the eaves in solid bucketfuls.

"Devil!" he muttered. "I wisht it was the middle o' nex'

week, I do. I wisht it always was the middle o' nex' week. Move over!"

The biggest elephant in all captivity—Asoka—moved, as meek as a mouse.

"You big bum!" Quorn addressed him. "You look like butter wouldn't melt in your belly. You look like a bishop, so blasted urbane that a traffic-cop ud treat you civil! Me, I'd hate to be the sucker if he didn't! As it is, I spend my whole time getting you quick out o' one trouble afore you get into the nex', so's to save other folks' tempers—'tain't no earthly use favorin' yours! You're the durnedest indiscreetest drunkard ever I see. Nobody'd blame you if you only got drunk same as me, now and then on honest rye. You get drunk on your own pride—you obsolete blamed ijjit! Well—there ain't no use us getting a howdah wet. Put me up."

Obediently, and as gently as if Quorn were a basket of eggs, Asoka curled a trunk around him and raised him into place—turned—paused in the wide opening to give Quorn time to duck and started squooging through the mud toward the compound gateway. The mud gave deliciously under Asoka's feet; the surrounding trees smelled wet and wonderful; the drumming rain sluiced off his glistening hide. He raised his trunk and whispered in his own left ear.

"You cut that out!" Quorn admonished and gave him a crack with the umbrella handle. "This ain't no picnic. You behave yourself sedate or I'll soak you a smack you'll remember."

AN UMBRELLA HANDLE, however, does not even suggest an *ankus,* the sharp elephant-goad; and Asoka knew from

The cobra's head appeared over the pillow

experience and with all his inner senses that he and Quorn would be friends in any event, until death did them part. Furthermore, a ride without the howdah on his back almost always meant a visit to the swimming pool or else a tour of inspection through the jungle to see how the grass was coming along.

There was jungle in three directions, so the fact that they started toward the palace made no difference to Asoka's temper; he broke himself a branch from a tree by the road and pretended to use it to swish flies off Quorn, although of course there were none while the rain came drumming down. Several times he almost smashed Quorn's umbrella.

Then there were incidents, mere nothings in themselves, that added minor touches of amusement, so that the sum-total was convincing. Narada's roads, since the ambitious young Ranee came to the throne, are better than they used to be, but they are not yet even moderately civilized.

There was a mud-hole fifty feet wide in which a local trader was stuck with a cart and four oxen; Quorn told

Asoka to shove the cart out of the hole from behind. He shoved with such a will that the cart came out, but the wheels stayed in and the tradesman rolled in the mud. Asoka rescued him by one leg, swinging him up to the roof of the broken cart, where he sprawled and prayed to fifty deities. It was immensely satisfying to Asoka, who enjoyed nothing as much as breaking things that had cost time and money to put together. Elephants in that respect resemble small boys.

And then there was the nipping dog near the palace gate; it belonged to a lady novelist in smoked spectacles and a long green mackintosh who was making notes for a forthcoming book on India's horrors. Asoka hated small dogs and he still had the branch in his trunk. He gave chase; and they deceive themselves who think an elephant turns clumsily. It was almost like a polo game, with the dog for an elusive and exasperating ball and the spectacled lady for referee, only she had a shrill voice instead of a whistle.

At last after a long time Asoka slew the dog and trod him deep into the mud. The lady's remarks were not original, but they were critical, to put it mildly; however, Quorn was wearing a turban and looked like a native, so he pretended not to understand; and Asoka, conscious of a goal well won, mistook her lamentation for applause.

So he went through the great iron gate into the palace grounds in a glorious mood, gurgling good will, inviting all the universe to show him something stronger than himself or something damnable that ought to be abolished.

There was an enormous clump of fancy bamboo near the gate; it was the sort of thicket in which pigs might hide or where a tiger might lie in wait; Asoka charged it like a locomotive, smashed every last stalk of it and trampled it into green trash. It occurred to him then that for some inscrutable reason Ben Quorn was annoyed, so he set forth to discover what annoyed him.

QUORN BROKE THE umbrella on his head—a symptom of impatience that called upon Asoka for intelligent investigation and swift removal of its underlying cause. Sure enough, in three long lines within sight of the palace windows, Asoka spied what certainly had not been there when he last had passed that way.

"You big bum, them's the Ranee's new frames for growing flowers!" protested Quorn.

Asoka put his foot through one of them to see. It smashed delightfully. It was brittle and it tinkled. Underneath there was a mass of soft dirt, warm and musky-smelling. There were wooden beams that cracked and came adrift. And something stung sharply.

That settled it; this must be the cause of Quorn's anger. The fact that six gardeners appeared suddenly from nowhere, waving their arms, throwing clods of earth and shouting like maniacs, confirmed what already was more than suspicion. Asoka began to smash with zeal and system, encouraged by the gardeners' frantic yelling and by Quorn's futile efforts with the broken umbrella handle.

"You fat-head, I hope you get stuck full o' glass like a cushion o' pins!"

It was hardly as bad as that. Not much glass pierced the tough skin, but a daring gardener took a long rake and attacked Asoka's rump with scandalous lack of discrimination so that Asoka's genial desire to please turned into fury and what had been a mere amusing interlude became serious.

He chased a gardener—not the man with the rake, but another one who had a long-handled hoe. The idiot dropped the hoe; Asoka trod on it; it rose and smacked him painfully. He knew then that a gardener is no good. He would slay them all, in the open or in their hiding places, no matter which. He would earn Quorn's loving gratitude or die trying.

The miscreant who had dropped the hoe took refuge in a dark shed full of flowerpots. The easiest way to dislodge him out of that was to destroy the shed and all the pots, so Asoka did it. Quorn stuck to him grimly like an insect on an earthquake, because the important thing was to be in at the finish and prevent some worse calamity.

The shed collapsed; the flowerpots became scattering bits of shapeless clay as Asoka dug among them. The gardener bolted like a rat, Asoka after him; and the fellow was lucky enough to vanish down a rubbish hole that was too deep and difficult for Asoka's further investigation at the moment, seeing how much other work there was to do. Besides, there might be cobras in the hole; so Asoka left him and chased another gardener.

The second man took to a lotus pond, that had a fountain in the midst—a statue of an unknown god forgotten in the mists of time, who spouted water from a thing on his head like a helmet. The fountain spouted furiously, because the water came from a natural spring and there was no means of turning it off.

The gardener climbed the statue and stood trying to

balance himself on the god's shoulders against a stream of water that would have done credit to a fire brigade.

Asoka plunged in after him and tried to demolish the statue, since he could not climb it; but that was too much even for his strength, so he turned away to chase another gardener.

THE THIRD MAN took to a wall and scampered along the top of it. First, Asoka tried to knock the wall down, but the blow that he struck with his forehead only battered a gap, and the gardener jumped it, so the elephant ran alongside, reaching upward. But the man's legs always seemed one scamper ahead of his trunk, and, at the end of the wall, the man jumped through a glass roof on the far side into a place where special kinds of cactus were being forced for the summer garden on the palace roof. So that was that.

A fourth man was running like a wetted scarecrow across the wide green lawn that faced the palace windows. That calling for nothing but speed, Asoka gave a squeal of thrilled anticipation and set forth in pursuit as swiftly as the fastest horse that ever set foot to a race track. But the lawn was oozy with all that rain on it; he slipped; for ten yards he slid on his rump, removing quantities of good, expensive grass and leaving an ugly brown smear. The gardener dodged.

Asoka, turning after him, skidded sidewise, plowing up the lawn. The gardener took to the flowerbeds underneath the palace windows. Asoka smashed about a thousand young begonias, and sank into the drenched earth almost to his belly. The gardener reached the palace steps, where an attendant, greatly daring, admitted him into the hall.

There were more than five tons of Asoka; even in that

mood he knew the responsibilities of weight, and did not dare to follow up the steps under the portico. So he stood at the foot of them, wondering what to do next, trying to make head or tail of Quorn's remarks.

"You lunatic! You've been and gone and done it for the last time! Any sucker 'ud forgive you strafing gardeners—them guys deserves any grief they gets—but all this damage? Where's your purse? Who's to pay for all that glass and all them flowers? You fat-head! Me and you are up against it this time, and no escape. What 'll we say to *her?* Tell her a gardener hit you with a hunk o' dirt? A lot o' good a bum excuse like that 'll do us. She'll—"

Quorn looked up. At the top of the steps the Ranee stood, surveying all the damage, and her beautiful young face was sorrowful. She dearly loved those flowers and the wide green lawn; the glass frames were the pride of her progressive heart that loved her little kingdom of Narada and intended it should be a still, quiet refuge for exotic beauty, in a world where ugliness and cheapness have increasing sway.

It was a dramatic moment, fraught with a feeling of tragedy; and it was borne in on Quorn that he must speak the first word, lest her first impulse should be one of vengeance. He could think of nothing, yet he must speak.

"Miss," he said at last in a tone of abject grief, "I've broke my new umbrella."

In proof he waved the handle of the thing.

Dignity is easy to mock; it is hard to imitate; it is impossible to come by without wisdom and a sense of humor welded by fathomless tolerance on to a far-seeing sense of values. The young Ranee, in a blue and crocus-yellow robe as Greek as Sappho's, instantly assumed a proper attitude toward this man who obviously grieved so deeply that he could only think of platitudes—who grieved more for his elephant, who must be punished, than for himself who only had a job to lose. She dismissed her own annoyance; her frown, that made a small, dark shadow on her forehead, vanished; and her eyes smiled, though her lips refrained from laughter lest it seem like ridicule.

"Thank you for coming so promptly, Mr. Quorn. Is anybody killed? I suppose the roads were too muddy for your new Ford? Kindly chain Asoka in the stables, get some dry clothes from the chamberlain, and then come in. I want to talk to you."

Quorn turned Asoka toward the stables. "You big bum! Maybe God could tell why elephants has dispositions as 'ud make a saint sick. Look at you now, acting as if you was teacher's darling on your way to Sunday-school!"

2

"I AM AFRAID YOU MUST DIE, MR. QUORN"

ARRAYED IN HINDU clothing because the chamberlain had no other with which to provide him, and therefore far more conscious than a woman would be that his legs were what he considered indecently exposed, Quorn let himself be ushered by obsequious attendants into the smaller palace reception room.

He sighed, leaned his forearms on the back of an ancient chair, and waited. After all, deep in his heart Ben Quorn was not a democrat; he was a small boy enjoying a fairy tale. He was an autocrat over elephants, a terror to the dissolute mahouts whom he ruled, and to the Ranee that most priceless of all assets, a devoted servant free from any illusions as to his employer's sanity. He preferred her merry madness to the dull stupidity of people whom the world calls wise.

"All the same," he was wont to mutter, "I'd as soon she was a mite more keerful."

When she entered, with two of her ladies following to preserve the fiction of respect for conventions that were as dead in that young woman's mind as dodoes, he came out from behind the chair; and because his manners were built on good will, not rule-books, again it was he who spoke first.

"Miss," he said, "I know there's the devil to pay or you'd never have sent for me on such a day as this."

She sat. Her ladies giggled and whispered in the farthest corner of the room. Quorn stood, until the Ranee signed to him to take the chair opposite hers.

"No, Mr. Quorn, not that," she said, "but politics again."

"Same thing, miss."

She gazed as if reading his mind. His agate eyes met hers without wavering. Quorn had nothing to conceal, although he wished his legs were more amply covered.

"That elephant," she began.

"Asoka, miss? He don't mean nothing by them tantrums. It's his little way, that's all. He busts things, but he's innocent o' malice. Him and me, we're two of a kind, we're liable to act a bit awkward with things that we don't understand. Now, them glass frames—"

"Never mind the frames; they're ruined. I was thinking of the gardeners. He might have killed one."

"He might ha' done worse, at that. Them thieves steal your flowers and sell 'em at cut rates for weddings. They—"

"It is very difficult for me," the Ranee interrupted, "not to order my troops to turn out and shoot Asoka."

"No, miss; it's easy. What's difficult is to find a new reason to tell them priests why you won't do it. Oh, I know 'em. They're forever telling you Asoka is as crazy as a mad dog and that I'm worse. But that's mild to what they say o' you behind your back. True, Asoka makes a bit o' trouble now and then, but he hurts hisself worst of all—likely I'll be picking bits o' glass out of his old hide for a week to come. And, miss, in his wussest tantrums, when he's smashing a high priest's automobile, or drunk and chasing pariah-dogs, he'll step aside not to injure a kid. Miss, he has saved your throne a time or two."

"You mean, *you* have."

"I don't mean nothing o' the sort. Asoka done it. Me without Asoka is a car without an engine. He's maybe obsolete, but he's the works."

The Ranee pounced on that.

"It is work that he needs," she answered. "Work would not hurt you, either, Mr. Quorn."

"Go ahead, miss. I knew there was the devil to pay."

"I WISH THE building of the summer palace to begin the minute the monsoon is over."

"Yes, miss."

"If Asoka is not to be shot, he must work. You are the only person who can make him work; so you must work, too."

"Yes, miss."

"I wish every man and every elephant in Narada to have plenty of work to do to keep him out of mischief. So you may take all the elephants to Panch Mahal. They are to work at dragging stone and at carrying timber and at clearing ground and rooting out stumps of trees."

"Yes, miss."

"And at any other task that presents itself."

"Ah! I knowed there was a string to it! Might I know the low-down? I mean, you and me's been friends this many a day. If you've enemies, yours truly is the guy you ought to put wise. Me and my buddy Asoka ain't so unquarrelsome we couldn't do your enemies a bit o' dirt."

The Ranee smiled. She looked guileless. "Secrets," she said, "are sometimes dangerous, Mr. Quorn."

"It's dangerouser, miss, to turn a decent team o' rooters for you loose without their knowing what they're up against. Might soak the wrong—the wrong politician. Miss, who's making trouble for you?"

"My ancestors," she answered with conviction.

Quorn whistled. He vaguely understood what that meant.

"More o' this here superstition?" he suggested.

"Don't be silly, Mr. Quorn. You know as well as I do that you and I and Asoka and all these people have lived a thousand lives together in the world, and very likely more than that."

"Me, miss! How should I be sure of it?"

"Because here you are, and here we all are, having to undo all the harm we did in days gone by—and make new *karma*, destiny, what you call luck, for future lives. Even a maniac could see that."

"Them what's blind can't see, miss, not though you call 'em all manner o' names."

"Certainly you did something wicked in a former life that caused you to be punished by being so blind in this one. However, you must have done some great good, too, because you're honest, which is always a reward for honesty in a previous incarnation."

"Well, miss, I reckon those lives are behind us, if we ever lived 'em. What's causing new trouble in this one? And what kind? I figure I'm alive now; that much gets by my stoopidness. And I can do a bit of honest dirt to any one what has it in for you. So say his name. Me and Asoka will go to the mat."

"I am afraid you will have to," she answered; and again Quorn sighed. He loved the Ranee, but he did wish she could come to the point without so much oriental subtlety and roundabout approach.

"I am afraid you must die, Mr. Quorn—you and Asoka—both of you."

"Yes, miss?"

"You see, you are supposed to be the reincarnation of the holy Gunga *sahib,* and I think you are. In fact, I know you are. And my name is Sankyamuni; so that I know I am the same princess who was in Narada a thousand years ago when you were the Gunga *sahib.* I have forced even the priests to admit that, though they try now to deny it. There stand our portraits together on the market-place wall, graven in stone a thousand years ago. And there is Asoka's portrait along with ours.

"In those days you were the greater and I the lesser. Nowadays that is reversed, but that is only temporary; you are being punished for some sin that you committed that you don't remember."

"THAT'S WHAT GETS my goat, miss," Quorn retorted. "If what you say is true, it ain't fair to make a guy forget and then to punish him for what he don't remember doing."

"Nonsense. Making him find out what it was is the whole of the punishment. The minute he knew what it was, there is no more punishment for that, and he can begin to be punished for something else. We only do wicked things and stupid things because we don't know. When we know, we awake and act wisely. I suppose that is why you must die—you and Asoka. I shall be very sorry."

"Me, too, miss."

"You see, the priests say if you actually are the Gunga *sahib*, all the prophecies concerning you must be fulfilled, not only two or three. You look like him, they admit that. You can ride the untamable elephant, they admit that. You rescued me from my father's clutches and enabled me to escape the seclusion of the women's *purdah* and all the other silly, stuffy ancient customs; they admit that—and it makes them very angry. So they say now that you and Asoka must die to save my throne."

"Well, miss, dying out o' turn ain't my idea of good sense. And if I die, them priests 'll have the laugh on us."

"They say you must come to life again," she added.

"Me, miss?"

"You and Asoka, both of you. You see, the priests like to make things difficult."

"For other folks, miss, yes. Them suckers like things easy for 'emselves."

"So I am sending you and Asoka and all the other elephants to Panch Mahal, where you will find that the dacoits are rampant. I shall come to Panch Mahal, too, when the roads are better."

"Them robber bands is dangerous," said Quorn. "You'd better stay here. You've only fifty soldiers. You can't take more than five and twenty with you."

"I will take ten."

"Miss, I never argue with a lady, but I think you're crazy in the head."

"The priests say I am crazy because you are an impostor and I trust you."

"Me? I never imposted nothing. 'Twasn't me who said I'm the Gunga *sahib*. I've said I ain't. I've said it that often I'm plumb sick o' saying it. I tell every one who asks me that I'm a taxi driver from Philadelphia. I show 'em my old license and the photo on it. I show 'em a picture o' me and the cab—I show 'em my birth certificate, an' my vaccination certificate, an' my passport. I show 'em the newspaper clippings where I'm fined for getting fresh with traffic cops. And all they do is smile and say the ways of the gods are wonderful. And now you want me to get— Miss, you spoke of politics. You want me to go to Panch Mahal and get killed by dacoits! That ain't politics."

"Yes, but I want you to come to life again—and that is politics. You'll see."

"I'm thinking a dead feller doesn't see much," Quorn retorted.

"**YOU WILL SEE** all you need when the time comes. And you must trust me." The Ranee was not imperious at that moment.

"Miss, I guess I've got to. But please be your age. Have a heart. Don't get too like that bird who wrote a book I once read out o' the palace library—what's his name?—Machiavelli. Try being more like honest Abe Lincoln or Florence Nightingale or maybe the Queen of Sheba. You ought to read about 'em."

"Listen," said the Ranee. "I am surrounded by three States, each of them larger than mine and each of them ruled by a rajah who covets my wealth and would like to marry me."

"How about Prince Rana Raj Singh, miss? Ain't you going to marry him? He's the goods. He's the okay-est gent this side o' the United States."

"I intend to marry him. But these other three rajahs intend that I shall not. And they are playing politics. They are rivals, but they are united in determination to defeat my purpose. Their idea is, they can defeat me first and then quarrel with one another afterward over the spoil."

"Yes, miss, that's politics."

"I am afraid they have bribed my ministers, Mr. Quorn. And I know they have bribed the priests. They would try to bribe you, if they thought they could do it."

"Them suckers haven't anything I want, miss," Quorn said, with an air of self-disparagement.

"So you are almost the only person I can trust."

Quorn, who never deserted a friend in his life, took instant advantage of that opening:

"Take my tip, miss: trust Asoka, too. He's ornery now an' then, but he's a wise old elephant; and if there's anything in this reincarnation stuff he's liable to do you a good turn when you're least looking for it."

"Asoka makes things very difficult for me," she answered. "However, listen: the British Government has been making a drive against dacoits lately. Rajahs of all native States have been practically ordered to take part in it and rid their territories of outlaw bands.

"I had no dacoits in Narada; all my outlaws were put to work last year policing roads, and they are much cheaper and more efficient than the uniformed policemen. So what have those three rajahs done but drive their own dacoits into my mountains—hundreds of them, as fierce as hornets. They have seized a village near Panch Mahal and butchered the inhabitants—soaked them with petrol and set a light to them—all that sort of savagery. They have auctioned off the women among themselves."

"And you're sending me there?"

"Naturally. Listen: those three rajahs are now complaining to the British Government that my little State of Narada is a hotbed of dacoits and consequently a very dangerous neighbor to their own peaceful and well governed States. They assert that with fifty soldiers, which are all that the treaty permits me to have, I can't possibly govern such unruly subjects. They demand that my territory shall be incorporated with one of theirs or else divided between the three of them in equal parts. And they suggest that if proper pressure were brought to bear I might consent to marry one of them and solve the difficulty that way."

"MISS, IF I were you I'd borrow soldiers from the English."

"Unthinkable! I would rather die! It would be plain proof that I can't govern. I must find some other way. And meanwhile, they have bribed my ministers that they give me bad advice and make all sorts of difficulties for me. And they know that I depend on you to help me in tight places, so they have bribed the priests, too; and the priests are once more accusing you of being an impostor. They think that if Asoka should be killed you might go back to Philadelphia in disgust, so they are demanding his execution as a dangerous nuisance. And they are telling the people that if you really were a reincarnation of the Gunga *sahib* both you and Asoka would die for the sake of my throne and would come to life again."

"Well, miss, why not talk to Mr. Brazenose Blake? He liked you and he's full o' good advice."

"He's helpless. Don't you understand that the Resident is the political agent of the British government? Besides, he has been summoned to Delhi, for a conference. If the British government should decide to abolish the State of Narada, Mr. Blake would have to give me the sort of advice that would lead up to that, whether he liked doing it or not. So we must have this situation settled before Mr. Blake gets back. There must be no dacoits and no problem. He must be able to report that to his government."

"Well, miss, it looks like we've got to pray for a miracle."

"We've got to make one."

"Out o' what, miss?"

"Out of almost nothing. But I have the excuse to send you to the Panch Mahal, that all the elephants need work, Asoka most of all. And fortunately, near the Panch Mahal there are at least a thousand dacoits."

"*Fortunately,* miss?" Quorn seldom showed surprise.

"It is always nice to know where you can reach your enemy. And I have secret information, which I hope is true, that the Rajah of Dumdumpore, who is the boldest of my three neighbors, has been seen in person not far from the dacoits' camp. He has no business to come uninvited into my territory. How soon can you start for the Panch Mahal with all the elephants?"

3

THERE IS POISON THAT CRAWLS

THERE WERE HINTS that very night that Quorn's continued presence in Narada had become dissatisfying to the priests.

For many months he had eaten nothing that was not first tasted in his presence by the cook, and he was equally careful about Asoka's food, examining corn and grass and sometimes feeding handfuls of the corn to cows, because he knew it would sadden the priests if a cow should die from poison of their brewing. Cows were sacred. But there is poison that crawls on its belly and sees in the dark.

The rain drummed down in torrents and Asoka fidgeted, swaying and plucking at his picket-ring. He was a little sore in spots where Quorn had pulled out bits of broken glass; and Quorn had a cot in the stall beside him as a precaution against tantrums that might send all four-and-thirty elephants into a midnight panic. It is always a cow-elephant that rules the herd, but Asoka could make even the old leader-cow so nervous that she would lose authority and be the first to pull up stakes and run.

"I'll put on something as smarts you worse'n iodine if you don't keep quiet, you sucker," Quorn admonished.

He lay smoking. There was no light except the glow of

his pipe. Two or three hours' sleep is all that an elephant requires and it was all that Quorn himself expected that night; he was waiting for Asoka to lie down, before putting out his pipe and dropping off to sleep himself, ready to wake again the instant that Asoka moved.

"What ails you, you big bum? You've been hurted worse 'n that a score o' times and made no fuss. There ain't a scrap o' glass left in you no-wheres. I've been all over you with a magnifying glass. Lie down and shut your peepers."

But Asoka would not lie down. He grew more restless, and after a while, even in the darkness, Quorn understood that the great sensitive beast was aware of some danger he himself could not perceive. He tried to think of what it might be, wondering for instance whether the rain had undermined the brick foundations of the long shed. At last he struck a match and found his flash light. He knew then in a second.

There were seven cobras crawling around the stall. All seven raised their heads and hissed the moment he struck the match. They were afraid of being trodden on, afraid of the light and, because afraid, they were alert and deadly.

To set his foot on the floor was to risk being struck, yet the only available weapon was the iron *ankus;* and the goad hung from a hook on the door, out of reach.

Quorn shouted, but his mahouts were all asleep in their quarters more than a hundred yards away and no one heard him; Then a cobra raised itself and began to weave at the end of the cot; presently its head appeared over the pillow. With his hair rising and his skin creeping like a snake all over him, Quorn stepped off the far end of the bed and tiptoed to the door, wishing that he had not taken off his boots before he lay down. He almost stepped on another cobra that writhed away.

Wondering how as many as seven of them could have got into the stall, he snatched at the chain that pulled the door-latch in the overhead beam, swung the door wide open and leaped into the night to avoid the downpour from the eaves and the torrent underfoot.

IT WAS WELL that he leaped. It was even better that he landed in his socks and slid, heels forward, in the soft mud, falling flat on his shoulder blades.

Something plunked into the opened door. Another something flickered over him and landed in a pool of water with a splash that was not in the least like the splash of a stone. Another something plunked into the mud beside him.

He lay still. There was silence, except for the din of the rain on the tiled roof and the stuttering splash of the puddles. He moved—and four more silent somethings quivered in quick succession through the air above him. He shouted—yelled—groaned as if in agony. He heard a man's retreating footsteps then go splashing through the puddles; Quorn lay still until they ceased in the distance.

Then he squelched through the mud to a shed where he knew he could lay his hand in the dark on a whalebone riding whip—a long one such as Indian trainers use who are too lazy to manage animals by the painstaking, patient way. He kept it to use on the backs of mahouts caught stealing grain; but there is no better tool in the world for killing cobras.

Then, dreading every step and sweating with fear, for a snake was a terror to Quorn that almost robbed him of his

self-control, he forced himself to return to Asoka's stall—
hoping against hope that the cobras would have escaped
by that time through the open door. However, they were
there. By the beam of the flash light he slew them one by
one. But he could not bring himself to touch them; he went
out again, trembling, and fetched a mahout, who was still
half-dreaming from his customary dose of opium.

"Carry 'em out. How do you suppose they got in?"

The mahout was anxious to please. He supposed that
unless he said something Quorn would blame him for the
cobras. India is fertile in excuses—always; it invents them
on the spur of any moment.

"Does the *sahib* not remember the green *memsahib* in
spectacles, whose small white dog Asoka slew? Many
people saw that. Many heard her curses. All knew that
her curses would produce some terrible thing. But this is
good now, since the snakes are slain without having accomplished anything. Therefore the curses must return to her
and smite her, for that is the law."

"Aw, rats!"

Quorn shoved him out into the rain with the broken
snakes still writhing in two bunches in his hands. He
followed—curious, now that the snakes were dead and
the creeping fear had left him. He examined the door that
had stood like a shield between him and something when
he leaped into the dark.

By the light of the flash light he found an arrow sticking
in it—not a very well made or particularly straight one; the
sort that the nearly naked Bhils use with a bow that will
only drive it fifty yards or so. He did not doubt that the
hammered wire tip was poisoned. Presently, he found six

similar arrows, most of them buried almost to their feathers in the mud.

"Seven snakes—seven arrows. Seven priests, I'll bet my boots!" he muttered. "I'll bet they had to pretend to make magic afore they persuaded some poor limping savage to take shots at me. They prob'ly paid him as much as half a dollar. Wonder how the snakes got in."

He found a small hole where a brick had been removed—marks of a man's knees in the mud where, outside, a sack was stuffed into the hole to prevent the snakes from turning back. He spent the rest of that night smoking on the cot with his legs drawn up under him, chuckling once or twice as he thought of the indignation of the literary lady in spectacles if she should be accused of attempting murder by means of magic curses.

AN HOUR BEFORE dawn he was up, arousing the mahouts to cook the big flat cakes for the elephants' breakfast, and brutally retorting to a dozen pleas for delay or leave of absence.

"I don't care if *all* your wives' mothers are dead—of if nobody 'tends to their corpses—I don't care if your bellies ache—or if the doctor says you have, the rheumatiz—I don't give a damn if you haven't a change o' G-strings. You can come along naked for all of me. The monsoon's over—no more rain. Breakfast, and then march! Them's the Ranee's orders."

But it needed more than words. He had to use the whalebone riding whip to stop their clamoring for advances of pay and permission to run into the city to make purchases. Even so, it was two hours after daylight before the procession began to move, Asoka leading, so there was time for a word with the *babu* Bamjee, who came floundering through the mud on a wall-eyed pony to seal up the stores and take official charge of the elephant lines in Quorn's absence.

Bamjee was the Ranee's purchasing agent and man of business—a small bespectacled *babu* in immaculate turban and gray silk suit. He and Quorn were friendly enemies.

They had saved each other's lives a time or two; they were at perpetual loggerheads about the quality of corn supplied to the elephants and about Quorn's parsimony. The master of elephants weighed out stores as if he were supplying gasoline and oil to taxi drivers, whereas Bamjee received a commission on everything bought; so there was no chance for peace between those two, although they liked each other.

Bamjee, wrinkling his face like a temple monkey because the morning sun was in his eyes, saluted Quorn.

"I wish you a pleasant journey. I wish I might come with you," he said politely.

"No pickings," Quorn retorted. "Stay where you can shave the shadow off a few rupees."

"I will watch the priests for you," said Bamjee.

"You'll wear your fool eyes out and see nothing at that. Them beggars acts too slick for any ordinary man to catch 'em at it."

"Am I ordinary?" Bamjee asked him.

"Aye, but I've met more ornery ones than you, at that."

"If I learn anything worth telling I will come to the Panch Mahal," said Bamjee.

"Meaning you know something now?" Quorn suggested.

"Yes," said Bamjee, "I know all about this new intrigue."

Quorn bit off a chew of tobacco. "Trust you to find out," he remarked grimly. "I don't doubt the Rajah of Dumdumpore has bribed you, among others."

"It is not receiving money, it is what one does that matters," Bamjee answered. "If there is money to be had for holding out one's hand, should I not take it? If there is information to be won by listening, should I shut my ears?"

"You never committed them two sins; you've took and you've listened. Go on."

"The point is, if I keep a lookout for you, will you scratch my back for me?" asked Bamjee.

"I've done it frequent. What's the graft now? I won't stand for no commission racket, but I'll do anything in reason."

"It is not much. It is only the use of an elephant at Panch Mahal," said Bamjee.

"WHAT FOR?" QUORN demanded with a frequently justified suspiciousness.

"There is a lady here—a spinsterish, unwise person who will write a book. She wishes to see for herself the real India, as she calls it. She wears green spectacles and a green coat—"

"Yes, I seen her."

"And she has asked me to conduct her personally on a tour into the heart of Narada where, as she puts it, she can get in touch with native life. She will pay me handsomely, although she thinks she is a very good woman of business. If I should take her to Panch Mahal, she would be well tired of bullock-carts by the time we arrived. I might charge her a very high price for a change to the back of an elephant."

"How about them dacoits?" Quorn asked.

"She says that is utter nonsense. She does not believe there are any robbers."

"Must be crazy in the head," said Quorn.

"No," said Bamjee—and then played his ace of trumps, a little way he had of doing suddenly when he was dickering with Quorn for favors. "She is cantankerous, not crazy. And she is critical; she believes the worst of persons. She has said, for instance, that our young Ranee is a despot and a person of loose morals—that being, of course, because the Ranee did not invite her to the palace. She says the Ranee is an anachronism."

"Meaning what?"

"It is a bad word," said Bamjee.

"The devil you say! Bring her along. Sure, I'll give her an elephant ride."

"And I will pay you ten per cent of—"

"No, you don't. The day you catch Ben Quorn accepting ten per cent of any kind o' graft you'll know you're seeing snakes and had better cut out liquor. Bring her along. I'll see she gets a ride. She called the Ranee a—what did you say?"

"I don't care to repeat the word," said Bamjee, who was Quorn's superior in certain sorts of finesse.

Then Quorn took to the road—the oozy, earthy-smelling road, with wet leaves of the jungle sparkling emerald in the sun, and lush green grass with flowers of almost every color thrusting their faces upward to be kissed by the breeze. There were bees—birds singing—monkeys leaping in dozens along the tree top lanes and shaking down showers of diamond raindrops—clouds of parrakeets screaming in sudden parabolas. The road—the road that reawakens all the primitive in man and makes him love the beast beneath him because the beast is nearer by a hundred eternities to the heart of nature and can send up true thrills to his rider from the rain-awakened earth.

Asoka led as if the doors of Noah's Ark had just been opened and all the other animals were following one by one to explore a brand new universe.

No sound escaped his restless ears, no scent of pollen or of young growth but his curious trunk detected it and passed the news along behind him to the others, that were noisy with pots and pans and yelling babies, shrill with the chatter of mahouts' lean womenfolk and shapeless with tents and stores and the mahouts' belongings. Quorn sat smoking on Asoka's neck, wet to the skin from the tree-drip, wondering at himself because he could not feel afraid or worried.

4

—

"DYING IN EXQUISITE PAIN"

PANCH MAHAL MEANS literally "playground of the ladies." So many centuries ago that no one knows his name, some ancient king had chosen that marvelous situation in the mountains of Narada for a palace where his private collection of feminine charm might be immured to enjoy his sublime society, without the impediment of heavy curtains on the windows.

Legend declares that the palace was a place of jasper ceiling and of design so perfect that the very gods themselves were jealous and destroyed it. There was nothing left when Quorn first saw it, but the excavated ruins of a limestone wall, some mounds of débris—and the view. Not even human vandalism could destroy that.

There was a view of mountains whose sunlit peaks, almost unclimbable, leaped toward a blue sky—of jungle as green as the jealousy the gods are said to have entertained—of rolling grass where *sambur, nilghai,* and black buck grazed—of falling water where Narada River plunges from a lake of hidden springs into a valley that snatches the breath and clutches the heart of the beholder, so intimate is it and yet so fathomlessly vast and filled with mystery.

The sound of cataracts comes echoing through pine

trees. Summits of chrome and red and purple rocks appear through opal mist that drapes itself in subtly changing form along the course of the winding river, which gleams like burnished silver where the mist breaks into fragments by a morning breeze.

It was no mean answer the young Ranee gave to the critics of old autocracy and of petticoat government, as her enemies called her steadfast devotion to decency and bright ideals. She was no believer in reducing all men and all methods to the lowest, that the low might praise old tyrannies with new names. Like the old cathedral builders, she believed in showing what aspiration can accomplish. She would build.

She would recreate that ancient palace, but without its idiotic purpose or its cruel battlemented prison wall. It should be a school; her own quarters were to be only one small part of it. She was determined she would teach ideals in a setting worthy of them, first gathering the teachers from all nations and from all the ends of earth, and thoroughly testing them before inflicting their stupidities on children.

Nothing of her visioned school was there yet, however, but in the camp of corrugated iron several hundred laborers waited to resume work in the quarries. It was they who showed Quorn the beginning of trouble to come.

"Build me shelters for my elephants," he ordered.

The foreman questioned Quorn's authority and Quorn had nothing to show in writing. However: "I'll have the shelters over yonder," Quorn said, pointing. "You begin in ten minutes or I'll set my four and thirty elephants to smashing your camp. I'll chase the lot of ye to the devil—

and let the Ranee get a new gang. If you don't believe me, jes' sit down for ten minutes and see."

So shelters were built—mere roof-and-pole affairs, protected against the prevailing night wind by a hillside, to make the elephants believe they were still civilized and not at liberty to wander where they pleased.

"WHAT'S EATING THIS outfit?" Quorn demanded, when the work was under way. He had a habit of translating American slang literally into Hindustani; and because slang is as often as not the simplest way of coming to the point, his astonishing idiom sometimes led him straight into the heart of information that a professional linguist might have hunted for in vain.

"We eat little, *sahib*. Presently the vultures will eat us," said the foreman. "No one dares to sell us victuals because the priests have said this work is sacrilege. They say we should let dead ruins lie and not build a palace where the gods have set their seal, saying, 'This is the last of man in this place.' Nor have we much left of the food we brought with us, because the dacoits took most of it, saying, 'Send to your Ranee for more—and lo, we will take that also!' So now we are gnawed by a yearning to go home. But if we do, we shall receive no wages and there will be no money with which to pay the taxes and the money-lender's interest. We are sad men."

"Where are your architects and your engineers?" Quorn asked.

"They have gone, *sahib*. They were afraid, and why not? These dacoits are Aos, who hunt heads. Their forbears lived in the hills of Assam, whence they were driven forth by the constabeels under British officers. They hunt heads, saying,

'He who takes a man's head has his victim for a servant in the after-life.' So our architect and his assistants ran, being educated men who do not wish to be the slaves of Aos in a life to come. But as for ourselves, it makes no difference whose slaves we are, in this life or another."

Quorn let the foreman lead him to a peak whence he could see the smoke from one of the villages that the dacoits had recently seized.

"And there, *sahib,* there are no men left alive, except the dacoits, who are not men, they are devils. However, the women carry wood and water for the Aos; and before long they will bear children to them, as a tame cat bears kittens to a wild one—and always those young are wilder than their sire. Thus there will be many dacoits in the days to come and may the gods take pity on our children."

"Anybody been around here lately?" Quorn asked.

"Nay, *sahib.* Who should come hither—at the risk of being filled with alcohol and red pepper? That is no death to be chosen. It burns worse than red-hot iron, but the burning is within, where water only adds to it, and the victim dies slowly."

Quorn turned on him suddenly. "You sucker! I'm mean, when a guy like you insults my intelligence! Do you suppose I'm fool enough to think you'd stay here if you didn't think it safe? You've had a talk with some one. Who is it?"

Quorn had agate eyes that almost hypnotized ignorant people with dread of his rumored intimacy with the gods. However, the foreman, though he shrank, would reveal no secrets. And experience had taught Quorn that succeeding direct questions, if the first one fails, only lead to lying answers that are more confusing than no information at all.

HE RETURNED TO his elephants, a little comforted by
Asoka's ponderous shadow, wherein he sat and smoked
his pipe until supper-time at sunset. He thought then that
even the elephants felt other-worldly, as the sun went down
amid the opal mists and all Narada River lay like molten
mystery, in silence.

When at last that crimson faded and the stars came
forth above the mist he had his cot carried out of the tent
and set beside Asoka's picket, where he ate his supper,
wondering whether he would see to-morrow's daylight.
There was death in the air. He could sense it; almost he
could smell it.

"I reckon a man gets like an animal from living close
among 'em," he reflected. "Elephants know when death is
sneaking up on 'em; I've observed that frequent. Wonder
why I hate the thought o' dying? I sure do, just the same."

Remembering the automatic pistol in his overcoat that
should be hanging from the ridge-pole of the tent he
knocked the ashes from his pipe and went to get it, walking first along the line of elephants to make sure they were
all securely fastened.

It was customary for the mahouts to wait, each man
beside his beast, until Quorn had made that routine
lantern-light inspection; thereafter they were free for the
night. By the time he reached his tent they were all huddled
up with their families in their own tents at the end of the
line, to all intents and purposes a mile away because the
din of conversation from the quarryworkers' camp outbid
all other sounds.

Some fool at the camp was tapping with a hammer on a

sheet of corrugated iron and two or three score were singing in time to it. The song, of course, was obscene.

As he entered the tent a cold hand touched him on the
neck and he shrank away from it with tingling skin. A sense
of horror almost froze him, paralyzing his natural instinct
to defend himself. A cold voice murmured into his ear, in
a language that he did not understand. He tried to shout.
He could not. He felt himself guided—shoved into the
canvas armchair. It was dark, but it grew suddenly darker;
he could see nothing but phantom spots of colored light
that were within his own eyes.

Suddenly a voice said: "Sit still," and he knew then that
there were two in the tent besides himself, although he
could not have told how he knew it. Nevertheless, he could
have sworn that the hand that had touched him and the
voice that now spoke were not of the same person.

It was several seconds before he realized that the last
voice had spoken English. When he did at last realize
it some of his self-command returned and he began to
wonder how to reach the automatic pistol without being
detected. Cautiously, little by little, he stretched both legs
and then his arms. They touched nothing.

Then he heard hands groping at the tent-cloth, as if they
were fastening something. At last a voice said "Ready"—
but that was in Hindustani, a language as unlikely as
English to be heard in those parts. He could sense some
sort of movement in the dark, although he could not hear
it, and his blood ran cold again. He sprang to his feet and
struck with all his might with both fists, but hit nothing.

A voice said "Make him sit." English again—a detestable voice, supercilious and bored by the owner's own arrogance.

He felt himself pulled by the neck from behind, not violently; the fingers of two cold hands touched the nerves of his back and he could no more resist than a hen in the hands of a hypnotist.

He sat down and stayed as if glued to the chair, until the fingers loosed their light hold; then he suddenly felt strong again, but good sense warned him to sit still and learn some facts before attempting any further action. It was so dark that he felt blind, and he noticed that the air was getting stuffy.

PRESENTLY A VOICE spoke from the farther corner of the tent, in English. It was the same hateful voice. It appeared to come from near the floor. He remembered there was a heap of blankets in that corner of the tent.

"You are Benjamin Quorn?" the voice asked. Then, after a long pause: "Make haste and answer me."

He knew then it was not a man's voice but a woman's, although again he could not have told how he knew it. A moment later he was conscious of a musky Eastern scent. He did not suspect that his nose had told him this truth in the first place. A man's senses are all far keener than his intelligence.

"It's none o' your damn' business who I am," he answered.

"Do you wish to continue to be Ben Quorn?"

"The likes o' you can't alter me, no matter who you are."

He felt a thin horse-hair noose about his neck. It tightened. Hands like the jaws of steel traps gripped his wrists.

"Do you wish to die? You shall be dead by sunrise, if you

wish? There is plenty of time between now and sunrise to learn all about pain. Do you wish that?"

"Who the devil are you? What do you want?" Quorn demanded.

"You would call me a witch. I am not one."

"What do you want? What are you doing in my tent?"

"I want, from Ben Quorn, certain services, for which I will pay."

"You can't buy me."

"You are already bought! You belong to the Ranee?"

"Damn you, I'm my own owner."

"That is fortunate—for you. Because, if you truly belonged to that unwise Ranee, who believes herself to be so clever, you would have to die with her. As it is, you may help her to live."

"I dunno who you are, but you're murdering swine!" Quorn answered. "Here's the first decent ruler Narada has had in about a thousand years, and there's half o' ye crazy to kill her! 'Cause why? 'Cause she's decent and you're that foul you can't abide decency! Half of ye are forever playing devils' tricks trying to prevent her from making her kingdom a proper place to live in. To the devil with you! Did you hear that? Did you understand it? To the devil with you!"

"Then you wish not to help her to live? She will die if you don't."

There followed silence so still that Quorn could hear the pulses drumming in his ears.

"You are the only person who can save her life," the voice resumed at last. "That is why you are to be allowed to live, if you are sensible. It would be so easy, Ben Quorn, to silence you and carry you away to die for the amusement of men and women who would be bored by the sight of any ordinary tortures."

"Huh! You want something that you can't get without my doing it. Well, I won't do it, whatever it is."

THE VOICE RESUMED—MEASURED, dull, unvibrant: "We could carry you off on the back of your favorite elephant."

Quorn was silent. He rather hoped they would do that. He would only have to give Asoka one hint that things weren't what they ought to be, and somebody would learn a lesson. But, whoever this woman might be, she knew Quorn.

"We could make a spectacle of you and your elephant dying in exquisite pain," said the voice.

The only time that Quorn had ever been in prison was for beating a man who ill-treated a dog. He would not have gone to prison then, only that he abused the police-court magistrate for refusing to fine and imprison the man he had thrashed. It made him savage even to think of an animal being tortured.

But anger had a way of calming him sometimes. He could pass in one spasm through sullenness into a mood in which an almost childlike air of stupid innocence concealed a deeper guile than anybody guessed.

He became ten times as dangerous as any serpent in the world, because a serpent strikes at random for its own sake and wastes venom, whereas Quorn, in that mood, used all his cunning to preserve himself, that he might strike the deadliest possible blow for his friends. But to see and to hear him he was only a weak man, ignorant and fearful.

"We-e-ell," he muttered, "what do you want? I'm sick of India. I want to go home."

"What is wanted is the Ranee. You can bring her to us."

"Me?"

"She is playing with deadly forces that will kill her unless some one interferes. Surrender her to me. She shall be married. She shall play her proper rôle as the wife of a great prince, to whom she may do her duty by bearing children. And as for that fool she is planning to marry—that penniless Prince Rana Raj Singh, whose castle on a hill-top has become a home of bats—you may surrender him to us, too. He shall be taught to stay in his own barnyard—taught so painfully that perhaps he may remember it the next time that he comes into the world. And when you have done your part, you shall be allowed to go home to America with money in your pocket."

"I sure am sick of India," said Quorn.

"How would a full pay pension suit you?"

"How would I know I'd get it?"

"A pension guaranteed by contract and indorsed by a very rich rajah—how would that be?"

"Which rajah? Them birds varies."

"Dumdumpore."

"Very well, I'll take his note for the full amount o' twenty-five years' pension, payable in annual installments, plus interest at eight per cent—value received writ plain on the face of it. And I'll have to have the note first, 'fore I'll do a thing."

"And you will deliver the Ranee to us?"

"Living." Quorn believed himself an expert at laconic answers that appeared on their face to commit him but left his conscience ample leeway. He was superstitious about wording a lie literally.

"You understand, of course, that if you fail us you will die very painfully and never again see the United States?"

"I know when I'm up against it."

"Stay in the tent until you hear a whistle—if you wish to live to see daylight."

"Aw—cut out threats," Quorn answered. "That kind o' talk don't cut no ice with me. You want from me what you can't get nohow else. I want a pension. I'm going to earn it."

Strange sounds began and presently it grew fractionally lighter; somebody was taking down a black sheet that had been draped inside the tent. However, it was still so dark that Quorn could only very dimly see two human shapes— then a third; he had not even guessed there were three in the tent. They vanished.

"Dumdumpore," he muttered. "Rich, eh? He's as poor as they tell me the Jew is in Aberdeen. But if he lives he'll pay that note, or me and my buddy Asoka don't know nothing. Huh! He thinks I'm a sucker. I say he's one. Reckon we'll know soon which of us is right."

5

"WHO SHALL DARE TO DEFY THEM?"

FAMILIARITY WITH GODS begets a sort of democratic insolence. Because of his agate eyes and his resemblance to the Gunga *sahib* pictured on the stone wall in Narada, not less than a million men and women regarded Quorn as some sort of minor deity. But that did not prevent their arguing with him or trying to play tricks on him, even though they made a mess outside his tent with offerings of flowers, and stuck sticky paint on his tent pole.

Even though they sometimes prayed to him—to his huge annoyance—they never hesitated to try to cheat him, so that in self-defense he had been forced to become observant, alert and drastic in his dealings with them.

As a special means of coaxing him to bless their scandalous intrigues with other people's wives or husbands, they sometimes even threatened to believe the scandal of the priests, who whispered calumnies about Quorn being no sort of god but a very mean human obsessed by a devil.

"Believe anything you like, you suckers, only don't blame me if I act up to your crazy beliefs," was his usual answer.

He had a theory that to carry weapons, as a rule, is a mistake. He kept the automatic in his overcoat chiefly to prevent ignorant villagers from praying to him outside his tent, the sides of which had many bullet holes. He had never yet hit any worshipers, but there had been some close squeaks.

That morning he almost hit the foreman. He had gone into the tent to shave himself before daybreak by lantern light, unaware that his shadow on the tent cloth took strange shapes as he scraped at his chin. The quarry laborers were hardly to be blamed for thinking he was making magic. They began to sing a sort of dirge to him, on their knees, outside the tent, and he fired a piratical shotted salute by way of acknowledgment.

"You heathen!"

He seized the heavy iron *ankus* and rushed out to break up the meeting.

"I'll change your religion for you damn quick! I'll use a Stillson on your consciences!"

But they were gone, because an angry god is nobody to trifle with. Only the foreman stood there, looking ruefully at a necklace made of beads on copper wire that he wore as a protection against unfaithfulness, his three wives being nearly a hundred miles away, in a tenement room in Narada City. A bullet had neatly cut the copper wire and there was one bead missing.

"Which wife is it?" the foreman asked, holding out the necklace for Quorn's inspection. Quorn snatched it and threw it away. However, good foremen are hard to get, and reasonably bad ones better than none at all, so Quorn did not brain him with the *ankus*. He grew suddenly calm.

"It's all three of 'em," he answered. "Get yourself another

batch. There'll be a stack of 'em to choose among, soon as them dacoits is settled with."

"Who shall dare to defy them, *sahib?*"

"You sucker, that's what I'm here for."

INSTANTLY HE WONDERED why he had said that and wished he had not said it. However, it was too late now to take it back; he tried to drive it out of the foreman's head by giving him something else to think about, bullying him to make him set the men to work in the quarry and then, the minute the chipping and hammering began, demanding an inspection of stores in the hope of finding shortages, for which he could worry the man out of his wits.

But everything was there except the food that the dacoits had taken; and at that, they had left about a week's supply for the hundreds of quarrymen. There was evidently some one in command of the dacoits who understood the art of living off a country, leaving enough to encourage production of more, in the same way that one leaves an egg in the nest of a laying hen. They had left the tools undisturbed too, so it was plain that they wished to encourage the quarrying.

"Why in heck didn't they take that dynamite?" Quorn demanded of the foreman.

"They did not know what it is, *sahib*. I told them it is sausages made from the blood of pigs in the United States. So they left that for us to eat, saying it is unclean and forbidden to such honorable people as themselves."

"What about them coils of fuse? What did they think they are?"

"I told them that it is rotten cord supplied by a cheating contractor. I explained we must send it back to be

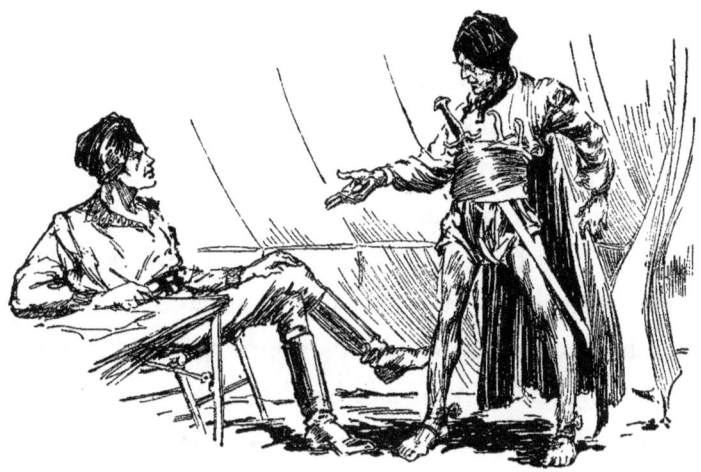

The dacoit chief held out the "magic" uncertainly

exchanged for stout, new cord. So they left that also, saying they will take the good cord when it comes."

Quorn returned to his tent to write a report of the situation for the Ranee and to ask her to send additional supplies of food. Writing was not his forte; it took him a long time, tearing up sheet after sheet of paper, inking his fingers and staining his turban when he stuck the pen behind his ear.

He was like a man making out an income tax report; it made him frantic; he found it next thing to impossible to condense his thoughts into any reasonable space or to arrange them in proper order. Several times he almost decided to tear up the report and to return on Asoka to say it all as a sensible man should, by word of mouth.

"But she'd think I was running away," he grumbled and resumed his writing.

It was afternoon, and the report not finished but beginning to resemble a coherent statement of the facts, when a party of dacoits came. Quorn, at his folding table inside the tent, observed their interest in the elephants. He smiled to himself as they gathered in front of Asoka.

"Maybe the suckers'll try to steal him," he muttered. "Let's hope. They'd find a red hot locomotive a heap easier."

They were all mounted on lean, tough-looking country ponies. Fifty of them, armed with assorted weapons, kept in something vaguely like a cavalry formation. Three had baskets filled with human heads, from which the blood was still oozing and forming a filthy plaster.

On foot in the midst of the party was a group of newly captured women, some with babies at the breast. They had finished their wailing; they were dumb with dread and nearly dropping with weariness; some were tied together by the wrists, but nearly all of them were too woebegone and spiritless to need more than a whip to keep them moving.

THE LEADER OF the party was a handsome ruffian armed with a naked sword, with a four-foot blade that he wore tucked into the cummerbund about his waist, which also held two daggers. His long black hair was coiled in a knot under a bright red turban. He rode without stirrups and had big spurs strapped to his bare heels.

His clothes looked as if they had been stolen from a wedding party—assorted sizes and colors, but every item new and hardly soiled, except where he had sweated through the striped silk shirt and where one sleeve was dyed dark crimson by the blood of some unfortunate.

In his own good time he rode to Quorn's tent, smiling, and dismounted by bringing up his right leg over the pony's neck.

"*Salaam,*" he said genially, hitting the pony on the rump

to make it move away. He came and leaned against the tent pole, peering in, appraising Quorn's belongings.

"What do you know about peace?" Quorn asked him. "*Salaam* ain't any word for a guy like you to use."

The dacoit did not understand. He signed to one of his followers, who rode forward to interpret. The leader tipped him off his horse and drove the horse away. They pranced for a minute or two, making mock lunges at each other with naked weapons, so that it appeared to Quorn their savagery was of the genial type—murder for mere amusement, without any special malice or hope of gain.

"You guys want to earn a dollar?" he asked, showing the one that he carried for luck. "Fight it out, then. I'll give this to the one that kills the other."

The leader snatched the coin, then asked what the talk was all about. The other told him. Quorn, grimly regretting his silver dollar, suddenly gave birth to an idea.

"Tell him," he said, "that's magic. Tell him, spit on it."

The outlaw spat voluminously, holding the coin in the palm of his hand, as far away as possible, and squirting an accurate stream between widely spaced teeth. Quorn made mysterious movements with his hands, closed his eyes and gabbled off two whole verses of the "Wreck of the Hesperus," the only poem he had ever learned by heart. He spoke too rapidly to be understood.

He paused, then turned to the interpreter. "Tell him he's all right now if he acts friendly and as long as he don't lose that piece o' silver. But if he loses it, swaps it, or throws it away—or if he does me any dirt—there'll come a devil in the night and gnaw his entrails. 'Twouldn't ha' worked if he hadn't took it from me. But he took it, so now he has to take the consequences. If I die afore he does, now, he'll be plumb up against it. Torture ain't nothing to what'll happen to him. But he's all right if he acts right by me."

The outlaw chief looked worried—naïvely credulous but resentful of being caught in such an unexpected trap. He grinned and scowled alternately, tossing the coin in the palm of his hand. At last he wrapped it in a corner of his loin cloth, along with all the earrings of the women he had captured, and walked away, taking the interpreter with him.

He went and stared again at Asoka, presently making his men round up several mahouts, whom he questioned arrogantly at first, then, little by little, with something almost suggesting courtesy. Quorn could not hear, but it was clear enough that the mahouts were trying to play safe by describing their chief as a master magician whom even gods obeyed.

THE OUTLAW RETURNED to Quorn's tent. For a minute or two he stood irresolute, as if he hated to feel beholden and yet did not dare to pass up opportunity. At last he touched the fold of his loin cloth in which the coin was tucked away and began shooting quick questions at the interpreter, visibly impatient with him when the man hesitated for the right word in English.

"This things is—how you say—good magic?"

"You bet."

"It—ah—it—protec' him?"

"Same as I told you already—perfect—one hundred per cent—unless he forgets hisself and loses it or takes a dirty dig at me."

"Good against any one?"

"Any one—anything—anywhere—rain or shine—day

or night. There ain't no kind o' predicament what that piece o' silver ain't minted to meet. Why, wi' ten o' those I've come free out of a judge's court, I have. With five of 'em I've stood off such hunger an' thirst as you've never imagined, let alone felt. With one like that—the very living spit o' that one—I've transported myself best part o' thirty miles without once setting feet on the ground. Magic? That's the marvelousest piece o' magic ever you seed."

"He is captain—yes—you understand me? He like be big man—how you say it? Sultan—yes?"

"I get you, su-u-ure." Quorn almost grinned. He only saved himself by looking at the basketful of human beads and at the group of abject women. "Wants to be boss, does he?"

"Ah, yes—that him—that word—how you say it?—boss, yes? Very big boss dacoit have not treat him much nice—understand me?"

"I get you. Say! You tell him a handsome guy like him ain't doing right if he goes taking orders from some one else. Tell him to look straight into my eyes." The bandit leader obeyed and flinched. Quorn's eyes were like a goat's, agate-yellow and mysterious.

"He's a born leader o' men," Quorn said. "He ain't doing his duty by hisself if he don't make hisself the boss dacoit over all of ye. That magic what he took from me 'd make a rajah of him if he'd act right. But he's got to have faith—use his wits and act crafty. And when the right time comes he'll have to hit hard wi' that snickersnee o' his."

"How soon he do it?"

"That depends," Quorn answered. "Let me look at the palms of his hands."

Knowing not even the vaguest rudiments of palmistry, Quorn was in no way hampered by tradition or that little knowledge that so handicaps the licensed wise men of the world. He scowled over the hands, followed the lines of the palms with the point of his pen, nodded, muttered to himself and at last pronounced his verdict.

"Keerful—keerful! He mus' first make sure he has a sizable good share o' men to back him up. Then smite sudden and without no warning. See? See here—ye see that split in the line o' life—ye see that? Any sucker knows what that means. That's where he splits the gang in halves. He does it surreptitious—see that curlicue? Then see here—see that new line coming in? That's where he cops the leadership. And soon, too. It won't be long now."

"THIS MAGIC—THIS GOOD only against mans?" asked the interpreter.

Again Quorn's wits saw daylight. "I should say not! Look here—look at this guy's lump o' Venus! Holy mackerel! Why, there ain't a woman living as can resist him—not with that there magic in his jeans. It's jes' the sort o' magic as the women fall for readiest. And there's no woman—"

He paused. A fortune teller is entitled to be told a thing or two.

"What if she has bigger magic?" the interpreter asked.

"There ain't none stronger. There's some that maybe *looks* bigger. But what he has there is one hundred cents to the dollar—you get my meaning? There ain't nothing in the world to equal it, exceptin' more o' the same kind. Howsomiver, there is several sorts o' women."

There was a whispered conference between the leader and the interpreter. Then:

"What if her name was Usha? Would that make any difference?"

Nothing made any difference to Quorn in that mood, but he suspected that this might be the name of the woman who had trapped him in his own tent. He proposed to find out.

"It might make a heap o' difference," he answered. "Let me see your hand again—the right one. Now—if she had dealings with a rajah, I should say," and he looked into the outlaw's eyes, "you'd better watch your step and come to me for good advice afore you act too definite. But if she'd had no truck with any rajah, then—"

"She is a rajah's spy," said the interpreter. "She is a rajah's dancing woman—"

"Yes," said Quorn, "I see she's that. You see this mark here on his lump o' Venus—all higgledy-piggledy? That's what that means."

"She is treacherous, and very clever, and most desirable. Her eye's are as a heifer's and her breasts are as ivory aged in oil of sandalwood. Her thighs are—"

"I should say he'd have to watch his step," Quorn interrupted. "My advice is, let him come to me and talk things over 'fore he takes a long chance. Maybe I might think up some more magic. What's this guy's name?"

"Narak."

"I'll remember it. I'll study out the proper sort o' magic for a name o' that exac' length. And you say the woman's name is Usha? I'll consider that, too. Run the two together and we get Narakusha, don't we? Well, that looks simple enough, but i'll have to study it. You see, that magic what he took from me works two ways. It obliges me to do him favors. I'd have bad luck if I didn't. Tell him he should come and see me rather frequent. And he'd better come by night, so's nobody won't know.

"And one more point—them women. No, I don't care for one jes' now. I don't want no women, they're a nuisance. But if this guy wants a lot o' good luck, seeing he has that magic on him, he must treat those women special extry gentle. You see, he had the women with him when he met me. Otherwise, I'd say treat 'em anyhow, and I don't doubt he'd do it. As it is, he'll play safe if he treats 'em kind. So long, then. Tell him to come soon, by night, and talk things over."

6

"SO YOU, TOO, HAVE BEEN PAID TO TALK ABOUT DACOITS?"

BLOOD HAD DRIPPED on the ground from the baskets of heads; Quorn ordered it cleaned up. Then he wondered again what made the quarrymen, and even his own mahouts, so fearless in the neighborhood of a camp of dacoits who did not hesitate to murder for mere amusement.

Quorn had plenty of time for meditation; there would be no work for the elephants until a lot more stone was quarried; it was evident enough that the Ranee had sent him there to cope with something very different from hauling stone.

"But I do wish she'd explain more to a feller," he regretted. He had a habit of soliloquizing with his head between his hands and elbows resting on his knees. "She believes in these here gods, but I don't. Die an' come to life again, eh? Dying is easy hereabouts. But the nearest I ever came to a resurrection was after I got drunk that las' time and Asoka pulled me out o' the river. Well, I'll say this: she's a good sport. Me and her has played many a game. I never knowed her not to rig the deck against a crooked dealer. She's the smartest, four-flushingest, squarest-acting bluffer I ever see. And she don't neglect her friends. Here's hoping."

So he helped himself to rye whisky and gave Asoka some, pretending to himself that the chill mountain air might otherwise give his favorite pneumonia. But the truth was, no man ever loved a dog more thoroughly than Quorn did that enormous beast, and he liked to share good liquor with him. He was even slightly jealous of the other elephants because most of them were better behaved than Asoka and received more gifts of sugar and sticky sweet-meats from people who came to look at them on fête days and holidays. He took another drink. Between them he and Asoka finished a quart of the stuff, and hope's barometer rose several degrees.

And then came the *babu* Bamjee, wonderful to see in European riding breeches and a big sun helmet that made him look like a trained monkey on horseback. The Ranee's guileful purchasing agent was riding a big gray mule that happened to be Asoka's special stable crony. The mule pitched Bamjee over his head and, after trying to kick the saddle off, strolled away to help himself to supper from Asoka's pile of hay—the only creature in the world that would have dared to do it. Quorn helped the plump *babu* to his feet and straightened out the helmet with his knee.

"Serves you right, you sucker," he remarked. "You ought to buy your own mule 'stead o' grafting off the Ranee's stables. A guy who grafts all the money you do ain't acting honest trying to save horse-hire. What's up?"

"She is. Up on a camel. Mrs. Galway."

"Who the deuce—"

"The literary lady in the green-rimmed spectacles, whose

dog Asoka slew—whom the Ranee refused to receive at the palace—whom the gods have made mad enough to write books—whom I personally guide at cut rates—cut rates, Mr. Quorn, believe me—to see India as is. Am sadly disillusioned babu; very. She is adamantine. Cash is the blood of her veins and it flows not forth. She knows price of everything, including the fact that the camel is out of the Ranee's stable; therefore she will not pay for same.

"First I tried to put her in a bullock-cart, believing she would not see quite so much, because a bullock-cart has canvas cover. But at the last minute she demanded a camel, from whose cursed hump she watches me like a vulture, overhearing too much.

"Fortunately she is camel-sick. She has spilled scent over the animal to make him smell less awful. And she is so stiff that she shrieks when she tries to gesticulate. She has to stop for rest at frequent intervals, so she may not be here for two hours."

QUORN GRUNTED. "AFTER dark, eh? Well, what of it?"

"Nothing—nothing of it. I am disillusioned, that is all. I had a dream of a great tourist enterprise that should grow from this small beginning. But when I spoke of it to her, she exclaimed she will write in her forthcoming book that tourists should stay away from India."

"Suits me," said Quorn. "I've druv too many o' them suckers in my taxi back home. Ought to be a law ag'in' 'em. Come to think of it, there is a law ag'in' 'em in Narada. She's out o' bounds, that's what she is."

"She says India is full of liars and unclean people, Mr. Quorn. She says that the natives who ride on elephants habitually butcher small dogs, presumably because the dogs are cleaner than themselves. She says there are no dacoits, but that we pretend there are because we hope by that expedient to cover up misgovernment of native States."

"And what was it she called the Ranee?"

"An anachronism, Mr. Quorn."

"She's a bad fare, that's what she is," Quorn said grimly. "What's the other news?"

"There is plenty. The Ranee has said to the priests that you undoubtedly will die and come to life again. So the priests are telling all the people you are already dead—or if not dead, as good as that—because you are a fraud and an impostor whom the gods will no longer permit to frolic on your vicious elephant at the risk of honest people's lives.

"There is a rumor, circulated also by the priests, that the Ranee is to lose her throne because Narada is to be divided into two, and one part added to the Rajah of Dumdumpore's dominions, one part to the dominions of the Rajah of Hathiabad, who, however, is a very decrepit person and does not wish it, so that the Rajah of Dumdumpore may perhaps get all of Narada.

"People are very excited. They are saying that the dacoits are a menace. There is talk of a petition to the British government. It is said that the dacoits have destroyed six villages and have slain upward of a thousand men. It is being said that the Ranee intends to build a palace here, most sacrilegiously upon the ruins of a building that the gods once cursed, because she intends to make use of the dacoits to enforce her power in defiance of higher authority."

"And you bring that there Mrs. Galway into such a mess

as this, to write her booke about it?" Quorn asked. "Ain't you sort o' nervy, for once?"

"*Sahib*, I would not have dared to do it, only we have an escort. No, not of police—not of the Ranee's soldiers."

"Good-job. Them guys 'ud get strung up by the dacoits quicker than butchers wring chickens' necks. Who is the escort then?"

"Prince Rana Raj Singh follows us, at a discreet distance, with four-and-twenty of his Rajput relatives, all mounted, and a train of mules with all their camp equipment. He appears to have come ready for a long stay. So, although there is a gap of at least a quarter of a mile between our parties, it may appear to the dacoits that we are a rather large armed column and I think they will let us alone."

"DOES MRS. GALWAY know who it is who is following her?" Quorn asked.

"No, *sahib*."

"Didn't she ask?"

"She has asked everything. If all the questions she has asked were printed they would fill a hundred books. So, since she proposes to write a book, I told her the prince and his party are bachelors riding in quest of virgins less than ten years old, whom they will seize and marry, such being our quaint custom."

"Why did you tell her that?"

"Because she likes to learn that sort of lie, *sahib*. And if she writes that in her book it may be people will understand she is a venomous liar. Then, perhaps, they will also disbelieve such few truths as she tells by accident. There are some truths, even about you and me, that we would not wish to be believed about us."

"Uh-huh. When's the Ranee coming?"

"I don't know, *sahib*. This *babu* has not her confidence."

"You won't have mine, you sucker, unless you come clean. You've had a talk with her. You've had a talk with Rana Raj Singh. And you'd never have dared to come here if they hadn't told you something special. Tell me—or I'll put the lid on this here one-hen tourist agency so quick you'll never guess what happened!"

"Mr. Quorn, be reasonable!"

"I'm the reasonablest guy that ever acted crazy for the sake of a sweet woman. Now—you tell me, or I'll put you on that there mule and send you to the dacoits along with my orders in writing that they must get off the lot. What they'll do to you won't bear thinking of."

"You know as well as I do, Mr. Quorn, that such personages as our Ranee and Prince Rana Raj Singh talk in subtleties. They say nothing that might be turned and used against them."

"Should I whack you with an *ankus?* Is that subtle?" Quorn asked. "What did they say to you?"

"Nothing—except that, unless I take great care, the dacoits may believe that Mrs. Galway is the Ranee. *She* said: 'Does she wear a veil against mosquitoes, Bamjee?' So I have told Mrs. Galway that our mosquitoes are very venomous, and I provided her with a long green veil. And *he* said: 'If it were thought she is the Ranee, rumor might travel ahead of her; do you know any way of stopping such a rumor, Bamjee?' So I think there have been rumors."

"Mebbe. Does Mrs. Golliwog look like any one on camel-back?"

"Most imperious, *sahib*. And she wields a silk umbrella

against the sun. Too tall by many inches to deceive any one, even at a distance, who really knows the Ranee. Nevertheless, to an ignorant stranger possibly convincing. Yellow dress and green umbrella—long green veil—she might indeed be any one.

"Her manner, when she is not being camel-sick, is arrogant, as if she despises all and sundry—as indeed she does. Furthermore, the ox carts follow, containing many tents and what not else, since she demands her privacy, being fearful lest prying eyes should behold her nakedness—which may mean she is chaste, although I doubt it. I believe that to her a woman is a secret sin in petticoats at war with all mankind."

"I've met 'em—lots of 'em," said Quorn. "They generally cuss you for driving too fast. Then they cuss you for missing the train. If they tip you, it's a nickel. After that they report you to the cops because the cab ain't clean. And if they lose anything, which they almost always does, they swear they left it in the cab and they have you pinched for not reporting it. When they find the thing afterward somewheres else, they don't apologize. I know 'em."

"SHE IS LOOKING for a husband, I believe," said Bamjee.

"What makes you suppose that?"

"She looks furtively, with the corner of her eye, at every handsome man of whatever race. But if he looks straight at her she is offended."

"Are them the symptoms?"

"Yes, *sahib*, because if a man looks not at all she is offended also."

"Ain't she ever pleased—not nohow?"

"Only when a man looks at her sideways. Then she is

either pleased or else she thinks he means to steal her purse."

"Steady," said Quorn. "I see her coming."

Her arrival was even more immodest than Bamjee had suggested that it might be. She was camel-sick and tired, so she had fussed until a mattress was spread in a cart to her liking and on that she lay, as assertive as a toothache.

Nothing escaped her acrid comments. If a driver hit his bullock, or if a bullock moved too slowly, she remarked on it in a voice that was penetrating and exasperating without rising more than half a note, but the half note was flat and numbing to the finer instincts of its audience. It irritated, wearied and left nothing pleasant to consider in the moments between one sarcastic comment and the next.

She greeted Bamjee with a curt laugh as he stood with his back to the setting sun and bowed to her through the canvas curtains at the rear of the cart.

"My good man, if you expect to conduct a tourist agency you will have to learn manners, at least. The idea of your running off and leaving me! I have ceased to expect ordinary honesty; the mere fact that you are being paid to look out for my comfort means nothing, of course. But don't gentlemen wait on ladies in this country? Are women mere beasts of burden? I assure you I am not of that kind."

Bamjee almost physically ducked to let his shoulders shed the flow of words. He was beginning to learn to endure without retort. She sat up and rolled one curtain back.

"Dark already—and no lanterns? Trying to save kerosene? Where do you propose to set my tent? Why aren't the coolies pitching it? How is the cook to prepare my supper?"

Bamjee indicated where her camp should be pitched. She differed. When the coolies at last had pitched the tent on the spot she chose she demanded to be told which way the night wind would blow. Bamjee told her. Promptly she ordered the tent taken down and repitched with its back to the wind. Then questions:

"Whose are those elephants? Who are those men in the sheds over there? Are you sure they haven't plague? Is it safe to camp so close to them? Where will you draw the water? Has it not been fouled by all those men with their unsanitary habits? The idea of braiding a palace in a place like this—and with so much that really cried out loud to be done with all that money! Who was that man I saw you talking to?"

"Mr. Quorn," said Bamjee.

"That's a strange name for a native."

"He is an American, *memsahib.*"

"An American! Nonsense. Then why does he wear a turban?"

Bamjee almost lost his self-control. He dropped the title of respect but managed to keep his voice in hand: "He believes it comfortable."

"Likes to see himself dressed up, I suppose you mean. Ask him to come and speak to me."

QUORN STROLLED OVER. "Hey, you—light that lantern for the lady." He handed the lighted lantern through the curtains. "Like to be a cool night. Better wrap up," he said politely.

"I am told your name is Quorn. Who are you?"

"Superintendent of elephants."

"Oh! Are you not the man who rode that monster that destroyed my dog?"

"I am, miss. Thet there dog come mighty near to killing me, a barking at my elephant and making him act crazy. There ain't no four wheel brakes on an elephant and that one's hard to manage at the best o' times."

"Then he ought not to be allowed in the streets. You say he is your elephant? Then I shall sue you for the value of my dog."

"No, miss, he's the Ranee's elephant. He come near busting up her palace after he was through with your dog."

"Then I will sue the Ranee," she said implacably. "I suppose there are law courts in India?"

"All kinds, miss. Have you any kind o' permit from a court or a commissioner, or from the Ranee, giving you leave to visit these parts?"

"I don't need anything of the kind. I have a passport."

"That don't cut no ice. You're out o' bounds."

"My dear man, I have as much right to be here as you have. More, I dare say, if the truth were known. You look like a dissolute person to me. Are you a drunkard? What right have you to question me?"

"I ain't interested to know nothing about you, miss," said Quorn. "But I'm in charge o' this camp. I'm responsible. There's dacoits not many miles away."

Her laugh was flat and nasty—superior, incredulous and rude.

"Oh! So you, too, have been paid to talk about dacoits? I suppose in order to prevent timid people from coming to see for themselves what misgovernment means? Or is it one of the horrors that strong drink makes you imagine? Well, I am not timid.

"Let me tell you this: I wrote to your Ranee, from that despicable *dak*-bungalow that is all the accommodation this uncivilized State provides for strangers. I suggested, very politely, I would like to call on her. As a matter of fact, I was intending to ask for her formal permission to travel all over the State. She did not have the courtesy to answer. She sent some flowers and a basket of fruit by the hand of a person who knew no English. And when I walked to the palace gate I was not admitted. So much for your Ranee! I intend to sue her for the value of my dog—even if I have to write to Washington about it."

"Would you care to see some dacoits?" Quorn suggested slyly.

"Certainly, if they were real."

"You shall," he promised.

CONTENTED, HE TURNED on his heel and went to put his elephants to bed, sitting smoking his pipe beside Asoka for a long time, watching him flick little finicky wisps of hay into his mouth; and Quorn talked to him, as he sometimes did when a turn of events seemed satisfying.

" 'Tain't often, buddy, that a fare like that one ups and asks for just what's coming to her. Mebbe our little Ranee ain't a wise one—mebbe! But what her game is this time, durned if I see! Wished you could talk, you fathead. Hello—here comes the Rana Raj Singh."

The Rajput prince had pitched his camp a mile away and came now riding a spare pony with an overcoat collar turned up to his ears. Quorn was always careful not to seem obsequious, but his manners toward a gentleman of courage and royal birth were a part of his own inherent dignity, so he got to his feet and took a stride or two toward his visitor, who drew rein. They shook hands in silence.

"Any news?" the Rajput asked when he had lighted a cigarette. The glow of the match betrayed his steady brown eyes and the aristocratic, rather stern face framed by a black beard.

Quorn told him all that had happened. "And now that female, she's here."

Quorn lit his pipe. By the match for a moment each could see the other's eyes.

"She is taking chances," Rana Raj Singh remarked. Quorn nodded.

"She don't believe in dacoits, sir. She allows 'at I'm a liar. Says she'd like to see 'em."

The prince drew at his cigarette until it almost blazed; then he suddenly threw it away. "Do you think that Dumdumpore might marry her, if he should catch her instead of—?"

"'Twould serve him good and right," said Quorn, "though yellow dogs like him ain't so easy to do justice to. Holy mackerel!"

"You understand me?"

"I get you, sir! When?"

"When occasion serves," said Rana Raj Singh. "But remember." He lighted a fresh cigarette and held the lighted match between his hands so long that he almost burned his fingers. He was one of those men who prefer to be seen distinctly when they speak of grave import. "Dumdumpore is the enemy. He has all to gain and we have all to lose. Therefore it behooves us to accept the long odds and take desperate chances. Take this."

He handed Quorn a folded document.

"That is your authority to arrest and detain Mrs. Galway if, as or when you think that necessary, either for her own protection or because she has no permit to wander at large in Narada.

"Bamjee is guilty of conspiring to break the law, by guiding her, well knowing that she has no permit. You may arrest him if you find that necessary in order to compel him to obey you. Bamjee is a useful little person, but he now and then needs reminding to whom he owes allegiance. Don't lose that document. Don't show it unless you must. Rather than let it fall into the hands of, say, the British authorities, destroy it."

"You bet."

"Because the Ranee might be criticized for having signed it."

"Right." Quorn nodded.

"WE UNDERSTAND EACH other," said the Rajput prince. "If by any chance this Mrs. Galway, through her own misuse of stolen privilege, should be mistaken for the Ranee and should fall into the dacoits' hands, it would be well not to let her true identity become too soon known— to Dumdumpore, for instance. You will find that I have dropped a package in the shadow near your tent. Make use of the contents."

"Yes, sir."

"I approve your strategy of dividing the dacoits by encouraging this man Narak to conspire against his chief. Continue that by all means."

"Means look sort o' skeerce."

"I had thought of that. So had the Ranee. Your reputation as a maker of miracles needs suitable building up, of course. I brought a box with me that I will send to your tent. Its contents are not profoundly magical, but they may serve your purposes; you will find a pamphlet of directions. And remember: these dacoits are very simple."

"Yes, sir."

"That woman Usha is not simple minded. She has been in the United States and England, touring with a one-act play. She has posed as a gypsy, among other things, and as a teacher of occult arts, and she understands a lot about deceiving idiots.

"She is the brains of the Rajah of Dumdumpore, who is obsessed by a belief that she can make him very rich and famous. He does what she tells him to do. It was she who put him up to bribing all these dacoits to invade our territory. The fool has followed her because he can't endure to be far away from her and he is somewhere in the neighborhood.

"The rajah's plan, of course, is to capture the Ranee and force her to agree to marry him, afterward absorbing all her territory with the consent of the Indian government, which he expects to be granted on the ground that there is no other way of ridding the country of these dacoits, whom he bribed to come here. Do you understand that?"

"Yes, sir."

"And you know that, including my twenty-four Rajputs, we have only seventy-five men, of whom thirty or forty are needed as palace guards?"

"Yes, sir."

"Then use your luck and every faculty you have. You may depend on me to keep in touch with you and to do my part. But remember: I have no legal authority. I am merely a prince without a kingdom. I have less authority than you have. Good night."

7

"I'M ACTING ON A BRIGHT IDEE"

THE PACKAGE LEFT near Quorn's tent contained clothing from the Ranee's wardrobe. It was faintly scented with the subtle perfume that she always used. Quorn examined it thoughtfully, smoked a pipe or two and sent at last for Bamjee.

"You're in bad," Quorn remarked by way of suspicious beginning.

"*Sahib*, I am always in bad. This *babu* is wealthy in Hope that springs eternal only to be bitten by the frost of bad luck. Am reduced to acting manager for this she-devil Mrs. Galway, who is seeing to it that my profit shall be in red ink, on the wrong side of the ledger. Ah me!"

"Care to see the inside o' the hoosegow?" Quorn asked.

"I would like to see the inside of almost anything. Am outside looker-on at profitable matters. What is a hoosegow?"

"Clink—chokee—coop—calaboose—jail—lock-up—dungeon—Royal Hotel Sheriff *à la* Ball and Chain. I have a paper here that bids me send you back in irons to Narada."

"What for?"

"Felony. High treason. Aiding and abetting an alien spy. Traipsing about the country with a female known by

you to be in quest of official secret information. Defense o'
the Realm Act. Minimum sentence ten years, and a fine o'
twenty thousand rupees. Want it?"

"*Sahib!* Are you joking? No? This is calamity! I have a
wife and children. Besides, I am innocent. I never knew
she—"

"Good job me and you is friends."

"Ah!" Bamjee sighed deeply. "*Sahib,* I have ever been true
to your heart's friendship. Not once have I ever neglected
one opportunity to do you a favor."

"No? Sa-a-ay, if I weren't a tolerant guy with understanding o' your weaknesses you'd ha' cheated me out o' my
eye-teeth long ago. And you'd ha' cheated the Ranee out o'
more money than 'u'd run the State, plus interest. So can
that line o' hooey."

"*Sahib,* I am struck dumb."

"Suits me. Dumb guys ain't obliged to be deaf—so you
listen. That there Mrs. Galway now—where does she keep
her wardrobe?"

"In her tent, *sahib.* Nightly she makes her servant unpack
two trunks and hang everything to take out creases."

"Good. Is she in bed now? What sort o' kit does she
sleep in?"

"God knows. Not even her servant has seen her asleep.
She keeps a screen beside the bed."

"You get a good blanket and keep it handy. Then you go
an' tell your camp crew that they know a dacoit when they
see one. Get me? No mistakes now—nobody goes and
recognizes my mahouts and gives the game away. Where
does she keep her money?"

"I believe beneath the pillow, *sahib.*"

"Well, you'd better grab that, so's to hand it back to her and get some sort o' credit for yourself. You'll need credit—bad. There ain't a moon yet. 'Fore it rises there's going to be a rush o' howling dacoits—and a elephant—which nobody don't recognize that elephant or your name won't be Bamjee, it'll be convict number umpty-um."

"SAHIB, WOULD A smaller elephant not do? Asoka is so difficult not to recognize."

"You manage your end and leave me to manage mine," Quorn answered. "Get this: she'll run. She'll run promiscuous, and you after her wi' that there blanket. She'll pro'bly fancy you're another dacoit, so she'll run like the devil. Don't catch her too soon. Give us time to get away with all her clothes and hide 'em. Then you cover up her shame and let her be a modest female—get me? Nex' you bring her back to where the tent was, though there likely won't be much tent, time Asoka's through with it. You help her hunt for her belongings, and you give her the money. Mind you now, you give her that money—all of it."

"Do you suggest I am a thief?" asked Bamjee, groping for shreds of dignity.

"I ain't suggesting nothing, excep' this: if she counts her money and some's missing, you make good. You get that? Time she's finished tossing off a few hysterics she'll begin to wonder how she'll look by daylight in a blanket and a flannel shift or whatever she sleeps in. Maybe then she'll throw another fit or two.

"You tell her I sometimes bring along the Ranee's trunk when she goes on a tour o' the country, so's the Ranee 'll have a change o' clothing if she travels too fast for her crew.

You say, it may be I might open up the Ranee's trunk if I was asked. Get that?"

"But, *sahib*, she is a she-devil. What if she does not run? She is likely to fight Asoka with her silk umbrella."

"All right. Better tell off two or three men to 'tend to it that she runs. Let 'em give her the bum's rush—nothing rough, you understand, but plumb persuasive."

"When is this to happen?"

"Quick and snappy. Get a move on now, afore the moon rises and spoils the circus."

Quorn's mahouts were breathless when he told them to take part in a deception. They were so used to his detecting and punishing their own constant attempts to get away with everything from theft to mayhem that a so-to-speak request performance stirred in them almost too much lawless zeal.

They armed themselves with sticks and bits of corrugated iron for making godless noises, pulled off their turbans and let their long hair straggle, offered countless idiotic suggestions of how to stage the show more horribly, made altogether too many torches of rags on sticks soaked in expensive kerosene, and at last submitted to being told exactly what to do.

The first thing they were made to do was to fasten all the elephants securely, with chains on both hind feet, because the noise was likely to send the whole long line into a panic.

Then there was the camp of quarrymen to be considered. Quorn sent for the foreman and told him to keep his men inside the long iron shed. But that was not enough; one foreman and a few assistants might not be able to control so many.

"Tell 'em the dacoits are coming to capture me. Say the magic what I'll make might send more than dacoits to Hades. Bid 'em lie still."

THAT WAS BETTER, but it might stir curiosity. One needs not be a quarryman in order to wish to see dacoits sent by magical means to the lower regions where they belong. Quorn wanted the absolute minimum number of witnesses; it was bad enough to have to trust mahouts to give no names away. So he sent his own cook with a message to Rana Raj Singh, inviting him to come galloping up with his Rajputs in order to keep the quarrymen within their iron walls.

"Tell him I'm acting on a bright idee and say I'm counting on him to do exac'ly what I ask."

Then he loosed Asoka, mounted him and waited until he heard the distant drum-beat of the hoofs of Rana Raj Singh's horsemen.

"Holy mackerel! If India had fifty men like him, that one and the Ranee 'u'd be the emperor and empress! Me, I'd get myself a harem and be a twenty-one gun rajah… Now, boys—soon as you hear me yell, you cut loose like a lot o' hell-cats."

When he did yell his voice nearly cracked. He remembered the little red schoolhouse days in Pennsylvania, when he and the rest of them played Indian and hookey, burning a farmer's hayrick and doing so much glorious mischief that the punishment afterward made them all feel like heroes.

Memory reproduced the old sensation. It conveyed itself by subtle processes along the nerves of Quorn's legs to the much more sensitive nerves behind Asoka's ears. The elephant became aware of mischief that would please his master and the long trunk straightened itself, sampling the air, before it curled up out of harm's way.

The timing and the din were perfect. Half a dozen whirling torches broke the black night into bewildering shadow. All the elephants except Asoka became frantic and screamed as they tugged at their doubled chains. Two mahouts, left for that purpose, all the mahouts' wives, and all their naked children rushed up and down the long line, shouting and commanding.

Quorn's men yelled their heads off, beating on their scraps of iron and prancing like idiots. Rana Raj Singh's horsemen, making no other sound than the hoof-beats, came on through the darkness like an avalanche of ghosts. The torches led the way; by their light and the bobbing and swaying of Bamjee's lantern Quorn saw some one in a long white shroud go fluttering between two men into abysmal night.

"Soak it to her good!" he ordered. "Smash that tent, you big bum!"

There was nothing in the whole world easier than to set Asoka smashing things. The difficulty was to stop him. Down went the tent in a bedlam of splintering poles. Crash went Asoka's forefoot through an open wardrobe trunk; it shut on his foot like a trap and offended him; he stamped it into pulp. Then the bed with its incomprehensible tangle of springs and folding framework angered him; he knelt on it, knew by its dying twang that it was something sinful, and abolished it with awful thoroughness, flinging the offending mattress sky-high and then hurling fragments of the frame to right and left.

That settled, he became aware of ox-carts standing with them poles in air; he shook the poles and the ox-carts came to pieces. He saw Bamjee's tent and flattened that. He broke and utterly abolished all the belongings and all the tents of Mrs. Galway's horde of servants.

Then he sought fresh fields to conquer; it was not often that Quorn encouraged him to break things; he would make the best of the unexpected picnic.

But the heavy *ankus* in Quorn's right hand steadied the monster at last. There was too much noise—altogether too much shouting near the elephant lines—too many torches. Quorn heard the sound of many more than two score horsemen. Through the clamor and din he could hear the thwack of sabers; he saw the dancing torchlight flash on steel—and suddenly he heard the voice of Rana Raj Singh rallying his men.

"DACOITS!" QUORN GASPED. "Holy mackerel! Them suckers come to pinch my elephant, I'll bet a year's pay! Steady, lad—steady—no use running thirty ways to come—steady, you ijjit!—gimme a chance to see what's doing—stan' still, durn you!"

Then the moon came up from behind a mountain, like a luminous amber lozenge on a blue enamel wall, suffusing half the camp in yellow light. Quorn on Asoka was still in shadow.

He could see a big party of dacoits, mounted on terrified ponies, gathering to resist a charge by Rana Raj Singh's men, who were only shadows forming in a solid phalanx somewhere near the place where Mrs. Galway's tent had stood. There was a line where the moonlight left off—all gloom on the hither side of it, all glow beyond.

Quorn edged Asoka toward that borderland. Then he heard what might have been a bugle note, but it was Rana Raj Singh challenging his Rajputs to charge into thrice their number.

"Now for your college yell, buddy! Us is the guns as saves this here picnic!"

Simultaneously, Rana Raj Singh and his horsemen, and Quorn on Asoka—two converging terrors—shot forth from the shadow straight at the heart of the rallying dacoit gang. Asoka's blood-palsying scream so scared the horses that even the Rajputs checked, and there was a low-voiced, cursing jingle-and-stab of spurs, clatter of colliding scabbards, kicking, plunging. Then forward, Asoka leading now by fifteen paces and moving like a five-ton cannon ball.

The dacoits ran. They melted like the sparks from a fire that vanish in the night, scattering in search of deeper darkness until they and night were one. But not all escaped.

Rana Raj Singh and his men cut down a dozen of them with the old-style saber-stroke that splits a fugitive from crown to chin and leaves the saber clear for more work, as a thrust seldom does. And Asoka overtook a fleeing horse, who swerved as his wild eye saw the straining trunk lick out of darkness, and spilled his rider.

The rider just missed being trampled on; he rolled and then crawled behind a rock, where a Rajput skewered him through the neck, as one splits tent-pegs at a tournament.

It took time to restore Asoka's mood to one of calm, superior dignity. He wanted to pursue. The fever of his strength was in him. By the time he was under control the Rajputs had gathered the dead and wounded, including two of their own men seriously hurt by knife-thrusts.

Rana Raj Singh was examining them, as best he could by lamp-light.

There were eleven dacoits slain and three so badly wounded that their death seemed certain. One other was badly hurt and groaning, but likely to recover. Between groans he could give an account of himself and there were two Rajputs putting him to question; in the darkness none but he could tell whether or not they added to his pain at intervals to make him talkative, but between groans his answers came in a hurry.

RANA RAJ SINGH looked up from examining his wounded men and his teeth flashed white in the lantern light as he grinned at Quorn.

"Any antiseptic in your tent? Good. I will find it. You had better go looking for beauty in distress. Was this just luck, or did you know dacoits were coming?"

"'Tweren't luck," said Quorn, "it was just my ignorance. Hark! That'll be my prohibition sweetheart singin' for a shot o' water!"

Agonized yells for help in a high-pitched feminine voice were repeated rapidly from several hundred yards away. They sounded much too angry to be symptoms of genuine danger.

"Would you pass me a bottle o' hooch, sir, out o' the lock-box by Asoka's stall? Here's the key—can you catch it? Thank you—either sort will do—rye or Scotch, it's all one. Yeh, I can get the cork out. Me and my Bucephalus will now ride forth and rescue the fire-breathin' virgin. If you could pull your freight, sir, 'fore we come along, you'll miss a funny scene, I don't doubt, but it might be tactics not to be here."

"What is she wearing?"

"Dunno, sir. Here's hoping. Cheerio, and thank you for the help. Come on, Asoka, head for that there noise o' nightingales."

8

"YOUR CLOTHES IS GONE. THE DACOITS TOOK 'EM"

IT WAS NO time to depend on Bamjee. The *babu* was petri-fied—utterly useless—numbed by the dynamic novelty of Mrs. Galway in her night attire. He and his two men sat in awe and contemplated her by the light of a hurricane lantern, in a deep depression behind a rock that hove its bulk against the rising moon and made ponderous shadow. Having nagged them into uselessness, she used her tongue now to bring other victims on the scene.

"Help! Help!"

She kept on screaming until Quorn came in sight on Asoka; and because his head was higher than the rock he was rounding, she saw that first, framed in a moon-made aura, like a god's face smiling out of nothing. So she screamed again, louder than ever.

"There, there, missy, nobody won't do you no harm. See, I brought along some magic for what ails you. No, 'tain't sinful stuff. It looks like it, and it smells like it, but it ain't, not by a long way, though it's in a whisky bottle, along o' my having no other kind."

Quorn made Asoka kneel and came to earth. He

knocked off the neck of the bottle with an old-time expert's sleight-of-hand. "Here, help yourself."

"Are you sure it isn't whisky?"

"Watch me prove it to you." He spied a tin cup tied to the waist of one of Bamjee's servants—commandeered the thing and filled it—passed that to Asoka, who sucked the cup dry with a snort, then injected the dose down his throat with a gurgle of satisfaction and demanded more.

"Can you suspect me after that, miss?"

"No," she said tartly. "I would suspect any man in this dreadful country, but animals are more to be depended on. Certainly I will not drink from that filthy cup. I must drink from the bottle. What is it?" She sniffed and drank.

"Be kind o' keerful not to cut your mouth, miss."

She swallowed, coughed, spluttered and drank again.

"You might leave some of it," Quorn suggested.

"Are you sure it's not whisky?" she asked. She tried again. Pre-Adamite instinct had control of her, perhaps encouraged by the fact that her costume was not so far removed from that of Eve in the age of innocence. It was true she was wearing a blanket and a long white nightgown underneath it, but her feet were naked and there was a vast power in suggestion. She began to feel nymphlike, if not positively bacchanalian.

"It mush be something won'erful," she remarked. "Is that the moon?"

Quorn rescued the bottle, nodded to himself and drank. Magnanimously then he gave a tot apiece to Bamjee and the two men, measuring it precisely into the tin cup, after which he took another drink himself and gave what was left to Asoka, who gurgled satisfaction over an evening well spent.

"Now, miss, seeing as how them dacoits wrecked your tent—"

But Quorn had spoken too soon; not yet had the nectar done its work; her vinegar was not yet wine. She interrupted:

"Don't you dare talk to me about your dacoits! If there's anything gone from my tent I shall know who took it! It was those workmen from the quarry—I know it was, and you're reshponshible—you shaid you are!"

"I mean to let you have my tent, miss—ain't no other thing to do. I'll turn in along o' the elephants."

"Do you mean I am to use your bed?"

"I guess so."

"Is it clean?"

THE FUMES OF unfamiliar whisky swayed her between a sort of sensuous feeling that she was in the midst of an adventure, and resentment that she must accept Quorn's favors. Also there was something suggestive of immodesty about the thought of Quorn's bed. But the fumes were quite familiar to Quorn and had an opposite effect: they made him genially courteous.

"I dare say, miss, it ain't no cleaner than it should be, but it's all you'll get because there ain't no other. Bugs is bugs, and I ain't more particular than most folks has a right to be in this here country, but you'll find 'em kind o' broke in. They've learned manners, 'cause I've scratched 'em so they had to. Mostly they lets you fall asleep before they—"

"I won't be told about your filthy inshex."

"All right, miss. Okay. I was only joking."

"Them guys have harems," Quorn warned
the lady novelist with a grin

" 'Shno time for joking. Make Bamjee bring shome of my clothes."

That was the last entirely sober speech she made that night. The dire news that Quorn now broke to her supplied emotion which was all the whisky needed to make conquest swift and sure.

"Beg pardon, miss. Your clothes is gone. The dacoits took 'em."

"Do you mean to tell me—"

But she could not finish it. She laid her face between her hands and wept with the noisy self-pitying unrestraint of a woman more used to forcing tears from others than indulging in such weakness on her own account. Between her hands she sobbed forth broken sentences, mixed with lamentation and threats of vengeance, drunkenness serving as a flux to meld the two together into one immodest boast of her importance.

She would sue the Ranee. She would sue Quorn. She would wire to Washington. She was ruined. She was a fool ever to have come to such a country. She would write to the Associated Press. She would put it all into her book—all the bugs and the dirt, and the cheating and lies, the diseases and the indignity of women.

She would have revenge. All India should pay in shame for her misadventure. Suddenly a worse thought than them all—a thought that almost, for the moment, sobered her:

"My notebooks?"

"Gone, miss. Every durned last scrap of everything is gone clean plumb to Hades!"

She refused to endure such calamity. She shrieked her anguish to the sky, reproving God for neglect of His hand-maiden. She demanded, with ever-increasing thickness in her speech, to be clothed in many blankets and led back to the nearest railway station on the camel.

"Can't be done, miss. Some guy cut the camel's throat."

She would ride in a bullock-cart.

"Carts is busted."

Then the deluge—anger and weeping followed by hysteria and hiccoughs that Quorn treated with the sort of friendly violence he would have used on elephants or a mahout who needed sobering. He pounded her on the back until her false teeth shook and her speech was less clear than it had been.

But bullies are all amenable to force; she succumbed to that treatment; she yielded to him.

"I'm sho shick."

"Give you a nice ride on an elephant," said Quorn. "That'll make you feel like you was Queen o' Sheba. Hey, you fellers, hold her while I climb up—then you pass her up to me."

HE MOUNTED ON Asoka's neck and signed to the three struggling Hindus to place her in front of him, so that he could hold her by the waist. A nightdress and a blanket are no costume for a ride of that kind, and a Hindu is no prude when it comes to nakedness; Bamjee pulled her nightdress up to let her legs hang freely behind Asoka's ears and the moonlight shone on a pair of very shapely limbs that would not have disgraced a chorus girl.

Against the elephant's dark skin, in that soft amber light, they were good to see. She saw them and struggled—almost struggled out of Quorn's arms. She was shocked so that the fumes of whisky almost lost their grip on het-brain. She screamed.

"Hush, hush—them ain't your legs," Quorn told her soothingly. "Them's mine."

She sighed, not daring to disbelieve him, leaning her head on his shoulder and looking up at the sky, ashamed and yet not altogether sorry to feel a strong arm holding her. Asoka swayed toward his shed, where he knew there would be extra hot cakes cooking as reward for extra work well done.

It was not unlike the motion of a small boat. The stars swung and swayed. There were two moons that kept on separating and then reuniting into something like the figure eight. She retained her dinner and her dignity with a will that habit had made automatic, but the weakness was there; it transmuted itself into self-reproach:

"Was I rude? I'm sho' shorry."

Quorn squeezed her. He hardly intended it, but sympathy is more compelling than the sense of caution. He was not a mean man, and he knew that she had suffered, more than some folk might under a hangman's lash. He imagined her sensations in the morning when she should awake and see the remnants of her tent and all the havoc that Asoka did.

It was only a friendly squeeze—a gesture of regret that she should be the victim of circumstance. He felt no guilt until she answered it by groping for his arm and pressing it with both her hands.

"Oh, holy mackerel!" he murmured then and whistled to himself a mite off-key.

She let herself lie loosely in his arms, her head on his shoulder, her body relaxed as if she had at last found some one in whom a vinegary old maid might confide without regret, she being much more virginal, though a widow, than some folk who have never entered the alleged blessed state of matrimony.

She was asleep before they reached the tent, so she was spared the shame of knowing how shapely and gleaming her legs looked when Bamjee and two others lowered her to earth.

THEY LAID HER on Quorn's bed and Quorn removed all of his other possessions to a comfortless lean-to made of sheets of corrugated iron beside Asoka's shelter. Then, when he had seen the hot cakes cooked that were Asoka's special reward, he mounted a pony left for him by one of Rana Raj Singh's men and rode to the Rajput's camp, a mile away, beyond a low hill.

9

"ONE TRAP WILL BE
BAITED WITH ME"

PRINCE RANA RAJ Singh, on a folded blanket, with his back to a rock in the moonlight, sat smoking endless cigarettes in silence. Quorn, borrowing a blanket, for a long time sat beside him, not even aware of privilege, so steeped he was in the spirit of true democracy that enjoys its own appreciation of the excellence of others.

He only wished the Rajput were not so taciturn; but there was compensation—his strength, his determination to do decently, his will to understand things' meaning, made his silence seem companionable. And when the Rajput spoke at last it was as if two parallel streams of thought had flowed into one channel, so that each understood how the other arrived at his point of view. There was no need for explanations.

"Those dacoits were misinformed."

"Sure, sir. It was me they was after—me and Asoka prob'ly. If they'd knowed which my tent was they'd ha' wrecked it."

"So it seems your trick succeeded. Narak has probably talked too soon, or to the wrong person."

"Weren't Narak with them?"

"No. Those were Lumding's men. We questioned one—thoroughly. Lumding is the acknowledged chief of all the dacoits. Narak, after his talk with you, sought to create dissension in the dacoit camp. He became insolent and rather reckless. He strutted like a peacock in front of the woman Usha and gave her all the earrings taken from the captured women. The prisoner says also that Lumding, learning from Narak's toasting what a magician you are, hoped to capture you and force you to make magic for him. You see, although it was the Rajah of Dumdumpore who persuaded them to invade our Ranee's territory, they don't trust him any more than they trust each other. They prefer magic."

"I've heard he's a terrible piece of cheese, sir."

"Dumdumpore is nothing without the woman Usha. She is the key to the situation—to his treachery and to the dacoits' plans, insofar as they have any genuine plans of their own."

"Where is Dumdumpore, sir?"

"Somewhere near where she is."

"And where is she?"

"God knows. But she is not far off. Our prisoner says that she has corrupted the quarrymen."

"I'd doubt that, sir, if I was you. Them quarrymen was bad eggs afore ever she came nigh enough to rot 'em."

"She has promised the quarrymen one year's pay apiece if they stand idle and let the Ranee be carried off. I have that from the foreman."

"Shows she's lackin' in business sense. Them guys 'ud stand idle all day for nothing. When is the Ranee coming, sir?"

They looked into each other's eyes by moonlight. "She is here now," said Rana Raj Singh.

QUORN WHISTLED—A STRANGE little tune of his own that he used as accompaniment to astonished thought. He was even more astonished when the tune was answered by another that he knew equally well, liquid and merry, apparently from a group of rocks some fifty yards away. But he could see nobody; the rocks were heaped in glistening white confusion; there was room amid them for a regiment to hide.

"She is here with ten men and a dozen servants," said the Rajput.

"Sir, it ain't safe."

"And the dacoits' spies will undoubtedly send word that she has left Narada City."

"Sure. We'll have them dacoits down on us," Quorn agreed.

"So the Ranee must go back home at once," the other said with an air of finality.

"Sir, it tickles me to hear you say that. But can you or I or any one make her do it?"

"She will go to-morrow."

"Good."

"Nevertheless, she will remain here."

Quorn, stroking his chin with his fingers, turned that over in his mind a minute. Then he knocked the ashes from his pipe and thumbed in fresh tobacco.

"I get you, sir," he said as he struck the match. "But it's risky. What good will it do us?"

"None whatever if Lumding captures her. But if Narak does, that is another story. Narak is an ignorant savage who can't even speak the Ranee's language. Narak wishes to be the chief of all the dacoits. Narak has no respect for Lumding or for Dumdumpore. But he has tremendous respect for the woman Usha; and he knows it is Usha who wishes to capture the Ranee, so that she may deliver her to Dumdumpore, who would then put the Ranee to death by poison unless she consented to marry him.

"So, to have the Ranee in his possession would give Narak a means of bargaining with Usha, who could, if she would, use her influence to make Narak chief of all the dacoits. She could turn Lumding's own men against him. She could frighten Lumding into running away. She has a gruesome reputation as a worker of black magic."

"Do you mean, sir, that if some one was speaking English to Narak, he wouldn't even know it was English?"

"Not he. He would only know it was a language he did not understand."

"But, sir—that there female ain't no more like the Ranee than cayenne pepper is like a cool drink. He's going to know she ain't the Ranee, soon as she starts talking at him. 'Twon't make no scrap o' difference that he's ignorant of English; she don't need no words to put her line o' goods across; she does it the same as a lemon does, by setting your teeth on edge. He's going to know he's caught a hot tomater."

"What then? He will have said he has the Ranee. Why should he then admit to any one except himself that he has made a mistake? Lumding and Usha will believe it, so will Dumdumpore; and his own spies in Lumding's camp will tell him they believe it. He can bargain for the chieftainship as easily with Mrs. Galway for a bait as he could if he had the real Ranee in his hands."

"Yeah—but Dumdumpore and that woman Usha ain't crazy. They'll want to see her afore they come to terms."

"Undoubtedly. But Lumding, who is also a savage, will resent the challenge to his leadership. Lumding will fight."

"You believe he will go after Narak?" Quorn demanded.

"Why not? Instantly, without any hesitation. What else is there for him to do? As a chief, whose lieutenant has stolen the prize he was after, and whose men are invited to join the lieutenant in open mutiny, he must either fight, or else resign and not only be mocked, but probably also put to death by malcontents who have a grudge against him. So there will be civil war among the dacoits."

"Yes, sir, that sounds okay."

"Thus the dacoits will destroy one another—perhaps with some slight assistance from ourselves; but it is they who will do most of the dirty work."

"HOW ABOUT DUMDUMPORE?" Quorn put in. "I'd liefer soak it to that sucker than to them ignorant savages. A dacoit, sir, is no worse than a wolf; he's ugly, but he don't mean nothing by it. Usha, she's a woman, so we won't say nothing about her beyond that she's a devil and don't know manners. But Dumdumpore has a salute o' seventeen guns. Them's seventeen reasons why that low-down son of a she-snake should be trod on."

"Let us hope," said Rana Raj Singh.

"Hope, sir? I've hoped for the moon when I was drunk enough. I've hoped Asoka wouldn't misbehave in public. Hope never got me nowheres."

"Dumdumpore," said the prince, "might learn, if we

use judgment, that the Ranee is really here, in our camp. He might learn that while the dacoits are fighting among themselves."

"And one trap," said a silvery voice, with a laugh, from a near-by shadow, "will be no worse for being baited with me myself in person."

The prince and Quorn sprang to their feet. The Ranee stepped into the moonlight, looking lovelier than Quorn had ever seen her, because the moon's rays glistened on the golden thread of her white silk *sari* and she shimmered in a golden glow. The dew on her sandals shone like diamonds.

In the faint mist she looked almost non-material, as if she were an apparition from an unseen universe. She was a reason why even an atheist had a right to believe in immortality, if only for one precious moment. Then she sat on the blanket that Quorn spread for her; he folded his own coat and sat on that, and they three formed a triangle, Quorn with his back to the moon.

"My men are on guard," said Rana Raj Singh.

"They are good men," said the Ranee. "I am grateful for their help and for your protection. But do they not take things a little seriously?"

"We are in serious danger," said the Rajput.

"No, it is Dumdumpore who is in danger," she retorted. "He and Ben Quorn. Dumdumpore is a coward and there is no safety zone for cowards. Ben Quorn has to die and come to life again. If he should take that too seriously he might be a long time dead."

Quorn made a movement of suppressed impatience. Rana Raj Singh nodded. The Ranee chuckled, removing her sandals to wriggle her toes in the dew.

"And so you and your Rajputs, my prince, must be pleased to regard this as funny. Otherwise we may be all obliged to learn too soon what life is after death. It will be very interesting, doubtless, but it would be just as interesting later on if we are not in too much hurry."

"What's the hurry about me dyin', miss?" Quorn objected. "I ain't such a lovin' crittur that the gods 'ud want to see me die young. Nor I ain't crazy. I got a good job. What'd I want to lose that for and go to where there maybe ain't no elephants, nor no Ranee, nor no whisky and tobaccer?"

"Don't you understand that the priests of Narada will poison you sooner or later unless we make it much more profitable for them to preserve your life as long as possible?"

"Them suckers 'ud poison their mothers and blame it on you," Quorn grumbled.

"LISTEN," THE RANEE said impressively. "They have said they will believe you are the Gunga *sahib* if you die to save my throne and come to life again. That was the prophecy. They have told that to all Narada. One half of Narada believes in you, as I do. One half doesn't, because the priests have called you an impostor. Consequently, all Narada is on tiptoe, waiting for the miracle. If you succeed—"

"But who's to prove it?" Quorn objected.

"We have all these quarrymen and all the mahouts as impartial witnesses."

"Them liars? Huh—who'd believe 'em?"

"People will believe when they say you are dead, won't they?"

"Yeah—most folks believe bad news."

"And the priests will believe it eagerly."

"You bet."

"The priests will boast that you are dead."

"Suckers! I'll come back an' haunt 'em!"

"You will do better than that. You will come back alive, on your elephant Asoka, and the priests will either have to eat their own boasting or else admit you are the veritable Gunga *sahib*. After which, they must preserve your life as long as possible, for the sake of their own reputation as custodians of sacred legend."

"Yeah, miss, that sounds okay. How about, though, if them dacoits puts it over on me an' I croak? I ain't the Gunga *sahib*. I ain't sacred. I can't work no miracles. I ain't so sure but what there may be something in this here theory o' being born and dying and coming to life again maybe a thousand times—"

"Many million times," the Ranee interrupted.

"Well, I dunno. What I do know is, I don't remember any past lives and I can't see ahead and prophesy no future ones. So I'm a sucker if I chuck away this here life, which ain't so troublesome but what I like it A-1 most o' the time."

"You are quite right, Mr. Quorn," said Rana Raj Singh. "Each life as we live it is the one to think about."

"All right. What then if a dacoit ups an' sticks a jabber in me?"

"Nothing," said the Ranee. "Only then you and I would have to wait until the next life we live on earth together, to finish the work that we began together, that is all. I wonder what you did in former lives to cause you to be punished by being so blind in this one. I was always Sankyamuni, you were always Gunga, and we always had the elephant. I can never remember all of it, but I get lots of little flashes."

"Well," said Quorn, "I'll tell you, miss. I'm maybe blind and I'm maybe stoopid. And my mother was a lady what did scrubbing for the saloonkeepers' wives in Philadelphia. That's me. That's the 'me' what I know. I ain't a handsome guy. I likes my likker. I don't hold with no bettin' on future lives nor with claiming I was some one special in days gone by. I hanker after peace in this here life. But I'm for you.

"You're a bag o' mischief, but you're bright, and you look awful sweet to me. You're wiser than what I am and you're on the level—'specially when it comes to standing by your friends. So I'll stand by you." He knocked his pipe out on the rock; it was like a hammer recording a final bid. "If there's anything I can do to help you play your game, you count on me to do it—with all my might."

"You are a—" The Ranee's voice quavered a half-note; it took her a moment to recover. "You are a dear. But how strange that you can't remember? Nobody but the veritable Gunga *sahib* could have talked to me like that."

"Them priests," Quorn began, but Rana Raj Singh interrupted him.

"Let the priests wait. We have dacoits to deal with."

"And Mrs. Galway," said the Ranee.

"WELL," SAID QUORN, "I left your clothes in my tent, miss. Them is all she's got, unless she elects to look more sporty in a night-shift. My belief is she will want to make herself look snooty, for to find out why I cuddled her a while back. 'Tain't a going to be no picnic. She's a woman with a will. I seen her legs—and they weren't bad-looking, neither. She'll figure any man as did that ought to marry her, I reckon."

"Why not?" asked the Ranee.

"'Cause, miss, there is limits. Death is something we don't know about, so we can face it. But I've seen poor suckers who had to live with her sort."

"You might pretend," said the Rana Raj Singh.

"Me, sir? Maybe *you* could do it."

Instantly the Ranee went into a gale of giggles. For a minute she could only seize her Rajput's hand; she had no breath for speech that any one could make head or tail of. But at last she forced words into sequence:

"You!" she said. "Of course, you! She doesn't know you. You don't know her. You pretend that you think she is me! You must ride to her tent in the morning—see her in my clothes—and turn aside at once because she has no veil. She has probably heard that I never wear a veil, but she has probably also heard that I scandalize all old-fashioned people by not wearing one; and anyhow, Mr. Quorn can tell her that. You choose one of your Rajputs who knows no English and send him to present your respectful compliments. Mr. Quorn acts as interpreter. Oh, this is perfect!"

"But what will I tell her?" asked Quorn.

"You must tell her that my Prince Rana Raj Singh is the Rajah of Dumdumpore, who proposes to carry her off and have her for his thirty-second concubine!"

"Hell's bells! She'll want to marry me to save herself!" Quorn objected.

"Not she! She will be thrilled more than she ever was in her whole life," said the Ranee. "She will insist on running away at once. Probably she will believe that her pleased excitement is genuine eagerness to escape from such a dreadful prospect. But deep in her heart she will hope he will follow and overtake her."

"Who is to help her to run?" Quorn asked. "She can't travel alone."

"Bamjee!"

"He'll be too scared."

"I will promise Bamjee anything in reason."

"He ain't reasonable."

"I will promise anything he asks for."

"He will ask for money," said Quorn. "That *babu* will do anything for money, excep' actually run out on you, miss, though he'll creep as close to doing that as he can shave a profit out of."

"You are quite right, Mr. Quorn," said the Rana Raj Singh. "We can count on Bamjee, though his services may be expensive. The Ranee must count on you and me to do the rest. We will succeed, if I can be as brave as you are."

"Hear that guy talk!" Quorn muttered to himself. "Them princes has manners, whatever else. That means I'm going to have to take all chances, so's not to look like ten cents to his dollar. Gee, I wish I was in Philadelphia. But I ain't. So here goes."

10

"FOR A LADY SUCH AS YOU ARE, THEY'D DRAW LOTS"

QUORN TALKED WITH the Ranee and Rana Raj Singh until the angle of the moon reminded the latter it was time to relieve the ring of sentries he had posted. The conversation was involved and intimate. Though they three trusted one another, even so habit asserted itself and a stranger overhearing them could hardly have understood their purpose and the plan they evolved in intricate detail, so oblique was their approach to it.

The Ranee now and then was forthright; energy exploded and forced plain speech; but the prince became more and more taciturn as they groped their way into the depths of intrigue; he hinted; he said very little that could have been held against him. Quorn took example from him.

They might have been enemies trying to reach a basis for negotiations. But the truth was, they were anxious not to limit one another by suggesting that any proposal that one or the other disliked was something to be literally carried out.

When Quorn at last swung up behind Rana Raj Singh's saddle and was presently dropped beside Asoka's stall, he understood the problem in all its bearings as well as the intricate means by which it should be solved, but he knew he was free to do exactly as he pleased in an emergency and that the others would not only trust him, but would instantly change their plans as far as possible to fit with any unexpected move on his part.

That is the secret of so-called oriental subtlety. It refuses to be limited or to limit others by so-called facts, which every one in the Orient knows may change into something else at any moment.

It was when the Rajput had ridden off into the night that Quorn began to peg himself down, like a chess player, to a definite line of assault on the dacoits, move by move.

He almost never trusted himself to pass final judgment until he sat beside Asoka. There was something natural and almost limitless about the enormous animal, his restful swaying and his interested sampling of the midnight smells; it made for clear thinking.

Superstitious in the ordinary meaning Quorn was not; but his ability to foresee and to reason when he had Asoka near him, amounted almost to the same thing. He slept while Asoka slept.

He awoke when Asoka did. He roused the mahouts with a pitchfork prong to set the hot cakes cooking and send the shivering grass-cutters to work. And at peep o' day he was smoking, on a stool beside his own tent, waiting for Mrs. Galway's anger to come nagging querulously through the tent flies.

He had to wait a long time, but he waited. There were strange sounds within there and he was glad he had left her his two-foot mirror, because he heard what could be nothing else than chuckling.

He could hear her trying on the Ranee's garments, and it seemed that she liked what she saw in the glass. She was unexpectedly, incredibly good-tempered. Even when she shouted at last for Bamjee to order the cook to bring her breakfast, she was only moderately unkind:

"I trust your sense of duty has not totally vanished? I hope you don't propose to let me die of hunger? Is the stuff the cook calls coffee ready? I suppose I will have to eat hard-boiled eggs again and that the butter will taste like margarine, but I am learning not to expect my likes to be considered." Then, at the top of her lungs: "Bring my breakfast."

SHE EMERGED FROM the tent as two men carried up a makeshift table, her own having gone to smithereens last night beneath Asoka's forefoot. And she stood with a critical frown to observe how they spread the tablecloth and laid the cutlery and plates that had been borrowed from Quorn's plebeian outfit.

But that was only a pretense—Quorn knew it. He understood perfectly. She was grimly suppressing delight in herself clad in the scented silken garments that tickled her vanity more than anything that she had ever worn.

Probably she had never looked so nearly presentable. Not even vinegary feelings and a morbid view of other people's sins could undo symmetry and flowing line. The colors suited her. The *sari* stole the hardness from her face, so that her critical eyes looked almost kind and the exacting corners of her mouth seemed almost guilty of good humor. Bamjee sized her up in half a second and *salaamed* with his forehead almost to the ground.

"*Sahiba,* so much loveliness will blind these eyes!"

"Huh! Fulsome flattery won't make me overlook last night's disgraceful doings!" she retorted. But she was pleased; she had never before been flattered by the shovelful, without an observant woman near to cause her to feel ridiculous. Quorn took his cue from Bamjee.

"Have to hand it to yer, miss. Some fixin's, I'll say. Suit yer to a T. Say, wouldn't you just knock their eyes out back home!"

"Nonsense!"

"Wish I may die if I don't mean it."

"These are your plates and so on, I suppose. Have you had breakfast?"

"No, miss."

Blandly, with an air of patronizing grace, she tripped into the net that Quorn had spent a long night fashioning from such stray thoughts as came to him. Over the way Asoka tossed his trunk to scatter hay-wisps on his back, but it looked like a triumphant signal and a laugh when she invited Quorn to breakfast.

He had counted on her doing that; there is a witchery of breakfasting beneath a blue sky when the birds are singing, even if the coffee is nothing to brag about. He did not dare to forego the least advantage. He depended on eating breakfast with her.

"Supposing them dacoits was to see you," he said. "Them suckers 'u'd carry you off as sure as they'd kill the rest of us. They'd think you was the Ranee. I ain't joking. They sure would."

She enjoyed it, but she bridled for the sake of modesty. "I don't believe there are any dacoits. After breakfast I intend to search the quarters of those quarrymen. I shall be much surprised if I don't find some of my belongings in there. There was an elephant; but that might easily have been one of our elephants."

"Meaning you accuse me, miss?"

"They could use one of your elephants, could they not? I accuse you of having given me something to drink that I would rather die than touch."

"Miss, that was medicine."

SHE DISBELIEVED HIM, but her eyes betrayed that she was grateful for the lie. "I must hope you are telling the truth. But you don't look to me like a truthful man."

Quorn judged it time to begin to take the upper hand: "Miss, I'm a first-class liar when it comes to not remembering things I've seen, what some one hopes I didn't see. I'd lie like the devil to hide a woman's embarrassment."

"I fear I was dreadfully sick last night. I have a slight headache now."

"Miss, if I didn't know better I'd swear you was drunk."

"I am glad you know better than that." She quickly changed the subject. "But you don't know me if you hope to make me believe in your dacoits. I shall sue the Ranee of Narada for the value of my belongings. Unless she offers me a sincere apology, I shall sue her for damages also. They were her laborers who attacked me in the night. I am sure of it."

"Miss, not only was them devils dacoits, but they thought you was the Ranee o' Narada, and if they'd found you they'd have carried you off as sure as my name's Quorn.

Why, miss, I'll show you dead ones, soon as you've had breakfast. I don't want to turn your stummick or I'd show 'em to you now. I've been a wondering all night how you'd ha' behaved if they'd ha' caught you."

"Why should they raid my camp?"

"Because, miss, they believed it is the Ranee's camp—and if they catch her, she's worth money. Lots of it. You see, it's known the Ranee travels light. She's known to be a daring young woman, who laughs at a lot o' the old-time customs. And it's known she intends to visit this here place, for to see how the quarrying's coming along."

"I sincerely hope she will come. I would like to meet her. I will give her a piece of my mind. I will stay here until she does come."

"Suit yourself, miss. You may have the loan o' my tent. But I was thinking, if the dacoits was to come again—"

"Why should they?"

"Spies, miss. I don't doubt their spies are lurking in the long grass. They'll have seen you. Any one who sees you dressed like that, a looking like a queen out of a story-book, can't be blamed for running to the dacoit camp and telling 'em you're the Ranee o' Narada. Why shouldn't they come—and you all unprotected?"

"Are you serious? Do you really mean I am in danger?"

"All that dangerous I never slep' a wink for wondering what you'd best do if they comes and ketches you. There's only one thing, miss, you could do; and that's pretend to 'em you *are* the Ranee. That way they'd keep you alive for ransom. If they was to find out you ain't the Ranee they'd kill you, if you was lucky. If you wasn't—"

"What?"

"Them guys have harems."

"Polygamy?"

"Yes, indeed, ma'am."

"Do you mean to tell me, Mr. Quorn, that there are men to-day in India who would dare to kidnap an American lady and—"

"You can't imagine. Ma'am, they wouldn't stop to think twice. Mostly they holds auctions o' their prisoners. But for a lady such as you are, they'd draw lots. That is, unless they thought you was the Ranee; in which case they'd figure they could sell you for more money to the Rajah of Dumdumpore than they'd care to lose by staging a debauch. You get me?"

"The Rajah of Dumdumpore? What has he to do with dacoits?"

"He employs 'em, ma'am."

"GOOD HEAVENS! WHAT kind of person is he?"

"The kind o' person what hires hellions to do his dirt. He's good to look at. He looks like one o' them sultans on a pickle-bottle label. First glance, you'd say he was that bold he'd take a tiger by the short hair. But that's all bluff; he can't say boo to his own shadder. So, seeing he wants the Ranee o' Narada for his harem, he has hired these here dacoits to ketch her for him."

"Is he leading them in person?"

"No, ma'am, he ain't that fond o' taking risks. He's all that surreptitious that he hasn't ever seen the Ranee. He's only heard she's a good looker, and he craves her kingdom and her money, which he figures might be had by clapping her into his harem and crushing her pretty toes with a ingenious device until she signs a paper saying she's his willing wife. You see, ma'am, marriage is all politics in these here parts, and politics ain't all they ought to be."

"But how did you learn all this?"

Quorn avoided answering that question, fearful of becoming too involved in skeins of imagination. "You should ha' wised yourself afore you came high-handed, and no permit, into a State where tourists ain't allowed," he answered. "There ain't nobody but me can help you now; and I can't do no more than give you good advice."

She smiled, so archly that Quorn's blood ran cold: "Since last night we are under obligations to each other. I hope I can count on your discretion."

"Ma'am, it's you what has to be discreet. If Bamjee can smuggle you back to Narada City, there's a chance that the British Resident might get back from Delhi in time to give you an escort to the railway line. If not, you're liable to have to use your wits. Supposing them dacoits *should* ketch you, kid 'em you're the Ranee o' Narada. They won't know no better.

"If you act discreet, they'll sell you to the Rajah of Dumdumpore; and by that time maybe I can get a telegram through to the British Government. There's some things can be said against the British, but they don't hold with letting no lady-tourists stay in a rajah's harem longer than it takes to send a airplane and teach him manners."

"Oh, I can't ride in those things. They make me ill. I've been up once. Nothing would ever persuade me—"

"Ma'am, them air-force fellers has a way with 'em. They'd take yer. Don't you worry. Mind, now, if the Rajah of Dumdumpore should see you—you're the Ranee o' Narada. Get that? Don't forget it… Oh, my God!"

"What?"

"That's him coming!"

Opportunely, from behind the hill at the back of the elephant lines, alone, on a beautiful bay mare, rode Rana Raj Singh. His black beard was brushed fiercely upward. His mustache bristled. His hot-mustard-colored turban had been pushed down low over his eyes. His shoulders were slightly hunched, as a man's might be who sought to do by treachery what nobler ruffians would do by force. He reined in, stared and then wheeled suddenly and rode away.

"There you are, ma'am. Now you've seen him. And he's seen you."

"But what a handsome man!"

"Ma'am, handsome is as handsome does. He's that ornery he's plumb unnatural. Do you know what? Do you know why he didn't ride forward? He's like all them Bluebeards, he's old-fashioned. He's shocked half out of his senses 'cause he seed you in the open without your veil on!"

NOW CAME A Rajput riding on a gray horse, using his right hand to cover his eyes, although he stared between his fingers. He dismounted, salaamed, then covered his eyes again.

"This, ma'am, will be his servant. You're in danger. I'd best kid the sucker you're the Ranee, hadn't I?"

"You know best. I can only hope you're right to—"

"Ma'am, it's almost wrong to be as right as I am. It makes you feel pre—what's the word?—presumshus."

Followed conversation in a language of which Mrs. Galway understood not one word. At last the Rajput bowed, walked his horse to a respectful distance, mounted and rode away.

"Ma'am, the pepper is in the hash and no mistake," said Quorn. "That sucker admits he knows all about last night's raid on your camp. What he wants to know is that you're here. Nex' thing you'll have his dacoits down on you again."

"Then why not tell him I am not the Ranee?"

"Because then, ma'am, he would tell the dacoits you are not the Ranee. You'd be their meat. They would come and get yer just the same. Only, knowing they had no market for you, they would draw lots for you among 'emselves and you would have to be a dacoit's mistress. How would you fancy that?"

"But wouldn't the British government interfere?"

"A fat chance! In among them mountains? Hell's bells! It 'ud take all their airplanes and a year o' time to find an army among them rocks an' jungles."

"I will go back to Narada at once then. Will you lend me that big elephant?"

"No, ma'am. You may have that littlest one at the far end o' the line. She's gentle and she can move fast."

"Oh, dear, I know the ride on an elephant will upset me. Isn't there a place where I could hide?"

"Bamjee might know of a place, ma'am. Shall I fetch him?"

BAMJEE WAS NOT difficult to find—he had been listening behind the tent. But Quorn walked to some little distance away and waited for him behind a rock. He wanted privacy.

"You sucker, are you all set?"

"*Sahib;* I am afraid."

"Have you been talking to the Ranee?"

"No, *sahib.* For two whole hours, until daybreak, her highness did me the honor of talking to me. I listened."

"Then you know what's what. Go to it."

"*Sahib,* I am terribly afraid. It is simple—oh, so simple to get caught by dacoits. But to get uncaught—!"

"Did she promise you money?"

"Yes, *sahib.* But to a dead man, money—"

"Are you all that skeered you couldn't feel if I should swat you?" Quorn asked.

"No, no, *sahib,* not that!"

"Do you kid yourself I won't swat you, if you run out on what the Ranee says for you to do?"

"But you and I are good friends—"

"Hell's bells, I ain't no friend o' yeller men! I like a guy wi' nerve. See here now, Bamjee: me and you have pulled off more'n one job that was pretty nigh as dangerous as this one, and I ain't denying that you always done your full share. But that don't prove nothing excep' that you've got to keep on doing it. You get me?"

"But I have a wife and children."

"So you always had, you sucker."

"And there are limits—"

"No, there ain't. What's more, there ain't no limit to my contemp' for a guy that'ud go green when he's counted on. You take that tourist agency o' yours and park it in a hiding-place and get it caught good by Narak—do you get me? And you keep on kidding Narak she's the Ranee—do you get that? And you count on us to get you out o' the mess, knowing not one of us ever went back on a friend—do you get that? After it's all over me an' you'll shake hands—so be no harm comes to that young elephant. Remember: that young elephant is in your charge and you're responsible."

"But the Galway *sahiba* is also in my charge. If harm should come to her—"

"Hell's bells—you can't kill her kind. The Almighty made 'em rugged, so's they could endure their own company."

"Oh, why was I born?" whiled Bamjee.

"Just for this, my little man. You do your job right. Then you'll maybe get trusted to do the nex' one. Go to it."

11

"YOU SHALL NEVER LIVE TO SPEND IT IF YOU PLAY US FALSE"

THERE WAS A man named Mulji, Quorn's prime favorite among the thirty-four mahouts. Quorn had offered the smallest, youngest elephant for Mrs. Galway's use in the scheduled abduction for no other reason than because Mulji was that elephant's mahout. A man who can be trusted with the education of a young beast is reliable in certain other matters, sometimes.

"Mulji, you're a bad egg, and you've three thrashings due you," said Quorn. He kicked away the little rags on bits of stick that Mulji had been preparing as bribes to the mischievous godlet who cooperates in the sinful schemes of dissolute mahouts. "That *memsahib* says you stole her overcoat las' night."

The overcoat, along with all of Mrs. Galway's other property that had not been smashed out of recognition by Asoka, lay in a locked box, back of the elephant line, and Mulji knew that Quorn knew there was nothing missing. So he pricked up his ears.

"It is unseemly for one so proud as that *sahiba* to speak lies concerning me, who am an honorable man," said Mulji.

"She says she's going to have the whole durned thirty-four of you clapped in quad, and you especial," Quorn informed him.

"Leaving your honor without mahouts to clean the elephants? Is she in her right mind?" Mulji asked.

"She's mean. You've got to take her to Narada City on that young elephant."

"On an elephant with sore feet?" Mulji asked, eager to please but not yet quite understanding the drift of Quorn's suggestion.

"You sucker! You know as well as I do that if that there young elephant had sore feet, what was left of you would be hunting a job what didn't call for no sitting down at no time for about a year to come."

"Her feet are as the feet of dancing girls," said Mulji quickly. "Never was an elephant that had feet in such perfect condition. She can carry ten *sahibas*—even to Narada City—if the *sahib* says so."

"Mebbe. Long way for a young elephant," said Quorn.

"A too long journey—terrible."

"Terrible my eye! That elephant could do it easy."

"Why not? Did she not come thence easily, bearing a load of tents and what not else?"

"Kept up good, eh?"

"*Sahib*, not even the great Asoka could leave that young elephant behind. She has a pride of workmanship, being well taught. Ever she loves to do her daily task."

"Hmm. Not skeered o' gettin' left behind?"

"Nay, *sahib*—frightened of nothing. Nevertheless, she loves company. Therefore, she is always on the heels of the next elephant ahead."

"Can't spare no elephants to keep her company," said Quorn.

Mulji began to see daylight through the mystery of many words. "She might seek to turn back," he suggested.

"Does she run away now and then?" Quorn asked him. "Say, if you show up back here with that English *memsahib,* I'll kill you!"

"The *memsahib* might fall off the elephant?"

"If she did, *she'd* kill you and save me the trouble. You take my tip and let her down gentle when Bamjee tells you where to halt for dinner."

"But the elephant is young," said Mulji. "If she should set down her burden she might suppose the task is finished. She might wish to return to the herd. It is not always possible to make an elephant obey."

"BAMJEE," SAID QUORN thoughtfully, "don't know nothing about elephants."

"Surely, *sahib.* That *babu* is totally ignorant of the ways of elephants. Doubtless both he and the *sahiba* will descend from the howdah at some place."

"Yep. They'll mebbe have a servant with 'em."

"He would descend likewise."

"Mebbe. He could climb back, couldn't he, to look for something in the howdah? I was thinkin' o' sendin' my cook."

Mulji grinned. "A great risk, *sahib.* If the cook should climb again into the howdah, surely a young elephant would be excused for thinking it is time now to return homeward. Is it not so?"

"Mebbe. I sure would hate to lose that cook. And I sure would hate to have to take your unsupported word for

*She was a toy queen,
tempted to prove herself
not such a toy after all*

anything, you sucker. Folks might say you'd run away o' purpose. So you should have a witness."

Quorn turned away to attend to other matters. He was not even present when the elephant kneeled before his tent and Mrs. Galway climbed into the howdah.

From a distance, on Asoka's neck, he watched, suggesting both to the young elephant and Mrs. Galway that he proposed to act as escort for at least a portion of the way; and the fact that his own cook, with a box of provisions and pots and pans, followed Bamjee into the howdah, also helped to create that suggestion in Mrs. Galway's mind. So there were no last-minute arguments.

Far in the lead, Asoka swung along the track toward Narada City and the young elephant followed, in no haste to overtake him, satisfied to know that the pride of the herd was somewhere along the road ahead of her.

But as soon as Quorn came to a gully he turned into it and hid behind a clump of trees. He did not move from there until the sound of Mrs. Galway's noisily complaining voice had died down in the distance.

Then he turned back; and when he had set the rest of the herd of elephants to work at carrying firewood for the camp, he turned Asoka's head toward the village, several miles away, in which the dacoits had established themselves. In a world of almost absolute uncertainties he was sure of one thing: that the dacoits would be keeping guard against surprise. He would be seen, and before long.

He rarely put the howdah on Asoka's back when he rode alone, but he had it now, although it was very lightly loaded, and its contents hidden under sacking. When he found a clump of trees that suited his purpose he made Asoka kneel, and with the aid of a shovel he did some very swift work, covering it neatly with dead leaves and loose dirt.

He was in no danger, he knew that Prince Rana Raj Singh and his Rajput horsemen—possibly the Ranee, too, since nothing could keep that young woman out of the zone of action—were watching him with the inimitable Rajput mastery of scouting.

WHEN THE HURRIED work was finished he chained Asoka by both hind legs to a tree not far away, allowing him scope enough to amuse himself breaking branches. Then he built a small fire, making it as smoky as he could, and sat down to wait.

He did not have very long to wait. There was a hill, much less than a mile away, with a fringe of bowlders along its summit, from which the dacoit watchmen saw him almost as soon as he lighted the fire. He saw one of them make a signal by removing a dead tree-branch that had been stuck into a crevice.

Plainly the dacoits suspected a trap. They were as cautious as panthers. They approached from three sides, under cover, showing themselves suddenly and then vanishing equally suddenly, to tempt an ambush to declare itself if one there were.

Most of them stayed under cover amid the rocks and scrub surrounding the clump of trees, but nine or ten came forward, of whom one was Narak. However, Narak was not the leader; he appeared to give grudging precedence to a man who might be eighty years of age, so gray he was and so sunken of cheek, although his muscular limbs looked active and he walked with an athletic stride.

"This is Lumding," remarked Narak.

Quorn stared curiously, almost as much fascinated by the famous leader's features as the dacoit was by the reputed Gunga *sahib's*.

Lumding had rather a refined look—cruel but sardonically humorous, and capable of far more intelligence than most of his followers; nevertheless, superstition had him by the brain. From his turban of twisted red silk to the toes of both feet he was covered with amulets of one sort or another—tigers' claws and tigers' whiskers, earrings, necklaces, wristlets, bracelets, rings on all his fingers— every one of them designed to guard against the evil eye or some other specific danger of the sort that creep by night and smite in daytime from an unseen world beyond a veil of mystery.

His only weapons, against visible opponents were a long sword and a jeweled dagger. He seemed offended because

Quorn did not rise to greet him. He spoke abruptly. A man near by interpreted.

"Stand up!"

But Quorn was sitting on the mechanism of his own material contact with the latent forces of an unseen world. If he had moved it might have cost him all his reputation as a wizard.

"Tell him," he said, in an off-hand tone of voice, "that it ain't the custom where I come from, to talk business standing." He thoughtfully thumbed tobacco into the bowl of his pipe. "Tell him he ain't here to pass no compliments, nor me either. What he wants he won't get—not unless he treats me civil. Bid him sit."

Lumding hesitated but the interpreter explained volubly and his men urged him, so he sat.

"Where's your rajah?" Quorn asked him at once. "Where is Dumdumpore and that writing on paper that the woman Usha promised?"

There was no immediate answer, but a lot of conversation between Lumding and his dacoits.

AT LAST THE interpreter pointed to Quorn and said abruptly: "You come with us."

"The devil I do! What for?"

"You get from Usha what she said you get."

"Nix! You go and tell that witch to keep her promises. She or else Dumdumpore himself can bring me, here, what she promised; or nothing doing."

"You bring your elephant and come or you get made to come," said the interpreter.

"Huh! You ask this boss o' yours if he knows what kind o' man he's talking to."

"He say," said the interpreter, "you choose. You come, or you get come along damn-quick!"

"All right. Tell him I'll make a monkey of him quicker'n he can beg me not to."

The interpreter perhaps was afraid to translate that threat too literally. There followed a lot of conversation and apparently Lumding was making up his mind to act sternly. Narak appeared anxious, as if he would like to speak to Quorn but hardly dared do so in the presence of his chief.

"See here," said Quorn, "I'll show you the kind o' feller I am—make you a bit o' magic. Ask what he'd like to have me do."

It was a perfectly safe question. Instead of answering at once Lumding took counsel with his men, giving Quorn the excuse to interrupt impatiently.

"Heck! I can't wait all day. Tell him I'll show him what I can just as easy do to him if he don't behave himself."

He pointed to a little pool of muddy water left by the recent rains. It was not more than three or four feet in diameter; it was possibly three feet deep. They stared at it.

With his heel Quorn shoved the switch that he had buried under dead leaves. Instantly a stick of dynamite that he had placed at the end of the wire in the pool exploded with a startling cough, and the water was muddy enough to make an astonishing spectacle as it leaped forth.

Asoka screamed, which made a fine addition to the panic in the air; Quorn had counted on that.

"Does he want any more?" he suggested. "Tell him to go and sit on yonder lump o' dry wood and I'll give him a free ride to heaven."

Lumding backed away from it. Quorn pressed his

heel against a second switch and blew the lump of wood to smithereens. He was now at the end of his magical resources for the moment, but he did not dare to admit that.

"What next?" he demanded.

"No more!" said the interpreter. "Lumding, he send for writing from the woman Usha."

"No. Tell him to go fetch it."

Terrified though he was, Lumding had dignity of a kind; he preferred not to be some one's errand-boy. He was afraid to refuse, but he tried to temporize.

"He say," said the interpreter, "if he go—maybe you—not here when he come back."

"All right. You tell him I'm not used to being put off by no argyments. What I say do, gets did—or else there's more o' that there magic, quick and snappy—I ain't guaranteeing where the next lot hits. You tell him, if he's all that unbelieving o' my being here when he gets back, he can leave this sucker here to watch me."

With his thumb he indicated Narak, who was as nervous as his chief. But Lumding seemed to think it a good enough idea to let Narak run the risk of being blown up. He commanded him to stay and Narak, fighting with his own fear, made the most of opportunity to prove in the presence of Lumding's men his own superior courage.

"Sure—he stay," said the interpreter.

LUMDING AND HIS staff took leave as hastily as shreds of dignity allowed, stepping very carefully around the pools of water and the lumps of rotting wood lest sudden magic speed them on their way.

About half of the men who had hidden themselves amid

the near-by rocks left cover at once and followed Lumding; but all of Narak's men remained and some of them even drew nearer. One of them called to Narak, urging him to beware of danger. Narak answered gruffly and the man who had served as interpreter at the former interview with Quorn came forward.

"Now," said Quorn, "you tell this feller Narak, if he wants to ketch the Ranee he'd better move quick. She's riding back toward Narada City on a young she-elephant, with a man named Bamjee, one mahout and my cook."

Narak asked a dozen questions in rapid sequence. Quorn answered them all in one slow, considered summary:

"Likely enough the Ranee will pretend she ain't the Ranee jes' to make you doubtful o' yourself. But don't you let her fool you, not even if she tries to kid you she's American or some such stuff as that. Treat her decent. Don't forget that spoiled goods ain't worth a tinker's dam in any market. Dumdumpore won't pay a price for her unless she's right side up and all in one piece. Get me?

"Soon as you've caught her, you beat it to the hills and hide. Make ready to defend yourself 'cause Lumding will try to grab her from you. Soon as you can, get word to the woman Usha saying what you've done; and then send that *babu* Bamjee to bring word to me. You can count on me to help you get what's coming to you. Hurry. Where are your horses? If you go on foot you'll hardly ketch 'em by the time they halt for dinner."

Narak ran and his men went after him like smoke before the wind. Quorn carefully coiled the wire and hid that with the battery and switches in the howdah, knowing that if Usha should come she would have heard the story of the magic and would certainly be shrewd enough to look for causes.

Then he made a fuss over Asoka, petting him and getting him to forget that the two explosions had been so terrible, before he undid the chain and hid that also in the howdah. Then he mounted and, guiding Asoka to the spot where he had previously sat, waited, *ankus* in hand, on the great beast's head—a living reproduction of the carving done a thousand years ago on the stone wall of Narada City marketplace.

The sunlight, broken by the branches overhead, cast shadows that completed the illusion—not that Quorn was conscious of it; he was wondering what he would have for dinner, with no cook to superintend the efforts of the pot-and-kettle boy.

IT WAS A long time before he saw returning dacoits, and Lumding was not among them. There were not more than twenty or thirty men, all mounted on ponies this time.

A woman on a small gray mule was riding in their midst and, on a horse beside her, a man rode looking as if he would rather have been doing almost anything than that. The woman was heavily veiled; only her eyes were visible above the edge of a silk scarf.

The man, too, had a colored scarf over his mouth and his turban pulled down low over his forehead, but even at a distance Quorn could see that he was puffy-cheeked, black-bearded and had heavy bags under his eyes. He kept glancing to right and left and behind him, not as if he expected pursuit, but more from a sort of guilty nervousness—or so Quorn diagnosed it.

"That guy owes money or else he's done his mother dirt,"

he muttered, tapping Asoka gently with the *ankus* to get him ready for action at a moment's notice.

The man and the woman approached. The others waited rather far off.

"Buddy, that bird has a gun in his fist," said Quorn. He always talked as if Asoka understood him. "If I prod you with the *ankus,* soak him quick and snappy, because I haven't got no weapon."

But the man kept his hand in his breast and let the woman ride ahead of him until her mule's nose nearly touched Asoka's trunk.

"I have brought you the paper," she said in good plain English.

"Let me see it."

Slowly the man drew his hand from his breast and passed a folded sheet of paper to the woman. Without glancing at it she held it toward Quorn, who ordered Asoka to take it. The elephant gave it into Quorn's hand.

"Jes' as I thought," he exclaimed. " 'Tain't legal. There ain't the name o' no bank written on it, nor no value received, nor no time limit. I'm a sucker, I am—mebbe. But I learned about notes along of having set my John Hancock on another fellow's to accommodate him—so I learned it good. Who's your fat friend?" He looked shrewdly at the puffy face behind the scarf. "Is this your hand o' writing? Are you Dumdumpore by any chance?"

He grunted and clucked to Asoka—gave into his trunk the folded note to hand back.

"Never you mind who that man is. It is not your business," said Usha.

Quorn had no doubt she was Usha, any more than he

doubted that the man was Dumdumpore, but both of them seemed to wish to play a farce of anonymity.

"Seems to me he come on business," he retorted. "You're a pair o' bright ones, you are! Here I am, all ready to do my bit and turn the Ranee o' Narada over to you—plans all laid—ready to deliver the goods on this here elephant— and you two come an' try to double cross me with a piece o' paper that ain't no more value than a canceled postage stamp. Huh! I've a mind to run out on you."

THE RAJAH MOVED his hand toward his breast again and Quorn made ready, in case of need, to use the heavy *ankus* like a javelin.

"You will not dare to disobey me," Usha answered. "I can send men to catch you at any time. If you don't deliver the Ranee to us—"

"All right—oh, all right. But what's wrong with acting honorable? Why not give me a proper promissory note, so's I can cash it at a moneylender's and make my get-away?"

"You shall have it," said Usha. She turned and whispered to the rajah. "Only you must cash it with the money-lender we name."

"Will he give me a fair face value?"

Again the whispering. "He will discount it."

"Then write the note for twenty-five per cent more money! I know them money-lenders. Say—see here, I'm sick o' argyment; you bring me that there note, writ proper, for the full amount, value received and payable without recourse, to-night to my tent. Get me? If you don't, the game's up—for I'll tip the Ranee to keep out o' your way."

The rajah's hand went to his breast.

"Nah-nah, you don't!" Quorn swung the heavy *ankus* and

the Rajah's hand dropped to his side. "You don't know the kind o' guy you're dealing with. You cut along back to your camp and write that note, or you'll lose out. I ain't afraid of you. I'm out for a piece o' money or I'd tell you both to chase yourselves."

"Your money you shall have," said Usha, "but you shall never live to spend it if you play us false."

"I'll be settin' waitin' for you in my tent to-night, after supper," Quorn answered.

They turned and rode away without the courtesy of taking leave, and Quorn sat still watching, to make sure that none of their followers stayed behind in hiding to keep track of his movements. He did not start back toward the elephant lines until they all vanished over the brow of a hill.

Then, when he had ridden perhaps two hundred yards, he became aware that he was watched; but he did not know who watched him until he heard the Ranee's silvery laugh and saw her ride forth, all alone, from behind a high rock by the side of the track.

"Gloomy?" she asked. "Why are you looking gloomy?"

"For one thing, miss, because it's dangerous for you to ride alone. There might be dacoits spying in the long grass."

"There were only five," she answered, "and the Rajputs caught them all. But tell me about your conference. Did all go well?"

"Went perfect, miss. The whole plan's working perfect, excep' there ain't no end to it!"

"Who knows an end from a beginning?" she retorted. "Did you know you were talking to the great Dumdumpore?"

"I guessed it."

"And Usha?"

"I guessed that, too, miss."

"You guessed well. But to outguess is better. Now what I want is Usha safe in my hands—and Dumdumpore at liberty, to guess himself into a quarrel with all the dacoits, so that they will hunt him like a wild beast."

"Yes, miss. Here's wishing 'em luck."

"Have you got that note?" she asked. "Well, get it. His estate will pay!"

12

"DID YOU STICK A STAMP ON HER HIDE AND MAIL HER HOME?"

"I WONDER WHO the sucker was," Quorn wondered aloud, "who invented that there rumor about the East not being in no hurry. Miss, do the earth turn fast enough to suit you? You should live in New York; them hustlers sets the clock forward an hour for an excuse to get up 'fore they go to bed."

The Ranee laughed. No serious discontent could exist within sound of that. Her fearless enjoyment of physical danger was contagious. And behind her laughter there was always judgment, shrewd and unexpected, though invariably daring and indifferent to anybody's comfort, her own included.

"Go ahead, miss. Shoot. I know durned well you're going to play me like a checker on a board."

"Oh, no," she said. "I think it's some one else's turn. My turn to tackle the danger—yours to stay behind the scenes."

"No, miss. Danger ain't no proper sort of employment for a young queen—"

"Don't be silly, Mr. Quorn. I am only a Ranee. I am a toy queen, tempted by fate to prove myself not such a toy after all. If I were a real queen you would see me at the head of armies. I have always thought that Joan of Arc should be spanked for having missed her opportunity—but probably the gods have done that to her. She should have laid all Europe under her heel, of course, and then governed it.

"My chance has not yet come, however—not yet. Perhaps it will. Perhaps I will do no better than she did. Meanwhile, I am only a toy queen, with an army of only fifty Sepoys, who are fed and paid so well that they are useless. One needs an army of starving malcontents to accomplish anything."

"Well, miss—what are you going to do about it?"

"Play-act! Watch me."

She stepped inside Quorn's tent and let the flap fall, so that he could not even guess what she was doing. In less than a minute she came out wearing his new blue turban and the Scotch tweed jacket that he kept for special occasions. She moved as he did, walked as he did. Save that she was wearing white riding breeches and spurred boots, any one at a distance might have thought that she was Quorn himself.

She copied every mannerism, even to his gesture when he squirted tobacco-juice through the gap between his front teeth. By an inch—perhaps more than an inch she was shorter than he, and she was much more lightly built, but perfect acting covered these discrepancies. Quorn hardly knew whether to laugh or feel offended when she mimicked his trick of scratching when he hitched his pants.

"TO-NIGHT I WILL be Ben Quorn."

"And me, miss?"

"You are Mr. X—the unknown quantity. I will sit inside the tent and wait for the woman Usha—"

"Miss, she'll spot you, sure! She'll split you with a knife as quick as packers split fish!"

"Not she. I will make a monkey of her! All the Rajputs, under Rana Raj Singh, will dispose themselves in hiding to deal with the dacoits whom Usha will certainly bring to help her make a monkey of you. You are to take your elephant Asoka and scout for Mulji, who ought to be back soon. We don't want Mulji and your idiotic cook to come bursting on the scene with news at the wrong moment. If Narak has captured Mrs. Galway and believes he has captured me, we don't want Usha or Dumdumpore to know that until they are separated and can't confer with each other."

"Miss, why separate 'em? Why not ketch 'em both and let Asoka kill 'em? He'd do it quicker'n a terrier kills a rat. They'd be two bad varmints done with."

"Don't be silly, Mr. Quorn. I want them separated, because Usha has the brains and Dumdumpore has only the resources. His resources are dacoits who will make nothing but trouble for him as soon as his brains are missing. I propose to use his brains myself, which is why Usha must be taken prisoner, not killed; but I don't want to take her prisoner until after I have learned enough from her lips to be able to make full use of all her information."

"Miss, she won't talk to you! Your voice ain't my voice; she'll detect that in the first six words you say."

"Oh? Did you never have a sore throat?" the Ranee retorted. She coughed in exact imitation of Quorn on a cold night when he had a touch of bronchial trouble. Then she spoke hoarsely, coughing again, with a handkerchief over her mouth.

"Holy mackerel! Ain't there no way o' feelin' easy without gettin' lit?"

Quorn laughed. He had to. It was his voice—his words—his mannerisms.

She resumed her own silvery speech. "Do you understand? It would be worse than useless for me to capture Dumdumpore because that would not settle the dacoit problem. If I should kill him, then the British government could declare it proved that I can't rule without murdering political rivals in place of hanging dacoits.

"How can I rid my territory of the dacoits with my little army of fifty incompetents, of whom I have had to leave forty in the city to help the police? There is only one course possible. Dumdumpore must be left at liberty. He must be made to believe that Narak has captured me. Then Dumdumpore—because he is a fool without Usha to tell him what to do—will probably fall foul of either Lumding's party or else Narak's."

"Very good, miss. But what if he doesn't?"

"Then we must see to it that the dacoits quarrel with *him*. But we will cross that river when we reach it."

"THERE AIN'T NO end to this plan, miss. There ain't no *finis* printed on the last page—not so far as I can see."

"Oh, yes, there is. The end will be when all the dacoits are either destroyed or driven out of my territory. That must happen before the British Resident returns from Delhi with power, perhaps, to force my resignation from the throne. And a new book begins—and a good one, Mr. Quorn—when you ride through the streets of Narada as the veritable Gunga *sahib,* risen from the dead. You have to die, you know."

"I'll die cheerful, miss, if that'll keep you from doing it."

"Nonsense! Can't I make you realize you are the Gunga *sahib?* I am no more important than you are—perhaps, in this particular incarnation, a bit more picturesque, that's all. You and I and Rana Raj Singh always come into the world together. Bamjee, I think, also, although I am not so sure of him; he hasn't the feel of an old familiar friend that you have. Now, you take your elephant and look for Mulji. It is nearly sunset. I will stay here."

"Miss, I'd hate to see you leave the world too rapid. I'll be lonesome without you to make me act like a doggone lunatic. Where are your ten soldiers? Have 'em near by."

"No, I have sent them to Rana Raj Singh."

"Well—'tain't my funeral. Mebbe 'tis, though! Well—orders is orders."

And so Quorn rode away on Asoka, silhouetted black against the setting sun. After a mile or so, because he knew there was only one track by which Mulji could return, he halted and stared at the caldron of cooling, fading colors in the Narada River valley, listening to the crashing echoes of the water tumbling through the rapids, until darkness at last conquered all but the echoes and the night breeze came sighing behind him to soften and subdue even the sounds.

Then starlight, luminous enough against the purple sky to tinge with almost indistinguishable opal the veil of mist that the breeze spread silently above the river and the dark-green forests on its banks.

"Heigh-ho!" he sighed, and yawned, both fists above his head. "Why ain't there somewheres a land like this, with a queen like her—and elephants—and decent likker—plus the morning paper and the movies and all a feller's old friends—and jes' an enemy or two to hate an' make you feel superior—and no snakes? Wow! What a world that would be! Why couldn't the Almighty have done it?"

His meditations were disturbed by Mulji and the cook— on foot—no elephant. They looked draggled and weary. As they stepped from the darkness like shadows they hung their heads.

"YOU MAYBE CHECKED your elephant in a parcel office," suggested Quorn with biting calm, "Or did you stick a stamp on her hide and mail her home? Did you use enough stamps? Sure she won't be returned for insufficient postage?"

"*Sahib*—"

"Goon. Spill your shame! You've lost your elephant. How come?"

"*Sahib*, dacoits came and took her from me."

"But I notice you stuck to your sweet life. I'd ha' sweetened it a piece more, mebbe, if you'd stuck to your charge instead and gone along with her and kept a bright eye for a get-away. I might ha' liked you for it—mebbe. A mahout without an elephant ain't worth a damn to any one. But go on—spill your grief."

"*Sahib*, that *sahiba* has a devil."

"Don't I know it!"

"*Sahib*, I could see the dacoits on a hill-top when she ordered me to stop that she might eat dinner. I said nay, because I knew my little elephant is swift, and we might escape them. But she said, you may tell the dacoits I am the Ranee of Narada and they will make no trouble. *Sahib!*

And I think that *babu* Bamjee told her to say that to me; he also has a devil."

"Ten of 'em," said Quorn. "But five of 'em are house-broke. Go on."

"So I stopped, and the elephant knelt, and she descended; but I remained seated on the neck of the elephant because I had foreseen what must happen, and I hoped to escape. Nevertheless, according to your honor's strict command, I waited for this thrice-accursed cook, who was busy with pots and pans and such-like foolishness; nor would he look at me, or he might have understood my signal.

"*Sahib,* I could hear the dacoits coming. So, because your honor had strictly ordered I should bring the cook back, I left my elephant to go and whisper to him beside the fire he had built. And even while I did that, dacoits ran between me and the elephant.

"So I seized the cook and he and I together jumped into a pool of muddy water, amid rushes, by the roadside, where we lay on our bellies because it was shallow. We could see little, because we dared not raise our heads except to breathe; but we could hear much—most of it the voice of that *sahiba,* uttering complaint."

"They hurt her!"

"Nay, but I think she hurt their feelings, *sahib.* For at first she protested she is not the Ranee of Narada, but she acted as it may be she thinks our Ranee might behave in such case—exceedingly arrogant. *Sahib,* there was one there who interpreted. I heard him say to the dacoit's captain, whom he addressed as Narak, that she is pretending to be a 'Melikanee. And the man named Narak was ashamed that any one should think him such a fool as to believe that.

"However, they asked Bamjee, and Bamjee said she *is* the Ranee of Narada—he being either in terror of the dacoits or pretending, I know not which. So then she changed her mind and began to pretend to be the Ranee, whereat the dacoits were even more offended, because they knew no Ranee would behave as she did, so they supposed she was mocking them."

"**WHAT DID SHE** do?" Quorn demanded.

"*Sahib,* I could not see. But I heard Bamjee beg her not to act so foolishly. He told her that not even peacocks strut thus. Then, in English, she commanded Bamjee to tell the dacoits that her army would presently come and destroy them all unless they allowed her to continue on her journey. But the interpreter overheard that, so he interpreted to Narak—whereat all the dacoits laughed and Narak said in a loud voice: 'Is she mad or art thou lying?' And then Bamjee said she is out of her mind for the moment because of great fear of their honors, which appeared to satisfy them.

"For a while there was a hunt for us two, but the water, as I said, was muddy and none could see us where we lay amid the reeds. Moreover, Narak was in haste. So presently they made her climb back into the howdah along with Bamjee, two dacoits also climbing in; and one of the dacoits took my *ankus* that I had let fall as I ran toward the pond—"

"Fine mahout you are, to let go your *ankus,*" said Quorn. "Kidded yourself you was Babe Ruth, I dare say, making a home run—chucked your bat away! I'll Babe Ruth you, you limping heathen! Go on—what happened next?"

"*Sahib,* that is all. They rode the elephant away. There were many dacoits and they surrounded the elephant on their ponies, so that the elephant had company and was not ill-pleased to go with them. And when they were out of sight this man and I came hither, hoping that your honor will believe our tale, which is the truth as I am your honor's servant and a living man."

"Aye, I believe every word of it, you sucker, and I'd like you twice as well if you was dead—a-losing your good elephant and coming back alive to face me cheeky as a dog what's lost his muzzle. Weren't you and your personal honor and that there young elephant one package?"

"*Sahib*, but you told me I should bring the cook, and—"

"Yep. That there's your alibi and I'm a reasonable man."

"Your honor is a confidant of many gods and therefore just and merciful."

"Mebbe. You ain't fired. Have you et?"

"Nay, *sahib*, not since morning."

"All right. Up you get behind me. I'll ride ye both back to the lines, where my cook shall fix you up a feed o' hash and he shall give you rations in a cloth for three days. And if either of you says one word o' this to any one—"

"*Sahib*, I will be speechless," Mulji interrupted.

"No, you won't, you sucker. You will tell your wife you're going somewheres and you won't be back for mebbe three days—mebbe longer. Then you go and find them dacoits. And you find Bamjee. And you bring Bamjee back to the lines on the back o' that young elephant."

"But how, *sahib?*" the man wailed.

"Damned if I know. But Bamjee can't manage an elephant. And a mahout without an elephant ain't no good. So you go get your elephant. If you come back here riding on him, and with Bamjee up behind, then me and you is friends again. If not—"

"I will try to do it, *sahib!*"

"You'd better! Give that cook o' mine a leg up—so. Now swing yourself up by Asoka's tail and sit behind the cook and hold him so he don't fall off. Most cooks ain't acrobats, and this one's awk'arder than most. Hang on, both of ye. *Cheloh*, buddy—step on her—give her the gas good!"

13

"THERE ARE WAYS OF PERSUADING"

BACK THEY SWAYED toward the lines at high speed. But when Quorn saw there was a dim light in his tent he slowed down. The light was suddenly extinguished. Presently he saw the shadowy shape of a mounted Rajput, so still that Asoka almost touched the horse's flank before a slight movement revealed the rider.

Without stopping, Quorn asked in a low voice. "Are they here?"

"They are here."

After that he made a circuit, in order to come at the elephant lines from the rear, around the hill, and escape observation. He passed figure after figure in the darkness; wherever there was a chance for dacoits or any one else to creep up unobserved Rana Raj Singh had posted either a mounted Rajput or else one of the Ranee's Sepoys; and the Sepoys were as silent as the mounted men, taking example from their betters. Quorn did not dare to chain Asoka in his proper stall, lest the dacoits should see him do it and make deductions; so he roped him instead near the quarry-men's quarters and routed out six of those rascals to bring a mound of fresh grass from the heap brought in by the grass-cutters. He himself went for more substantial fodder.

It was on his way back from the store-shed with a bag of unhulled rice on his shoulder that he encountered Rana Raj Singh, who was standing beside his mare in darkness so deep that his voice seemed to come from another world.

"Usha has come."

"What now, sir?"

"She is in your tent and the Ranee is also in there. She entered the tent less than five minutes ago, after posting three men in the darkness outside."

"God, sir, they'll kill her!"

"No, no. Three of my men are there. One is in the tent, under a heap of blankets; two are outside; all the others are within hail."

"Then why not close in on the skunks and ketch 'em?"

"Give the Ranee time. She has an automatic and she is well protected. Besides, Lumding and at least two hundred dacoits are in hiding near by. Probably Dumdumpore is with them. We have to be careful, we are so outnumbered. Besides, fighting in the dark is difficult."

"Ain't there going to be no fight?" Quorn asked him.

"Perhaps. Perhaps not. The dacoits may wait until daylight. We will capture Usha presently, without the dacoits knowing what has happened. They are afraid to attack in darkness. Last night taught them that much. And just now I loosed our wounded prisoner after letting him overhear a conversation in which I said the quarrymen have all been armed."

"SIR, WHY NOT take the fight to 'em and get it over with?"

"We are too few. And it will be better to have them fight with one another. Has Narak captured Mrs. Galway?"

"Yes, sir."

"And believes she is the Ranee?"

"Yes. Trust Bamjee for that."

"Good. Now you go to the tent, but go quietly and don't be seen or heard."

"Sir, I ain't no Rajput."

"No, but you are Ben Quorn. You can do it. Listen until it seems to you that the Ranee has all the information she needs. Then enter and make all the noise you like. The moment they hear that noise my men, outside the tent, will kill two of Usha's attendants and capture the third. My man inside the tent, with your aid possibly, will deal with Usha. Then take your orders from the Ranee."

"What if your men think I'm one o' them dacoits, sir, and split me like a fish?"

"They expect you. They will see and hear you. But come at the tent from behind. There is a horseman posted between the two big rocks fifty yards back of the tent. Go close to him, but don't speak. Whistle that little tune of yours. When he hears and sees you he will imitate the voice of a jackal and my men near the tent will understand. Now feed your elephant and go."

Quorn, normally the least extravagant of men, gave Asoka the whole bag of rice.

"Help yourself, you big bum. Maybe that's the last meal that ever I'll give you. I'm more skeered o' them Rajputs in the dark than I am o' dacoits! Me and you belong in Hades, I reckon; anyhow, here's hoping that we both goes to the same place! You're a ornery, cantankerous, destructive typhoon in a haybag, but I like you fine. So long to yer! And Heaven pity the guy that has to be your boss when I'm gone!"

He approached the tent with a cold wind on his spine. But it was a cool night wind that favored him, sending a sigh through the grass and filling night with scores of sounds that served to absorb his stealthy footsteps as he cat-walked from one shadow to the next.

He came on the mounted Rajput from behind, flattering himself that he had come unheard and telling himself for his own encouragement that Ben Quorn was no such duffer after all. But before he could touch the man's stirrup the Rajput whimpered like a jackal without even turning his head to confirm who it was. Quorn's boast died within him. From there to the tent he crept on all fours, because now the moon was rising.

There was litter around behind the tent—boxes not yet opened, sacks of canned goods, cans of kerosene; it was easy to lie unseen when he reached his goal. The tent could be opened at either end, and only one of the flaps at the rear was actually fastened, though they were both closed, so it was easy, too, to hear what passed within.

THE FIRST VOICE that he heard so exactly resembled his own in a bronchial mood that he had to use will and memory to make himself believe that it was the Ranee talking:

"This here note seems okay—but—who's going to give me money for it?"

"The money-lender Tul Din of Dumdumpore," said a voice that he knew as Usha's.

"Mebbe. How do I know this signature ain't forged?"

"You are a suspicious fool."

"I'm running risks. Suspicion ain't unreasonable."

"You are running no risk whatever unless you fail to do what you have promised. Fail me and take the consequences! I have given you what you demanded. Now do your part." Usha was stern.

"But the Rajah o' Dumdumpore should ha' come. I'd sooner see him sign a note; then I'd know for sure it was him as wrote it. I'm sick of all you four-flushin', double-crossin' folks that—"

"Listen: isn't the Ranee in Rana Raj Singh's camp?"

"I ain't saying."

"She is. We know she is. Those Rajputs are like a nest of hornets or we would go in and seize her ourselves. Now listen: you have that note, which was all you demanded. But if you will deliver the Ranee to us to-night, instead of waiting until to-morrow, you shall have two thousand rupees extra, in ready money."

"Who will pay it?"

"He will. The Rajah of Dumdumpore will pay it. He has the money with him. Take your elephant, go to Rana Raj Singh's camp, and persuade her for any reason you can think of to climb into the howdah. Then carry her off."

"How far would I have to take her?"

"Only a little way. The minute Dumdumpore sets eyes on her you shall have two thousand rupees. And if you are afraid to return to the camp after that, you may come with us."

"I'm skeered. What will you do with her?"

"Take her to Dumdumpore, of course."

"For what purpose?"

"He will make her his wife."

"What if she refuses? She has sperrit."

"There are ways of persuading her to change her mind. But that is none of your business. You will go to the United States and forget all about her—and all about this. If you don't, you will die more painfully than you can imagine until it overtakes you. Hurry up now; will you or will you not bring her to us to-night?"

"Mebbe she won't come."

CAREFULLY QUORN'S FINGERS felt the tent-flap. Then he tried to peer within, but it was pitch-dark. However, he could tell by the voices that the Ranee sat on or near the heap of blankets in the corner at his end and Usha was on the mat that faced his cot, in mid-tent. She would see him against the moonlight as he entered.

There was nothing for it but to act noisily and boldly, trusting to the Rajputs, outside at the far end, to act swiftly and make no mistakes. So he threw the flap over the guy-rope suddenly to let the moonlight in.

"Heck, no! She won't come!" Quorn said—and ducked. A dagger missed him by an inch. He leaped, feet forward, landing with his heels on Usha's shoulders; and before he could recover himself he felt himself thrust aside by some one who pounced on her and gripped her by the throat and one wrist. Quorn seized the other wrist, and none too gently.

The Ranee, removing Quorn's new blue turban from her shapely head, gagged Usha as artfully as a surgeon bandaging a broken skull. Outside all was silence.

"Do you suppose them guys have made their get-away?" Quorn wondered.

He opened the front of the tent and went outside to look. He stumbled over a corpse that lay face downward. There was another corpse within six feet of it—face upward, this one, with a throat split vertically and the wide-open eyes staring at the moon. Some fifty feet away from that there were three men struggling on the ground, making almost no noise. He went to lend a hand, but there was no need; already the two Rajputs had a turban around their victim's throat and he was growing weaker. Suddenly his tongue protruded and he lay still.

They tied him hand and foot and then gagged him artfully before loosening the noose, by which time he was unconscious.

"A mite too rough with him?" Quorn asked.

"Nay. Tell the Ranee all has been done as she commanded."

Quorn returned to the tent, where the Ranee had lighted a candle and sat close to Usha, studying her face.

"Two dead, one taken," he announced.

"Did that one see you? Did he recognize you?" she demanded.

"No, miss. He ain't recognizing nothing except birdies and a lot o' sparks. Them Rajputs done him up a plenty. He'll lie still for quite a while, I reckon."

"They know their business and they know what to do. He will recover presently. They will carry him to Asoka's stall. Is Asoka in there?"

"No, miss."

"Excellent. They will sit near him and talk to each other of how Asoka is to trample him to death before morning. By the time you go to him he will be in a mood to listen.

Help me now with Usha. You loosen her right hand while
I cover her with the pistol."

THEN SHE SPOKE to Usha pleasantly enough, but with
the nearest iron in her voice that Quorn had ever heard:

"I hope you will be sensible. If you are not, you will have
to be killed, although I don't like killing people—even silly
people. If you please me, by obeying me exactly, I will very
likely find employment for you in Narada later on; but
that must depend on yourself. Now—you have told me
the Rajah of Dumdumpore is somewhere near. On that
box are pen, ink and paper. Write to him. You can write?"

Usha nodded. The Ranee began to dictate and Quorn
held the candle.

"It is as we might have foreseen—Narak has stolen her.
Already he has escaped with her to the mountains. The
man they call the Gunga *sahib* is much upset, because he
will receive no money unless we capture her. I tore up the
promissory note; I would not give it to him."

The Ranee, pausing to give Usha time to catch up, looked
into Quorn's eyes, smiled and handed him the note. "You
had better take it. Keep it, and cash it as soon as you can.
It is a valid note." Then she went on dictating.

"The Gunga *sahib* captured one of Narak's men in the
scuffle. He questioned him, as I have also. Narak loves me.
For me, he would exchange the Ranee. So I go to him. The
Gunga *sahib* will take me on his elephant. The prisoner will
guide us to the proper place.

"I can manage Narak. But I cannot manage him unless I
go to him first with none other than the Gunga *sahib* and
perhaps one servant. One day later you must come with all
of Lumding's men and fall on Narak. Kill him and all his

scoundrels. Perhaps it shall be I who kill him, but come you and Lumding to destroy the others. I will put her in a safe place so that you may have her after you have destroyed those rogues."

The Ranee watched each word go on the paper, then took it and examined the large, almost childlike handwriting to make sure that Usha was playing no tricks. But Usha, her eyes glittering like a snake's, had obeyed with suspicious accuracy; it was impossible to believe she should be so obedient and not have a trick in reserve. However, the Ranee dictated again:

"It is safe for me to travel with the Gunga *sahib*, because Narak wants him, thinking him a great magician who may help his cause against Lumding, whom he hates and hopes to overthrow. And this is a good thing, because it will enable you to destroy this fool, who knows too much about you, instead of giving him a promissory note, which might be dangerous evidence.

"Therefore, I beseech you, take no steps to find or to overtake me until after I arrive at Narak's camp. And above all, do not attack this camp, because Rana Raj Singh, who is a devil, has armed the quarrymen and has persuaded them, by means of false promises, to break their word that they would be as your servants in this matter. It will be time to teach those quarrymen their lesson after you have dealt with Narak."

THE RANEE PAUSED, then resumed:

"Rana Raj Singh is alert and his men are posted so that it would not be possible, by day or night, to surprise this camp or to assault it successfully without any more men than you have with you. Two of the men who came with me are dead; the Rajputs slew them. The third is a prisoner, but he will presently escape and be the bearer of this letter.

"Gunga *sahib* has concealed me in a stack of sugar-cane near where the elephants are tethered. He will release the prisoner and let him go to you. Thereafter, he will escape with me toward Narak's camp as soon as possible.

"What Rana Raj Singh intends to do is doubtful; but the Gunga *sahib* believes he will probably take all his men and all the quarrymen, along with the elephants, back to Narada City, whence he may send a telegram asking the British government to interfere. But he does not know— he does not even guess that you are in this neighborhood, so such telegram can do no harm; it can only convince the British government that it is high time to include Narada in your territory for the sake of a better administration.

"Go away now, I beseech your highness, and go swiftly, so that Rana Raj Singh may relax his vigilance and I may slip away unseen to Narak's hiding-place. As you have trusted me thus far, now trust me to the end of this affair, that it may bring to your highness wealth and happiness and honor."

The Ranee then commanded: "Sign that."

Usha signed it. She could not speak, because of the gag, but her eyes blazed indignation and Quorn utterly mistrusted her.

"Watch out, miss," he warned, "there's a trick o' some sort. She's too dog-goned obedient."

But the Ranee only smiled. "You don't understand such people, but I do. They are never to be trusted, but they understand defeat. This woman would turn on me in an instant if she had the chance; but for the moment she will do anything that will save her from torture.

"You see—she has seen so many tortured. Haven't you, Usha? Have you seen them with salt in their mouths, Usha, and cool water dripping just out of reach? Was that what Dumdumpore would do to me, to make me agree to marry him? I wonder whether I could have endured it. You know you couldn't—don't you, Usha? Wise woman! But if you ever disobey me—"

She shook the letter until the ink was dry, Quorn wondering, as he watched her, whether she really would apply torture to a prisoner. He was undecided—would have hated to have to bet on it either way. He knew very well that he himself would torture any enemy to save the Ranee's life. She folded the letter and gave it to him.

"Take this to the prisoner, Mr. Quorn. But before he sees you, send the Rajputs out of sight. Undo the gag then and talk to him, telling him all that is in the letter. Once you are sure he believes you, loose him and let him go. But go with him as far as our farthest sentry, because Rana Raj Singh's men might possibly mistake him for an enemy and kill him, which would be inconvenient."

FIRST QUORN SUMMONED some mahouts to drag two corpses out of sight, because he knew the Ranee's superstition about bad men's bodies that, according to her theory, attract the vilest sort of elemental spirits from an unseen world and so become a mental and a spiritual menace as well as a material horror.

He did it tolerantly; she had his permission to think anything she pleased—even that he was the Gunga *sahib*— if it might help to uphold her courage. For his part, he did not actually disbelieve her theories; he merely could not understand them.

"But I don't believe in this here plan," he muttered. "It's too dog-gone complicated. Seems to me, the whole thing blows to bits as soon as Narak learns he hasn't ketched the Ranee but a hot tomater. Well—orders is orders."

He was swift with the prisoner. He feigned excitement. The man understood Hindustani, so Quorn had no difficulty telling him all that the letter contained. And the fellow was so scared by the Rajputs' talk of crushing him beneath Asoka's feet that the relief Quorn brought him upset any judgment that he might have had.

He swallowed the story whole, and he swore undying friendship. By the time his feet and hands were loose a stranger might have thought him Quorn's blood-brother from the way he took leave; he was as affectionate and fawning as a stray dog somebody had fed.

So, still feigning excitement and fear to impress the man, Quorn led him to the farthest limit of the Rajput ring around the camp and sent him hurrying with the letter.

"And give the Rajah o' Dumdumpore my best respects," he insisted, by way of a last artistic touch.

14

"SHE SHOULD KILL ME. THAT IS WHAT I WOULD DO"

THERE WAS DEADLY danger now and no doubt of it, because Usha was one of those much too numerous women who have brains and live by being dangerous. She knew her value—understood perfectly all of the complicated maze in which the Ranee was snared.

Usha knew that her death could do the Ranee no good, whereas her intimate knowledge and skill in intrigue might serve the Ranee's purpose. So she was a prisoner who might still make terms and might end, if she played her cards correctly, by being better off than ever.

She was probably of gypsy origin, at least in part. That gave her the subtly mercurial quality of yielding instantly to force and, on the surface, of agreeing candidly to any argument that she could not refute or oppose at the moment.

But it also made of her an opportunist, a genius so totally indifferent to conventionalized morals and standards of desire as to be unpredictable. One could not guess what hidden purpose underlay her open motive. It was certainly not safe to take her word for anything; worth less than any other promise that she might make was her parole.

So Quorn fixed up a cell for her in a cave hewn by the

quarrymen, building up the front of it with big stone blocks. And the Rajputs mounted guard.

Dumdumpore would never have had brains enough to send the dacoits into the Ranee's territory. It was Usha who had thought of it and who had persuaded the dacoits to do it; it was she who had foreseen that the resulting anarchy would get the Ranee of Narada into difficulties, to the subsequent profit of Dumdumpore.

Without her, Dumdumpore was incapable of managing the dacoits—equally incapable of the skillful conduct of negotiations that should end in the Ranee's deposition by the British government and the surrender of her territory to him.

Usha was sure that the moment he knew she was the Ranee's prisoner, Dumdumpore would hasten to the rescue with every resource he could command. Usha knew too many of his secrets for him to dare to do anything less.

The dacoit chief Lumding also wanted her. Lumding was aging and conscious of losing his grip on the lawless ruffians over whom he had ruled so ruthlessly for half a century. Lumding counted on her cunning; she was sure that Lumding would not leave her long in the Ranee's hands without a violent attempt at rescue.

Lumding was nearly as superstitious about her as was Narak, who counted on using her magical arts to overthrow Lumding and assume the leadership. So she knew that Narak, too, would lose no time in coming to her rescue the first moment he should learn she was a prisoner.

That much the Ranee also knew and understood. And the Ranee understood equally well that Usha's death would be avenged as terribly as savages could do it, as soon as

"You old misnamed son of a crazy earthquake," Quorn said affectionately

possible, but patiently if need be; year after year, if they must, the dacoits would wait for their chance to slay—because Usha, to them, was a priestess of magical arts, and to take her away from them by force was the same as interfering with religion, the most dangerous of all the deadly snares of politics.

SO THE RANEE took counsel with Quorn and Rana Raj Singh, seated in the quarry amid the din of hammers that made it impossible for any one to overhear them.

"What I hope," said the Ranee, "is that Dumdumpore will buy Mrs. Galway from Narak, either thinking she is me or after learning that she is Mrs. Galway."

"In either event," said Rana Raj Singh, "we could compromise him. We have that note. We have Usha for witness—"

"What I dread," the Ranee interrupted, "is that Lumding and Narak may learn what has happened, patch up peace and join forces to march against us instead of fighting each other."

"We would have to retreat," said Rana Raj Singh.

"I will not retreat! I have a throne and I will defend it to my last breath."

"Good for you, miss!" Quorn felt at the moment as if he were on the bleachers rooting for his favorite. Enthusiasm obliterated the thought that he would have to play, too.

"In this place they could too easily overwhelm us," said the Rajput prince. "Rashness and death go hand-in-hand."

"I am resolute, not rash. But if the gods say I am rash, then I will die here—and that is my last word on it."

"Then we die here also," said Rana Raj Singh, "so that is settled. What then?"

"The key is Usha. If they unite to rescue her, we are done for. But if Usha turns against them, and they know it, anything may happen."

"Yes, but how?" the Rajput asked patiently. The tap of a whip on his riding boot hinted, though, that something underlay the patience and his eyes glowed ominously. "Do you wish my men to—"

"No, I don't," she interrupted. "Torture sometimes uncovers secrets. Sometimes. It is useless for making people change their minds. They only resent what you did to them and turn on you when you least expect it—as I would, too, if anybody tortured me. Usha must act of her own free will. Do you think you could persuade her, Mr. Quorn?"

"Me, miss? Mebbe. If you let me take my *ankus* in there. I've persuaded elephants. Even Asoka agrees, free-willing, time I've showed him it don't pay to free-will contrary to my judgment. Say the word—I'll change that hussy's religion or fix her so's she won't have any for a while."

"You leave your *ankus* here," the Ranee answered. "Go in and use your wisdom."

"Miss, I haven't any."

"Nonsense. You are the Gunga *sahib,* so the gods will give you wisdom—just as they give it to me, too, when I need it, because I am Sakyamuni."

"How about you bankin' on the gods, then? Why not you go in to her and let them gods tip you what to say?"

"No. My wisdom tells me to send you in. Go in now and talk to her."

"For a guy whose job is bossing elephants, I'm some—"

"You are the Gunga *sahib.* Go on in."

QUORN WENT, DREADING the task. He could think of no argument, nothing to say that would influence Usha's mind. She was probably bitter against him for having tricked her, and if she listened to him it would only be to give him lying answers, he did not doubt.

He supposed that to tell her the truth would only make him seem ridiculous in her eyes; whereas to lie to her would be to enter into competition with a past mistress of lying, who would catch him in his own net.

"Don't I wish them gods o' hers weren't hooey!" he muttered. "If there was any gods around I'd listen to 'em like I was a sponge a mopping up rum from a barrel."

The Rajputs had to pull down heavy stone blocks to admit him. Usha, blinking at the sunlight, sat on a folded blanket with her back to the rear wall, looking humorously abject, as if she were amused at bitter luck that had snatched her hope away.

She was a handsome woman, much too wise to let anger spoil her looks and rob her of that advantage. It was her shoulders that drooped. Her eyes shone curiosity and welcome.

She betrayed no hint of ill-will, even when Quorn, with his hands on his hips, stood before her and stared with grim distaste that he made no effort to conceal.

"You unfriendly?" she asked.

"No. Anything I can get yer? Do you chew tobaccer? Care for a shot o' Scotch?"

She shook her head. "Why do you come?"

"Durned if I know." He sat down beside her, cross-legged, his back to the wall. "I'm supposed to dicker with yer."

"Oh! She sent you?"

"Yep."

"Why did she not come herself?"

"Mebbe she thought I'd stand a better chance o' makin' you believe we ain't so rotten as you think. She may ha' thought you'd hate her too bad to listen to reason."

"So she thinks I'm difficult?"

"Aw, she knows it. We all know it. I'll be frank to tell you, we don't know what to do nex'—what to do wi' you, I mean."

"She should kill me. That is what I would do to her if we were in each other's places."

"She thought o' that," said Quorn. "We all did."

"Then why don't you do it?"

"Durned if I know. I'd ha' voted for it, but she was set ag'in' it; she wouldn't have you tortured, neither. So you see, you ain't dead yet."

"But I don't see why not," Usha answered.

"No. No more do I," Quorn admitted ruefully. It appeared to him that he was getting nowhere.

"**DO YOU THINK** it possible there is something that she wishes me to do?" Usha suggested.

"Mebbe."

"Perhaps she wishes me to tell her how to defeat Dumdumpore?"

"Mebbe."

"Would she make that worth my while?"

"Mebbe. Depends what you want."

"Would she trust me?"

"Mebbe."

"Why do you trust her?"

"For the same reason that you would, if you had any sense, you durned fool. Me, I trust her 'cause she's okay— 'cause there ain't no yellow streak in her—'cause she never goes back on a friend. I trust her 'cause she's on the level, an' plucky, an' generous—'cause she has the courage to defy them priests and nerve enough to stand up and scrap with a treacherous sucker like Dumdumpore. Say—how much did them priests o' Narada pay you to persuade Dumdumpore to do this foolishness?"

"Who told you I know those priests?"

He had stumbled on something! Why had he suddenly asked her that question? He did not know, any more than he knew what to say to her answer. If the Ranee's gods had prompted him, he wished they would carry on the good work instead of starting something and then leaving it.

"I know 'em too. I ain't plumb ignorant," he answered. "Me, I'm bettin' on our young Ranee to win against that gang o' suckers. You, you're bettin' on the wrong side."

"You think? What will she give me if I help her?"

Quorn tried almost frantically to imagine what might tempt such a woman as Usha, but his mind was a blank. He could think of nothing except money and, somehow, money seemed the wrong thing to suggest.

"Lord love yer," he said suddenly, "what more do you want than a chance to come clean and act honest? Don't you want a chance to slam that sucker Dumdumpore—to double-cross a four-flushing hawg that 'ud doublecross you for the sake of his hide any day o' the week, same as he has every other fool who ever trusted him? And what more do you want than a chance to make a sucker o' them priests? Ain't they the jackal's yell? Won't it look sweet to see them eatin' crow and having to tell the populace that the gods have given judgment between our young Ranee and the Rajah o' Dumdumpore, who has met with his just deserts? Could you beat that?"

"Dumdumpore is a pig," said Usha, "and the priests are vermin."

"Then why do you keep 'em company?"

"I keep the company of him who trusts me. Would the Ranee trust me?"

"Who said not? And anyhow, what do it matter—so long as you can trust her?"

"It matters everything. If she trusts me, it matters everything. I die for any one who trusts me. If she trusts me not, I do nothing for her. Dumdumpore would be better, because he trusts me a little, but he trusts me very little out of sight. Lumding would be better. Narak would be better. They trust me a little because they fear my magic. Any one who trusts me, I love him—I do him much good. No trust? My enemy! I stab him!"

"**DO YOU KID** yourself that Dumdumpore is anybody's friend? Do you kid yourself he's your friend?"

"I no 'kid' myself. Dumdumpore is vermin. I no trust him. But he trust me now and then—a little—now and then a lot, when he can't help it. That is better than not to be trusted at all."

"Would you trust me?" Quorn asked.

"Yes. You are the Gunga *sahib*. You are a fool, but what you say, you mean, I know that. You would die for your Ranee because she trusts you—is it not so? I would die for any one who trusts me."

"The heck you would!"

"I speak true."

"Do you know what I'd do," Quorn asked her, "if you was to kid the Ranee she could trust you, and she did it, and you let her down intentional? I'd hunt yer till I found yer. And I'd do you dirt. Do you believe that?"

"Why not? But why you say I kid the Ranee? Is she such a fool she would talk about trust and not mean it? Should she not mean it, I would know; then I would—what you call it?—double-cross her. But if she mean it, I would know that and Dumdumpore and all those dacoits can go to the devil—*phooth!* If she is what you say she is—"

"I haven't said the half of it."

"Then she will look into my eyes and she will trust me. If she is good, as you say she is good, I will know that when I take a good look in her eyes—"

"Yeh—but you ain't good. You're a bad 'un," Quorn said dubiously. "What right ha' you to be pickin' and choosin'?"

"I would rather that a good one trust me than that all the power in the world is mine."

"But you've a rep, you know. You're dangerous."

"That is all that I am good for—to be dangerous. And I am dangerous to her if she is bad. If she is a hypocrite, I hate her. If she is good talker and bad doer, then I spit. If she is a coward, I spit; and then I lie to her, because a coward can't trust any one—she only pretend. And I kill maybe. And I spit on her when she is dead. But if she—what you call it?—if she got nerve, then I love her. Then I am more dangerous than ever, not to her but to her enemies."

"You're a heck of a good talker. You could sell a line o' Bolshevism to a bishop," Quorn admitted.

"You are not good talker. You are damn fool. Now you go outside and tell it all wrong; and she smile up the side of her mouth and never trust me."

"I wouldn't trust yer a yard," said Quorn. But Usha only nodded, peering at him from under half-closed eyelids.

"You are no such fool as you pretend," she said after a minute's silence.

"The heck o' me," said Quorn, "is that I ain't pretendin' nothin'. I'm jes' plumb skeered. And I'm skeered o' you. I'd vote to have you trod on by my elephant, and I'd eat my dinner twice as easy afterward. I ain't kiddin'."

"I think you are remarkable nice man," said Usha.

"You mean you'd like to stick a knife in me."

"Not often I kill nice men," Usha answered. "But if the Ranee trust me—and you not do right for the Ranee—then I kill you. Maybe I stick knife then in your kidneys."

"And you don't touch whisky or chew tobaccer? Ain't

much I can do to make you comfortable 'fore they shoot you, is there?"

STICKING HIS HANDS in his pockets, Quorn strolled out, believing in his honest heart that he had mystified the woman more than she had puzzled him.

The Rajputs put the stone blocks back in place, Quorn superintending because he trusted no man with a black beard and a dark skin to do a proper job at any kind of careful work. Then he walked to the midst of the quarry and stood silent in front of the Ranee and Rana Raj Singh. For more than a minute the Ranee said no word but gazed into his eyes. Then:

"Tell me," she commanded. "Tell me in a telegram of ten words."

"Miss," he answered slowly, "since you ask me, I should say yes."

"I can use her?"

"Yes, miss."

"Trust her?"

"Miss, you'll hev to trust her. Same as I trust Asoka. If I didn't trust him, that old bag o' tantrums 'ud finish me quick as a cook can wring a chicken's neck. There ain't no kind of evil that old son of a typhoon hasn't wrought, and I've forgiven him as frequent as the priest did Pat Maloney, 'cause there weren't nothin' else to be done. But I trust him, miss. I hev ter. And it sets good on my stummick, 'cause he's saved you half a score o' times by doin' dirt to other people; which that is his religion. And you can't blame man or elephant for his religion, if he sticks to it and does his durnedest. Usha ain't no dangerouser than Asoka."

The Ranee nodded. "Ask those Rajputs, Mr. Quorn, to remove the stones again."

She waited in silence, Rana Raj Singh tapping irritably at his riding boot, until the opening gaped wide. Then she approached the cave mouth.

"Usha," she called, "you may come."

Usha stood framed in the opening. Their eyes met for the space of half a minute.

"I will be your friend as long as you are my friend," said the Ranee. "I will trust you just as long as you trust me."

"So? Then you will trust me until death," said Usha.

15

"TAKE THE ELEPHANTS AND FLEE!"

FOREBODING FELL WITH darkness like a pestilence, and one by one they shuddered until even the Ranee fought with tears that all but conquered her. They were so few, against so many; and so much depended on the outcome.

They sat around a fire in front of Quorn's tent because Quorn would not desert the elephants for the safer seclusion of the Ranee's camp amid easily defended rocks. Every fifteen or twenty minutes Rana Raj Singh mounted and rode to visit one or other of his sentries, speaking bold words from a hollow heart and returning to sit with his chin on his fist.

Usha, with a fixed stare at the cherry-red heart of the fire, was letting glimpses of the truth about herself appear amid skeins of lies. She spoke as the mood of a moment seized her, in Hindustani, English or the mongrel dialect that passes current in the villages.

"And why I tell, no matter. Nobody would understand. But the priest who is coming—I say to you: give me a knife and let me mutilate him."

Near by, with a Rajput guarding him, there sat a temple servant who had come to announce with brassy insolence that one of Siva's priests was on his way with a message and demanded audience. He had been whipped by Quorn to teach him manners, and sat whimpering with his head beneath a blanket Quorn had given him to hide his shame; the mahouts had laughed and that had hurt more than the strokes of a rattan cane.

"For I hate those priests," said Usha. "But to fight them is useless. It is they who desire to destroy Narada for their own ends. Dumdumpore would yield to their influence. You stand against it."

"Even if I die, I will stand against it," said the Ranee.

"Surely you will die, as do all their enemies," said Usha. "That is why I bid you let me knife that murderer who comes. He is a murderer with clean hands. It is his tongue that poisons. It is always others who do the slaying and who pay for the slaying, in prison and on the gallows—but with never a Brahmin to give them comfort when they die. The priests sow; we reap. He who comes is he who caused the hanging of my father and two brothers."

"Are you telling the truth?" the Ranee asked.

"Enough of it. If I told all, the Mahabharata and all the Vedas and the Lay of Alha would be but a tinker's song compared to it. That priest who comes engaged my father to slay the Rajah of Moolnuggah, who had mocked the priests and said their mysteries were less than nothing—even as you do, Daughter of the Dawn."

"I say their claims are lies and their authority is false. I love their mysteries," said the Ranee.

"No matter. They accuse you of atheism because you mock their lies; that is ever their way. That Rajah of Mool-nuggah had no son; his cousin was his heir, and he craved the throne, so he promised the priests great tribute and authority. Because he was the heir to the throne and made unseemly haste to claim it when his cousin died of what was said at first to be a hunting accident, suspicion fell on him. So that priest who comes to-night betrayed my father and two brothers to the police. And they were hanged."

SEVEN TIMES, AT measured intervals, Usha spat into the heart of the fire before she continued:

"I sought vengeance. It was not enough to kill one priest, in exchange for three lives. I sought to ruin all of them. But that is not easy. I lent myself to their devices, suffering all indignities until they believed I am their fearful servant. They think—those fools!—they think I believe the lies they tell about the gods. They think I am afraid to disobey them lest they curse me and I die to become a worm forever. But I have learned all sorts of magic from them, and I know their ways, so at last they sent me to Dumdumpore to persuade him to do this treachery against you."

She stared moodily at the fire and spat again.

"How would that have given you revenge?" the Ranee asked.

"I hoped Dumdumpore would kill you. What did I care about you? I had never seen you. Let Dumdumpore kill you or carry you off—and then turn on the priests when I betray him. I have two other witnesses of his conspiracy with the priests. But it is too late now for that. I think that we four are to die here. That is why I ask for a knife, with which to mutilate that dog of a priest who comes to mock you."

"Why do you think we will all four die here?" asked the Ranee.

"That is something that I know. I do not need to guess that." Usha answered. "Did I not write to Dumdumpore at your dictation? That was before you promised you will trust me and we were enemies then."

"Nevertheless, you wrote what I dictated," said the Ranee.

"Why not? Could I have done otherwise? You watched me, did you not? Yet—although you held it to the candle-light you did not notice that I pierced the paper many times. Perhaps you saw that and supposed I always write so heavily. But I can write as lightly as a shadow on the paper if I wish. That piercing with the penpoint is a trick that I learned from the priests. And I taught it to Dumdumpore. He is a flabby fool, but he will read that letter fifty times, and at last he will see the pen-pricks. Soon after he has seen them he will understand."

"What did they mean—those pen-pricks?" asked the Ranee.

"Not much—only that the letter is a lie. That was the prick on the first line. The prick on the second line means I am in danger. That on the third line means his enemy is weak. And the prick on the fourth line urges him to act swiftly—on the fifth, with violence—on the sixth, with the aid of his friends. He could not misinterpret that, because he has no other friends than dacoits.

"The prick on the seventh line means that a deception has been practiced, concerning which he must undeceive himself as fast as possible; the prick on the eighth line means that the same deception has been practiced on his friends. Thus he may put two and two together and arrive at understanding. The prick on the ninth line means the deception relates to a woman; and that on the tenth infers that his friends are divided against each other and he must plan at once to reunite them. If I had made the pricks in other places on the same lines they would have had other meanings. It is a simple code, but none who has not the key can read it."

RANA RAJ SINGH kicked a brand into the fire and breathed sibilantly. He made no other comment, but strode to where his mare was tethered, near by, and presently trotted off to ride the rounds again. But he did not go far. Suddenly Asoka's stablemate, the mule, brayed hideously and all the elephants tugged at their pickets, tossing their trunks in air—a row of big black phantoms swaying in purple darkness.

Quorn sprang to his feet. The mahouts shouted. There came a challenge from the outer night—and suddenly another phantom burst into the zone of firelight, wheeled and sped toward the empty end-stall. Then, as suddenly as they had shown excitement, three-and-thirty elephants grew still.

"Young she-elephant's back. Here's hoping she ain't harmed," said Quorn and started to investigate.

But he, too, did not get far. Mulji met him, and Bamjee on Mulji's heels. The mahout knelt, touching Quorn's feet, but Bamjee ran into the firelight, where he stood breathless for a moment.

"Lo, I bring my elephant," said Mulji. "Heavenborn, am I a true mahout?"

"You'll do. What's wrong with her?"

"Nothing. As I live, no harm has come to her, save that she is perhaps a little weary, having run far."

"All right. Feed and water her, then look to her feet. After that you may come to my cook for your supper."

Quorn returned to the fire, where Bamjee stood recovering his breath. He had broken both the lenses of his spectacles, so the shadows baffled him and he could not tell which was the Ranee and which was Usha.

Quorn enlightened him, shoving him out of reach of the mare's heels; Rana Raj Singh stood beside the mare and, as his custom was, said nothing until he knew what there was to discuss. Nobody spoke until Quorn put a hand on Bamjee's shoulder and his restrained voice broke the tension.

"Speak your sorrow, little man. We know it ain't no good news."

"Daughter of the Dawn, Highness, Heavenborn—my news is dreadful. Take the elephants at once and flee before the dacoits come! It is better my story should wait—I can tell it as we run toward Narada."

"There will be no running," said the Ranee. "Speak up, Bamjee."

But she was wrong. Mulji had told the quarrymen enough to send them into headlong flight. Like giant bats, their bundles on their shoulders, they began to stream in a long line southward, and not even the foreman came to make pretense of asking leave or to explain the panic.

"Let them run," said Usha. "If Lumding's men or Narak's men pursue them there will be the fewer for you to deal with."

"Bamjee, tell your story," said the Ranee.

"Glory of the Moonlight, I am undone! These knees oscillate with remembrance. In memory I see the horror that I left behind me. It will overtake us presently—and then what? Mrs. Galway, I assure you, is a detonator! Spark in powder-magazine, compared to her, is as harmless as old-fashioned squib on a rajah's birthday! She is like a detonator in a barbed-wire factory full of TNT! By Krishna, she is! And Dumdumpore—he hit her with a hammer on the nose and set her off!"

Quorn put a hand on his shoulder again: "Cut all them preliminaries. Spill the beans," he ordered.

"SHE INSISTED ON lunch," said Bamjee, "so the dacoits under Narak came and took us, as per story very likely told by Mulji the mahout and Mr. Quorn's cook. But they were much too terrified to see it all; their terror, spurring atavistic instinct, set them back a hundred thousand aeons. Mulji and the cook were suddenly reborn as tadpoles and took to the water.

"But that woman—oh, my God! First she was not the Ranee. Then she was the Ranee. Then she was the Ranee's aunt. Then, oh my God, she was the Queen of the United States with an admiral and fifty battleships at anchor in Bombay Harbor! The interpreter told all of that to Narak, who was naturally curious.

"The interpreter at one ear, she at the other, swaying on the back of a balky elephant, I had to try to reconcile all her statements with your highness's instructions to me and the probably opportunist policy of Narak, Lumding, Usha, and the Rajah of Dumdumpore, to say nothing of indignation of the British government. I fell back on the Einstein theory of relativity and said she was mad. That worked perfectly for thirty minutes—by my wrist-watch."

"Time?" said Quorn. "There ain't no such thing as time

in this here Orient. Everything happens at once or never. Try shoving your tale out side-wise, Bamjee. It'll take too long if it crawls out head first."

"Speak on," said the Ranee. "We are listening."

"She was so annoyed by being thought mad that she set to work to prove herself sane. Can you imagine that? To prove to Narak she is sane! As if it mattered! So she made use of the interpreter to ask Narak about his religion and about what chance he thought he had of getting into heaven when he dies if he practices having more than one wife at a time.

"That woman was simply unbelievable. I could do nothing about it. I even threatened to slap her mouth, but she complained to the interpreter and he told Narak; so Narak laughed and had me pulled down off the elephant and put on a pony behind a ruffian who stank like a hyena. After that, of course, there was no stopping her at all.

"And of course, the more she talked about Narak's personal affairs with women, the more convinced he became that she was certainly not the Ranee of Narada, whoever else she might be. Even that ignorant dacoit knew that a royal lady would not talk with men concerning such intimate matters.

"So Narak changed his mind about her. He decided he would not carry her off to the mountains, since she might not be worth all that trouble. He decided to give her to Lumding. And he rode alongside me and threatened to tear off all my toenails if I didn't tell the truth about her. I cannot endure to have my toenails torn off, so I told him she is a sorceress who can turn men into lice-infested crows. I thought he would be afraid and let us go when

I told him that, but no, he thought she would be excellent for Lumding, who would probably annoy her and be punished for it.

"After that he was only interested in two things: Could Lumding be turned into a louse without the crow? And did I know of a protection against her spells? He said I must know, because he had seen me annoy her; yet I was still a *babu*, not a crow. So I told him he must say his own name backwards whenever she looked at him and must always carry a hair from a horse's tail inside his turban." Bamjee paused a second for breath.

"I AM AN optimist," he resumed. "This *babu* then saw possibility of so manipulating superstition as to bring on internecine warfare between dacoits, and thus Kilkenny-cat the whole outfit, to the everlasting glory of your highness. Said much, making many promises to Narak, who in turn assured me that he will torture all my enemies to death if I should turn out not to be a liar. All would have gone nicely, I believe, but for an accident. Whom should we meet but the Rajah of Dumdumpore, himself, in person! Oh, my God!

"It was dark by that time, moon having risen, but we were in a valley of black shadow—very hungry, I remember. Still am, having eaten nothing and vomited much from fear and topsy-turviness of too much thinking. Terrible!

"For sake of alibi, no doubt, or possibly because he, also, fears the dacoits, Dumdumpore had ordered his camp removed into that valley, where there is a haunted ruin of which the dacoits are afraid. Servants pitching tents in the dark—confusion—panic as we arrived—talk, lies, explanations, argument—and suddenly the rajah on a very hot horse—foaming at both mouths—the rajah foamingest.

"He had a letter in his hand—disgust on his lips. He said Usha was a certain sort of female—said which sort— said it often. That not being news to me, this *babu* turned attention elsewhere, seeking to discover why we waited. Suddenly obvious—young she-elephant now weary and demanding supper. Ponies also not so fresh as formerly. Narak ordered the dacoits to seize fodder and provisions from the rajah's camp, making rajah's servants very angry. Pitch-dark. Rajah in his big tent, studying a letter by the candlelight.

"Even so, all might have gone well, I believe, had that she-detonator Mrs. Galway not gone off suddenly like watchman's rattle. Fat was in the fire then. 'Who is he? What is he? Why is he here? I wish to see him! Help, help! Rescue!'

"Out then comes the rajah and demands to know what fuss is all about. Narak tells him—his version. Mrs. Galway tells him—her version. Presently I tell him—my version. I say, both of them are liars and that Mrs. Galway is a fugitive from justice on whose head is a reward of a *lakh* of rupees that has been offered by the British government.

"Thus I hoped to cause the rajah to lay his hands on her and detain her, this involving him in legal difficulties. Head in a whirl—everything upside-down and could not think collectedly—must make up new plans on the instant and could not do it. Pity me and be not angered. Did my utmost."

"I forgive you, Bamjee. Go on with your story," said the Ranee.

"O Everlasting Joy, I stood there. And the rajah asked me where your highness is, and how many soldiers are with you, and why you should practice deceit on himself and these innocent men by substituting for your royal self this female alien whose voice is like the clashing of cymbals. And he threatened to have my finger nails removed with pincers. Then he read me Usha's letter. Nevertheless, I perceived by his manner of reading it that there were other meanings to the words. It was as plain to me as that the moon was in the sky, that Usha had put one over on us and that I must do something about it—but what?

"Glory of the Morning, oh, the whatness of that what! This miserable *babu* could imagine nothing! I looked up at the sky, and there was nothing there but stars; they told me nothing. I looked at the ground, where was nothing but darkness all around me. And I looked into the eyes of the Rajah of Dumdumpore, where was cruelty, treachery, greed—and hatred, at that moment aimed at me! I was the target of it. Pity and forgive me! I deplore the unwise words I said to him. But they are said—oh, woe is this *babu!*—beyond recall.

"I said to him: 'Thrice Nobly Born, this futile *babu* believes her highness loves you and has sent this shameless, cymbal-sounding female to you as an irritant—to make you see how worthless any other woman is and oh, how easily a woman may be pounced upon and carried off!' I know not why I said it, Daughter of the Moon and Stars. I think some devil slipped the words into my mouth."

QUORN SWORE FERVENTLY, and Rana Raj Singh drew an inward breath. But the Ranee smiled, her eyes like jewels in the firelight.

"It seems to me that you spoke very wisely, Bamjee," she said in her silvery voice. "What else could you have said? He will come for me now, I suppose? Will he bring all the dacoits, or only Narak's men?"

"All—all of them, *sahiba!* He persuaded Narak there and then to go to Lumding and to summon him with all his fighting men in that valley at dawn! He said the gods have given you and all Narada into his hands, since he can now prove to the Indian government that he was forced to invade Narada to save the life of this alien lady, whether or not she is a fugitive from justice! Also he spoke of the *lakh* of rupees reward that in a moment of madness I invented, and he promised Narak that he and Lumding shall divide it all between them! Furthermore, he spoke to Narak about Usha, saying Usha is in peril. Therefore Narak went away in haste to summon Lumding, leaving only six men to guard me and Mrs. Galway and the elephant.

There in that valley I still would be, *sahiba,* had not Mulji the mahout come looking for his elephant. Because the elephant was weary it was lying down. But it seemed to forget its weariness when Mulji came up like a shadow. I, too, forgot my fright when Mulji whispered to me in the darkness. Mulji cut the heel-rope. He and I together climbed on to the elephant's neck and lo, it was a long way and a hard ride, but we are here—"

"And here we die!" said Usha. "I can hear that priest approaching. Give me a knife and let me kill him!"

16

"A TUB O' TNT ON FOUR FEET"

SUBWAY RUMBLINGS SHAKE a city's roofs. Spasms from an earthquake stir the eagles' feathers in the sky. Age-long warfare in Narada between church and state had its unmistakable surface indications, and the Brahmin priest from Siva's temple made a more than royal progress, not because he liked it—dabblers in the darker mysteries prefer to attract less notice to themselves—but because political plans demand noise or they die.

The bray of the conchs, the tomtoms, cymbals, and a gleam of torchlight announced him through the darkness while he was more than a mile away. Usha repeated her demand:

"Give me a knife and let me kill him!"

There was more than one knife within her reach; but what she wanted was the Ranee's confidence. She craved that. She was willing, like Charlotte Corday and many another, to take all blame and all the consequences; but the price was the Ranee's blessing.

She had never been blessed by any one for whom she had sincere respect. She craved it like a criminal about to feel the public hangman's rope. Less than a dozen hours ago she would have slain the Ranee just as willingly, but at the price of a blessing from some one else. She was in the market. Her price for the commission of any crime whatever, was the sensation of being in the confidence of some one better than herself. For the sake of some one better than the Ranee she would turn again. The Ranee understood her.

"Nonsense!" said the Ranee. "Let him think he sees a victory. His insolence will kill him. Let death choose its victims. Why should we?"

"Nevertheless, I will set some sabers near," said Rana Raj Singh. He rode away into the darkness.

"Mr. Quorn is the one who is chosen for death. The legends chose him," said the Ranee. "It is no bad thing that priests are here to witness that. When he returns to life and rides into the city on his elephant, what shall the priests of Siva say then? They will be petrified."

"Them suckers won't be petrified no more than me," said Quorn. "I reckon I can die as slick as any man, but—"

"Before they have time to think of new evasions they will stand committed," said the Ranee. "Publicly committed. Ben Quorn thereafter is known as the Gunga *sahib*. No man will dare to deny it. So the priests shall take a back seat."

"Do you mean I am to kill Quorn?" Usha asked. She was perfectly willing—a new convert to a new religion—very eager to earn approval.

"No, indeed. You kill too permanently... You know this priest. He knows you. You are the one who must deceive him with his own intrigue. I said, let him think he sees a victory. If you should say you have persuaded me to yield— if you should tell him I am willing to become the wife of

Dumdumpore, because I see how utterly impossible it is for me, with only fifty men, to rid this land of dacoits who will presently destroy me unless some one who can control them calls them off, will he disbelieve you?"

"No," said Usha.

"Why not?" The Ranee's characteristic sudden rapier trick of wordplay had pricked many an immature plan and so had saved her and her friends from many a disaster. But Usha was on her own ground now and knew her business.

"Who doubts the bird that he sees in his hand? Was I not sent by the priests to do this very thing? Is he not coming here to-night to try to talk you into this surrender? Will he not take credit to himself for having won for the priests without having actually to employ the violence that almost certainly would cause a scandal? The priests detest a scandal, even though they use it to their own ends at the last."

"You are right," said the Ranee. "Remember, I trust you. Do it."

Then, although she knew her liberty, her life and throne were all in Usha's keeping for the next few hours, she lighted a gold-tipped cigarette and smoked it without bravado and without a trace of nervousness. She had faith in her intuition—faith and a fencer's love of finely measured hair's-breadths between destiny and death.

QUORN, HOWEVER, WAS no such lover of the feel of death's breath in his whiskers; he wished he had shaved that morning, because every bristle on his face was stirring as if living fear were crawling on his skin.

"Better not wait for him here, miss," he suggested.

" 'Twon't look good. 'Tain't far to your own camp. You can get there 'fore he comes."

"No," she answered, "I will wait here. My tent is silk and the servants will have lighted all the lamps. The place will look much too splendid. Here all is shabby—I look more like a defeated Ranee. It is better so."

"I'll be right back, miss."

Inherent mistrust of the priests and a feeling, akin to instinct, that the dacoits and the priests were likely to know of each others' movements and to act suddenly without warning, sent him to where Asoka stood swaying in darkness at the end of the long line of swaying shadows. Each man to his own—his own argument, his own weapon and his own friend in a crisis.

Quorn could think, with Asoka's fool trunk searching in his pockets. He could feel, as it were, the impending drift of things, in contact with that enormous tonnage of living natural force that included love, anger and intelligence far greater than a man's in some respects, if pitifully less in others.

Quorn's own pride in the strength and dangerous reputation of the huge beast that obeyed him came to his aid in such moments, loosening the floods of sentiment that save a man from blind logic, the loveless god of the intellectuals who would destroy the human race if only men would logically worship him.

"You big bum," Quorn muttered, rubbing his cheek against the restless trunk. "You old bag o' tantrums, me and you's been buddies; but it looks as if we're near the end now. Shall I write you a recommendation, you old sucker? What 'll I set down: honest? Shall I say you was a tub o' TNT on four feet, what never went off exceptin' at the wrong time? What for did they call a guy like you 'Asoka'? *That* means free from sorrow. I'm that sorry at the thought o' losing you that I could blub about it—no kiddin'—only I'm ashamed for her to see me with a wet eye.

"What a sensible guy should like you for I'm durned if I know. Maybe I ain't sensible. I like ye fine—you old misnamed son of a crazy earthquake. Who was the cocky optimist who first called you Asoka? If I'd been there when you was broke to heel-ropes I'd ha' named you Dynamite— and you're that contrary you'd prob'ly have—"

He stiffened. "Dynamite!" he muttered. Then he looked along the swaying line of elephants. They were like dark goblins' laundry hanging on a line, in a phantom wind that blew unfelt, unheard.

He went to see whether the quarrymen had robbed the tool-shed before taking flight. He found the padlock on the door, but no key, so he smashed the lock. The tools and dynamite were all there—nearly a hundred boxes of the stuff, with a barrel of caps and quantities of fuse, some coils of insulated wire and a box of dry-cell batteries.

He closed the shed door, returned to Asoka, loosed his heel-rope, mounted him and rode with measured dignity toward the camp fire. He could see the glow of the Ranee's cigarette.

"It's funny," he muttered. "I don't feel skeered no more. I'll bet she's thinkin' what I'm thinkin'. She looks calm, but, heck, I know her! She's just boiling with excitement. So'm I! Durn her gamblin' instinct! I believe she'd sooner die than have things safe and easy!"

THE PRIEST CAME, carried in a chair on poles, surrounded

by servants, blood-red in the torchlight, barbaric in his
insolence. His thin-lipped smile suggested that he thought
the Ranee a mere newcomer, whose line of ancestors was
traceable only for a scant two thousand years or so, and
who was human at that.

His dealings were with gods, his rating a divine sub-re-
gent. He let an ominously long pause elapse before he bade
his toiling porters lower the gilded chair and stepped to
earth apparently expecting homage.

But he was met in silence. He received a stare from Rana
Raj Singh that might have chilled the blood of any one not
shielded and made arrogant by the custom that accords to
priests immunity from personal chastisement. Quorn spat
into the fire—a wondrous long-range shot from his seat
on Asoka's neck. Usha sat still, her eyes smoldering with
what might be triumph.

"You bring me a message?" asked the Ranee.

If that priest could read her mind or motive he was wiser
than he looked; voice, gesture, nothing indicated what her
mood might be. His own impassive face betrayed in the
torchlight a hint of suppressed irritation. Pausing before
he answered, he appeared to decide to try what mannerless
impudence could do.

Instead of answering her, he addressed himself to
Usha—in a low voice. Quorn could not catch what he
said. Usha answered in almost a whisper, her lips scarcely
moving, her eyes fixed in a burning stare on his. The priest
left his chair on the ground in the midst of the torches and
retired into the outer darkness. Usha followed him.

The Ranee smiled. But there was no word said around
the little camp fire, until at last the priest returned into

the zone of light, more mannerless than ever, with a curl of contempt on his lips, and his glittering eyes alight with malice. Usha did not come with him; Quorn saw her whispering in the dark with one of the priest's attendants.

"So you yield?" The words were cruelly inflected. It was clear he proposed to spare her no indignity. He turned to Rana Raj Singh. "What are you doing here?"

He received no answer. His eyes looked like an alligator's as he turned again toward the Ranee. The suggestion—not intended, he meant to hide it—was that he felt so sure of having Rana Raj Singh at his mercy that he did not need to advertise the fact; nor did he need to hint how little mercy lay within the triumph of his mood.

"So you see, you must turn to the gods in spite of all your sacrilege and neglect and insolence toward us, the gods' faithful worshipers," he said. "And the gods will help, because they see in terms of centuries. Your mockery means nothing to them. The inevitable punishment that you have brought upon yourself will be your own affair, during many lives to come. But what of this man?"

He did not look at Quorn; he indicated him with the smallest possible backward and upward gesture of the head.

"Well? What of him?" asked the Ranee.

"The impostor, said to be the Gunga *sahib!* What is to be done with him? Will you take him with you when you go to Dumdumpore? To die there and to be reborn?"

Quorn's voice answered him from up in the torch-light-tinted gloom above Asoka's solemn head:

"Did you never hear what happened to the cockerel that crowed afore sun-up?"

That was the one touch needed. It gave the priest the

satisfaction of ignoring Quorn, and it egged him on, lest his treachery reveal itself too soon. He slipped a cog or two of his intrigue in his haste to make events march as he wished them to.

"I WILL ESCORT you now to the camp of the Rajah of Dumdumpore," he told the Ranee.

Quick work—too quick even for the Ranee of Narada, who could think more swiftly than the summer lightning! She laid her chin on her hand as if, perhaps, she had not understood; but from his height above the ground Quorn's eyes could see what the priest's could not because of the smoky splendor of the torchlight that created baffling shadows.

In the velvet darkness at the Ranee's back knelt Usha, whispering—or at least, Quorn thought she whispered; he could see a shadow that he knew was Usha, and whether or not her lips moved was impossible to tell.

Rana Raj Singh took a few strides nearer to the Ranee, doubtless to determine whether Usha had a dagger in her hand. He was a man of parts, but he lacked that vivid understanding which enabled the Ranee to trust a murderess. However, the effect was to provide a screen between the priest and Usha and to divert the priest's attention for the moment to the Rajput prince.

"Since you and your followers have made yourselves a sort of outlaw army, you had better continue to protect the Ranee's camp," said the priest with a sneer that was like acid. "Or will you desert her in extremity? It is true, her belongings are none of your affair."

"I will not go with you," said the Ranee suddenly, "but

Dumdumpore may come for me. You may, if you wish that, go and tell him I have yielded."

"Am I your messenger?" the priest retorted. "And is it likely he will come without a following, into a trap set by these Rajputs?"

"Very well," she answered. "Let him bring his following. Are you afraid to go to him?"

The priest raised his head haughtily; his arrogance forbade an answer.

"Then you may go to him and tell him he may come at daybreak. He may bring as many as he pleases. He shall go with me, or I with him, whichever you determine after we have talked together. Though I yield, there is nevertheless a bargain to be struck."

"He will bring a dacoit army with him," said the priest. "Do you risk that. Your possessions—"

"What do I care?" she retorted. "Go to him and return and tell me what he promises if I yield. Go, I tell you—go! I tire of all this talking about a thing that must be."

She covered her face with her hands, and the priest saw fit to let his lip curl at what he imagined was her gesture of despair. Then he turned his back. If he remembered Usha he must have decided to leave her there to keep watch. He climbed into his chair and was carried away into the night amid a din of conchs, drums and cymbals, in a smoky crimson glare of torchlight.

The Ranee arose and came near to Asoka, putting her hand on his trunk that reached out for the sugar that she usually gave him. It was difficult to see Quorn's face, but he could see her in the firelight.

"Is the dynamite all there?" she asked him.

"Yes, miss."

"Could you load it on all the elephants—some on each elephant?"

"Yes, miss."

"Kindly do—then come and talk to me."

QUORN TURNED ASOKA end for end and rode away into the darkness, as usual when he was puzzled, muttering to himself: "It's a rum go. Durned if I savvy the hang of it. Is this here cackle o' hers about the gods a good brown egg under an honest hen? Or are she and me both crazy? She and me—we seem to think o' the same crazy idees at the same time—good, ridic'lous, silly-lunatic idees that come off! Durn all mysteries! If it ain't a hook-up with the gods, what is it? Where do idees come from all of a sudden?"

Matter-of-fact to the verge of dullness, in spite of a bewildered mysticism, Quorn had left nothing to guess-work where his routine duty was concerned. He had trained the mahouts with an almost Prussian zeal for exact obedi-ence; all four-and-thirty of them, thieves and drunkards though they might be, obeyed him always, without argu-ment; and did it swiftly, no more noisily than shadows, and at once.

Thanks to his unimaginative and drastic but just disci-pline, obedience had become such a fetish with them that they never even stole unless they could invent some way of doing it that was new to Quorn and that he had therefore not denounced and specified among the things forbidden.

He commanded silence; even the shrill tongues of their quarrelsome wives and naked brats obeyed. He commanded that the elephants be saddled; it was done so skillfully that even in the darkness there was no confusion.

Just as in a dream things happen without having to be done, so it seemed that the elephants suddenly stood, all harnessed and as curious as goblins on parade to learn what business was afoot. The prospect of a night march, in the cool, with the dew on the ground, aroused only their willing interest. They knelt to receive their loads as silently as gray ghosts, obeying gesture, without the shouting that they sometimes needed in the light of day.

The dynamite, well packed in sawdust in the regulation wooden export boxes, was carried out and carefully stowed on the howdahs and pack-saddles—a mere nothing for the elephants, who understood they were to march light and so were good-humored and easy to manage.

Then a long, low-murmured conference in which Quorn, normally the law and all the prophets to that primitively minded gang, assumed authority that made the hair rise on his own neck, so impious it sounded to himself—but, nevertheless, so satisfying to their hunger for unreality.

"You've heard me say a heap o' times I ain't the Gunga *sahib*. That was to keep you blamed ijjits from gettin' too pepped up and cocky—do ye get that? Savvy what I mean? If I'd ha' confessed and said, 'Sure, I'm Gunga,' you contrary-minded heathen 'ud ha' got that snooty there'd ha' been no gettin' a day's work done.

"You'd ha' felt so important, takin' your orders direct from a feller that's allowed to keep his shoes on in the presence o' the gods, that you'd have upstaged the Ranee herself and I'd ha' had to punish ye worse than I like doing.

"But I'm tellin' ye now. Ye're a dissolute bunch o' low-down, ornery, lazy, no-account liars and bums and thieves. But I admit you've done your best a time or two.

And though you've fretted my temper something horrid, and made me 'shamed o' having a thing to do with you, most days o' the week, it's only fair to tell ye that you're the decentest mahouts in India. That maybe ain't sayin' much, but it's the plain truth. So I like ye pretty good; and I'm admitting to ye, for the sake o' fair play, that I am the Gunga *sahib!*"

THEY WERE EYES in the dark—eyes and a tide of breathing—he in their midst, sitting as they sat, on his heels. The rhythm of the breathing broke a little; many an owner of credulous eyes in that group had flinched from the flick of Quorn's whip for having dared to call him Gunga *sahib* in a moment of thoughtlessness. They had known he was the Gunga *sahib*. The surprising thing was that he now admitted it.

But the ways of the friends of the immortal gods are nearly as surprising as the ways of the gods themselves, and it is foolish to expect them to behave like common mortals.

"Speak on, *sahib!* We be willing men. We and our wives and little ones—we will obey!"

"Ye'd better! If ye don't, there won't be one of ye alive to-morrow noon. Ye'll not only be dead; ye'll be reborn again into the bodies of them filthy green flies that buzz around where bad smells are. Now do ye get that?

"And when ye've been green flies for a million years, ye'll turn into a stink and blow away along the wind. Mind—I'm not kiddin' ye. Not many suckers get an opportunity in this world to make sure o' being rich nabobs in their next incarnation. But that's the opportunity I'm handin' out to-night to all of you—in return for jes' a simple bit of strict obedience.

"If ye act right, if ye obey good, there won't be nothin' too good for ye in the nex' life—ye can have it easy—anything ye want. But the penalty for loafin' on the job or makin' one mistake is corresponding—well, I'd hate to be the sucker who slips up on this night's job o' work."

"Gunga *sahib*, we are poor men, but your honor's servants. We will do our utmost."

Then he drilled them—first all of them together, and then one by one, making each man memorize his orders and repeat them, until there was not much chance of their forgetting what to do.

"And remember, if one of ye makes a mistake, not one of ye but the whole damn' lot will be blown into fifty or sixty million filthy flies—and flies you will be forever until fly-time's up and ye become a stink to put inside rotten eggs. Ye never knew where that stink came from, did ye? It's the souls o' guys like you, who got their chance and fumbled it. But when ye see a nabob with a harem and lashings o' cash—that's a guy who, in his las' life, saw a chance and took it. He ain't lucky, he's a guy who's gettin' what he earned."

Bamjee heard all of the last of the discourse. He had forced himself into the crowd, but Quorn was not aware of him until he had exhausted his last expletive and had squeezed the sponge of his imagination dry.

Then, when he dismissed the throng, each man to wait by his elephant, he turned and saw Bamjee's eyes—felt Bamjee's trembling hand that touched his wrist.

"MR. QUORN, I do not know what you intend—but do you think you can do it?"

"You come and lend a hand, you sucker! I've got a job for you to-night that 'll suit you perfect."

"Suit me—but can I do it? Can I do it?"

"What's your religion?" Quorn asked him.

He knew, but he wanted Bamjee to create his own dilemma.

"Religion? None. I am agnostic."

"Don't believe in a nex' life?"

"I have enough to do to cling to this one!"

"And you like this life—and your good graft—and all that money you've got soaked away? And when your time comes you want to die easy, in bed? Good enough. To-night I'm giving you your choice o' three chances. You can die at the hands o' dacoits—and they'll enjoy that more than you will. Or you can die quick along o' me and my men—so sudden that it can't hurt; and the way to do that is to make a mistake, for then it 'll be you that kills us all. Or you can collect that money the Ranee promised you, and live to enjoy it, by actin' like the good guy that I think you are. Or—you've one other choice. You can take a licking. Shall I have at you with this *ankus?*"

Quorn took him by the scruff of the neck roughly enough to shake up the little man's courage that had settled somewhere near his heels. They two had shared danger too often for Quorn not to know that Bamjee only needed crowding; he had plenty of last-ditch courage; it was only the beginning of a thing that almost paralyzed his wits.

"Mind, I'm not kidding. I'm a man o' few friends and you've been one of 'em. You mean a heap to me—and if you'd fail me in a pinch like this I'd break ye with this *ankus* so you can't run, and leave you for the dacoits to torture to death. Are you coming? Me and you have got to remember to-night more than we ever knew about a heap that Edison and Tesla never learned."

They were a hot team. Quorn as a former taxi driver, who could make his own repairs, and Bamjee as an ex-te-legraphist, who had hoped (until he was fired for turning secret information to his own advantage) to win his way to the top by understanding every branch of his profession, could between them, even in darkness, do a marvel of a job with batteries and insulated wire. Clumsy, indeed, it might look. But it worked.

And in the box of tricks that Rana Raj Singh had sent to Quorn's tent there was a bottle of phosphorescent paint of the kind that miracle makers use in all lands where the gullible pay money to see spirits come forth from the dead. There was enough of it to paint great rings around the eyes of all the elephants.

17

"THIS NIGHT, AMID THIS DARKNESS—"

UPON WHETHER OR not your opponent believes or disbelieves what you intend he shall believe depends the outcome of all warfare; and the essence of all artistry in warfare, as in many other matters, is to foster self-deception in your foes.

"That priest," said the Ranee, "is so besotted with pride that he believes I will wait here for him."

"Those dacoits," said Rana Raj Singh, "have been promised so much that they believe your camp is full of gold and jewels."

"That priest's confidant," said Usha, "ordered me to stay and watch you, and to make a signal when the dacoits come, so that you may be seized and not slain by accident."

"Me and Bamjee and the elephants are ready," said Quorn. "You give the word, miss, and we're off."

"I am coming with you," said the Ranee.

Rana Raj Singh watched a solid mass of cloud that filled the entire sky to the southwest. It was the rearguard of the monsoon, hurrying to overtake the remnants of the main host that was shattering itself in tempest on the crags of the high Himalayas beyond the northern skyline.

"In an hour," he said, "the moon will pass behind that cloud and we shall have darkness filled with confusing shadows. Furthermore, the dacoits are afraid of darkness. But they will come, because that priest will tell them we are likely to escape unless they do. He is bitterly bent on killing me and all my men along with Ben Quorn."

"If they come in the moonlight, then we are lost," said Usha. But the "we" was not lost on the Ranee.

"If we die together bravely we will win each other's love," the Ranee answered. "What is a handful of troubled years, compared to that? Stay you here, Usha. You and the mahouts' wives must keep the fires burning. If the mahouts' wives become terror-stricken, tell them the dacoits don't kill women. But I think that the dacoits will never reach this camp."

"They will not," said Rana Raj Singh, "if they come in darkness through the Burra Ghat, which I believe they will. It is the only easy road in darkness, though a little longer than any other. It is darker than death in the Ghat when there is no moon."

"Do you think that death is dark?" the Ranee asked him. "Shame on you! Death is the goal of destiny. To die well is to go home gayly."

"That there priest and the Rajah o' Dumdumpore shall have a one-way ticket if I can find 'em," Quorn said grimly.

"Would you rob me?" the Ranee asked him.

"No, miss."

"Then kill neither of them if it can be helped. If we rescue Mrs. Galway, who can say there is no protection for a stranger in my kingdom? If we capture Dumdumpore, in my territory, with a score of witnesses to prove he was in league with dacoits, he will have to submit to whatever penance I inflict or else be dealt with by the British Raj. He will prefer my punishment to theirs. But if we should kill him, it would be we who would have to explain our conduct to the British—and of all this world's indignities an explanation is the most embarrassing. As for the priest, the humiliation of him and his friends will amuse me more than ever his dead tody would. So above all, spare that priest."

"But it is time to go," said Rana Raj Singh. "Let us do our work, and let the gods spare whom they will."

THERE WAS NO aside between the Ranee and Prince Rana Raj Singh. They two were a pair whose loyalty was based on mutual faith and understanding. Though with equal fervor they repudiated the time-dishonored rule that women should be veiled and lovers never see each other until the marriage day, they were sincere and old-fashioned enough to obey the spirit of the rule with far more strictness than if the customary veil and eunuchs had invited, while forbidding, trespass.

They observed a regard for each other's dignity that they understood if no one else did. They were not even noticed to glance at each other. But as Rana Raj Singh mounted his mare, the Ranee set her foot into his stirrup, stepped thence to the saddle behind him and sprang into the howdah on Asoka's back.

"And me?" asked Bamjee. He sounded lonelier than an owl in the wilderness—lost, like a small toy. Vividly intelligent and wrinkled with nervously felt experience, Bamjee nevertheless had never grown up; he was an incorrigible

Enormous eyes glowing in the night

child, precocious, to whom dignity was a tinsel suit to be torn or taken off as easily as a magpie can ruffle its feathers.

Quorn commanded and Asoka swung his huge weight like a liner leaving moorings. The long trunk licked into the dark—a liner's derrick—seized and encircled Bamjee, hoisted him squealing like a caught rat, and dumped him into the howdah at the Ranee's side.

"Am a synonym for nothing much," said Bamjee. "Am a frightened baby—believing in no deities to whom to pray—less fortunate than Mr. Quorn who prays to Holy Mackerel and is comforted… *Ting-a-ling!* I ring bell. You may go now, coachman."

The only animal on earth who can adjust his own load is the elephant. The evolution of intelligence has caught him in the same snare in which man struggles toward the goal that he neither sees nor even dimly understands.

The long line of swaying, ghostly, phosphorescent circles that Quorn had painted about their eyes, which almost frightened Quorn himself, meant nothing to the elephants, but they understood that there was something serious about the mystery of wires that connected them one with another. Each of them in turn had lifted up a coil of the stuff and set it in the howdah on his back.

They were aware of the tangible link that in its own way symbolized the instinct of a herd to keep together. It was something they must not tangle or break; although Quorn had taken good care to prevent that by adding ropes that would have to be broken before the wire could take the strain—and even then, there was a coil in every howdah, so that the system had an emergency reserve of elasticity.

All wires led to one coil, which Asoka now lifted and passed to Bamjee. It was the longest coil of all. And when Bamjee had taken a couple of turns of it around a stanchion on the howdah he fastened its ends with thumb-screws to the switch that was already connected to a box of dry-cell batteries.

"Am now in league with much fine death. Am godlike personage," the *babu* said. "One move of little finger and—to the devil with friends and enemies at same time! Difference is, that gods are reputed to destroy only others, not themselves, whereas—am personally sitting on box of dynamite. Proceed!"

IT WAS NOT so silent, that procession, as its leaders would have liked. Its beginnings were pursued by wailing from the wives of the mahouts, who were in no way mollified by any mystery of painted eyes on elephants that were the be-all and the end-all of their drab existences.

The toilers behind the scenes of pageantry are not impressed by its familiar details; they look for results. The wives had seen that inexplicable paint put on. They saw their bread and board go, shadowy and dumb, away into the night. They knew the dacoits were at hand.

It meant nothing to them that Usha commanded silence; she was a strange woman, who had borne no brats and knew no aching emptiness of the sort that is felt by mahouts' women or soldiers' wives in the dust of departing columns on the march.

So there was lamentation. But the Ranee's spirit was the sort that rises loyal in repudiation of ill-omen. Some one's agony is some one's ease, so long as there are two sides to a dollar.

"This night, amid this darkness," she said to Quorn and Bamjee, "Narada, this little kingdom, is reborn into its infancy; perhaps—who knows?—to grow into a better kingdom than it ever was. Some day, when a son is born to me at midnight, there will be fear and crying. But there will be a new man in the world; and the fear will turn to hope and happiness; the crying will become laughter and a noise of trumpets. And so with this."

Simple words to say, but magic in the mind of any one who says them, believing, reserving no subtleties of doubt; magic that stirs its equivalent in the hearts and minds of others, because courage is a thousand times more alert than fear and more contagious. Even Bamjee could substitute for panic, if not eagerness, at least excitement, as he clutched his electric switch in dread lest devils (that his brain repudiated, but his keen subconscious heritage accepted with every breath he drew) should snap the contact home before the proper time.

In truth it was a reassuring spectacle to its masters, that ponderous, almost noiseless column on the march behind

Asoka. Phosphorescent eyes in the dark—enormous eyes, traveling in column, four by four. A stealth of strong feet, silent on the rain-wet earth. Dim, enormous outlines— endless because the end of them was lost in darkness. And behind them, a jingle of spurs and a clash now and then, as a scabbard struck stirrup.

With the Ranee's ten men counted, there were only four-and-thirty swordsmen under Rana Raj Singh; but to Bamjee—and Quorn and the Ranee—it seemed as if all history, and legend, too, had sent its heroes to lend a hand in that night's work.

"I can't see gods," said the Ranee, "but I can sense them. They are all around us."

"It's ag'in' religion and it ain't moral, to agree wi' you on that point, miss," said Quorn. "All the same, I believe ye, I'm damned if I don't."

THEY WERE, HOWEVER, human beings, though they might have invisible hosts to aid them and incarnate devils to overcome. It is not human to permit the unseen gods to lay the eggs from which the gods, it may be, are to hatch the chickens.

Human ingenuity has pride of place, if only that it may arrange a puzzle for the gods to straighten out, and the Ranee's young brain was electric with foresight. Crusader though she was for the ideals of a storied past, she was alert to every living moment, with an eye to the future, always.

"That priest," she said, "is in a bad predicament. If he should lag behind the dacoits, they might possibly destroy me. But he dreads that, knowing that the British would investigate. So, though he hates me, he must protect me if he can and marry me to Dumdumpore. But on the other hand, he is determined to destroy you, Mr. Quorn, and my beloved Rana Raj Singh. So he must loose the dacoits against us.

"No one in his senses, and most certainly no priest, would trust Dumdumpore, who is likely at any moment to get panic-stricken and run home denying everything and everybody. And certainly, to curry favor with the British government and to blind them to his wickedness, the Brahmin would like to get the credit for having rescued Mrs. Galway. So I think he will come in advance of the dacoits. I believe he will bring with him Dumdumpore and Mrs. Galway.

"I expect his plan is to permit and encourage the dacoits to plunder the camp, take all the elephants and kill every one except myself; after which he proposes to let Dumdumpore escape with me—perhaps with Mrs. Galway also, while he himself will return to Narada to write a report to the British government."

"Sounds sensible," said Quorn.

"No," said the Ranee, "it sounds silly. It sounds silly enough to suit that fool. If it is his plan, I have him, because Rana Raj Singh's horsemen will catch him easily."

"And then?" asked Bamjee. "Your highness, it is wonderful to have the gods on whom to blame a slaughter of so many innocents—including me!"

"You guessed that sucker right, miss. I see him coming," said Quorn.

Rana Raj Singh's eyes had also instantly detected the faint tinge of torchlight in the darkness above a ravine into which the track descended. He and his horsemen all came streaming by at a canter, and at a sign from him Quorn halted all the elephants, that closed in on their leader on level ground a quarter of a mile from where the road began to dip down-hill.

It gave Quorn a chance to repeat instructions to the mahouts, although there was a dire risk that restless trunks might damage the system of wires, or that legs might become entangled. In the dark they looked like fisher-men toiling at nets as they hauled in the slack, grunting commands to their elephants to make them keep curious trunks out of mischief.

18

"INTO HIDING! THERE IS A GOOD PEACE BEHIND THE BOWLDERS—"

RANA RAJ SINGH led his horsemen circling to the right in order to cross the ravine by a track higher up and reënter it from the far side. Taking the priest from the rear in that way, he could also throw out scouts to learn which route the dacoits took and how near they already were.

The Burra Ghat, of which the Rajput prince had spoken, was a winding wide valley with a level floor that led into this ravine at a right angle, more than a mile lower down to the left. If the dacoits should come by that route, as expected, there was a level ground of many acres in extent, where the Burra Ghat, suddenly narrowing to a passage hardly ten feet wide, opened and spread with equal suddenness. It was a perfect place for a pitched fight, darker than the belly of darkness, now that the moon was hidden.

"I believe in the gods," said the Ranee. "I trust them."

Bamjee sighed. "*Sahiba*, I believe in you and dynamite. I wish I trusted either of them. I am terribly afraid."

"There's a law," said Quorn. "Burned if I know who made it, but it's religion. It says: Never give suckers a chance. That there priest is a sucker. Dumdumpore's another. Them

dacoits is suckers. They haven't no earthly chance whatever."

"You have called me a sucker fifty thousand times," said
Bamjee.

"And I was right," said Quorn. "But the Ranee ain't one.
You stop fiddlin' with that there switch and ride in on the
Ranee's luck. Here they come, miss."

Toward them, over the lip of the ravine, rode Rana Raj
Singh and beside him, on a small mule, Mrs. Galway. Next
rode a half a dozen Rajputs; then the priest in his litter,
surrounded by his torch-bearers and attendants, all looking dreadfully tired. Then Dumdumpore, dejected, in the
midst of his own unarmed attendants—six or seven rather
wild-eyed men whose surrendered weapons hung from the
saddles of Rajputs who brought up the rear.

Rana Raj Singh cantered forward and Mrs. Galway
tried to keep pace, but the mule was more than she could
manage; the prince's mare, well used to elephants, was
terrified by the goggle-eyed herd confronting her and
had to be skillfully managed; the mule spun around and
scattered the priest's attendants before two Rajputs could
subdue the animal, one on either side.

Rana Raj Singh was about to speak when a drumming
of hoofbeats interrupted him. From the direction of the
Ranee's camp there was a rider coming belly-to-the-earth,
in spasms, the mount failing and being flogged to another
effort. Suddenly the mule that was Asoka's stable-mate
came staggering out of darkness, sought Asoka and stood
heaving alongside him, foundered. Usha, leaping from his
back, caught the rail of the howdah and scrambled in, as

breathless as the mule. It was a minute before she could speak and be understood.

"Narak's men! They come from the north! They sent a spy. I saw him. We had word together. He told me Narak steals a march on Lumding—for the loot. He will seize the loot and run with it. He hopes that Lumding's men will join him in the mountains, because Lumding will have no loot, so his men will say that Narak is the better leader."

"How far away are they?"

"Near. They are very near now. They make haste, to be ahead of Lumding."

"Where are the mahouts' womenfolk?"

"I hid them in the quarry."

"Where is the spy?"

"In Quorn's tent. I took him there to show him where the gold is hidden. He asked too many questions. I slew him with his own knife."

THUNDERING HOOFS AGAIN—FROM the ravine ahead, this time. Six horsemen coming hell-or-hallelujah: Rajputs racing in with information. He who won the race drew rein beside his prince like a shell going into the mud. He spoke in low tones. He was a shadow; the whites of his eyes and his horse's eyes were visible, not much else.

"Lumding comes along the Burra Ghat," said Rana Raj Singh. "Three or four hundred men are with him, on ponies."

He sounded pleased; but that was merely the correct mood for a Rajput gentleman who realizes that a crisis is now on top of him. He glanced over his shoulder at Dumdumpore, who was talking to the priest amid the torches, nearly a hundred yards away. His speech, if he intended any, was forestalled by Mrs. Galway, who persuaded her mule at last to approach the elephants.

"Are you the Ranee of Narada? I am Mrs. Galway. Are these your horsemen? I will have you know they have behaved abominably. That priest is a gentleman. He came and rescued me. He persuaded the Rajah of Dumdumpore to take me away from those horrible dacoits, who he says are your subjects.

"They had confined me in a hut surrounded by human heads on poles. The goings on in that village, within your jurisdiction, were simply incredible, as I intend to let the whole world know.

"And on top of that, no sooner am I rescued than your ruffians come and inflict gross indignities on this gentlemanly priest and his friend the rajah. They took away the weapons of their men. They—"

Usha interrupted. "Cut her head off! She is crazy. What now? Tell me and I do it!"

"Can you ride a spirited horse?" asked the Ranee.

"I ride a whirlwind—I ride anything!"

"I will give you Dumdumpore's. On his own feet he may make less trouble for us. Ride toward the Burra Ghat and tell Lumding you come at Dumdumpore's command to warn him that Narak and his men are stealing a march on him. Tell him that Narak knows where all the money is that was meant for the pay of the quarrymen; and say that Narak intends to escape with the money and elephants and seize the leadership. Add that if he hurries he may come in time to catch Narak off-guard and inflict such a beating on him and his men that—"

"Good! I go!" said Usha. She was down out of the

howdah in a moment—spitting heartily at Mrs. Galway, who was about to speak again; dodging the heels of Rana Raj Singh's mare; running toward the torchlight. It was Usha who seized the rajah by the spurred boot and tumbled him out of the saddle. In a second she was on the horse and galloping away into the darkness. Mrs. Galway sputtered fury at the new indignity to Dumdumpore.

"Remember, I was a witness to all this," she repeated again and again.

Then Rana Raj Singh cantered back. "Toward the camp and into hiding!" he commanded. "Leave the prisoners to me. There is a good place amid the bowlders beyond the quarry, where—"

QUORN KNEW THAT place and the elephants also knew it; they could find it in the dark because it was there they had rested between spells of dragging trees to be sawn into cordwood. But it was a serious business to turn that herd of monsters end for end without tangling or breaking his system of wires; it was as difficult as managing a liner in a narrow channel with the wind across the tide. It took him several minutes, but by dint of blasphemy that scalded the mahouts and patience that pleased the elephants, he did it. And then off, to reach the camp ahead of Narak's men, praying aloud to Holy Mackerel that the speed would not shake loose the dynamite purposely lashed none too securely to the howdahs.

The elephants went like smoke, believing they were going home. There was a moment of near disaster when Asoka tried to take the wrong track and return to the elephant lines. The whole herd milled behind him. But the guard-ropes held and in the nick of time Asoka understood and led in the right direction; not a wire broke, not a box of dynamite was shaken loose—so that the Ranee laughed and said the gods were holding things in place. But Quorn corrected her:

"It was me and Bamjee, miss, that tied them hitches."

They safely reached their hiding-place within a ring of enormous bowlders that some glacier had let fall against a flank of a hill a hundred thousand years or so ago.

"Expressly for our purpose," said the Ranee. "Destiny is never in a hurry."

But then danger found another way of bringing each one's heart into his throat or boots, according to his disposition. The mahouts' wives heard—smelled—sensed the nearness of the elephants that meant more to them than law or even husbands—since an elephant means bread and business, whereas a husband is a mere expedient. Or perhaps it was that one woman saw the phosphorescent goggles in the dark and told the others.

They came running, shrilling, carrying their brats and so alarming all the echoes that even Rana Raj Singh's horsemen rode into the ring of rocks unheard. The Rajputs made the priest's attendants throw away the torches; they were treating Dumdumpore to low-voiced ridicule because he had been made to ride on Usha's foundered mule; and the porters who carried the priest's chair were almost dead with fatigue, although the priest had been made to ride behind a Rajput's saddle—a soul-scarifying, shameful sin against the law of caste, amusing them as much as it offended him.

19

"THEN LET US GO!"

NOW AN AGONY of waiting. Then the blare of Narak's brass horns and a hailstorm drum-beat as the dacoit leader sought to exorcise a dread of magic and underworld devils, such as always robbed his superstitious followers of their aggressiveness by night, particularly when the moon was hidden.

The dacoits had suffered one defeat already from the hornet-horsemen who inhabited the darkness of the Ranee's camp and, loot or no loot, they were none too eager for another. If the spy that Narak sent had but returned with information—but he had not. It was neither the storm of Narak's drums and horns nor Narak's urging that impelled them in the end. It was Lumding hurrying to jump their claim. Rivalry, jealousy, resentment did what the leadership of Narak could not.

Lumding made no secret of his coming. He was red rapine, encrimsoned by the smoky glare of torches—black and blood-red, weapons and eyes and horses' legs all swimming amid bloody shadows—sounding like a tidal wave of horror, howling and hollow, dreadful, merciless, as all-devouring as a sea that surges inshore at the summons of an earthquake.

And the two tides met in mid-camp, Lumding at a disadvantage because his torches revealed his men as a target and a hundred arrows hummed into the massed ranks, striking down men and ponies, before they could beat out the torches or hurl them into the ranks of Narak's men. Then total darkness with only a dim light here and there where a thrown torch sputtered to its death-cries and a shuddering crash of weapons—warfare of worse than animals, men who fought unseeing, tearing at the throat of friend and enemy alike.

"Ready? Then let us go!" commanded Rana Raj Singh. He had a voice like a war-lord's trumpet when he chose at last to let his Rajput passion loose and slay for the love of old ideals. His was no heroism that night; it was anger hurled on vermin.

"And now, oh, my God!" said Bamjee. But he had no time for terror after that; he had to cling in darkness to the swaying howdah, feeling his switch with his thumb and listening with both ears for the voice of Quorn to tell him, in the midst of all that din, to make the contact—and then the signal to the following mahouts.

Asoka, at Quorn's urging and stirred in every nerve of all his five tons weight by the thrill descending to him through his master's legs gripping him behind the ears, became a typhoon suddenly condensed to solid matter and directed by a ruthless will.

He was a smasher, tusked with ivory—a leader of destroyers, spreading out behind him in a line nearly shoulder to shoulder, that followed through or over, not around things. Civilization had gone and dreams were true; they were a herd again, crashing as they used to crash through jungles in the wake of the stoutest leader when a forest was alight and there was no way out but through it—through the flame.

And the elephants had glowing goggle-eyes. They were a mystery of phantoms—such a horror as no dacoit ever saw until that moment when they burst on the flank of the viewless fight and moved across its midst a swath that closed like water again behind them because the dacoits were hand to throat, mob-mad, fighting to reach the midst of things.

MIDWAY OF THAT yelling frenzy, with the arrows flickering around him, Quorn shouted the command; but Bamjee could not hear him. The Ranee leaned and struck the *babu,* pointing at the switch. Bamjee made the contact, but he lost his head then and forgot the next thing; it was the Ranee who snatched the automatic pistol and fired three shots into the air—the agreed-on signal. The electric spark had fired the fuses. There were exactly sixty seconds in which to dump the dynamite and vanish out of range.

The Ranee and Bamjee between them dumped their dynamite. Three and thirty mahouts behind them did the same thing and all the elephants except Asoka wheeled and scattered—which was the greatest miracle of all. Instinct, habit, excitement impelled them to follow Asoka; but for once they obeyed orders, snapping the ropes that linked them together.

As they sped away outward in all directions the dacoits, obeying instinct, flowed toward the center again, to be behind them. Some one seized a dying torch and shook it into flame. It flared over an inferno of maddened devils who stabbed at random while they fought for the boxes of what they probably supposed was gold, though nobody ever was to know what they supposed.

They had torn open at least a dozen boxes of the stuff before a fuse burned home; and most of them went that instant to a less material Hades, whence neither dacoits nor any other men return to argue.

It was as if all the big guns of the world had exploded in one dazzling thunder-clap. Asoka had run another hundred yards before the crash and thump of falling débris fell on deadened ears. Then on the utter darkness silence fell, unbroken except by the thud of Asoka's hurrying foot-fall, until, from far behind, there came the intermittent shock-and-worry of the Rajputs "cleaning up," pursuing fugitives.

Asoka laid the long leagues underfoot. The biggest, strongest elephant in India, he was the most indignant and the least amenable to orders when abnormal noise offended him or shocked his dignity.

Once frightened, he was afraid of his own terror in addition to the unknown awfulness that had made the night a thing to flee from and the daylight something to be found, perhaps, beyond a limitless horizon.

An elephant in terror runs like nothing else that lives; he attracts to himself such elemental forces as include the unreasoning rage of landslides. He is a herd in himself. He is something almost absolute. He changes terror by some chemistry into titan-strength intolerant of obstacles, devouring distance. Mania makes him a super-elephant. He knows nothing, feels nothing but a concentrated super elephantine vehemence and hunger and will to use it.

Fifty, sixty, seventy miles are nothing to him—until

weariness, almost suddenly, overwhelms his nerves and he becomes a mere tired animal extremely sorry for himself. Then, if he is a wild elephant, he is deadly dangerous because he has begun to think. But if he has been trained he remembers his master and reaction makes him crave the comforts of obedience.

FALSE DAWN WAS flickering in the sky before Quorn even attempted to control Asoka; he simply sat still, hoping there would be no jungle in the path with overhanging branches that might smash the howdah and kill its occupants. However, then the end came swiftly, at a stream with the faint light flickering on a pool amid quiet rushes where the wild ducks were beginning to squawk a sleepy greeting to the daylight. There Asoka hesitated, turned, thought better of it and made up his mind to drink.

"Down with you!" Quorn shouted. They were his first words since the dynamite exploded. He did not know he shouted. "Get down any way you can, miss."

Bamjee and the Ranee slid to earth by holding to Asoka's tail; but Quorn stuck to his post. He knew well what was coming.

"You big bonehead! If you had any sense you'd wait for us to dump the howdah. But I dassent take a chance. You'd run a million miles afore I'd catch ye, and Lord pity any other sucker who tried to round ye up."

Asoka drank. He waded deeper. He felt the delicious wetness on his legs and the good brown mud under his feet. A squattering flock of ducks took wing as the first breath of the morning wind went sighing through the rushes. He knelt. He lay. He rolled. He wallowed. He let Quorn scrub him.

He lay still until Quorn undid the buckles of the straps that held the howdah. Then he rolled clear of it, wallowed again, let Quorn scramble back into place, and waded toward midstream, where he swam and let the long night's terror vanish from his consciousness as if it were a dream that went with daylight. He even obeyed when Quorn commanded him to lift the howdah and set it to dry.

"And now, miss, breakfast?" Quorn suggested. "Asoka can rustle all he needs. But how about you? Can you eat air?"

20

"GUNGA SAHIB!"

NOBODY KNEW HOW Bamjee reached Narada, and not
many people saw him; those who did were cronies whom
he knew he could trust to keep all credit to themselves for
the success of any enterprise whatever. They were thieves of
ideas, of reputations, of mysterious authority. Thus Bamjee
was left to his own devices while amazing rumor multi-
plied itself and the swarming city became too expectant
of unreality to notice real movement on the checkerboard
of unsuspected intrigue. Bamjee, in other words, was in
his element.

The stage was well set. Rana Raj Singh had returned at
the head of his horsemen, but he held his tongue because
he had no right to meddle in Narada politics or even to
police the hills; there might be trouble for him if he told
his doings.

Dumdumpore had ridden to Narada with him; but
Dumdumpore was even more morosely silent; he, too,
had no imaginable business in Narada, and the priests of
the temple of Siva, who were well known to be friendly
to him, were afraid to receive him or to make as much as
a gesture of recognition. Also Mrs. Galway came, on a
mule, as fussy as a wet hen and as angry as a dry drunkard

because Dumdumpore would have nothing to do with her. Dumdumpore had troubles enough of his own.

The priest of Siva rode in also in the train of Rana Raj Singh, saying nothing with ecclesiastical restraint, which is a sort of overloaded silence suggesting portents. He, too, repudiated Mrs. Galway. She had caused to be interpreted into his scandalized ears, hour after hour on the way to Narada, all of her passionate plan for the redemption of three hundred million people out of sloth and dark perversity by means of her forthcoming book, which should pillory their shame before a sinless world.

She told him many of the vicious sentences she meant to write into her book; she had stolen all the dirty linen out of India's hamper and she meant to brandish it beneath the noses of the proud and pure. The Brahmin was so offended he could hardly contrive to be rude to her; however, he pulled himself together and did a first-class job, through the interpreter, who had his face slapped for his pains.

It was Mrs. Galway's story of the dynamiting of the dacoits that first gained currency. Not being in on the secret, she had drawn her own deductions, to the effect that a meteorite had fallen, by the act of an outraged God. She with her own eyes saw it fall; she saw the hot parabola of its swift descent into the midst of warring savages.

The elephants had also seen it, had been panic-stricken and had fled in all directions after following Asoka far enough to plunge into the mêlée, where they lost even the instinct of a herd to keep together. All this, she declared, was burned into her memory by the vivid flash of the descending meteor, so that it was impossible she could be mistaken.

Then, with those same unmistaken eyes she had seen Asoka struck by the exploding meteor that blew the elephant, the Ranee, Bamjee and Ben Quorn to unrecoverable smithereens along with such a horde of dacoits that the unfeeling inhumanity of Rana Raj Singh and his horsemen had been almost futile.

Nevertheless, and she would write it in her book that all the world might know his ignominy, Rana Raj Singh had pursued the remnants of the dacoits, slaying any that he or his men could find in darkness.

Worse yet: Rana Raj Singh, reeking with the sweat of bloody murder—on a frenzied mare whose heels in the darkness almost killed the narrator, missing her face by only half an inch—had sought a most immoral female by the name of Usha and had promised her a job at court or any other reward she craved if she would find as many dacoits as she could and put it into their heads to flee into the neighboring State of Dumdumpore.

"A most ungentlemanly piece of malice," Mrs. Galway spat. "Just like dumping garbage on a neighbor's lot!"

IT WAS ANNOYING to be told, as she was by several people who approached her to betray the secret for purely humane reasons, that a plan was already on foot to have her lynched in order to forestall the anger of the British government, who would want to know why she had been permitted to wander at large and to represent herself as the reigning Ranee, with the natural result that dacoits had seized her and offered her bribes to help them lay waste all the neighboring States.

It was explained to her that Brazenose Blake, the British Resident on leave of absence, had been wired for and was coming in an airplane to investigate the rumor that she was a Soviet agent in disguise. However, should she hurry to the coast and take the earliest outbound steamer, possibly the British government might let the matter drop.

She was not told that Bamjee had been talking; if she had been told that, could she have believed it? She herself had said that she saw Bamjee killed by the bursting meteorite that destroyed Asoka.

And so she never knew that it was Bamjee who supplied the motor car and the persuasive driver who offered to sneak her away, by night, for nothing, to the railway station seventy miles away; nor that it was Bamjee who started the riot outside the State guest-bungalow, from which she narrowly escaped, mistaking mocking laughter for the yelping blood-lust of assassins.

By wire from the railway station she engaged her passage on a steamer that allowed her fifty minutes to buy clothing in Bombay; but she kept the Ranee's clothing, since it would make a fascinating costume in which to deliver lectures. And her book, in which she says she saw the Ranee of Narada die, will be published shortly.

The mahouts of three and thirty elephants that had returned with Rana Raj Singh never admitted having spoken to Bamjee after the disaster, or even to having seen him. Nevertheless, they all declared with one voice that they had seen Quorn die and that the Ranee had been with him on Asoka. They stuck to the story.

As a result, the priests, being so delighted to believe that Quorn was dead and hoping the Ranee might be dead too, arranged a royal funeral. Their best magicians worked like the devil meanwhile in the temple crypt to assist the chief astrologer, who recast the Ranee's horoscope and found she could not possibly have lived beyond that minute, since her Saturn was in trine with Uranus, with Mars in the ascendant and a full moon.

And besides, the populace was so excited about the death of Ben Quorn, and the legends, and what the priests had said about him, that they bombarded the priests with demands for a downright statement.

Did the legend not say that the Gunga *sahib* would have to die to save the Ranee's throne? And had the priests not said that if Ben Quorn should die and come to life again they would believe he was the Gunga *sahib?* Was he not dead? Had a priest and a half a hundred other witnesses not seen him die? What about it?

THERE WAS NOTHING the priests could do but stand by what they had already said. They simply had to stick to it. Too many people nowadays were accusing them of vague evasiveness and of trimming their sails to every stray wind. And had not one of them, a man of promise slated for preferment on the ground of orthodoxy, seen him die?

It was a safe bet, and the magicians were at work to cinch it. So the priests said yes, Quorn was dead, slain by an act of Siva. They cursed him solemnly. They numbered him among the homeless souls of evil-loving infidels who shriek and flee forever through the astral gloom from vampires and the fiends that invented infamy and pain. They cursed him eloquently and in detail. They pronounced him dead and damned.

But it was strange how rumor circulated, although nobody admitted having heard from Bamjee. There was a story, a little vague and various but constantly gaining credence as it leaped from mouth to mouth, about the Ranee staying in a village in the hills where she was said to be reorganizing village life and discovering homes for the women whose husbands had been murdered by the dacoits. Even the priests admitted she was capable of that; but the priests said the story was hokum.

However, a few of her elephants with Mulji in command were sent to look for her; and it was noticed that the elephants were loaded rather heavily with packages that were brought forth from the palace. Not that any one saw Bamjee. If he had been seen there might have been suspicions, Bamjee being what everybody knew he was; however, the palace attendants held their tongues. And when the elephants returned with no news, but without the packages, there was the public funeral to think of; and nobody thought of asking Mulji what had become of the elephant loads. If they had asked, he had an answer ready, but it was a rather lame one and as well not risked.

It was the priests' idea to hold the Ranee's funeral on the day that Brazenose Blake arrived. The British Resident was as irritable as a porcupine because, like every other sportsman who had ever met her, he idolized the little Ranee of Narada and would almost rather have died himself than know that she had met such hideous disaster.

His only satisfaction in the circumstances was that now he would not have to order her to rid her land of dacoits or resign from the throne. He had an ultimatum in his pocket, signed by the government before the telegram had come announcing the Ranee's sudden death.

As her friend and very worshipful admirer he had dreaded having to hand it to her. He was not exactly dry-eyed as he took his stand, surrounded by the Residency staff, on the steps of the new town hall that the Ranee had built, to watch the sad procession file by and salute the bier, on which they had laid a wooden image of her, to be burned at the *ghat* by the river.

Brazenose Blake gritted his teeth; and he hated the hard, ironic smiles on the faces of the priests, who sang sweet hymns and swayed so truculently. They were at no pains to disguise their pleasure.

Nobody saw when Bamjee came and whispered to him from the gloom of the columned porch behind his back. Nobody noticed when the grief that had made him pallid changed to a gasp of incredulity—a gape of stark astonishment—and then a grin that he hid behind his hand until his face was under control and masked by an official British stare.

And the priests knew nothing—not yet; though, as they went by Blake they were beginning to be puzzled by the tumult that gradually became louder behind them, at the end of the long procession, which thundered between the high walls of the winding, narrow street.

They could not see, because the long parade came serpentwise along a street as crooked as their politics. They might not learn, because it was impossible for any messenger to struggle through the swarm of men and women who lined the street on either hand. They could only hear what must have sounded to them like a cosmic cannon thundering salutes, as griefless as a sunny morning, thundering the doom of their own influence, saluting progress.

"GUNGA SAHIB! GUNGA *sahib!* Gunga *sahib!"*

At the tail of the long procession rode the Ranee, on

Asoka, behind Ben Quorn seated on Asoka's neck; and Asoka was swaying with all the ponderous dignity that he loved to display to a crowd, Quorn had gilded his tusks and had smeared him with vermilion paint. In secret somebody had brought out the jeweled howdah of state for him; and Quorn, in a brand-new purple turban, sat as solemn and still as any of the images graven on ancient walls. He was the Gunga *sahib,* to the last, least mystic detail.

But the Ranee was smiling radiantly, dressed in the brilliant robes of state and wearing all her jewels—mischievous, merry, and glad to be home. Behind her, four by four, arrayed in new clean cotton clothing, many of them carrying their babies, were the women of the villages, whose husbands had been butchered by the dacoits. They were not so sad that anybody noticed it; to the last lean wondering woman, they were grinning, shrilly echoing the crowd's shout:

"Gunga *sahib!* Gunga *sahib!*"

As she drew abreast of Blake, the Ranee called a halt and, leaning from the howdah, waved to him:

"Cheerio! Glad to see you! Ultimatum for me? Keep it! Not a dacoit in all Narada! No, not one!"

www.ingramcontent.com/pod-product-compliance
Lightning Source LLC
Chambersburg PA
CBHW070757030726
47504CB00003B/587